S.N.U.F.F.

Special Newsreel Universal Feature Film

A Utøpia

Victor Pelevin

GOLLANCZ

LONDON

The author would like to express his gratitude to Svetlana Payne and Victor Pelevin for their contribution towards the novel's translation.

Original text copyright © Victor Pelevin 2011
English translation copyright © Andrew Bromfield 2014
All rights reserved.

First published in Great Britain in 2015
by Gollancz
An imprint of the Orion Publishing Group
Carmelite House, 50 Victoria Embankment,
London EC4Y 0DZ
An Hachette UK Company

A CIP catalogue record for this book
is available from the British Library

ISBN 978 1 473 21302 9 (Cased)
ISBN 978 1 473 21303 6 (Trade Paperback)

1 3 5 7 9 10 8 6 4 2

Typeset at The Spartan Press Ltd,
Lymington, Hants

Printed and bound by the CPI Group (UK) Ltd,
Croydon, CR0 4YY

The Orion Publishing Group's policy is to use papers that
are natural, renewable and recyclable products and made
from wood grown in sustainable forests. The logging and
manufacturing processes are expected to conform to the
environmental regulations of the country of origin.

www.orionbooks.co.uk
www.gollancz.co.uk

Jour après jour
les amours mortes
n'en finissent pas de mourir.

Serge Gainsbourg

[Day after day, old loves just keep on dying.]

PART 1.

A DAMSEL IN DISTRESS

Certain pastimes can be salutary in moments of inner tribulation. The perplexed mind understands which actions to perform in which sequence and for a while it finds peace. Such occupations include, for instance, playing patience, trimming one's beard and moustache, and Tibetan meditative embroidery. In this category I also include the art – almost forgotten in these times – of writing books.

I am feeling very strange.

If anyone had told me that I'd be sitting here in front of a manitou, like some lousy sommelier, stringing together little blocks of words, trimmed and polished on a creative articulator, I'd have spat in that person's face. Figuratively speaking, of course. I haven't become an Ork yet, although I'm more closely acquainted with that race than I might wish. But then, I didn't write this brief memoir for people. I've done it for Manitou, before whom I shall stand at some time soon – provided, of course, that he wishes to see me (he might turn out to be too busy, or perhaps a whole slew of people will show up for the meeting along with me).

The priests say that any appeal to the Singular should include a detailed exposition of all the circumstances. Slanderous tongues claim the reason for this is to hike up the charge for declamation: the longer the supplication, the greater the cost of having it read out in the temple. But since it has fallen to me to tell this story standing face to face with eternity, I shall expound it in detail, explaining even those things that you might already know. For soon these jottings may be all that is left of our familiar world.

When I started making these notes, I didn't yet know how the whole story would end, and for the most part events are described as I experienced and understood them at the time they occurred. Therefore, in telling the story, I often stray into the present tense. All this could have been corrected during editing, but I think my account appears more authentic like this – as if through some quirk of fate my story had been imprinted on temple celluloid. So let everything remain just as it is.

The protagonists of this story will be the young Ork Grim and his girlfriend Chloe. A series of circumstances led to my observing them directly from the air, and virtually all their dialogues quoted here were captured through the long-range microphone of my Hannelore. That's why I'm able to tell the story as Grim saw it – which renders my task far more interesting, without undermining the veracity of the narrative.

To some people my attempt to see the world through the eyes of a young Ork might seem unconvincing, especially to the extent that I aspire to describe his feelings and thoughts. I agree – a civilised individual seeking to immerse himself in the nebulous states of the Orkish soul does look like a suspicious sham. But then, I'm not attempting here to paint the inner portrait of an Ork in the totality of his being.

An ancient poet once said that any narrative is like fabric stretched over the blades of several precise insights. If my insights into the Orkish soul are precise – and they are – the credit for that is not due to me. The credit doesn't even belong to our sommeliers that have spent century after century structuring the

4

so-called 'Orkish culture' so that its mental horizon would be absolutely transparent to appropriate oversight and monitoring.

It's simpler than that. The fact is that a substantial part of the work on these notes was carried out when the fates determined that Grim would be my neighbour, and I was able to ask him any question that interested me. And so if I write 'Grim thought...' or 'Grim decided...' that's not conjecture on my part, but a slightly edited transcript of his own telling of the story.

It's a difficult task, of course – trying to see the world familiar to us since childhood through Orkish eyes and show how a young savage, who has almost no concept of history and the order of the universe, gradually grows into civilisation, becoming accustomed to its 'miracles' and culture (I could quite happily set the second word in quotes too). But trying to see oneself through someone else's eyes is even more difficult – and I shall figure in this memoir in a dual role, as both the narrator and one of the characters.

However, the central role in this doleful tale of love and revenge belongs neither to me nor to the Orks, but to her whose name I still cannot call to mind without tears. Perhaps after ten or twenty pages I'll summon up the strength to do it.

A few words about myself. My name is Damian-Landolpho Damilola Karpov. I don't have enough manitou to spare on a full genealogy of the name – all I know is that some of these words are closely related to Church English, some to High Russian, and some have roots going back to ancient, forgotten languages that no one in modern Siberia has spoken for a very long time. My friends call me simply Damilola.

As for my cultural and religio-political self-identification (this is an extremely notional sort of thing, of course, but you need to understand whose voice it is that you're hearing across the ages) – I'm a post-Antichristian lay existentialist, a liberative conserval, a humble slave of Manitou and simply a free non-partisan spirit, accustomed to using my own reason for thinking about everything in the world.

And as for my job, I'm a reality creator.

But by no means am I some sort of madman who imagines he's a deity, the equal of Manitou. On the contrary, I'm quite sober in my appraisal of the work for which I'm paid so little.

Any reality is a sum total of information technologies. This applies equally to a star, divined by the brain in the impulses of the optic nerve, and an Orkish revolution, reported in a news programme. The activity of viruses that have colonised a nerve tract also falls into the category of information technology. And so I am simultaneously the eye, the nerve and the virus. And also the means for conveying the eye to the target, as well as (here I lower my voice to a tender whisper) the two rapid-fire cannons on its sides.

The official name for my work is 'live news cameraman'. It would be more honest here to replace the Church English word 'live' with 'dead' – simply to call things by their proper names.

But it can't be helped – every age invents its own euphemisms. In ancient times the happiness room used to be called the privy, then the lavatory, then the toilet, the loo, the bathroom and then something else – and every one of these words gradually became impregnated with the odours of the latrine and needed to be replaced. It's the same with the forcible taking of life – christen it what you will, the essential nature of what is happening requires a frequent rotation of tags and labels.

I'm thankful that I have the words 'cameraman' and 'video-artist' to use, but in the depths of my soul of course I understand only too well what it is that I do. All of us understand this in the depths of our soul, for it is precisely there, in the uncreated darkness, where Manitou dwells, and he sees the essence of things through the ragged tatters of words.

My profession has two aspects that are inseparable from each other.

I'm a visual artist. My personal studio is called DK V-Arts & All – the serious professionals all know its small, unostentatious logo, visible in the lower right-hand corner when the frame's blown right up.

And I'm also a combat pilot for CINEWS Inc. – a corporation that films news and snuffs.

This is a structure entirely independent of the state, which the Orks find rather hard to understand. The Orks suspect that we're lying to them. They think any society has to be structured along the same lines as theirs, only even more cynical and sordid. Well, what can you expect from Orks?

Our state is no more than a shady operation that plasters over the cracks at the taxpayer's expense. The whole world and his dog spits when the President goes by, and every year it gets harder and harder to find candidates willing to run for the post – these days state functionaries have to be kept hidden away.

But the guys who really have everyone by the throat are in the Manitou Reserve – they don't like people talking about them for too long, and they've even come up with a special law on 'hate speech': if you check it out, it covers just about any mention of them at all. That's why CINEWS couldn't give a shit about the government, but there's not much chance of it going head-to-head with the Reserve. Or with the House of Manitou, which under the law is not subject to control by anyone or anything, apart from the truth (so better not go searching for it too energetically – they might get the wrong idea).

I'm certainly a pretty good artist, but there are plenty of those.

But I'm also the best pilot there is, and everyone in the company knows it. I've always been given the most difficult and delicate assignments. And I've never, even once, disappointed CINEWS Inc. or the House of Manitou.

There are only two things in life that I really love – my camera and my sura.

This time around I'll tell you about the camera.

My camera is a Hannelore-25 with full optical camouflage, and it's my own personal property, which makes it possible for me to conclude contracts on far more favourable terms than steedless knights can.

I read somewhere that 'Hannelore' was the call sign of the ancient ace Joshka Rudel from the Green SS Party, who was awarded the Red Cross with Crowns and Hemp Leaves for his heroic exploits on the African Front. But I could be mistaken, because the historical aspect interests me least of all. For me personally, the word is a reminder of the name of an affectionate and intelligent guinea pig.

In appearance the camera is a fish-shaped projectile with optical lens systems on its nose and several stabiliser and rudder fins jutting out at various angles. Some think the Hannelore resembles the streamlined racing motorcycles of ancient eras. The camouflage-manitous covering its surface give it a matt-black colour. If it was stood on end, I would be two whole heads shorter than it is.

A Hannelore can manoeuvre through the air with incredible agility. It can circle around a target for a long time, selecting the best angle – for attack or recording. It does this so quietly that it can only be heard when it flies right up close. And when its camouflage is engaged, it's practically impossible to see. Its microphones can detect, differentiate and record a conversation behind a closed door, and it can see people's silhouettes through walls with its hyperoptics. It's ideal for surveillance, low-altitude attack and – of course – filming.

The Hannelore isn't the newest thing on the market. Many think the Sky Pravda has superior characteristics in most areas, especially in relation to infrared porn shoots. It has much better

8

optical camouflage – a 'split-time' system with silicon-based wave guides. The Sky Pravda's quite impossible to spot, whereas my Hannelore uses traditional metamaterials, so it's not a good idea for me to fly in too close to a live target. And it's always best to approach downsun.

But, firstly, my Hannelore is much better armed. Secondly, its customised features make any comparison with standard models meaningless. And thirdly, I feel as much at ease with it as with my own body, and it would be very hard for me to switch to another camera.

When I say 'combat pilot', that doesn't mean I fly through the sky myself, fat paunch and all, like our hairy ancestors in their kerosene-burning gondolas. Like all the progressive professionals of our age, I work from home.

I sit beside the control manitou, with my legs bent at the knees and my chest and stomach resting against a heap of soft cushions – people ride high-speed motorcycles in a similar posture. Under my haunches I have an absolutely genuine Orkish prince's saddle from ancient times, bought from an antique dealer. It's black with age, with precious embroidery that can barely even be made out, and it's fairly hard, which provides effective prophylaxis against prostate problems and haemorrhoids if you work in a sitting or half-lying position.

I have lightweight glasses with stereoscopic manitous perched on my nose, and by swivelling my neck I can see the space surrounding the Hannelore as well as if my head was attached to the camera. Hanging above the control manitou is a woodcut print by an ancient artist, *The Four Horsemen of the Apocalypse*. I got a sommelier I know to remove one of them, to transform my workstation into a continuation of the metaphor, as it were. This sometimes inspires me.

Aerobatic flying is a complex skill, like horseback riding; I have a handlebar with curved levers in my hands and silver

Orkish stirrups under my feet – I bought them together with the saddle and attached them to the control manitou. The complex, dancelike movements of my feet control the Hannelore. The buttons on the levers are responsible for the camera's combat and filming systems: there are scads of them, but my fingers have them all off pat. When my camera's flying, I feel like I'm flying myself, adjusting my attitude in space with super-light movements of my feet and hands. But I don't feel any g-forces: when they reach a level that's dangerous for the camera's systems, the reality in my glasses starts turning red, that's all.

Interestingly enough, a less experienced flyer is also far less likely to smash the camera, since it has fail-safe idiot-proofing. But I have to disable that system to perform certain highly intricate manoeuvres – and also to acquire the capability to descend almost to ground level. If the camera gets wrecked, I'll still be alive. But it would cost me so much manitou that it would actually be better if I died. That's why I really do all the flying myself, and for me the illusion is absolutely genuine reality.

I've already said that I carry out the corporation's most complex and delicate assignments. For instance, starting the latest war with the Orks.

I need to tell you about them right at the beginning, of course, or else you won't understand where the word came from.

Why are they called that? It's not at all that we despise them and regard them as racially inferior – we don't have any prejudices like that in our society. They're people, the same as we are. At least physically. The fact that the word is formally identical to the ancient word 'ork' (or 'orc') is purely coincidental (although, let me remark in an undertone, there's really no such thing as a coincidence).

It's all a matter of their official language, which is called Upper Mid-Siberian.

There's a science that goes by the name of 'linguistic

archaeology' – I took a slight interest in it when I was studying Orkish proverbs and sayings, with the result that I still remember a whole slew of all sorts of curious facts.

Before the collapse of America and China, there was no such thing as an Upper Mid-Siberian language. It was invented in the intelligence service of the narco-state Aztlan, when it became clear that the Chinese eco-kingdoms fighting each other behind the Great Wall wouldn't interfere in events if the Aztlan naguals decided to have the Siberian Republic for lunch. Aztlan chose a traditional approach – it decided to dismantle Siberia into a series of Bantustans by forcing each of them to talk its own dialect.

Those were times of universal decline and degradation, so Upper Mid-Siberian was invented by moonlighting migrant dopeheads from the shores of the Black Sea, who were paid, following the custom in Aztlan, in narcotic substances. They were members of the cult of the Second Mashiah, and in remembrance of him they based Upper Mid-Siberian on Ukrainian, larded with yiddishisms, but for some reason or other (possibly under the influence of those substances), they tacked on an extremely complicated grammar, an erratically wandering hard consonant sign and seven past tenses. And when they thought up the phonetics, they threw in an aberrant vowel reduction from 'o' to 'u' – apparently they couldn't think of anything better.

So now they've been 'u-ing' away for about three hundred years, if not all five hundred. Aztlan and the Siberian Republic have been gone for a long time – but the language is still there. In everyday life they speak High Russian, but the official language of the state is Upper Mid-Siberian. Their own Department of Cultural Expansion keeps a strict watch on this, and we keep an eye out too. But we don't really need to, because the entire Orkish bureaucracy feeds entirely off this language and is ready to wade through bloody corpses for it.

An Orkish bureaucrat has to study the language for ten years at first, but after that he's the lord of the world. Every official document must first be translated into Upper Mid-Siberian and then officially logged as received, following which a decision from the executive authority must be appended, in Upper Mid-Siberian – and only then is it translated back for the petitioners. And if there is even a single mistake in the document, it can be declared invalid. All the Orks' official commissions and translation bureaus – and they have more of those than they have pigsties – live and grow fat off this.

Upper Mid-Siberian has made virtually no inroads into colloquial speech. The only exception is the name of their country. They call it the Urkainian Urkaganate, or Urkaine, and they call themselves Urks (apparently this was a hasty revamping of the word '*ukry*' – a High Russian name for an ancient Slavic tribe – although there are other philological hypotheses). In everyday speech the word 'Urk' is unpopular – it belongs to high-flown, pompous style and is regarded as fusty, bureaucratic and old-fashioned. But it was the origin of the Church English 'Orkland' and 'Orks'.

The Urks, especially the urban Urks, who absorb our culture through every pore of their skin and try to follow our lead in just about everything, have called themselves Orks, after the Church English manner, for centuries, deliberately exaggerating the 'o' sound. For them it's a way of expressing their protest against authoritarian despotism and emphasising their own civilisational preference – all of which suits our motion picture industry just fine. And so the word 'Ork' has almost completely supplanted the term 'Urk', and even our news channels start calling them 'Urks' only when the dark storm clouds of history gather and I am ordered into the skies.

When I say 'ordered into the skies', that doesn't mean of course that they instruct me to carry out the initial attack. Any novice can handle that. The task I'm entrusted with is filming events on temple celluloid for the news immediately before the war. Anyone in the information business will realise how important this work is.

In fact, an immense number of people work on every war, but what they do is invisible to outsiders. Wars usually begin when the Orkish authorities suppress the latest revolutionary protest too harshly (they don't know how to do it any other way). And it just so happens that the latest revolutionary protest occurs when it's time to shoot a new batch of snuffs. About once a year. Sometimes not quite so often. Many people can't understand how it is that the Orks' revolts break out at precisely the right time. That's not something I take care of myself, of course – but the mechanism is clear to me.

To this day people in the Orkish villages still have fits of religious terror at the sight of microwave ovens. They can't understand what's happening: there's no flame, no one touches the hamburger, but it keeps getting hotter and hotter. It's very simple to do – you just have to create an electromagnetic field that induces violent agitation in the hamburger's molecules. The Orkish revolutions are cooked up in exactly the same way as hamburgers, with one difference: the field that makes the particles of shit in Orkish craniums vibrate is not electromagnetic, but informational.

We don't even need to send any emissaries to them. It's enough for some global metaphor or other – and all of our metaphors are global – to hint to the proud Orkish countryside that if the love of freedom should suddenly awaken there, certain people will be on hand to help. And then the love of freedom is guaranteed to awaken in this countryside, purely in the hope of making a profit – because the central authorities will pay the village elders more and more every day not to awaken completely, but the advance of history will be impossible to halter. And what's

13

more, we won't spend a single manitou on all this, although we could print absolutely any amount for them. We'll simply sit back and observe the events with interest. And when the process attains the required intensity, we'll start bombing – whoever we need for the footage.

I can't see anything especially reprehensible about all this. Our information channels don't lie. The Orks really are ruled by exceptionally vile scumbags, who deserve to be bombed at any moment, and if their regime isn't actually evil in its pure form, that's merely because it's significantly diluted by degenerative senility.

In any case, we don't have to justify ourselves to anyone. Condemn us if you like, but unfortunately we're the best thing this world has to offer. And we're not the only ones who think so – the Orks do too.

Informational support for the revolutionary movement in Orkland is provided by sommeliers from a different department, and I'm responsible solely and exclusively for the video footage. Which is substantially more important, from both the artistic and religious points of view. Especially at the very beginning of the war, when the high tide of the initial headlines has already receded ('THE WORLD HAS WARNED THE ORKS...'), but there isn't any decent feedback as yet.

For the last few wars I've worked as a team with Bernard-Henri Montaigne Montesquieu – a name that you've probably heard. In fact, Bernard-Henri was my neighbour (the rumours of his lavish lifestyle are greatly exaggerated). We didn't become friends, because I didn't approve of some of his habits, but we were close acquaintances, and in the professional sense we made a good, solid team. I doubled as trailing wingman and cameraman and he was the frontman-gunlayer (or, as he himself once dubbed it in some esoteric mix of Church English and Old French, the *aimer d'aimer*).

14

He preferred to call himself a philosopher. That was how he was presented in the news. But in the payroll register, which is kept in Church English, his job title is given unambiguously as 'crack discoursemonger first grade'. In actual fact he's another military man, just like me. But there's no contradiction in this. We're not children after all; we understand that the power of contemporary philosophy lies not in syllogisms, but in close air support. And that's the reason why the Orks frighten their children with that word 'discoursemonger'.

Just as every genuine philosopher is supposed to do, Bernard-Henri wrote an obscure book in Old French. It's called *Les Feuilles Mortes*, which means 'Dead Leaves' (he himself translated it slightly differently, as *Dead Pages*). Crack discoursemongers pride themselves on their knowledge of this language and trace their family trees back to Old French thinkers, inventing similar names for themselves.

Of course, this is unadulterated travesty, burlesque – pure and simple. They, however, take the matter very seriously – their special assault group is called *Le Coq d'Ésprit*, and in public they constantly toss around incomprehensible phrases punctuated with guttural 'r' sounds. But I know for certain that Bernard-Henri knew only a few sentences in Old French and even listened to songs with a translation. So, putting two and two together, the book must have been written for him by a creative articulator with a French language module.

We know how these treatises in Old French are composed: take some obscure ancient quotation, stick it into a manitou, tap your fingers on the menu for a couple of seconds, and it's done – heap the blocks of words all the way up to the ceiling, if you like. But the other gunlayers of our aerial strike force don't even go to that much trouble. So Bernard-Henri was a conscientious professional, and if it wasn't for that grim hobby

15

of his, the on-screen dictionary would devote a lot more space to him.

To this day many people regard him as some kind of altruistic knight of spirit and truth. He wasn't. But I don't condemn him for that.

Life's too short, and the sweet drops of honey along the way are all too few. A normal public intellectual prefers to spin his lies comfortably along the force lines of the discourse, which start and end somewhere in the upper hemisphere of Big Byz. Sometimes, in a safe area, he allows himself a free-spirited crow – usually in Old French, to avoid accidentally hurting anyone's feelings. And also, obviously, he denounces the repressive Orkish regime. And that's all.

Any other behaviour is economically unjustifiable. In Church English this is called 'smart free speech' – an art mastered to perfection by all participants in the global Spirit Pride.

It's not as simple as it might seem. A certain internal flexibility isn't enough, you also need to know something about the way these force lines actually curve, which the Orks can never understand. The lines also have a persistent tendency to shift their position steadily, so the work is almost as edgy and risky as a stockbroker's.

Ah yes, by the way – the creative articulator surmises that the word 'smart' (meaning 'astute'), was formed from the ancient sign for a 'dollar' (as a manitou once used to be called) and 'mart' – an abbreviated form of 'market'. It could well be true. But on its own, a mastery of 'smart free speech' is a rather low-paid skill, since the supply significantly exceeds the demand.

Don't get the idea that I look down on all these guys, though. Basically I'm no better than them. As a commercial visual artist I'm undoubtedly a cowardly conformist – a state of affairs that I'm just fine with. But I'm also an audacious and experienced flyer, and that's a fact. As well as being a resourceful and ardent

16

lover, although it's unlikely that she to whom my love aspires will be able to appreciate that adequately. But more about that later.

Anyway, it all started with Bernard-Henri and myself being given an assignment for the newsreels – to film the formal video-pretext for War No. 221, the so-called 'casus belly' (the dictionaries claim that this Church English expression derives from an ancient idiom meaning 'to tear [the enemy's] stomach'). To film actually means 'to organise'. Bernard-Henri and I understand this without it needing to be said, since we have already started two wars together – No. 220 and No. 218. As for No. 219, it was started by our creative competitors.

Organising a casus belly is an esoteric, delicate assignment and by no means easy. An assignment that is only entrusted to the very finest specialists. That is, to us.

The most convincing and indisputable video-pretext for a war, on which absolutely all the critics, commentators and pundits in modern visual culture are agreed (as they have been for centuries) is considered to be the so-called 'damsel in distress'. I apologise again for the Church English, but there's no other way to say it. And I also actually like the sound of these menacing words that positively reek of gunpowder smoke.

A 'damsel in distress' is not simply 'a young woman in anguish' as this phrase is translated. Let's just say that if an Orkish maiden is sleeping in a hayloft somewhere and has a nightmare that makes her break out in a sweat and sets her trembling all over, you can't start bombing because of that. If the young Orkish maiden has fallen into a pile of shit, been given a thick ear by her granny and is sitting in a puddle, roaring her head off, that's no help to you, although her anguish might be entirely sincere. No, a 'damsel in distress' presupposes, firstly, offended innocence and, secondly, heavily armed evil hovering over it.

Generating a scene like that at any required degree of resolution is a simple five-minute job for our sommeliers. But CINEWS Inc. only does that sort of thing in its entertainment schedule. Everything that finds its way into the news clips must actually happen on the physical plane and become part of the Light of the Universe. 'Thou shalt keep thy newsreel wholesome,' said Manitou. Well, perhaps he didn't actually say it, but that's what we've been told.

It's for religious reasons that news clips are shot on temple celluloid film. Photons burn their way into a light-sensitive emulsion prepared according to ancient formulae by votaries of the House of Manitou, precisely as it was done many hundreds of years ago (even the width of the film is devoutly reproduced).

The film has to be flammable – because the Formulations contain the phrase 'it blazes like the blood of Manitou'. And the reason why a living imprint of light needs to be preserved is explained during initiation into the Mysteries, but I've been out of short pants so long now that I can't remember it – and anyway, I don't wish to stick my nose into questions of theology. The really important thing here is that a film camera takes up an awful lot of space in my Hannelore. If not for the camera, plus the rockets and the cannons, the rest of the technology could be tucked away in a container the size of a standard dildo – but there's nothing to be done, if that's what Manitou wants.

When it comes to the news, we can't falsify the representation of events. But Manitou, as far as the theologians' understanding goes, won't object if we give these events a little nudge to help them happen. But no more than a mere smidgen, of course – and here you have a borderline that can only be sensed by genuine professionals. Such as Bernard-Henri and myself. We don't falsify reality. But we can arrange a caesarean section, so to speak, to reveal what it's pregnant with – in a convenient place and at the right time.

We waited several days for a suitable moment for the operation. Then an informant in the Urkagan's retinue informed us that Torn Durex, whose hands were already stained with the blood of rebel Orks (a wing of combat cameras had managed to forestall a massive bloody massacre with a missile strike, but the Kagan still had the collateral casualties on his conscience) was returning to Slava (that's what the Orkish capital is called) by the northern road.

Bernard-Henri and I immediately flew out on an intercept course.

When I say 'we', it means that my Hannelore flew there, armed with film and shells, and taking my conscious perception with her, while my body stayed at home, swivelling its head in combat glasses and pressing buttons on levers. But Bernard-Henri was actually delivered to Orkland in person. That's his job: it's a risk, of course, but with my Hannelore there, only a very small one.

The transport platform dropped Bernard-Henri off at the side of the road a couple of kilometres from Slava – and then rose back up into the clouds to avoid wasting its battery on camouflage.

The mission had begun.

Bernard-Henri told me to survey the terrain and locate some suitable material while he prayed. Prayed, indeed... In reality the old satyr was simply tanking up on dope, the way he always did before a combat shooting. But the senior sommeliers turn a blind eye to that, because it makes Bernard-Henri look better on camera. And it goes without saying that the most important thing of all in the work of an on-screen discoursemonger is the way he looks while he's talking. Expansive gestures, open posture, a calm, slow speaking voice, a confident manner. No scratching your head or sticking your hands in your pockets. We live in a visual culture, and the semantic content of on-screen babble accounts for only fifteen per cent of the overall effect. All the rest is in the picture.

Bernard-Henri's substances start taking full effect after about an hour, or an hour and a half – exactly when the Kagan's convoy was due to appear. There was plenty of time, but I couldn't afford to waste it – I had to get everything set up urgently.

I climbed higher.

The terrain was rather depressing. That is, on one side of the road it was actually quite picturesque, as far as that word can be applied to Orkland – there were hemp and banana plantations, a little river and a couple of stinking Orkish villages. But on the other side lay Orkland's most dismal jungle. It's not dismal simply on its own account, but because of what comes after it. After only a few hundred metres the trees thin out, giving way to an immense swamp which also serves as a cemetery.

The Orks call it the Swamp of Memory – this is where the whole city of Slava buries its dead. From the air it looks like a murky, grey-green lake, with the veins of narrow streams running into it. It's dotted all over with dark specks – from the air they look like freckles. These are floating Orkish coffins, the so-called 'sputniks' – round boats covered with a roof of straw with four sticks jutting upwards. The Orks believe that in these garbage pails their souls fly off into outer space to Manitou. I'm not so sure about that.

The Orks deliberately planted the forest along the edge of the swamp (yes, such things really do happen – an Ork planting a sapling). They did it to drive back the stinking, bluish-green slurry from the road and their vegetable gardens. When the Kagan passes by, he's always accompanied by bodyguards, since it's easy to set up an ambush here. And the area is thinly populated in any case: the Orks are afraid of their own dead. Someone once hammered it into their heads that each generation inevitably betrays the one before it, and fear of their ancestors has assumed the proportions of a collective neurosis for them. A neurosis supported by the fat crocodiles living in the swamp, although they don't bother to come out of the water: the sputniks are more than enough for them.

In ancient times, so-called 'sages' used to settle here in an attempt to enhance their spiritual status by daily proximity to death. And the urban Orks used to come to them to have their fortunes told from *The Book of Orkasms* – they believed that in this way they could ask Manitou Himself a question (I'm not joking, the Orks really do have such a book, although it was very probably written by our sommeliers).

But under the Orkish emperor Loss Solid, the free-trading sages were abolished, and all fortune tellers were made subordinate to the General Staff. Since then the only people who go into the cemetery forest are young couples who have nowhere to be alone. They're afraid of dead people and crocodiles, of course, but love is stronger than death. If I was a philosopher, like Bernard-Henri, I would definitely sing a hymn of praise in Old French to the secret festival of life that blossoms so brightly in these thickets of decay.

I could search for suitable material near the villages, where Orkish wenches of a tender age wander, pasturing their cattle. Or I could fly above the margin of the jungle, along the road. I chose the latter course, and after flying literally for only five minutes, I came across what I needed.

An Orkish couple – a boy and a girl of the same age, about sixteen or slightly older – were walking along the verge of the road. I can be so confident about their age, because this is the Orkish 'age of consent', and if either of them was younger, they would almost certainly never have dared to be seen together. The Orkish authorities imitate our mechanism of sexual repression with obtuse zeal – they'd adopt our age of consent too, if our advisers would only allow it. Apparently they think that's how they'll get on the road to a technotronic society. In any case, there's no other road left open to them.

21

The couple was carrying fishing rods. That immediately made everything clear – for young Orks 'fishing' takes the place of a back-row seat in a movie theatre.

I switched to maximum magnification and studied their faces for a while. The boy was an ordinary Orkish lad, with clean good looks and flaxen hair. They're all like that, until they start drinking *volya* and shooting up *durian*. But the damsel was absolutely ideal.

She looked just great in shot. Firstly, she didn't look like a child, and that was good, because they'd shown minors before the last two wars, and the audience was tired of them. Secondly, she was very pretty – I mean for a biological woman, of course. I was sure that Bernard-Henri would immediately get the urge to protect a little piggy like this from any kind of distress.

I glanced at my manitou. The Kagan was still a long way off, and I had time to spare. But there wasn't really any point in looking for other material. I informed Bernard-Henri briefly about my find and transmitted the damsel cutie to his manitou, and he was hooked instantly, I could tell from the way he was breathing. Then I engaged maximum camouflage, cautiously flew round the couple, came up to them from behind and started following, listening to their prattle.

They turned into the forest and soon found a clearing on the bank of one of the streams flowing into the swamp. And there they immediately started... fishing. Apparently the lad was a keen angler, and he was trying hard to put other ideas out of his head. The girl soon became conspicuously bored, and so did I, but he just kept on fishing. And the fish were biting.

When there was half an hour left until the convoy arrived, they started getting into more interesting things. But by then, unfortunately, it was time for me to interfere.

Grim looked up at the immense sphere of Byzantion hanging in the sky.

If he leaned his head over and screwed up his eyes, he could see it as the nest of some huge bird that had made its home in the next tree. If he screwed his eyes up even tighter, he could imagine it was a ball from a game of soccer being played by Titans – flying towards him out of the distant ancient times, before there were any palm trees here, when snow fell for many days of the year and hairy mammoths strode across the virginal white land . . .

Grim looked at Chloe.

'I've got to do it right now,' he thought. 'It'll be too late afterwards . . . But how? What the hell, just get up, go over and put my arms round her? Then she'll go and ask – what's this, all of a sudden? Why now, and not earlier? Damn these fishing rods . . .'

All the signs were that Chloe wanted the same thing as he did. She hadn't put on any make-up before their date, and in the implicit code of teen ritual that was a hint that she was expecting decisive action that could leave her make-up seriously compromised.

And it was good that she hadn't done her face up.

He liked her round head (with its funny protruding ears, pink cheeks and skin as tight as the head of a war drum) much better without any make-up. And Chloe smelled really nice too, not Orkish at all – she'd probably folded away her clothes overnight with sweet-scented herbs. Or bought the fashionable perfume of the season, Ancient Serpent – her family certainly wasn't poor.

She was dressed trendily too, in a new school dress that was simultaneously a reminder of childhood and an invitation to forget it. And over that she had a sleeveless waistcoat with pictures of Nicolas-Olivier Laurence von Trier in various roles from his long career. Waistcoats like that, with the slogan 'Two Cultures – One World', were made in the Yellow Zone, and they cost at least a hundred manitou. In Grim's family they didn't spend that kind of money on trinkets. And the little cosmetics purse hanging over Chloe's shoulder was made out of Doberman skin – that wasn't cheap either.

'Wake up, you've got another bite.'

Grim jerked his rod up, took the fish off the hook and tossed it to Chloe. She caught it and smacked its head lightly against a rock. Then she giggled and did it again. And again.

Exasperated, Grim walked over and took the flapping fish from her. He stunned it with a single blow and went back to his rods.

He didn't feel like cussing her out – in comparison with other Orkish girls Chloe was really kind. She never tortured mosquitoes before she swatted them.

'What's go you so cranky?' Chloe asked, putting the fish in a plastic bag filled with water, where two others were already languishing. 'I'm bored. Can't think why I bothered coming along really.'

Grim's blood suddenly ran cold. That's it, he thought. And afterwards she won't...

'If you're bored, then let's talk,' he suggested.

Fortunately he had something to keep his hands busy – he had to skewer a fresh worm on the hook.

'Come on then,' Chloe sighed and hugged her knees.

Grim cast his line, walked over to Chloe and sat down beside her, making sure he didn't touch her accidentally.

'Have you written your essay already?'

Chloe nodded.

'I cribbed it. How about you?'

'No,' said Grim. 'I haven't even started.'

'Then you're screwed.'

'No I'm not,' Grim objected. 'I'll write it in a day. I'll rip it off from the *Free Encyclopaedia*.'

'You're always boasting about that encyclopaedia of yours,' said Chloe. 'You twist the conversation round every time, just so you can mention it. How would you like me to boast about my dad having a motorbike?'

Grim blushed – she'd hit the bull's eye.

'Don't be daft,' he said. 'That's not why I brought up the encyclopaedia. It's because there are so many things I can't find even there.'

'Such as?'

'Why are the names of all the Orkish rulers chosen up there at Big Byz? Take the Torns, for instance. Durex or Skyn – those aren't Orkish words, are they?

'No, they're not Orkish,' Chloe agreed.

'They take words from the ancient times, ones our people don't remember. Maybe they mean something insulting, and we don't know about it. And they invent our soldiers' uniforms. They just send the pattern down to us before the war starts. There isn't a word about that in the encyclopaedia. And they were saying at the market that the Torns keep the entire Orkish treasury up there with *them*. Otherwise they wouldn't print manitous for us.'

Chloe cuffed Grim gently on the back of his head.

'Better keep your mouth shut about that,' she said. 'Or they'll boil you in shit with the *orktivists*. Some great hero from the Yellow Zone you are!'

She gave him a thump on the ear and moved closer – close

enough for Grim to feel her side touching him. It was very pleasurable. But for some reason he pulled away. Chloe sighed.

'All right then, look at this,' said Grim, sticking his hand in his pocket and pulling out a five-manitou note.

Folding it in an intricate sequence of movements, he managed to transform the holographic giant with the multi-cornered hat, supporting the sphere of Byzantion on his shoulders, into an incredibly repulsive dwarf with legs that sprouted from his armpits.

'You've worn me out with your politics,' said Chloe. 'And you've got another bite.'

Grim put his money away, ran over to the rods, deftly jerked the fish out and tossed it to Chloe. This time she stunned it with a single blow.

'That's the fourth already,' she declared, putting the fish in the plastic bag of water. 'Maybe we should go before a crocodile eats us?'

Grim nodded stoically.

'I'll just put some make-up on, then,' said Chloe, giving him a look of frank derision.

Grim looked away.

After tying the plastic bag of fish with a sturdy double knot, Chloe opened her dog-skin purse and started dolling herself up.

Glancing sideways at her, Grim started folding away his rods. If only he didn't have such a sick, dismal feeling, it would really be funny. He knew the entire sequence of actions that would follow now – he'd seen it already on his last, equally fruitless fishing trip.

Chloe took a charcoal pencil out of her purse and drew three jagged zigzags on her forehead: they looked like an old woman's wrinkles – the so-called 'wisdom lines'. Orkish girls believed that the lines made them look clever, but Grim had his doubts. Next a white-clay pencil appeared in her hands. After applying a thick layer of white to her rosy cheeks, she put the pencil away, took out her rouge and drew two round crimson spots over the white clay – they were supposed to represent the healthy, ruddy bloom of young cheeks.

To complete the procedure, she carefully positioned on her face a pair of massive black spectacle frames with no lenses, and held together at two points with thread – the very latest chic streak of girly fashion.

But even after all these procedures, in Grim's eyes there was still something attractive about her – although now Chloe reminded him of the piglet Snort, the heroine of an Orkish fable who wallowed in mud and hay on the eve of the Great Gluttony, so that she could pretend to be an old rat and cheat her fate. The moral of the fable was simple – they ate all the other piglets in silence, but cracked jokes and told funny stories while they ate Snort.

Chloe put away her cosmetic tackle, raised her little face and shot him an entrancing glance from under her thick ginger lashes.

'We can go now,' she said.

And at this point – perhaps because now he thought Chloe looked much less attractive – Grim finally made up his mind.

He took a step towards Chloe, embraced her resolutely and kissed her – at first on the cheek, and then on her upper lip.

'What are you up to...? What... Ooh... Go away, will you, you idiot. I've got my make-up on already... I mean it...'

But Grim didn't back off, and after a few more minutes of intense snuffling, Chloe was lying on her back with the triumphant Grim on top of her, and everything he had previously only dared to do in his imagination was actually taking place.

Chloe didn't do anything to encourage what he was doing, but she didn't actually object – she looked off to the side, puckered up her face and sighed contemptuously, as if she'd been sick and tired of this sort of thing for years. Grim wasn't really very adept, since he had almost no experience at all, but eventually all the necessary buttons had been unfastened, the bands of fabric had been parted and he realised that now it was really going to happen.

In fact it had already started happening, when Chloe suddenly slapped him on the back.

'Look,' she said, and nodded towards the clearing.

Grim looked up.

There was nothing there. But from the way Chloe's body had tensed up, he realised that she wasn't joking.

Then he saw it too.

A kind of trembling in the air above the clearing. A vague, quivering patch. And it wasn't the only thing quivering – the trees on the other side of the clearing were too, like when you look through a current of heated air on a hot day. It was almost impossible to spot at first, but the longer Grim looked, the stranger the trees in that patch seemed – as if they weren't genuine trunks and branches, but only reflections, distorted in a corridor of mirrors.

'Do you see it?' Chloe whispered.

'Uh-uh.'

'What is it?'

'Just a moment,' said Grim.

Trying not to let Chloe slip out from under him, he grabbed a lump of earth and grass in his fist, hoisted himself up a bit and flung it at the quivering circle.

He really shouldn't have done that.

Instead of flying through the circle, the earth scattered and fell. The impact was only very light, but it was followed by absolutely astounding changes.

In a split second the circle shrank in towards its centre and disappeared. And at the point where it had just been, Death appeared.

Grim realised straightaway what it was – as if someone had already shown him the scene and explained what their final meeting would be like. He recognised it and was hardly even scared at all.

Death was matt-black and looked like a long, low motorbike – with no wheels, but lots of asymmetrical headlamps on its nose. Some of them were transparent and some were white, like a blind man's eyes. There was no rider on the motorbike, but that seemed quite natural for Death. Death had short black wings jutting out crookedly at the sides, and its asymmetrically assembled body consisted of a host of smoothly swaying plane surfaces – like a series of valves constantly opening and closing.

Death even had a tattoo – red arrows that came together towards the nose, and zigzagged at the centre of the fuselage. There were little symbols under the arrows, recording victories – large and small human figures and some numbers, very substantial numbers. Right behind the numbers on the fuselage there were sooty steel brackets with the short muzzles of cannons protruding from them. And Death hummed too – but very quietly: if Grim hadn't deliberately listened, he'd never have noticed it.

'A camera,' Chloe gasped, and Grim realised that Chloe was right.

But that didn't mean he'd been wrong about Death.

He'd never seen a combat camera from so close up. Only in pictures.

'Stop shaking like that,' Chloe whispered. 'If he wanted to kill us, he'd have done it by now. He wants something. Let's get up, only slowly ... And put your hands up.'

Trying not to make any sudden movement, Grim got to his feet – and realised the full seriousness of his situation. It was easy for Chloe: once she got up, all she had to do was adjust her

29

dress. But his trousers fell down, and he stood there, red-faced with shame, looking into the wall eyes of the black motorbike suspended in the air in front of him.

Suddenly loud music started playing: the camera's external speakers had come on.

The music was strange, not Orkish at all. It was menacing and piercing, and it reminded him of ancient times, forgotten glory and death. It carried on playing for a whole minute at least, and towards the end of it Grim felt such a surge of valour in his chest that he bent down, pulled up his trousers and fastened the button.

The music stopped and the camera swayed smoothly in the air, as if it was indicating which way to go. Grim took an indecisive step in that direction and the camera immediately nodded its white nose, exactly like someone expressing agreement.

Grim took another step, and then another. The camera moved along with him.

'He wants us to go out on the road,' said Chloe.

'I realised that,' Grim answered. 'Maybe we should run into the forest? How's he going to catch us in among the trees?'

It was hard to believe it, but the camera seemed to have heard what he said. It swung round towards the forest dividing the clearing from the road, and Grim saw the complex curve of its body in profile. On one of the stabilisers he could clearly make out the emblem of Byzantion – two capital Bs reflecting each other, looking like a figure eight with a vertical line drawn through it.

There was a loud crack. The camera was shrouded in smoke, and incredibly fast-moving red threads went hurtling into the forest, leaving a smoky trail behind them. When the threads collided with tree trunks, yellow clouds of wood dust swirled up and the tall old trees went tumbling in different directions, sliced through like wax candles.

Then the camera stopped firing, turned back to Grim and Chloe and moved its nose from side to side several times – exactly like someone shaking his head. When it stopped, they could still hear the cracking of trees toppling.

'That's how he's going to catch us,' said Chloe. 'Got it?'

'Got it,' Grim replied, not really knowing who to – the camera or Chloe.

Now there was a smoking corridor leading straight out to the road, and choosing which way to go was easy. The camera let them go ahead and floated after them.

Out on the road, Grim and Chloe stopped.

'Now where?' Grim asked.

'He'll explain that in a moment,' Chloe guessed.

Grim turned towards the camera.

The camera did something very strange. Without taking its wall-eyes off them, it floated up and off to the side, towards the sun – and suddenly disappeared. Grim realised it had activated its camouflage again. Immediately there was no way of telling where it was – he couldn't spot any trembling in the air.

Grim gazed up into the sky for a few seconds.

'Maybe it's flown away?' he suggested.

No one answered.

Grim turned round and saw Chloe lying in the road, curled up in a neat little ball. She looked as if she was sleeping serenely, and there was some kind of green dart sticking out of her arm. Grim was just about to lean down when he heard a click and felt something sting him. He saw the same kind of green dart sticking out of his chest. He pulled it out – the plastic stalk ended in a short, flexible needle, so thin that no blood came out.

'No big deal,' he thought.

Then he suddenly felt an overwhelming urge to sit down in the road, and the desire was absolutely impossible to resist. And once he sat down, he realised he had to lie down, so he did.

Chloe was lying beside him: he could see her dress, her shoulder and part of her face. Her eyes were open, but she was looking away from him.

Grim didn't really understand what was going on. It seemed to him that if he just made a bit of an effort, he could stand up. He needed someone to help him, give him a nudge to get him started, and then the numb stupor would release him. But there wasn't anyone to help.

The sun seemed to have moved across the sky a bit. And then he felt another prick, in his leg this time, and the paralysis instantly disappeared. He turned his head and saw that Chloe had revived too.

She was almost on her feet when she suddenly got a blow in the back that sent her sprawling in the dust again. Grim had the impression that the sun had gone behind a cloud. He looked up.

Half the sky was blanked out by the armed horsemen towering over him. There was an entire cavalcade behind them, and Grim and Chloe were blocking its way.

Obviously someone very important was travelling in it. He was being guarded by Ganjaberserks from the Slava garrison – grey-bearded giants with dusty false dreadlocks and short bone pipes in their mouths. They were dressed in camouflage battlesuits with black armour and carrying heavy spears. One of the riders had just dug Chloe in the back with the blunt end of his spear – and now he was turning it round to strike with the sharp end. The berserks killed without a second thought, so Grim froze in horror.

Suddenly a brief command rang out and the berserk lowered his spear. The line of horsemen parted, and they moved off the road.

'Get up!'

Grim and Chloe scrambled to their feet.

There in front of them was a black motorenvagen – with

a long wheel-base and folding roof, the most expensive kind. Only top brass could have one like that. But the men sitting in it weren't Global Orks – they were morose Right Protectors, wearing black cloaks. Another motorenvagen was standing a bit further away – also black, even lower slung and more imposing, only with a closed top. And towering up even further away was a red palanquin covered in gold spastikas with a wonder-working Visage of Manitou hidden behind a curtain. It was held up by sweaty musclemen in velvet shorts, four on each handle.

The top of the second motorenvagen opened smoothly, folding into a shell behind the seats. Skipping in his zeal, one of the court secretary eunuchs, dressed in a heraldic body stocking and a cockerel mask, immediately darted over to the door.

The man sitting in the motorenvagen was...

Grim couldn't believe his eyes.

Sitting there in the motorenvagen was Torn Durex, the Urkish Kagan and sovereign ruler, the great hero of seven wars. On his left, sprawled out on the back seat, was his sweety-boy favourite, his little face smeared with candy. On the Kagan's right, glittering with gold chains, was a rubber woman, the kind they make in Big Byz. The Kagan didn't like women, everyone knew that. It was merely a status symbol, a declaration of tolerance and willingness for intercultural dialogue.

The leader's sullen face, with its sideburns trimmed on a slant and grey bags under the eyes, boded no good at all. He raised one hand and yawned, straightening up his body, encased in a long, black silk frock coat.

'What's going on?'

The secretary sagged down to bring the beak of his mask closer to his lord and master's ear, and started talking in a low voice, pointing to Grim and Chloe.

The wrinkles on Torn Durex's face smoothed out and he laughed.

33

'In the road?' he asked.

The secretary nodded.

Torn Durex looked at Grim appraisingly, as if he was pondering whether to take him on as a pageboy. Grim noticed that the Kagan's favourite was looking at him intently too. Durex shifted his glance to Chloe, then back to Grim, and evidently changed his mind.

'Scram!' he said, waving his hand.

And then something unexpected happened.

'*J'accuse!*'

The words rang out over the road in an imperious tone.

Frightened as Grim already was by what was happening, this frightened him even more. No one dared to speak in that tone of voice in the Kagan's presence.

No one except discoursemongers.

Everyone in Urkaine knew that exclamation, whistling and cracking like a whip. They frightened children with it, because it brought death in its wake. '*J'accuse*' meant 'I accuse', only not in Church English, but the language of some other ancient tribe, from which the discoursemongers traced their lineage.

A man who had appeared out of nowhere walked quickly towards Chloe – he must have approached the procession while all eyes were fixed on the Kagan.

The man was tall and radiated majesty, although he was dressed very simply, even poorly, in a cassock of sackcloth belted with rope. The majesty was supplied by silver curls down to his shoulders and an aquiline nose. That was how knights and heroes looked.

Somehow Grim was immediately reminded of an ancient coin with a gold border – the 'One Oiro' from the Museum of the Ancestors, which had the outlines of two human figures merging together stamped on it, with their arms and legs spread out to the sides. There was so much freedom and proud dignity in the design that the coin obviously hadn't been minted in Orkland or even Byzantion. The explanation on the card read: 'The so-called "Vitruvian Sodomites", an engraving by Leonardo da Vinci'. Despite the denunciatory caption, the coin had made a powerful impression on Grim. And this discoursemonger aroused pretty much the same kind of feeling.

He himself was apparently quite agitated by what was happening – his lower jaw was trembling slightly, as if he was pronouncing tiny little words very fast, and his eyes glittered brightly. He was holding a staff with a curved handle and a leather strap wrapped round it. When he raised his arms the gap in his robe revealed a bulletproof vest chosen to match the colour of the cassock precisely. Only the upper people had those.

The Kagan said nothing, staring morosely at the stranger – according to the rules of etiquette he would have dishonoured himself by responding to a preamble like that.

The cockerel-secretary was the first to recover his wits.

'Who are you?' he asked coming to his sovereign lord's aid. 'What are you doing in the land of the Urks and by what right and authority do you block the way of the Urkagan?'

The man took a step towards Chloe and put his free arm round her shoulder.

'I shall answer you,' he roared, raising his staff even higher. 'I am a philosopher. But if you do not understand what that word means, then for you let me be simply a concerned passer-by. A passer-by who has no authority other than that granted by his own conscience...'

Grim noticed that the man wasn't looking at the cockerel-secretary, but in a completely different direction – into empty space above the forest. He guessed the camera must still be hovering somewhere over there. It finally became a little bit clearer what was happening.

'But though I may have no authority, I have news!' the man

roared in a well-trained voice. 'News that will not be to your liking. Your band of torturers and murderers shall do no harm to this child, and not one more tear shall fall from these eyes of blue!'

Grim thought that it obviously wasn't him who was being talked about – his eyes were yellowish-grey. And then he saw the man gradually turn Chloe towards the invisible camera and nudge her to one side, so that Grim was left behind her. And an ancient Orkish instinct suddenly told Grim that in order to survive, what he had to do now was not run away from the camera, but stay in the frame any way he could. He took a step forward and stood beside Chloe. The discoursemonger gave him a dark look, but there was nothing he could do. Meanwhile his voice carried on rumbling melodically across the road:

'Every man is born free, as Manitou conceived him! And I cannot, I will not stand silent when some monster, some insatiable, malicious beast, tramples down the bright festival of childhood with the black tyre of his limousine, bought with the tears of countless widows. I do not know – although it would indeed be extremely interesting to know, and without further delay – how much longer the free world will put up with this dark strangler of freedom, pretending that it does not notice the innocent tears and the blood spurting straight into our optical devices! Nothing can justify the mockery of defenceless innocence, no plugs in indifferent ears will muffle the pounding of a child's heart, tossed to the dogs and the pigs to be devoured! Today I accuse the Orkish Urkagan of being his own people's executioner. How long will we carry on pretending not to notice the atrocities committed by this pervert, this serial killer, this psychiatrist's dream and most dangerous of sadists? But I do not wish to speak any more of this degenerate, because he makes me feel sick. I wish to save this... This... These youngsters, whose harsh homeland has denied their right to childhood and youth... I proclaim that henceforth they are under the protection of Byzantion! They are granted the right to enter Big Byz!'

He pointed to the distant dark sphere in the sky, at the same time turning his head to the side. There was nothing but roadside bushes where he was looking, and Grim realised the discoursemonger was simply displaying his noble profile to the camera.

'No one can talk like that to the Kagan!' the cockerel-secretary whispered in amazement.

The stranger turned his visage, radiant with transcendent joy, towards the secretary for an instant and then turned away again towards a section of sky that was empty – for those not in the know.

'And who does speak to him anyway, this Kagan of yours?'

It seemed to Grim that everything suddenly went very quiet.

The Kagan remained gloomily silent, looking straight ahead. But this was too much for the cockerel-secretary.

'Dishonour!' he gasped, pulled his teeny little sword out of its scabbard and started walking towards the discoursemonger.

The stranger waited calmly, with his staff raised high in the air and his face still set in the same confident smile of a man unafraid to die for his words. And just when Grim thought that was about to happen, there was a crack in the sky, and the familiar red threads sliced the cockerel-secretary in half. Tall fountains of dust rose into the air on all sides.

Everyone standing on the road froze.

But a second later everything started moving.

The first to dart off was Chloe – she tore herself out from under the man's arm and ran for it.

Then the soldiers surrounding Durex's motorenvagen came to their senses – they pulled out their weapons and went for the man. But as soon as they reached the secretary, floating in a red puddle, they were cut down by the same blurred red arrows – although the soldiers were moving quickly, the cannons pulverised their rush with ease. A cloud of dust rose up over the road, so thick that the Kagan's motorenvagen was almost completely hidden, the heap of shattered bodies on the ground grew higher and the man, still standing there smiling in the same way, raised his staff toward his attackers.

Grim finally realised this was the right moment to get off the road. There was no one holding him back. He dashed past the berserks, who were trying to restrain their frightened horses, and hurtled into the forest. After running for a few minutes, he stumbled over a root and fell. He stayed there, lying where he had fallen, trying to control his wildly pumping lungs.

For a while he heard shooting behind him. Then it stopped.

After waiting for half an hour, he walked through the forest and out onto the road. The ambushed column was behind an outcrop of the forest. He couldn't see the corpses from there.

'Chloe!' he called.

He was afraid to shout loudly, but even so he decided to try just once more.

'Chloe!'

'I'm here!' he heard her answer.

Grim saw a figure detach itself from the line of the trees and Chloe came out onto the road about a hundred steps ahead of him. Grim set off towards her, screwing up his eyes against the sun.

He had already opened his mouth to start telling her about the nightmare he'd just seen, when it turned out the nightmare had no intention of ending just yet.

A transparent shadow quivered behind Chloe's back. Then a triangular hole appeared in empty space and a tapering set of steps extended downwards out of it. The discoursemonger in the brown cassock appeared in the hole, then walked down and

38

before Chloe even noticed him, swept her up in his arms and tossed her into the black triangle.

Grim went dashing after him, but the discoursemonger was already climbing the steps. Grim managed to grab hold of his leg, but lost his balance and almost fell. The discoursemonger looked down at his feet. The sun lit up the hair cascading over his shoulders, and for a moment Grim thought it was some sun-god looking down from the heavens at him here on the earth. And then the sun-god pulled his foot free, raised it – and shoved Grim into the dust with his sweet-smelling sandal.

I mean, the shots were simply astounding. One series for eternity, with the sun blazing straight into the camera over the ranks of soldiers with their pikes. And another, without any fancy flourishes, for the news.

I was recording simultaneously on all media, and now I had almost a minute on temple celluloid, with one frame showing Torn Durex lounging in his motorenvagen, with his shoddy rubber woman (not even animated, and its skin was the cheapest kind of bioplastic), the wild-looking bearded warriors with their weapons raised, and the kids standing in front of them. And Chloe had turned out especially well, because she kept blinking her immense eyes all the time, trying to turn on the tears, but she just couldn't, and it looked as if she really didn't understand where she was and what was happening. And her Orkish paint-job was just right – those zigzags on the forehead are the coming fashion with our youngsters too. That will be good for the empathy, any sommelier can see that.

The bearded Orks were spot-on too.

The Orks have two types of elite guards, two brigades that are supposed to form up on the right and the left of the Kagan – the 'Right Protectors' and the 'Ganjaberserks' (they don't call them 'Left Protectors' because Orks believe the left side is unclean). In combat terms they're more or less equally matched, but the Ganjaberserks' pipes, beards and dreadlocks make them look a whole lot more impressive. It was lucky for me that they were the ones who started dealing with the children – Right Protectors wear long black cloaks with spastikas, and they look more like priests than soldiers.

Grim also ended up in the shot, which I hadn't been trying for at all. But there were about fifteen seconds with Chloe fluttering her eyelashes all alone, right beside a jagged spearhead, with a slightly blurred Kagan in the background. They could cut Grim out now, or they could leave him in the shot, with an eye to the gay audience – he was really quite handsome. But I don't decide things like that.

And then that clown Bernard-Henri sprang into the thick of the action – to be quite honest, I'd completely forgotten about him – and started running through his routine. I'd never seen him so zonked before, but I had to film it – it's my job, after all. Basically, he gave the young Orks a quick hug and waved his staff at the soldiers, and that's the moment when he should have got off the road. Everything would have ended neatly – the Kagan's no fool, he understands very well what's going on. But the blockhead overdid things, and I had to fire.

I can't stand working in conditions like that – it's like an elephant having to dance in a china shop. At all costs I had to avoid hitting the Kagan or the young Orkish couple who'd already been photographed on temple film. And obviously I couldn't fire at Bernard-Henri either, although I almost wanted to. There was only a narrow gap left between him and the

Kagan, so I had to fire my cannons through that, and naturally there was no guarantee about the ricochets passing dangerously close to the automobile.

'Get out of the directress, you cretin,' I shouted to Bernard-Henri over the comms link.

But it was as if he didn't hear me – or maybe he'd just switched off his comms unit. I was already thinking I'd end up snuffing the Kagan and lose my job – but I was saved by a lucky fluke.

The Kagan was on the comms link, too, at the time – and although he knew no one was supposed to fire at him, he got scared. As soon as the shooting started, he huddled up against his rubber woman. It was a pure reflex response, because he's an experienced man and knows how he should behave in front of the camera. But it looked funny.

And after that things got even funnier.

'Directress' is our professional jargon word: it means a free corridor for the line of fire, and members of the production team have to keep out of it. But the Kagan, the stupid Ork, decided that must be what people called rubber women, and he was spoiling my camera shot. So he promptly flung himself aside. And just in time – one of the ricochets passed straight through his rubber bimbo and red dye splashed out of her in all directions. That immediately told the attentive viewer a great deal about the Kagan's intimate preferences. The folding roof of his motorenvagen started moving up, but it was too late already.

Only then did Bernard-Henri realise it would be a good idea to get off the road, and quick. A circle of guards bristling with sharp pikes closed round the motorenvagen with its roof up, and the procession crept on along the road, straight over the bodies – in order not to break formation. Bernard-Henri was still brandishing his staff in the air, but I wasn't filming him any longer. And since no one was attacking Bernard-Henri now, I didn't have any reason to carry on firing.

41

When the Orks had passed by, there were at least forty soldiers' bodies lying on the road. They were black, trampled underfoot, and they looked terrifying, there was no point in filming that for the news. The youngsters who'd been saved were nowhere to be seen – they'd managed to sneak off.

I glanced at the manitou and saw the system had credited me with a million and a half for these fifteen minutes. Apparently our sommeliers had found a lot of what I'd shot extremely useful. If I earned that much for every flight, I could buy an external villa in the lower hemisphere, I thought. I could repay the loan for Kaya in just three more years...

Bernard-Henri was still standing on the side of the road, obviously still struggling to gather his wits after his M-vitamins. I called his trailer and decided to wait until he got into it – after all, he was my responsibility until the operation was over. I didn't bother to lay into him, because everything had turned out fine in the end, and the military tradition in cases like that is to leave the contentious post-flight debriefing for later.

But then he decided to speak to me himself.

'Where's the little slut?' he asked in a hoarse voice.

'How should I know?' I answered. 'I didn't watch where she went.'

'I hadn't got finished with her,' he said.

That was just too much – because I knew exactly what he really meant.

'I just almost killed the Kagan because of you, you cretin,' I roared. 'And I'm supposed to look out for your little bitches?'

'Who do you think you're talking to, you flying lard-arse?' he roared back. 'I'm Bernard-Henri Montaigne Montesquieu! And a cretin was your papà for not coming on the floor...'

And that set us off – before his garbage bucket arrived, we were able to say what we thought of each other a dozen times. Then he went off to look for the girl, and soon informed me that she'd shown up, she'd been hiding in the forest. He loaded her into the trailer and took her off to the Green Zone – an old, tried and tested routine of his. But this time his girlfriend had a chance of living longer than usual – Bernard-Henri had contracted to rebuild the post-war world and could get stuck down there for a long time.

Now I was perfectly justified in putting the camera on auto-pilot and park. The camera set off back home, and I was free.

The moment I clambered down off my combat cushions and took off my glasses, Kaya looked up at me and said,

'You butcher.'

At this stage I'd forgotten that I sat her at the control manitou to follow the flight – because I hadn't been planning any shooting. Who could have known everything would turn out like that? And of course, my girl had seen plenty of bad stuff.

'Flying lard-arse,' Kaya continued in a spiteful voice. 'What did you kill all those people for? I feel sorry for them. You fat brute. Bloodthirsty moron. I'm never going to watch you fly again. Do you hear me? Never!'

That hurt my feelings, because I really am on the stout side. Bernard-Henri always hits below the belt. And so does Kaya.

Anyone who mocks another person for being overweight must be a mental lightweight, as well as a physical one. So how could they understand that Manitou only allows his elect to put on a solid middle-aged spread? It's no accident that a fat man laughing has been the symbol of riches since time immemorial.

Your mass is your presence in the universe. If there's a hundred and fifty kilos of you, the life included in you is enough for two average citizens. So it's hardly any wonder if you're smarter than the average individual or superior to everyone else in one area or another. Of course, fat people aren't always geniuses, but generally speaking they're interesting, amiable and extremely useful members of society. I'm a good pilot precisely because

43

when I'm controlling my Hannelore, I rely on my instincts – that is, I fly with my gut. With all of it.

It's true, of course, that for engineering reasons most of the pilots of ancient times were small and thin, but even here I can point to famous aces like Herman Göring and Benito Mussolini. And it's no coincidence that they were both distinguished statesmen too. But Kaya couldn't give a damn about all that.

By the way, I've noticed something interesting. When she calls me fat, I don't get offended, I'm used to it.

When she calls me an imbecile, all I do is laugh. But when she calls me an imbecile and fat at the same time, I feel hurt and resentful. And there's nothing I can do about it.

But I've only got myself to blame. I was the one who set her bitchiness to maximum; no one forced me to do it.

That's one of the settings in her 'red list'. I've got 'bitchiness', 'seduction' and 'spirituality' all set to maximum simultaneously. But I'll tell you what that means a little bit later.

Anyway, I took offence and went to the happiness room – the manitou from which Kaya is controlled is in there. I entered the password and put her on pause.

The reason I adjust her settings from this place isn't because it holds some sort of cesspit symbolism for me – it's just that Kaya never needs to use it. There's less risk of her ever getting her own hands on the control system. But I feel it's time for me to clarify a few points here.

Kaya is the sweet blossom of my life, my main investment, the light of my heart, the happiness of my nights and many, many years of loan payments still to come.

Kaya is my sura.

Let me explain immediately that in my sexual orientation I'm a hundred per cent gloomy. A gloomo, gloomball, doll-shagger, pupophile – call me whatever you like. If you're a pupophobe and you have prejudices about all this, that's your problem, but there's no way you're going to make it mine. We fought for our rights for centuries – and the result is that nowadays the word 'gloomy' occupies a place of honour beside the word 'gay', with only a comma to separate them. But that's the politically correct term, we call ourselves pupos.

In case you don't happen to know, 'pupo' (from 'pupophile') is a formerly insulting term for gloomy people, derived from the Old Latin *'pupa'*, meaning 'doll'. We took it over – in exactly the same way as gays once transformed the insulting name 'queer' into their own term of ironic self-identification. On Big Byz it's an eminently respectable expression. Nowadays only the Orks use 'pupo' as an insult, and they confuse it with 'pedo'. But for them these terms don't necessarily indicate sexual orientation, more often they signify a person who flouts the accepted moral norms (although what those might be for the Orks is another story altogether).

Of course, I've got nothing against biological partners, I've even tried them a few times in my life. But it's simply not for me. My choice is a sura.

I absolutely love the word itself. It sounds to me like the name of a song, or a prayer, or some bird with bright, paradisiacal plumage. But it's simply an abbreviation of the Church English 'surrogate wife' that has come down to us from the times when pupophiles could still be subjected to public humiliation. Only I'm not sure it's correct to call suras surrogate women (especially 'rubber women', as we sometimes call them in our slang).

In fact, in these times it's the live women who are more like surrogates. Especially since the age of consent was raised to forty-six. And for them the term 'rubber women' is entirely appropriate – with all the implants they get done almost every-where now.

The most significant thing the cinemafia and venerable feminists have been doing since they seized power in our aging society is to raise the age of consent. Now they're planning to take it up to forty-eight. For gays and lesbians the age of consent is forty-four at present, because they have a powerful lobby, and they won an amendment through affirmative action – but the plan is to raise them to forty-six too. If it wasn't for GULAG (and I've been a member of that movement for nine years now), the age of consent would have been increased directly to sixty.

Our association is essentially the final anchor point for the remnants of freedom and common sense in society. But I'll tell you about GULAG some time later – it's a long story. For now let me simply remark that it's the only genuine social force capable, if necessary, of opposing both the state and CINEWS Inc. – what's known as 'grassroots power'. And the battle lines, ha ha, run straight through my heart.

Actually, of course, things aren't all that bad – the strict prohibition doesn't apply to sex, only to filming it. As far as sex itself is concerned, the juvenile rule 'don't look – don't see' applies. But it's only high-flyers like Bernard-Henri who can derive practical benefit from this on a daily basis.

The cynics claim that the venerable feminists raise the age of consent in the hope that someone will be seduced by their own over-mature charms. That's nonsense, of course. The attempt to deprive others of their sexual rights is an extreme form of sexual self-expression, something like sex with an old shoe or anal exhibitionism. Just take a look at the faces of the champions of the cause, and you'll get the full picture. Of course, it's cruel to deny them the right to realise their sexual fantasies, but the problem is that the egotistical actions of a single aggressive sex-minority create a problem for a huge number of people.

But it's not even a matter of these hysterical women – they're just a blind in all this. Their exclusive function is as talking heads, but the work is directed and financed by completely different forces.

The powers that be raise the age of consent in response to constant pressure from the movie industry, which lobbies furiously on this question. Admittedly, the cinemafia's efforts to raise the age of consent also meet with a positive response from society, because they're in line with its hypocritical morality. The contrite gerontocrats think they can win Manitou's good favour by sacrificing other people's joy to Him. But we don't delight Manitou with these gifts. We merely insult Him.

When we, the free people of the new age, go to the temple on Sunday to watch a fresh snuff, we come face to face with the boundless hypocrisy that pervades our morality. Convex, 3D, full-colour hypocrisy.

No, our offering isn't totally mendacious. We pilots are pure in the eyes of Manitou: the death in the snuffs is entirely honest. But the love that we offer to His pure rays of light is phony through and through. And when Manitou punishes us – and it will happen sooner or later – the beneficiaries of this sacrilege will find no salvation in their bank accounts or their treasure hoards.

It all looks perfectly decent and proper. The actors don't provoke disgust, their bodies are still beautiful (although with a rather overripe, glossy kind of beauty), their movements are meticulously choreographed, the general presentation is flawless. But even though plastic surgery has scaled unprecedented heights in our times, nature is not easily deceived.

As far as the men go, it's not so bad. After all, the male sex is fairly ugly by its very nature – instead of beauty, as they say, it has testosterone and money. But the actresses...

For instance, there in front of you is a girl with little blond plaits, sitting on a bed, holding a teddy bear, and you believe that what you're seeing is the tender dawn of youth – and then a faint pterodactyl-like crease suddenly twinkles briefly on the neck of this creature, patched together out of scraps of herself,

47

and you immediately realise that she's an old woman, and the surge of warmth in your lower belly is replaced by a shudder of revulsion that runs through your entire body.

A woman is a magical flower, a mere glance at which should be enough to derange your mind, inspiring you to endure the trials and tribulations of procreation. That's how Manitou wanted it to be.

And then on Sunday you arrive at the temple, but instead of a flower, they show you a pair of high-budget breasts, inflated with implants, which by all the laws of nature should have disintegrated into silicone and proteins half a century ago. Then they apologise for all the other petals still being swathed in bandages, and they expect you to respond with an ardent bacchanalian frenzy of love for life.

The main point here is that everyone knows there are some genuinely beautiful young people among the male and female 'disciples' of this caste of actors accursed by Manitou. Well, not just beautiful – very beautiful. And everyone realises that they'd look a lot better than the old guard on the temple celluloid.

And that's exactly why the age of consent has been hiked up to forty-six. Porn actors are extremely rich, because the rate paid for temple film work is incredibly high. It's no exaggeration to describe these people as a powerful mafia with a mighty political lobby and extensive social support – owing to the fact that the average age of the inhabitants of Big Byz is fairly advanced. Everyone in the cinemafia understands each other implicitly, and the last thing they want to see is young competition emerging.

In an open information society no one can criminalise filming. But with powerful lobbying it's perfectly possible to criminalise what's filmed. This won't have much impact on citizens' lives because of the 'don't look – don't see' rule, but it will immediately make it impossible to shoot temple porn with young actors – as a self-evident, documentable breach of the law.

That's the paradox of it.

Therefore young actors – meaning those who are more than twenty or thirty years old – have to remain disciples for decades, which means they simply grow into this mafia. But the parts in temple porn are played by old men and women who are fifty, sometimes even seventy years old. If they were filmed on digital, all the problems could be solved by processing the material on a manitou. But you can't do it that way with temple celluloid, because snuff's a sacred mystery. That's why I say our offering is impure. Yet our society finds it too painful to discuss subjects like these. There are things that are just not talked about. And this is one of them.

Fortunately, gloomy people's lives are entirely unaffected by the age of consent, because it only applies to what happens between two or more humans. But we use suras, and with them no legal problems like 'consent' ever arise – in this case no consent is required, either from the sura or from the man engaging in intimate contact with her. It's forbidden to film suras in snuffs (they can't be party to a religious ritual) or in porn (they 'imitate individuals who have not attained the age of consent'). But if you use a sura at home, you won't have any problems. That is, of course, until you start sharing video clips of your conquests on the personal front: that kind of thing happens every year, and the unfortunate dopes are immediately sacrificed on the altar of public morality, to strident jeering from the grey-haired feminists.

Suras can be very different – from the rubber dolls filled with red dye used by sadistic deviants and Orkish Kagans (for Torn Durex, mind you, they're just a status symbol) to such absolute miracles as my Kaya: a 'self-maintaining, biosynthetic, premium-1 class machine', as the manual proudly calls her.

As I've already said, my camera might not be the best there is on the market. But Kaya is the very best. And I don't think there'll ever be anything more perfect. All the innumerable ancient technologies that animate and motivate her little body can only be imitated and replicated now – there's not much chance that anyone will ever be able to improve on her. Especially since there's no particular need for it.

A top of the line model like my Kaya is an indulgence that very few inhabitants of our crowded little world can afford.

What she has inside her, I don't know.

That is, of course, within certain limits I do know, and very well, but I don't wish to descend into vulgarity. What I mean to say is that I don't have any clear idea of how all her electronic and mechanical insides work. I don't even really know what it all looks like, although I do have a vague inkling – several years ago a crazy lunatic sawed a sura of the same class into pieces, and by pure chance a few photos ended up in my manitou.

That young guy, I believe, was a member of the Film Burners sect. They said on the news that he wanted to take out his girl's atomic battery and make a bomb out of it, or something of the kind, but that's nonsense. Because the battery's entirely safe and shuts itself down automatically at the slightest attempt to gain unsanctioned access. It's the green atom, the same principle as in all the ancient machines. It produces no pollution under any conditions and it's extremely expensive – not even my Hannelore has a battery like that. Critical technology – it's not installed on combat equipment that could fall into enemy hands.

Sheer idiocy, of course. Firstly, a sura could defect to the surface – in theory, at least. Secondly, if the enemy did pluck the battery out of a broken camera, he still wouldn't be able to do anything with it. The whole business is just a conspiracy between the makers of the cameras, who don't want to step up another level on the spiral of competition. That's why a Hannelore has to be recharged every now and then, but Kaya doesn't. Atomic batteries last for centuries, and a sura always outlives her owner. So I can understand that young guy.

I don't know how that atomic battery and all the synthetic biology inside her body work. I only know that externally her body's indistinguishable from a youthful, ideally healthy and freshly washed human being. She even has a biofield simulator.

In physical terms she's hardly superior to us at all – she can't run too fast or perform all sorts of acrobatic tricks (although I should mention regretfully that she can give this fat individual a hundred points start in that department too). She's a domestic creature, designed primarily for moving calmly round one's home. But she can walk, gesticulate and perform any minor household task as well as a human being.

She breathes – or rather, she goes through the motions. Air constantly enters her body and leaves it, and she speaks exactly the same way we do.

There's almost nothing she needs, not even repairs – if you damage her delicate skin, the wound soon heals over on its own. The instructions tell you not to give her anything but water and two or three maintenance pills a year (these are little plastic spheres that look like vitamins). She can also swallow them in much greater quantities, if you want her, for instance, to grow her hair long or put on a bit of weight.

You can manage without the maintenance tablets – feed her compressed fish-food, or any other organic concentrate, and her internal structure will pick out the substances it requires. And at a pinch, she can manage without that – even if you tear a little piece out of her body, she can still restore her previous shape. The poor wee thing will simply lose a few grammes of weight.

Self-restoring, quasi-organic nano-fabric – I think that's what the manual calls it.

She only needs water on those magical days when we make

love – or if she wants to torment me by crying – but that brings us back again to a delicate subject that I'd rather not broach.

However, I've been talking too long about what's on the inside of her – it's time I told you what's on the outside.

When you purchase a sura of this class, you spend a lot of time with a team of sommeliers, carefully considering all the intimate details of the future product. You hypercritically inspect every square centimetre of the body – you'll be spending the rest of your life with it. The discussion covers the kind of nuances that no one talks about, even with their very closest friends. Eyes, nose, chin, the line of the cheekbones, the form of the nipple, the navel – and everything lower down. Every one of these details can take hours, or even days. But the final tweaks go in at the debugging stage, and all this is still not the most important thing about a sura.

The most important thing about her is that devastating blow she strikes at your senses every time you lay eyes on her. The sommeliers tried to explain to me what's happening here, and I think I understood.

Viewing the human female in the most cynical light – and that is precisely how the manufacturers of suras view her – she is simply a biological machine that can conventionally be divided into two functional systems: the 'hypno-emitter' and the 'sperm receiver', as the consultant surologist who worked with me put it.

The reproductive system is the assembly line for the production of new human beings, and everybody already knows everything about that. But the information system...

At this point I run into difficulties articulating the concept. Let's just say it's a totality of signals which the woman broadcasts in order to facilitate (or, on the contrary, exclude) the likelihood of reproduction. Or rather, she thinks that she's broadcasting them, but nature actually does ninety per cent of it for her, and couldn't give a rotten damn for this particular female. And this, of course, is the primary source of woman's ancient woe.

Why is female allure so very powerful? Why is this force, dwelling in a young creature, capable of shattering empires?

The reason is that the beauty of a young girl is the future, scrolled up tight in the present. It's a message, stating that the door into a distant tomorrow can quite easily open here and now – one of the doors through which Manitou has been escaping from Himself into times to come for so many millions of years. Manitou enjoys seeing a door like that through our eyes. We are merely His servants and pawns. And all we can do is carry out His orders respectfully and promptly. Even in those difficult moments when His glance halts on boys or lambs.

Now let me try to repeat the same thing less poetically.

The informational signals intended to ensure reproduction impinge on each of the six sense organs. The effect involves elements of smell and touch, the taste of someone else's lips, the sound of words, and the thoughts aroused by those words – but even so the most important channel, of course, is visual.

From the scientific point of view, female beauty is nothing more than summary information about a woman's genome and reproductive capacity, which is analysed by the male brain in a split second: a man realises from the very first glance if he finds a woman attractive or not. And if she is attractive to him, this feeling acquires extreme intensity immediately, for the man could be killed by wild beasts five minutes later, and nature doesn't want to take that risk.

But we live in a society, not in caves. And therefore the religious moralists were absolutely right when they made women cover both the sperm receiver and the hypno-emitter with a special piece of cloth. For a woman's primary sexual organ, of course, is her face. It's no accident that the Orks, with their sensitive ear for the quiet voice of nature, use the word 'fuckface' for 'a likeable girl or woman of reproductive age'. Of course, this is all very obvious – I don't even need to cite the existence of such a paradigmatic genre of temple porn as the facial. Not to mention the significance of make-up.

Our offspring from certain women have a better chance of surviving (or for some other reason they seem preferable to the huge biological programme of which we are all part). These women are more attractive to us than others – that is, not to us, but to that very programme, and with its intrinsic cynicism, it plunges us first into a state of romantic inebriation, then into long, agonising emotional torment, and finally into tedious legal turmoil.

The creators of suras exploit this bioinformational mechanism. First they take a sample of your DNA. Then they calculate the type of female beauty that will be perfectly congenial to your genome. Your sura will have almost exactly the same effect on others – we're all fairly similar in genetic terms. It's just a question of the nuances. But, as everyone knows, they're what make all the difference.

Of course, beauty like that is absolutely stunning: it's something you have to experience for yourself. All that's left for you to do is choose the virtual age of your destined partner and polish up the fine details.

When it comes to the optimal age, there isn't any real consensus in the pupophile community – just as there isn't any among the straights. Bernard-Henri, who has a thing for Orkish juveniles, claims that the blossom of human beauty withers rapidly and you have to hurry to pick it while it's still fresh. In some ways, of course, he's right. I think Chloe's age is the best for women – sixteen, the boundary line that nature herself has laid down (addressing us in the language of criminal codes, among others, for she is many-tongued). And after all, it's no accident that this is the age of consent for the Orks, who have retained a conspicuously close kinship with the natural world.

Women under the age of sixteen are only of interest to children and deviants. Women older than that already understate their age, to make it easier for the hypno-emitter to entice a client into the sperm receiver. And since the women behave this way, it must be the voice of nature speaking.

But Kaya will never have to understate her age. Kaya is a blossom that will never fade.

A sura isn't some bedroom dummy with looks perfectly suited to your taste. No, she can talk. And she doesn't just pronounce words, she engages you in full-blooded personal interaction. Her behaviour can be modified across a wide range, but I'll tell you all about that next time. For now I'll just explain what I did when I succumbed to blind resentment.

Well then, after putting Kaya on pause, I opened her emotional and volitional parameters screen on my private manitou and thought for a while about whether I should take her off maximum bitchiness. But the words 'flying lard-arse' had already stopped reverberating in my ears, and I decided not to.

However, since I was already in the fine-tuning menu, I did make one minimal intervention: using a few secondary controls in an auxiliary window, I adjusted her for heightened interest in my work – so she wouldn't even think of carrying out her threat. Maximum bitchiness means she bears grudges for a really long time. But I like it when she sits at the control manitou while I'm flying.

I didn't bother to specify which particular aspects of my work she should be interested in, leaving the entries 'any' or 'self-orien' in all the fields. It wasn't a particularly risky operation. And anyway, at that moment I was still seething with resentment and I needed to do something to keep myself occupied.

At the end of the procedure, I remembered I'd already promised myself twice not to interfere with her tuning, since that transforms her from a unique life partner into a wind-up toy.

A genuine pupo doesn't do that – he tunes his sura just once, for life.

I swore solemnly once more that this would never happen to me again. And to make sure my oath would be more than just a load of hot air, I limited tuning module access by setting a compulsory half-hour delay – so now, if I put her on pause, I had to wait thirty minutes to get to the controls. This is an extremely valuable feature of the programme, introduced following numerous requests from users. While I'm waiting, I thought, my gloomy pride will awaken.

Then I took her off pause.

When I got back, she was looking into the control manitou.

The camera had already parked itself in the maintenance bay and the control figures were scrolling across the screen.

'I was scared, but fascinated,' she said, looking up at me with her dark eyes. 'Thanks, sweet buns. That was entertaining. But I want to know what happened to those Ork youngsters afterwards. Especially to that boy. Will you show me?'

Now, why couldn't she say that in the first place?

'And what will that get me?' I asked.

'The usual,' she said, lowering her eyes.

'When do you want to take a look at them?'

'Today. Right now. Please, okay?'

I just love it when this girl asks me for something.

I looked at the control manitou. My Hannelore was standing in the charging and loading queue – the whole procedure, including replenishing the ammunition, shouldn't take more than half an hour. But I didn't want to spoil her too much.

'There's no way it can be today, honeybunch,' I said, tugging on her sleeve. 'Later. In about three days. If you behave yourself.'

'But why not now?'

'My Hannelore needs to take a rest. And Kaya here still has a little job to do...'

She nodded and blushed slightly. And even though, when we'd only just got to know each other, I personally spent two evenings fine-tuning that effect, my heart started beating noticeably faster.

Grim couldn't concentrate because they were making such a racket downstairs.

The boozing had been going on down there for hours and hours – Uncle Khor, a cobbler invalid, had died two days earlier, and they were seeing him off on his final journey. First, there had been a long quarrel between the relatives, and a lot of foul language was reaching Grim's ears. Then everyone downstairs had made peace and started singing Orkish folk songs.

The first song they rendered – with deep feeling, almost weeping, was 'No Fucking Way to Break Out from This Shithole'. And when they struck up 'My Bloody Homeland Really Sucks' they hit such a raucous note that Grim upstairs, trying to do his school homework, had to stick plugs in his ears.

In two days' time he had to submit his graduation essay on the topic of 'What I know about my Fatherland and the world', and it wasn't ready yet. But Grim wasn't particularly worried, because what they had in the house was the paper edition of the *Free Encyclopaedia*, published in the time of Loss Liquid. He usually copied all his essays straight out of there, distorting the language a bit – to make it more believable, missing out minor facts and adding in a few mistakes. He got away with it, because his teachers didn't have an encyclopaedia like that – the only place you could find one now was in the Yellow Zone.

He resolutely copied out the first section of his essay from the historical outline:

In the age of Ancient Films there were two great countries, Ameriza and Tchina, which towered above worldwide Chaos and fed each other. When antiquity fell into a state of decadence, Tchina cut itself off from the world with the Great Wall and disintegrated into separate kingdoms. In Ameriza wars broke out between Hispanics and Blacks, and it was divided into several feuding regions.

Now the most powerful country in the world was the narco-state Aztlan, which included the Spanish-speaking south of Ameriza and the former state of Mexizo. The people living there were blessed to see Manitou the Antichrist, who took on human form in order to give them the New Law. Of his own free will, the Antichrist took for Himself this name and the sign of the spastika, in order to cleanse the minds of men. For He purged with His Light all that was most abominable and appalling and declared that the past was no more, and from henceforth the voice of Manitou would speak from out of the darkest corners, so that men would know that there was no place which was not the Home of Manitou. And Aztlan killed Him and took His blood upon itself.

Aztlan was a sinister despotism, ruled by a cruel and immoral elite. The states of Yamato, Brazil, the Kingdom of Sheng, the Siberian Republic and Eureich were the same – those were the countries that had raised their offglobes above the land's surface.

Now he had to write about the offglobes. Grim got up from the desk, put the gold-and-black volume of the encyclopaedia back on the shelf and took another. Opening it at the article he needed, he sat back down at the table and carried on writing.

Initially, the offglobes were tax-free extraterritorial zones where terrestrial laws did not apply. They appeared when the President of Aztlan, Jorge the Horrible, granted the whole world Aztlanian citizenship and compelled everyone living on earth to pay taxes, under the threat of nuclear holocausting. The offglobes, tethered above the earth on a gravity drive, were not formally subject to this law.

The movie industry, science and finance sector gradually moved to them – and the ancient dream of the bankers of all the earth, an offshore money-printing bank, became a reality. The offglobes began turning into huge flying cities, where the elite of mankind lived without any fear that some 'Occupy 'em!' movement would break in with their tents, loudspeakers and revolutionary banners. All the technologies of social protest known in the past became powerless. When, for some obscure reason, a great war of mutual extermination broke out between the terrestrial states, the offglobes were not affected because they were declared a peace zone and nuclear weapons were not used against them...

Grim looked across to the next page, ran his eyes over it in bewilderment and cursed. The next five or six pages had been torn out.

Someone in his family had done that – for a common, everyday purpose that was quite obvious. And what's more, they had done it quite recently, because Grim had read the article only a few months earlier. It was so interesting he'd been looking forward to reading it again – in vain, as it turned out.

Searching for inspiration, Grim looked up at the wall in front of his workspace.

His great-uncle Mord's business card was hanging there – Mord was a deceased relative of his mother's who had somehow contrived to become a genuine lawyer in Big Byz and work for the rich Global Orks from there. The letters and numbers on the card looked simple and austere:

Mord ITN 1 7012 00 126 01 8
Attorney-at-Law
Big Byz 093 457 890-3288

The business card had been hung up there by Grim's mother when he was still very young, so that every time Grim looked up he would remember what an ordinary Ork could achieve through his own hard work. Strangely enough, the example did help. At this moment, for instance, Grim decided that he could manage perfectly well without the torn-out pages.

He still remembered a few things. Especially the story of the destruction of the great offglobes of the past – lots of interesting and spine-chilling stuff there. For instance, the offglobes of Eureich and Yamato were scuttled in the sea after their commanding officers had committed suicide (he even remembered that on Eureich the entire elite had taken cyanide after listening to an ancient opera, and the offglobe had fallen into the Baltic Sea where it still towered up out of the water like a dead black mountain). The colossal offglobe of the Kingdom of Sheng, with more than a hundred million people living on it, was flung out into the outer space when the incorrectly copied gravity drive ran out of control. To this very day that was still considered the worst catastrophe in the history of mankind, and the Warring Kingdoms behind the Great Wall had changed their development model largely under the influence of this tragedy.

There were rumours that the last two offglobes, belonging to Aztlan and Brazil, were not destroyed by modern weapons but by the power of magic. Nobody knew anything for sure about Aztlan, because after Manitou the Antichrist was killed that land was believed to be cursed. But they said that the Brazil's offglobe was supposedly brought down by a boy, wreathed in flowers and driven there in a chariot made of jaguar skulls – and he did it by playing on a reed pipe.

All in all, Grim had managed to squeeze out enough information for a few sentences only – but that would have to do.

After that he had to say a few words about the world's last remaining offglobe – Byzantion, or Big Byz. And even though Big Byz was hanging right over his head, this task turned out to be the hardest.

It wasn't clear what tone he should adopt in writing about it. The meticulously balanced blend of servile submission and rabid hatred that made up the Orkish news didn't easily lend itself to imitation. And he only had to overdo it slightly with the hatred (or, indeed, the respect), and there could be problems.

Grim decided to present the dry basic facts and leave it at that:

Big Byz has a population of about thirty million. The political regime is a liberative democraship in the form of a Manitoual Demarchy (or the other way round, no one really understands what these words mean anyway). The state language is Church English, but High Russian is also current. The political system is tripartite ritual. The Frontman of the Manitou Reserve, aka the President and the Auspex General, is chosen from the Whitefaces, Augustes or Hobos for a term of six years. By provision of the Constitution, no one ever knows his name or sees his face; it is also forbidden to mention him in the news.

The precise size of the offglobe is classified [we can't even measure that for ourselves, thought Grim], *but it is the largest*

61

that has ever existed, since everything that could be un-
coupled from the offglobes of the past, before they had been
destroyed, was transferred to Big Byz. That was the reason for
its barely perceptible asymmetric hump. The offglobe, as you
have already guessed, hangs above our beloved capital city,
an ancient cradle of civilisation, where there was once a late
Barbed-Wire Age offshore settlement, wiped out by a nuclear
explosion during the war between the Siberian Republic and
Aztlan ... The Orkish city of Slava now stands on the site of
that explosion, and directly above it is Big Byz, which was
moved here several centuries ago.

Grim pondered. So was 'offshore' the same as 'offglobe' or not?
That was the second time he had come across the word. He
didn't think so – someone had once mentioned that this confusion had been perpetually tripping up the school-leavers: in the
Barbed-Wire Age, a civilisation of this kind did exist. It was
even mentioned, briefly, in the curriculum on our native land's
history, but when it was time to sit graduation exams no one
remembered a thing about it.

He could also add a phrase from a propaganda broadcast
that had stuck in his mind: Big Byz was doomed to remain
forever moored above the Orkish capital, so in the final analysis
the Orks and the upper people shared the same fate, a fact
that the arrogant oligarchy of Byzantion had so far failed to
appreciate. But that was for later, to be placed right at the very
end.

It would be good to throw in something technical, something
intelligent and serious as well, but one had to be careful not to
overdo it ...

He found a suitable phrase in an article on the gravity drive
– and ripped it off in full.

Unlike the offglobes of the past, Byzantion cannot fly to an-
other site or gain altitude – above it lies a zone of powerful
winds where it could be ripped off its ring-shaped concrete
footing that conceals the solenoids of the gravitational anchor.
The anchor is essential because the gravity drive is overloaded
with excessive mass.

Elegant and incomprehensible.

In the article entitled 'Religions of the World' he discovered a
paragraph about the reformed religion of Byzantion:

Movism is a hypocritically distorted form of Manitouism that
regards Manitou the Antichrist as only one of many incarna-
tions of Manitou that have trodden the earth. The esoteric
doctrine of Movism is kept a deep secret by its adepts...

Well, he also had to say a couple of words about the name.
' "Byzantion" used to be the ancient name of a city that was
simultaneously the last capital of the West and the first capital
of the East, and this symbolic role, la-di-da-di-da...' In short,
that part was clear enough.

Grim put another volume of the *Free Encyclopaedia* back
in its place and took down an economics textbook – the essay
definitely had to include a passage about economic life. This,
again, was something that he could crib without worry.

The original strategy for the development of the Orkish
economy is to catch up with and overtake Big Byz in terms
of major stock indices. There are two schools of Orkish eco-
nomic thought, which propose diametrically opposed ways to
achieve this goal.

The first school, known as 'Byzantism', believes that we
should adopt the Byzantine stock indices and then, through

modernisation, ensure that their values would rise higher for the Orks. This is regarded as the classical tendency in economic thought.

The second school has come into being only recently. Its founder was the scholar Cosm, who had worked on an internship on Big Byz and was considered a natural genius by the economists there (to them he was known under the pseudonym of Adam-Smith Wesson Malthus).

Cosm asserted that for several centuries the world had already been living in the Age of Saturation – when technologies and languages (both human tongues and IT codes) hardly changed at all, since the economic and cultural meaning of progress had been exhausted. This should not be regarded as stagnation – it is a normal state of society. In the Palaeolithic age, people had lived like this for many hundreds of thousands of years; the age of 'progress' accounts for no more than one per cent of human history. There is every reason to expect that the Age of Saturation will be long and stable – but of course, a lot happier than the past historical plateaus. Cosm accepted the possibility that in the distant future it would be replaced, yet again, by a spiral of frenetic growth – but that is all in Manitou's hands.

Many of Cosm's views, especially in the area of political economy, seemed revolutionary to his contemporaries. He claimed that Orkish stock indices could not outgrow those in Byzantion in principle, since the Orks did not have a stock market. And what's more, the Byzantines had not had one either, not for a long time – they determined their indices during the solemn divination held in the House of Manitou, and in our time that is simply one of the religious rituals of Upper Manitouism (so-called Movism).

In addition, Cosm asserted that it was pointless for Urkaine to compete economically with Byzantion, since the offglobe

and the lower territories presented a single cultural and eco-
nomic system, a kind of 'metrocolony'. His statement that
the true capital of Urkaine was London (a sector of Big Byz
where the highest-ranking Global Orks had long since been
acquiring hover-estate) provoked universal indignation. Shortly
before Sacred War No. 216 (when Orks wore a carnation in
their breast pockets), Cosm was hanged in a market square
to boost the morale of the general public.

    Subsequently, Cosm was rehabilitated. The second tendency
in economic thought, Cosmism, has arisen on the basis of
his ideas: it calls on the Orks to develop their own stock
indices – in such a way that those would be the right ones
from the very beginning. But to many this doctrine seems too
bold and simple, and so the state's economic strategy is based
on an amalgam of the two approaches.

That incomprehensible word, 'amalgam', worked perfectly well
as an ending. Everything became clear now – another day or
two to polish it up, and he could hand his essay in. Only he
would definitely have to add something about global warming
and the death of the Gulf Stream, about the high-altitude winds,
and the fact that all the black holes were one and the same
Singularity – 'the Body of Manitou, the same point of reference,
and it only seemed to us that they were scattered across the
sky ...'

Having annotated his text, Grim sighed in relief – homework
was over for the day.

As he was putting the book back in its place, a piece of
paper, folded up to look like a pleat and covered with his own
writing, fell out of it. It was his own crib on the past tenses
of Upper Mid-Siberian, written in mischief two or three years
ago:

Ay u føker
Ay u føken
Ay u føkend
Ay u føkender
Ay u føkenden
Ay u mav føkendend
Ay u mad føkendender
Ay u man føkendenden

On the other side, in blue ink and the same schoolboy writing, were examples of correct usage – mnemonic rules for scribes and translators, some of which had long since become popular expletives:

Ay vey yur ma føkend
Ay vey yur grundma føkender
Ay vey yur grundgrundma føkenden, ohh wehh

Grim sighed. The piece of paper had survived, but Grim, the happy, carefree Grim who had written it before that long-ago exam – he had already disappeared, melted away like a cloud at the summer noontime, and there was no way back.

His relatives were still singing – more and more aggressively with every minute. Grim decided to watch something on the manitou.

Unfortunately, the old snuff that was on could hardly be called a radical cultural alternative to what was happening downstairs. Especially since Grim had already seen it a couple of times.

I wonder, he thought, why they never set us essays on snuffs? We don't even write that they demonstrate the moral bankruptcy of the rotten Byzantine elite. But we could... It's probably because of the censorship...

The battle scenes in the snuff had been brutally cut. The

only part they showed in full was the Orkish army lined up for battle, in their felt helmets and leather coats meant to look like 'Parthian armour'. There were occasional fleeting glimpses of the enemy – long shots of upper people, dressed in multi-coloured togas. But as soon as the electric catapults appeared in the frame, there was a gap so crude that scissors seemed to flicker across the screen.

But they showed the Orks in felt caps, as they were being killed by the concrete balls, very generously – at great length and in great detail, to the accompaniment of tragic music that seriously spoiled Grim's mood.

Fortunately, the battle fragment came to an end and a love fragment started – a relatively young Nicolas-Olivier Laurence von Trier appeared in shot with an Elizabeth-Nathalie Madonna de Auschwitz who looked still quite fresh.

The great actors were standing, by a bed, in front of a wall painted with mysterial frescoes, gazing at each other, damp-eyed, and holding hands. Nicolas-Olivier was wearing a purple toga and a diamond coronet, and Elizabeth-Nathalie had on a pink ancient-Greek-style robe with countless bijouterie knick-knacks. They kissed with feeling, and suddenly youthful servants and maidservants started flitting about – some removed the stars' numerous items of jewellery, some fluffed up the bed, and some lit the oil lamps. Grim watched all this for the sake of the maid-servants – some of them were really very pretty.

Unfortunately, Nicolas-Olivier and Elizabeth-Nathalie were almost undressed already, and as soon as Elizabeth-Nathalie reached for the clasp of her pearl-embroidered brassiere and Nicolas-Olivier raised his strong hand to clasp her flawless bosom, a logo appeared on the screen with a caption in ornate lettering:

SPIRITÜLØ CENZØRSHEEP DUH ÜRKAINØ

Only the upper people had the right to cut a snuff – but they never touched the erotic scenes, they only removed their military secrets from the shot. But even though the Orkish censorship couldn't cut anything out, it had the right to obscure the image temporarily with its logo. The logos kept changing all the time – Grim hadn't seen this one before.

Glowing brightly below the inscription was a golden spastika – a cross with three ends bent counterclockwise and one long leg with a stroke across it. The spastika was animated – sunshine sparkled across its golden surface, and below the long leg, which ran into a frizzy drawing of a forest grove, jolly little animals were dancing: little piggies skipping about on their hooves, little monkeys fighting playfully and little chickens flapping their wings.

Grim felt certain that all the Orks watching the screen at that moment were performing, just like him, the same mental calculation – figuring out how much the guys in the Department of Cultural Expansion had pocketed on this order. And they must have pocketed a lot, because animation work like that, even with a tacky five-second loop, could only have been produced above or in the Green Zone. Or maybe, at a pinch, in the Yellow Zone. And all the prices in those places had lots of zeroes on the right.

As soon as the languid sighs started up in the speakers, the original soundtrack was cut off too, and replaced by jangling Orkish music. It was a three-stringed cross between a mandolin and balalaika, introduced by Loss Solid to unify Orkish and Byzantine music – an instrument initially known as *mandalaika*, but renamed *mondolaika* by the Department of Cultural Expansion. In those days, not many Orks had their own manitous, so they mostly watched the snuffs in the army barracks, and when the screen was obscured by the spiritual censor's logo, a military musician amused the soldiers by playing a mondolaika. The tradition had caught on and was still followed. Loss Solid had been planning to catch up and overtake the upper people – but after his eleventh military victory he was killed on the Hill of the Ancestors by a coconut that fell off a palm tree, and his entire legacy was declared accursed by Manitou. But the mondolaika had survived.

The other channels were also showing two snuffs censored into total incomprehensibility – one really old, from the time of Loss Liquid, when the Orks went into battle in suits and ties, and the other one relatively recent, from the time of Torn Skyn, when they fought in doublets and wigs. It was all deadly boring and Grim had seen it all many times before. He turned the manitou off.

And then he swung round sharply towards the window.

If there really had been a Byzantine camera hovering out there, Grim wouldn't have been able to see it against the sky in any case. But after that nightmare on the road, he kept getting the feeling that someone was watching him. It was probably a consequence of nervous shock.

The scene outside the window was the same as before – shabby three-storey buildings from the time of the late Losses, a few scraggy palm trees and a funeral wagon, with Uncle Khor already lying in his sputnik.

Two of his relatives were smoking beside the wagon – Uncle Shug, in his black cloak of a Right Protector, and a visitor from the south whom Grim hadn't seen at a family gathering before.

Uncle Shug wasn't really a Right Protector. He worked at a classified factory where they made 'Urkaine' mopeds – everyone there was issued an officer's uniform.

Both men were well drunk – they were carrying on with some kind of conversation that had started at the table.

'Why haven't we got any technologies?' the visitor from the

south was asking vehemently. 'Not even the ones that were in place a hundred years ago. What do you call that if not sabotage?'

Uncle Shug laughed as if he was talking to a child but – at least to Grim's mind – the answer he gave was perfectly serious.

'Who needs sabotage? No sabotage is required. In the first place, engineers are regarded as an inferior caste round here. And the hero of our time is a Global Ork with a hangout in London. Or maybe, at a pinch, some shiterary philolophile who spent seven years at the uni being taught how to give the Kagan a royal blow-job. Especially if he's wheedled his way into the Yellow Zone and blows upper people as well. I'm just a kind of mechanic, a servant. So now just try and think – why would I, an engineer, go and give myself a hernia, hoisting those schmuks up into the sky? They can go drown in shit, and take their *Word on the Word* with them.'

Uncle Shug swayed, but the visitor managed to keep him on his feet.

'And in the second place...' Uncle Shug went on.

'What?'

'We Orks are always torturing each other. Our way of doing things is through underhand deception and fear. And we try to dominate matter in exactly the same way...'

'Don't the upper people do the same?'

'The upper people treat material like a woman. They cajole it and persuade it. They rouse its interest. But Orks try to cheat it or shag it to death. And they can't even do that right. They start shagging it to death before they've finished cheating it. Or they start to cheat it after they've already shagged it to death. They yell at it, like they do in prison – barge over, you bitch! I'll give you what for! And all the time they're smashing it with this imaginary sledgehammer. The same way they've been beaten themselves, ever since they were kids. That's why all our things

70

look so horrible and don't work properly. Atoms and molecules stopped being afraid of our powers-that-be ages ago ... Aagh ... So how can we suddenly go and make something beautiful and useful, when ...'

Uncle Shug swept his arm round in a wide arc, as if adducing the panorama of the world around him as his final point. The argument was rock solid, of course.

'Our forefathers made microchips,' said the visitor from the south.

Uncle Shug spat.

'Have you just fallen out of a palm tree, or what? That's all propaganda. Every civilisation has its technological limits. You've read *The Book of Orkasms*. What kind of microchip can you make in an Urkaganate, listening to criminal songs? The only thing we can produce to a high quality here is Church-fearing philolophiles. And we can trade in corpse gas, too. Or saw up a pipeline and sell it over the Great Wall.'

'What pipeline?' asked the visitor.

'It's this legend. Under the first Losses a certain redhead of a Global Ork was put in charge of gas. And in the first year he sawed up all the old pipelines and sold them to the Kingdom of Sheng as scrap.'

'And he stole the manitou?'

'Why bother stealing it? He paid it to himself as a bonus. For profits in the annual returns.'

'And what happened to him?'

'Ha, what do you think? He flew off to London. And since then we've been selling gas in cans. At least we still make the cans ourselves. And you talk about microchips ...'

They put out their fag ends and went back in the house. Grim sighed – Uncle Shug was right about everything, he didn't want to be an engineer either. Chloe wouldn't have gone into the woods with a future engineer, that's for sure.

71

The lid of the sputnik had already been closed – it was a hot day, and they'd said their farewells to his uncle early, to avoid taking any risks with the smell. Following an old superstition, the two halves of the sputnik were sewn together with consecrated cow's tendons (so the dead man wouldn't climb out into space before he reached Manitou – no one believed that, of course, but they observed the custom anyway). The sputnik was of the cheapest kind – with four white-painted sticks jutting up crookedly towards the sky from a crudely woven sphere that looked like a large inverted basket. They were burying his uncle without any pomp or ceremony.

There was no camera anywhere around, of course.

Grim laughed.

'Ah, who's interested in me anyway?' he said loudly.

The words had a strange ring to them in the empty room, and Grim immediately realised that he really shouldn't have spoken them.

In actual fact, the yard didn't look exactly as it did before. A new object had appeared beside the wagon, one that he hadn't noticed at first against the background of the freshly dug vegetable patch.

It was the black motorbike that belonged to the district public prosecutor, Chloe's father. And although the motorbike didn't look particularly streamlined or menacing, Grim still thought it was a bit like a Byzantine battle camera.

And just then there was a knock at the door.

Standing in the doorway was Grim's aunt, dressed up for the funeral, in a new green sarifan that had already come unwound across her stomach. She was drunk.

'Let's go down, Grim,' she said. 'It's almost time to go.'

'I'm not going,' Grim replied.

'Come out and say goodbye then. And the public prosecutor's arrived too. He wants to talk to you about something.'

72

The funeral feast was laid out on the table in the main room. Grim's kinfolk were sitting round it – his uncle, his aunts, a couple of cousins and even a little nephew from the country. It occurred to Grim that there could have been more food on the table, and fewer bottles of rice *volya*.

As he walked in, the prosecutor, with a glass in his hand, who was sitting under the image of Manitou, was just concluding his farewell speech.

'... times were different from ours. In those days, brothers, people had cast-iron rhinoceroses, and the Urks went after them with bamboo bear spears. Because there was treachery, of course, on all sides. But that doesn't cancel out the heroes' great deeds at all – on the contrary. And our folks today should remember that their turn will come soon. It's not everyone who could do what Khor did – lose both legs and still feed a family. So here's to his memory. Fly to the chambers of Manitou, Khor, and may outer space be sweeter to you than *volya*. And may all be well with us too. And it will be, because our faith is the true one. Manitou is on our side.'

'Manitou is on our side,' they repeated raggedly round the table.

After drinking up they all got to their feet – now, according to custom, they had to get a move on, in order to catch up with the spirit flying off into outer space. Grim exchanged kisses on the cheek with faces reeking of onions and *volya*, gave his country cousin his old baseball cap, with the intertwined letters 'BB' on it, as a present, promised one of his unknown relatives to visit more often, and was left alone with the public prosecutor.

With his dreadlocks and grey beard, the prosecutor looked exactly like one of those warriors who had almost finished off Grim and Chloe on the road. Except that he was dressed differently – he didn't have any black armour on, and instead of field camouflage fatigues, with leaves and branches, he was wearing urban fatigues, featuring a brick wall with dried-up gobs of spit, small pits and various drawings: a heart pierced by an arrow, a spastika with its arms blasphemously straightened out and the Siberianism 'beaver' (with the item named depicted above it, so that no doubts could remain). He had a parapublic medal hanging on his chest, and two earrings dangling from his left ear – probably to improve his contacts with the younger generation, Grim concluded morosely.

The prosecutor set two chairs face to face, sat down on one and pointed to the other for Grim.

'Sit down,' he ordered.

Grim shrugged and sat down – he had no reason to object.

The prosecutor took a bone pipe out of his pocket, clicked his lighter and took a pull. The air was filled with a smell of burnt rags and some other kind of nauseating muck. The prosecutor beckoned Grim towards him with his finger and turned the stem of the pipe towards him.

'I don't want any,' said Grim.

'I'm not asking if you want any or not,' the prosecutor said with a grin. 'I wish to blow your brains clean as a matter of legal procedure. Or else you won't understand a thing.'

'It's against the law,' said Grim, making his final attempt to resist.

'I *am* the law,' said the prosecutor.

He wrapped his fist round the pipe, grabbed Grim's ear abruptly with his other hand and pulled him towards himself. When Grim's face was close to the pipe, the prosecutor pressed his lips to his fist and breathed into it hard. Grim was forced to breathe in the plume of smoke that shot out of the stem, and the acrid fumes seared his lungs. He started coughing. And when he recovered his breathing and looked up, nothing in the world was the same.

Firstly, the world was terrifying. It had become incredibly

dangerous. Danger, bright and iridescent, emanated from everything: from the windows, with the Orkish capital city lurking behind them, from the table, heaped up with leftovers and empty bottles, from the dresser with the cheap blue spirits glasses, and even from the icon with the image of Manitou – a symbolic representation of a black hole with an accretion disk and two narrow fountains of grace being emitted into the void. It didn't look like Manitou was on Grim's side at all.

Secondly, the world had become not only dangerous but also blatantly, unspeakably vile.

Thirdly, it had become irrevocably hopeless, a dead end. There was nowhere to hide. And nowhere to run to either.

But what seemed most terrible of all was the prosecutor – sitting opposite him, with a drawing of a woman's crotch on his chest and a medal pinned directly onto its hairs.

Grim suddenly realised that the condition that had terrified him was habitual and comfortable for this man. He entered it voluntarily. More than that, Ganjaberserks entered it every time they were advancing into battle, towards death. It was incomprehensible. Grim felt absolutely powerless to resist that kind of spiritual power.

The prosecutor was apparently well aware of what was happening to Grim. He took another pull on his pipe and asked,

'Right then, do you get it now?'

Grim nodded, and then he nodded again several times, afraid that the first time hadn't expressed his thought clearly enough. The nods drifted towards the icon with the black hole in a staccato rhythm. But one or two of them got through to the prosecutor anyway.

'Then let's have a talk,' the prosecutor said. 'I know about you and Chloe. Everyone who watches the news knows it too. Of course, Chloe's gone up in the world pretty sharply. She's in the Green Zone now, and that discomongler's with her.'

'Discoursemonger,' Grim corrected him.

The sound of his own voice dumbfounded him and he immediately started explaining, stumbling over the words, that he hadn't meant to offend the prosecutor at all by correcting him, but quite the opposite, he only corrected the people he respected and loved, and his own mum, when she was alive, used to say 'fishcoursemonger', and he couldn't get her out of the habit. Fortunately, he soon realised that the only word he had spoken out loud was 'discoursemonger'.

But the prosecutor seemed to have heard everything anyway.

'I couldn't give a fuck,' he explained.

Grim glanced at the medal and believed him immediately.

Neither of them spoke for a few minutes. The prosecutor carefully studied a poster hanging on the wall with the profiles of Torn Durex and Torn Skyn superimposed on each other above a slogan in gold:

TIMME DUH MAN DESIDENDEN, BRÜ HITHERØ ABOR THITHERØ!

The poster was a rarity, because very few of them had been printed when they were planning to hold an election between Skyn and Durex, the latter at the time being still young. In the end, the transfer of power was effected in a different manner: Torn Durex thumped the previous Kagan on the ear during a parade, and the Ganjaberserks and Right Protectors immediately swore allegiance to him. Of course, the Orkish intelligentsia was outraged by it all to the very depths of its collective soul, but in those days Slava was being bombed almost every day, the paper manitou was falling in value at a terrifying rate, and they tried not to argue with the topside stylists.

Many years had passed since then, but to this day the elderly Orks still recalled the time when democraship seemed just around the corner. This poster was regarded as slightly rebellious, and it was only hung on the wall in the very boldest liberative homes with contacts in the Yellow Zone.

Grim was about to start explaining that he hadn't put it up, it was the deceased cobbler Khor, who had managed to get that high up without any legs when the other cobblers came to his place at night, gave him a hoist up and immediately went away again – but when Grim was already completely tangled in his web of lies, again, it turned out that he hadn't even opened his mouth.

The prosecutor waited for him to realise that and started speaking.

'They showed you in the news too. But only once, the very first time. And in all the repeats it was just Chloe, all by herself. That was what they decided up there,' – the prosecutor nodded upwards. 'And even though the discomongler promised both of you a pass for the offglobe, you haven't actually got one. Because no one's going to let you into the Green Zone – the first ring of security is ours, and you haven't been put on the lists. And if they won't let you into the Green Zone, then how are you going to get up *there*? In short, Grim, no one up there's interested in you.'

Grim agreed with every word – even slightly before, it seemed, it reached his ears.

'According to my information, they've only issued a pass for you to the Yellow Zone. That is, you could go to them and be an *orktivist*. If I were you, I wouldn't do that. Because the war's coming very soon. And you won't have long enough to qualify for a pass to the Green Zone.'

The prosecutor took another pull on his pipe. The pause allowed Grim to arrange everything that he had just heard somewhat more tidily in his head. The prosecutor was saying very rational and clear things.

'And then,' the prosecutor continued, 'what's so good about being an *orktivist*? Fair enough, upper discomonglers are clever people all right. But ours, the ones in the Yellow Zone – they're just crap, they stink. One of them made a discovery recently. Urkaine, he says, is a cryocolony of Big Byz.'

'A cryptocolony,' said Grim, surprising even himself.

'Yeah, right, like I said. The way they control us, he says, is by allowing one man to hide everything he's nicked, but not allowing someone else to the same. It took less than a thousand years for that jerk to catch on. Where do they get grass like that from?'

Grim guessed that the phrase about grass was a Ganjaberserk joke – the prosecutor wanted to show that he was talking to him like one of his own.

'Being brain-dead is bad every which way,' the prosecutor continued. 'Did you know that Rott? He used to live in our district at one time.'

Grim shook his head. He'd only ever seen Rott once in the news. It was just before the last war.

'The lad joined the *orktivists*. Got himself registered in the Yellow Zone. They gave him a T-shirt – "Witness of Tyranny" – issued him his own personal camera, everything tip-top. He wandered round Slava for a whole year, with the camera flying over his head. The moment he saw a turd, he'd run up to him from behind and lash him up the backside with his foot. The turd turns round, and he sees everything straight off, he under-stands, and there's nothing he can do about it, he just smiles and salutes. Well, the lad did plenty of showing off, right enough. But in all that time nothing more intelligent ever occurred to him. And they never gave him a pass up there. And when the war started, they did for the chump on the first day. And it wasn't even the turds, mind, it was the porters from the market; they were pissed off with watching him in the news every day. Is that what you want?'

Grim shook his head again. He hadn't realised at first who the 'turds' were, but then he remembered that was what the Ganjaberserks called the Right Protectors. The Right Protectors also had a whole heap of insulting names for the Ganjaberserks, of which the most affectionate was 'butts'. The two branches of power clearly didn't like each other – despite the official clichés about their 'separation and symphony'.

'Then listen. Soon there'll be another war. And what's more, it's going to be a tough one, they're making almost twenty kinds of uniforms. So we want to draft you into the ranks. And give it wide publicity, so the people can see that not all of our lads have sold out yet. So they'll show you on the manitou, we'll take you on as an orderly for the Urkagan. You'll be delivering the orders. Your own "Urkaine" moped. Almost all the orderlies come back, if they don't let their chance slip away. And afterwards you'll start on a career that will carry you higher in the offglobe than all those yellow and green turnip tops, including my own daughter. Don't you believe me?'

Grim shrugged.

'Look. If you join the *orktivists*... Well, let's say, even if they let you up *there* – what are you going to do? Go prick-fishing with your lips? You haven't got a manitou to your name, who needs you up in those parts? So you'll just be somebody's errand boy. But follow our line and you won't believe how much you can earn, if you've fitted in right. And there...' he nodded upwards '...it all goes into the accounts. And they have a law – steal a hundred million manitou, and you're an honorary citizen of London outright, and an Orkish investor. That's what all the serious Global Orks do. Figure it out, what's better, kicking turds up the backside until they wring your neck, or getting into serious business? Quietly, without any stink?'

'Getting into serious business,' Grim managed to repeat.

'That's what I think too...' The prosecutor took another pull. 'There are two paths through life, Grim. You can strive towards Manitou in your imagination. Or you can fly to Him like Uncle Khor. In a sputnik. But you can also ascend to him while you're still alive – straight up to London. And not suck dick for your food, but stand above the river for real, with your own bollocks in the window...'

The prosecutor started coughing and flapped his hand in front of his face to drive away the smoke.

'Just recently I saw this Global Ork off on his way up there,' he continued. 'I won't mention the name. It's not that I know him personally, I was just detailed to guard him. A serious man, motorenwagen black all over, no way of telling where the window or the door is. And up in front, a public prosecutor on a motorbike. Me, that is. We reach our destination. It doesn't seem like anything special – a crooked palm tree at the side of the road and a rice field. This guy hasn't even got any things with him, just a small bag. The way he's dressed is nothing special either, a cavalry cloak, like they wear topside. You or I could dress like that. Only there's a chain on his chest, with a little gold gas can hanging on it. And it's not as thick as a finger, either, it's slim and really tiny – simply to point out that he's in the gas line. We wait. I reckon there's only a minute left until the appointed time, but there's no one there. I start getting nervous, but he's just standing there calmly, smiling – I can see this isn't his first trip. And as soon as it's time, this kind of triangular door opens up in empty space in front of us, and lowers itself down onto the ground, making these kind of steps. And I can see that there's a little room inside there, with chairs. But if you look from the outside, there's nothing there at all. In other words, a porn actor's personal trailer, can you imagine that? And it's our

80

Orkish chum that's got the use of it! He climbs inside, waves to me to say everything's cool, the door closes – and that's it.'

'I've seen that too,' says Grim.

Apparently he could already speak.

'So you've seen it, it's good,' the prosecutor responded. 'That means you know the way this world works. That's the way clever people travel to London. But not everyone can do that. You have to start small. Do you want to be a Global Ork? We'll teach you how. But first you have to spend a bit of time in the barracks with the simple folk. And just before the war we'll shift you over to Durex's headquarters! Don't be afraid, he won't shag you – they pick up the queers for him through a different connection. You're only needed for propaganda. Have you got all that?'

'I'm under eighteen,' said Grim.

'We'll register you on the sly. Don't you fret, we know how to fix things. Here, take your draft notice, I'm delivering it in person.'

The prosecutor got up off his seat, leaving the sheet of brown paper in Grim's hands.

'You seem like an intelligent lad,' he said. 'I think that's all got through to you. If it didn't, it will, when you read that again in the morning. The address and the time to arrive are in there. I wish you a soldier's luck. And I'm off to the district office.'

The sun appeared in the window again. The prosecutor got up and walked towards the door. His head was caught in the beam of sunlight, and for a moment Grim imagined that the thick tangle of musty dreadlocks had turned into the fluffy, silver curls of the Byzantine discoursemonger.

When the prosecutor went out, Grim collapsed straight onto the floor. For some reason he felt like lying on something hard for a while.

The prosecutor's weed gradually released its grip. The sinister component that rendered the world repugnant and terrifying passed off quickly, but the leaden torpor stayed with him right up until his relatives came back from the Swamp of Memory.

They returned satisfied and touched. Some were crying. It turned out that when the funeral procession was passing through the village before the cemetery, they met a Byzantine child-dealer coming the other way. That was a sure sign that in the next life the sputnik would raise the dead man up to the offglobe.

'In a black cloak, with a little metal case,' his aunt told him tenderly. 'With a gauze mask over his face – as if to say: I can't bear to smell your stench. The country folk have already put their brats out on the tables for him. And everyone's trying everything to jump the queue and hand him their little pisser to be examined, they're almost fighting even . . . Or else he buys one, two if you're lucky, and then nothing from him for a solid year. Ooh, Grim . . . What are you doing napping on the floor? Did you finish up the *volya* on the table?'

Then she turned serious, hoisted Grim up onto his feet and led him upstairs, so the relatives sitting round the table and making a racket wouldn't disturb them.

'Now, sweetums, listen to what's happening. The prosecutor said you'll be off to the war soon. They've just explained to me that this new law's come out. It's called "On Defending the Defender". They're putting the country to rights now – basically anyone whose documents are being held up by the authorities, if they get stained by the crimson blood of battle, the orders are to resolve the matter without delay, and they won't dare demand a bribe. Grim dear, I want you to come back in one piece, but in case, Manitou forbid, you do get a scratch – can I give you a little folder to take with you? It's got a few documents in it in Siberian, ours for the barn, and some from the relatives in the village. They're taking forever to lay in the water pipes. People've been carrying water from the river in buckets for years now; a cobra just recently killed two girls. Okie dokie?'

In order to understand how suras can engage us in full-blooded personal interaction without possessing a personality, consciousness or soul (or whatever we might call that which makes us human), you have to be an erudite sommelier. I'm not one of those, and my retelling of their explanations might prove not entirely accurate. But I don't intend to devote very much space to the theory.

To put it briefly, suras deceive us.

But in exactly the same way as we deceive each other.

What happens when we talk to someone? We evaluate the words that we have heard, select an appropriate response and pronounce it out loud. If we want to offend the other person, we make our words barbed and biting, if we want to flatter him, we sprinkle them with sugar, and so forth. This is simply the processing of incoming information on the basis of cultural codes, biological imperatives and personal intentions.

The cultural codes are the simplest part of all this – it's no problem at all to pour into a sura the most detailed encyclopaedia and all of its cross links, multiplied by themselves ten times over. Subjects for conversation, phrases and turns of speech, the circumstances under which they should be spoken, the intonations and so on – that's not really such complicated science. And in any case, a real woman only opens her mouth to divert your attention. On this point, I liked an extract from the glossy manual for Kaya:

A woman of reproductive age making small talk at a social function usually controls the process of interaction not along the parameter of meaning, but in accordance with entirely different indications, and after assessing an immense array of input information, she decides the question of biological contact quite apart from any connection with the content of the conversation, and the other person immediately senses this...

Precisely so. This is the source of all those legends about the irrationality of a woman's heart – what rubbish, may Manitou forgive me. There is nothing more rational than a woman's heart, it is simply a rationality of a higher order – the role the woman is playing here is not that of a little fool at a party, but living out an impersonal aspect of nature and eternity. This socio-biological mechanism also lends itself to simulation and programming without any particular problems, since it is based on entirely calculable parameters – this fact, in my opinion, is quite clear.

But the matter of the intentions of the human heart is a bit more complicated. I mean the emotionally coloured desires that make us dash around in ambient space from the moment we wake up until we go to bed.

Many users don't want to believe this, but a sura simply doesn't have anything of the kind, because she lacks the internal subjectivity for such desire. You can wrestle with this as hard as you like, but in this respect a sura will always remain the insensate rubber woman from which she originated at some time in the ancient country of Nippo. A sura can only simulate feelings. But the most important thing is the quality of the simulation.

Do they have a personality? Yes and no. It all depends on how you understand the word. Suras of Kaya's class are unique. This is achieved by a special configuration of internal data connections. They are as distinctive and individual as different locks of the same make – the design is the same, but in each case a lock has its own key. If you buy a second sura and give it the same settings, it will be a rather different being. Or, more correctly, a different simulation. Experiments of this kind have been conducted.

The most important and subtlest part of a sura's internal organisation is what is called the emotional and volitional block. The algorithms built into it are very complicated and based on sophisticated interactions between the database of cultural codes and a random events generator, which is controlled, in turn, by another random events generator – which means that a sura can be made genuinely unpredictable. Of course, within strictly defined limits – as in the case of a live woman.

All the biological mechanisms that have been invented by remorseless nature over millions of years in order to deceive living creatures are exploited by a sura for a single purpose – to give you the maximum possible pleasure. But along the way to this pleasure you may possibly also have to experience pain. Such, the operational manual asserts, is the dialectics of ecstasy.

The company offers about a hundred standard 'characters' – emotional and volitional modalities, each of which has been checked using numerous tests (I suspect that biological women can be divided up into a significantly smaller number of real types). If you use any of the factory presets, your sura carries a long-term warranty and you have nothing be afraid of.

The warranty is voided if you switch to the manual adjustment of settings. You can only do this after you have read and signed an addendum to the licensing agreement, under which the company ceases to be responsible for the sura and for your life. A sura on manual settings really can be dangerous. Especially if you don't know how to use her properly.

But this is precisely where genuine happiness awaits the owner of a sura.

The point is that this is the procedure that transforms a sura from an item of furniture to a living, unpredictable life partner, who can kill herself or dispatch you to the next world. Such things have really happened. It's highly improbable that you will die, though. The greatest danger is that the sura might run away or shut herself down.

The point here is not that she really wants to leave you or to die. She doesn't want anything. And she can't die either, since she's not alive.

But she simulates with extreme precision the behaviour of the emotional and volitional type that you have chosen, on the basis of the templates that she possesses – and your craving for verisimilitude in the relationship can easily lead to a conflict with the harsh facts of life. Take a look at yourself in the mirror, and you'll understand what I mean. But then, suras that have run away from an ugly owner are quickly found – their spatial blocking doesn't allow them to get far away. This happens often, and it brings the owner only a few additional minutes of joy.

Things are more complicated with so-called 'nirvana'. This is a kind of internal short-circuit that often happens under manual control when owners set their suras to maximum spirituality. In this case the sura doesn't simply run away, she hides and switches off all her systems, falling into a hibernation-like state – which can make finding her rather difficult. I'll say a couple of words about this later.

While you are adjusting the settings, what you see on the manitou is something like a large control panel with numerous knobs that can be moved up or down – as if you were tuning a multiband equaliser. There are many of these screens, so the number of actual settings is absolutely countless, and the parameters often have funny names, such as 'reddening of the cheeks', 'drowsy affection', or 'intermittent yawning'.

It all seems intuitively understandable – for instance, you increase the parameter 'drowsy affection' and when your sura is

86

simulating falling asleep, she doesn't simply stop moving about in the bed beside you, she moves up close to you and presses her warm, tender little body against your side, or something of the sort. The result is that you get the reassuring impression that you're adjusting a safe and simple domestic electrical appliance, such as a bed warmer, and you already understand everything about it.

Nothing could be further from the truth.

It really isn't very difficult to make sense of the settings for minor behavioural characteristics. Let's say you like your sura to yawn from time to time. No problem. She'll do that every thirty seconds if you like, and it won't affect anything else.

But with parameters like 'spirituality', 'bitchiness', 'seduction, 'frankness', 'coquettishness', 'duplicity' and all the others that make up the so-called 'red block' (the adjustments marked with a little red star), things are much more complicated.

On the subject of quirks of sura behaviour, there's an age-old saying: 'every knob has its flop'. As the dictionary explains, in ancient times a knob was not just a visual element on your manitou, but a real round handle that you had to turn to adjust the tuning of an electronic device. The control screen for the red block is arranged exactly like that. This isn't simply the sommeliers playing games or a nod to the fashion for antiquity, but a stern reminder to the client of the seriousness of what is taking place.

The point is that in changing the parameters of the red block, you influence all aspects of behaviour simultaneously. If, let's say, you set 'bitchiness' and 'drowsy affection' both to maximum, then your sura can squeeze up against you so hard that you'll fall out of bed.

I'm exaggerating slightly, of course, but 'behavioural pattern interference', as the manual puts it, can really lead to unexpected results. That's why a live woman, for all her capriciousness, is far more transparent than a sura in manual adjustment mode.

The most insidious parameter is 'spirituality'. When it's set in positions close to the maximum, all the sura's behaviour, everything she says and all her reactions resonate with the ancient wisdom of mankind. And in addition, the database is updated from time to time. When your control manitou tells you something like: 'Downloaded: five books of the Pali Canon and the Gospel of Barnabas', and you haven't got the remotest idea of what that is, you'll be left guessing whether you might get a fork in the eye in response to some indelicate request.

That's precisely why all the professional tuners recommend not raising spirituality above forty, or at most, fifty per cent of the maximum, and in the factory settings it's never higher than five per cent. This guarantees that the sura's internal references to sacral meanings will not lead to tragic consequences. To put it crudely, if your sura does run away, her intention is to make you find her and press her to your heart – she doesn't plan to fall into nirvana in some forgotten ventilation shaft that isn't on any navigator.

But all the genuine connoisseurs are freaks. And I'm one of them.

At maximum spirituality our interaction has become incredibly interesting and exciting. When she tries to explain something important to me in the course of our tender embraces, when she tries to rescue me from the abyss of my degradation, it awakens an incredible power in my loins. She, so to speak, preaches and exhorts, and meanwhile I... You can guess that for yourselves.

Some people might think that spirituality is not all that important in a sura. But for the less sophisticated users there are rubber dolls, filled with red dye. The genuine connoisseur knows that to take possession of a lovely body is one thing, but to take possession of a highly spiritual and lovely body, a

88

divine blossom, in which the ancient heart of mankind beats, is something quite different. It is something that has to be experienced; you can't explain it in words. And if you have already tried this poison, the question for you is not whether to switch your sura to maximum spirituality or not, but how to make use of this mode safely.

I solved the problem simply.

Kaya can't move beyond the bounds of my home – her spatial displacement block is engaged. To call things by their proper names, she runs around the bed on an invisible lead, but the lead is long enough for her not to notice it until she tries to cross the threshold of our little nest.

Kaya has already fallen into nirvana twice, but as long as she's at home, dragging her back out again is no problem. It's done by using 'restore defaults', after which the manual settings have to be entered all over again. But that's not such a long process – that is, of course, if you kept a backup of the latest configuration. Fortunately, the memory is saved.

If I add that, simultaneously with spirituality, I keep bitchiness and seduction on maximum, you'll realise what an explosive mixture is heaving about beneath my little doll's delicate skin. You can't relax with her for a single second.

In my mind I understand that her thrilling existence is only a distorted reflection of my own, a pure illusion – in essence, I am simply clowning about in front of a sophisticated mirror. But for me Kaya is a far more real living creature than any of the Orks that I see in my flying goggles. And to be quite honest, I could say the same thing about people.

Some people assert that a sura is simply a complicated means of erotic self-deception. That may be so. But I would much rather deceive myself than let it be done by Stepmother Nature, smashing me over the head with her hormonal club, or hypocritical social morality, which is preparing to raise the age of consent from forty-six to forty-eight.

After Kaya began simulating interest in the two young Orks, I stopped being afraid that she would fall into nirvana – the simulation was taking up too much of her software resources. I remembered, of course, that it was sheer pretence – but it was precisely my clear understanding of that particular circumstance that transformed Kaya into a living woman. And although manual adjustment mode meant losing the warranty, our relationship was approaching the kind of harmony that all the sex encyclopaedias talk and all couples dream about. The game was worth the candle.

True, every now and then I had to fly Hannelore to Orkland when work didn't require me to – simply to amuse my little darling. Searching for Grim and Chloe wasn't difficult, because my markers were still in their bodies – the manitou could locate them from far away. Cruising around above Slava, I took several evocative close-ups of Orkish degradation, for which I was paid rather well.

There was another pleasant consequence. When she'd seen enough of my camera gliding along above the narrow little Orkish streets, dodging posts and pillars, rounding advertisement hoardings and squeezing in through gateways, Kaya finally realised what kind of pilot had chosen her for his companion in life. Effects that I had not personally programmed started manifesting themselves in her attitude to me.

It was that 'pattern interference' again – and I was all for it. Everything now was exactly the same as it was with people. When I caught her rapturous glance after returning from a flight, all evening long I felt like weeping and singing.

So far, I didn't know why it was these two Orks who had caught her attention and not, for instance, the technical aspect of capturing images on temple film in conditions of poor visibility.

Evidently it was the outcome of her entire set of preferences. Especially spirituality, which makes her simulate extreme compassion for all living creatures that appear in my sights (what she saw on the control manitou was exactly the same as what I saw in my flying goggles).

Of course, every day before the war started I was deluged with reproaches. In a way they were just – but precisely to the extent that an Ork can be reproached for trampling on ants when he ploughs his field.

'Do you realise that you're a butcher?' she used to ask me. 'That time on the road – why did you kill those poor Orks?'

'Poor? They were men in military uniform with weapons in their hands.'

'Yesterday they were peasants. They were simply drafted into that ... I don't know what it's called, into that administration. And they were ordered to put on those idiotic costumes invented by your sommeliers. And that gives you the right to kill them?'

'They have to think for themselves about why they have that form of government. Let them fight for freedom. We'll help them from the air.'

'You started the war.'

'Don't exaggerate. A war starts because it's the will of Manitou. The nature of Manitou is such that sometimes He demands blood. We artists and philosophers have only one choice – to earn money on this, or not. And money is always needed, my little darling. If only to pay for your fit of righteous wrath. Well, and all the other things that you and I like to do, he-he-he ...'

'You filthy, lecherous, fat monkey.'

Insults are incredibly arousing.

'Not only did you kill those unfortunate soldiers, you also shattered the lives of those two, Grim and Chloe. They'll probably kill Grim now as well ...'

At that point I got really angry.

91

That's extremely unusual for me. I analysed my feelings – and there was a genuine discovery in store for me.

I was starting to feel jealous about her.

That was stunning – as if suddenly it turned out that I also had a control manitou on which my little doll could move the settings with her own delicate little fingers. I was in ecstasy, in genuine ecstasy – and the poor little thing had to share it with me yet again right there on the floor.

An unforgettable moment.

However, there was some basis for what she had said. By that time things were getting rather difficult for the Orkish couple. I suppose they had even ceased to be a couple. Grim had joined the army and was sitting in the barracks, waiting for the war – it wasn't clear now if he would be able to make use of Bernard-Henri's invitation or if it was only his soul that would soar on high. And Bernard-Henri himself evidently didn't remember him very often, because he was spending most of his time with Grim's girlfriend.

My comrade-in-arms was still in Slava, in the extraterritorial Green Zone, where all our people live. I think he was involved in some murky political business, with an eye to the next post-war period. They issued a green pass for Chloe, and she spent all the time with him (in order to speed up the procedure, Bernard-Henri adopts his little girlfriends in the Orkish administration – it's cheap and it only takes a minute at the outside). I occasionally edged Hannelore up to the window of their loft. Bernard-Henri, like all philosophers, instinctively adores lofts – probably because it's easier to direct aerial strikes from there.

I was interested in Kaya's reaction to what she saw. That is, I realised that she wasn't reacting at all to what was happening, whereas what I had in front of me was only the simulation of a reaction – but Kaya only had to say a few words and before I even noticed it, I was drawn into a conversation.

'But it actually suits her,' my little darling said, eyeing Chloe. 'Boots, whip, leather. And best of all, it's entirely in the spirit of the Orkish national tradition. Pretty authentic. And very agreeable work – I'd take pleasure in whipping that scumbag too – until he bleeds...'

She really is such a sharp-tongued bitch that it's a great relief when her snide remarks are redirected at someone else. But this sarcasm of hers is somehow combined with an almost childish naïvety. I was often puzzled by what this was – a gap in her education or part of the game.

'But why does she tie him to the bed?' she asked with a serious air. 'So that he won't run away when she's whipping him?'

'Where would he run to?' I laughed.

'No, really.'

'Bernard-Henri has an entire programme,' I replied. 'The sequence ramps up the action. First he asks his Orkish girlfriend to tie him to a bed somewhere in the Green Zone. It's safe there, and if necessary he can call for help. If everything goes all right, he asks his girlfriend to take him into the forest and tie him to a tree. Then they hide away, deep in his secret Orkish lair, which he keeps especially for this purpose, and she ties him up there. And what's more, Bernard-Henri removes all his radio beacons and identification markers. So that no one will know where to look for him.'

'Why does he do that?'

'Danger is arousing. Exactly like with you, sweetie pie...'

'Repulsive, slobbery baboon. No, not him. You.'

It was only an illusion, of course, but it seemed to me that there were moments when Kaya spoke to me more sincerely than usual.

'And what do they do afterwards?' she asked. 'After the lair?'

'Bernard-Henri has a very interesting and unconventional

93

continuation of the plot. But I'll tell you about that sometime later, sweetheart.'

On the whole, however, Kaya wasn't particularly drawn to watching Bernard-Henri and Chloe. Clearly she didn't want me eyeing that beautiful little Orkish fool for too long. She was far more interested in Grim.

I think that at first she simulated curiosity about him in order to provoke my jealousy, but when I started showing annoyance, bitchiness got involved in the action. So now I had to hover for long periods in front of the Orkish barracks, peeping at Grim through a chink in the little window – or drifting invisibly through the air behind him when he came outside for a stroll.

The army chaplain Goon walked into the barracks and climbed up onto the white dais that had been prepared for him under a banner with the red inscription:

HØLISHER WØR No. 221

The entire barracks fell silent – the cleric looked so impressive. It wasn't even a matter of the brocade robes and the spastika with three cross-pieces, which indicated a colonel's rank.

The priest's greyish-white hair was combed in a special style – the so-called 'fringe of wisdom'. It entirely covered his face and merged into his beard. In front of his mouth, nose and eyes, there were stains on the hair left by tears, snot and food, and those transformed the fringe of wisdom into a mask that expressed some kind of calm, along with exalted, entirely unOrkish state of the spirit. And although Grim knew that hidden behind this otherworldly visor with its yellow eye blotches, there was an ordinary, coarse Orkish mug with a brass ring in its nose, he still felt a thrill of respect.

Then the Holy Views were carried through the barracks – these were a pair of standard little pictures, covered with glass to keep the kissing hygienic. First came the icon 'Manitou in Glory' (the wonder-working black hole was painted in the meagre ancient manner: a side view of an accretion disk with two fountains of emissions, a pink Eros and a brown Thanatos). That was followed by an image of a canyon filled with candle wax, the place where Manitou the Antichrist was shot: cliffs rendered garishly colourful by the items stuck on them – incense burners and auto-prayers, flowers, paper cranes and the traditional blue biscuits lying on every rock.

All in all, the start was drearily yawn-worthy.

The priest spoke for a long time about the *Urkaganatum Lossum*, which is resurrected from out of the ashes of the centuries; about Urkaine on guard over Spirit and Will; about the sacred sacrifice of the Urk warrior, rescuing the world from self-destruction; about a gang of rabid perverts, once again imposing war on the Urks – all the usual stuff. When he reminded the audience that the Urks were created by Manitou not for philistine idleness, but for the glory of battle and the ecstasy of prayer, Grim suppressed his first yawn. When he started droning on about the true faith ('What they have, lads, is only Manitouism by name, eviscerated of its very essence, but what you and I have is the primordial azure path...'), Grim started dozing off. And when he started reciting the hour-long *Word on the Word*, Grim actually fell asleep.

He wasn't the only one. Everyone had heard *Word on the Word* many times, starting from their preschool days. Many of them knew it by heart – and there was nothing they could do about their sleep-reflex response.

Grim knew how to doze off without offending against the social proprieties, and he even managed to register the familiar patterns of sounds through his sleep. Although the ancient words meant nothing to him, he could tell from them how far off the end was, as if they were surveyor's markers.

However, this time the markers let him down. Grim fell more deeply asleep than he wanted, and only opened his eyes when the army divination for which he had stayed in the barracks had already begun.

By that moment the priest Goon had practically lost his face from working so long with his mouth, and now his tangled mask of hair didn't look so exalted: one of its eyes had narrowed, as if the sage was winking furtively.

Grim wanted to have his fortune told too. He raised his hand. Thank Manitou, so far there were only two eager soldiers ahead of him – a village lad who looked like a boar with sideburns, and another, as skinny as a rake, who belonged to a traditional military dynasty – which could easily be seen from the tattoos on his naked torso.

The priest was holding an old divinatory book with a spine of iridescent blue fabric. Grim was sitting close enough to make out the small polished ivory plaques on the cover and the name written in letters reminiscent of a noble ancient age:

THE BOOK OF ØRKASMS

Most of the young Orks only remembered about the divinatory book before a war, when the soldiers decided whether to ask about the future. They were afraid of the divination. Many believed that it could call down the wrath of fate, so it was regarded as one of the most terrifying of army rituals. Those who decided to do it were either daredevils or simply fools. But Grim thought that for an orderly everything might turn out not so very terribly.

Just then the priest Goon was divining for the village lad. He shook three little sticks with numbers on them out of a little cup, looked at them, then tossed out a fourth and a fifth, and started counting something, bending down his fingers as he went. Working out the number was a complicated procedure that had almost nothing to do with the law of probability: certain predictions came up very often and others almost never.

Goon finally determined the answer. He lifted the book up so that his audience could see the numbered column of angular letters on paper that was yellowed with age. Then he started reading out loud.

Fifty-Six. On Flies.

How can I condemn flies for fucking? However, when it is on my head, it infuriates me. Likewise it is with queerasts. When they perform that which is the inclination of their hearts in quiet solitude, who shall object? But they hold torch-lit parades and chain themselves to lamp posts on the embankment, tooting tin whistles and shouting aloud, so that all might know of their disposition – that they do lash it into the orifice and hammer it up the backside. In truth, they are worse than flies, for flies only rarely sin on my head, while the queerasts do strive from day to day to copulate at its very centre. The flies out of folly, but the queerasts with cool deliberation.

And through this do I perceive that they do not wish to shaft each other, but everyone, and moreover, do it by force, and their mutual sodomus is for them merely a pretext and a pretence.

Now the entire barracks was looking at the village lad, and he was batting his eyelids in bewilderment.

It was a bad prediction. The very worst possible. It was believed that if Manitou 'handed you a queer' in the divination before battle, it signified certain death. Even the word 'fly' boded no good.

The tattooed scion of military men was still stretching his hand up into the air, and the priest turned towards him. The procedure with the little sticks was repeated. Then Goon showed the audience the column of text and read it out.

One Hundred and Eight. On Music.

Those who have dwelt for a long time among queerasts say that they are secretly ashamed of their sin and strive to astound with all kinds of tricks. Thus do they think to themselves: 'Yes, I am a queerast ... It has just turned out that way, what can be done about it now ... But perhaps I am a queerast of genius? What if I write incredible music! Will they really dare to speak badly of a brilliant musician ...?' And therefore they strive constantly to think up new music, in order not to feel ashamed of carrying on shagging each other in the hole. And if they did it quietly, in a special place lined with cork, then everyone would care as little about it as they do for their shafting of the ass. But we are obliged to listen to their music every day, for it is played everywhere. And therefore we hear neither the wind, nor the sea, nor the rustling of the leaves, nor the singing of the birds. But only one and the same mechanical dead sound with which they seek to amaze, launching it into the sky at various angles.

There are times, it is true, when the queer music machine breaks down. At such moments, make haste to listen to the silence.

The hereditary military man turned pale. And it wasn't just his face, but his entire body – which made his tattoo (depicting a tank battle at Orkish Glory) stand out incredibly clearly, right down to the last spastika on the banners. But a cold smile continued to play on his face as before – his soldier's breeding showed.

Deafening silence descended in the barracks hall.

Now they were all looking at Grim. When the priest turned towards him, Grim was seriously tempted to lower his hand. But it was already too late – Goon cast the little sticks with numbers onto the floor in front of him.

After completing the divination, he read out:

Forty-Eight. Where Everything Comes From.

Out of yourself. And I shall prove this very simply. What is all this? It is what you see, hear, feel and think at this moment, and nothing more. Only you, and no one else, could have created this, for it is your eyes that see, your ears that hear, your body that feels and your head that thinks. Others will see something different, for their eyes will be in a different place. And even if they should glimpse the same thing, a different head will think about it, and in that head everything is different.

Sometimes people prattle, saying that there is a 'world in general', which is the same for all. I shall reply, 'The world in general' is a thought, and each head thinks it differently. And so in any case, everything comes from ourselves.

But surely it cannot be that I have created this torment for myself? From this I conclude that all this cerebration is merely the venomous sting of the mind, and the mind itself is like a wild beast guarding me, and is only mine in the sense that it has been set to guard me. Human reasoning can never pass beyond this.

They say that one should contemplate darkness with lights until the looker and the observed mingle together. Then the wild beast will cease to understand where you are and will itself be visible from its slightest movement. And afterwards the path to the Light of Manitou will be opened, but I myself have not been there.

Grim caught his breath. He'd never heard this fragment, but he remembered that drawing the 'wild beast' together with 'light' was considered a sign of a fortunate destiny. This combination was only encountered very rarely – in the hall they started whispering and someone slapped Grim on the back approvingly. Immediately there were more soldiers keen to have a reading – lots of hands went flying up.

The strain of the last few minutes had been too much, and Grim felt short of air. He got to his feet and set off towards the door, brushing against the soldiers sitting on quilted jackets and straw mattresses.

In the corridor he discovered that the main door was locked. It was a greeting from his childhood – for as long as Grim could remember they always did that so that the youngsters wouldn't scamper off while the priest was reading *Word on the Word*. Fortunately there was an open window close by – the soldiers climbed through it to have a smoke. Grim clambered over the windowsill and found himself in the inner yard: on the other side of the fence there was a mud-covered wasteland in front of a pig farm.

Standing beside the window was a large red barrel with the word 'Sand' on it. For all that, there wasn't any sand inside. Instead there was some stinking slurry composed of soaked cigarette ends – the water probably hadn't been changed since the times of the previous dynasty. Orks drafted at the same time as him were standing around, excitedly jabbing their fingers up at the sky, where the black spots of two Byzantine cameras were suspended in the air.

Grim listened to the conversation for a minute or two. The new recruits believed that the people were holding a pre-war air show – to put psychological pressure on the soldiers. But an experienced sergeant laughed as he explained that nobody was interested in them (he expressed himself more succinctly and colourfully).

Novice pilots hovered here every day to get a panoramic shot of shit and pigs for the news. The pilots loved this spot because there were several pig farms together outside the fence, and also a mass grave from the time of Loss Solid that had been rooted up, so the pigs often ended up in shot together with human skulls. And the pilots disengaged their camouflage to avoid draining the batteries.

Grim shifted his gaze to the camouflage cloud concealing Big Byz. Today the offglobe couldn't be seen from the city, above which it hung, but the cloud seemed to have absorbed all of its weight – it looked as if it was made out of a twisted spiral of lead.

From the spot where Grim was standing the city seemed to ascend in terraces towards the cloud – both the market square and the gigantic ring of the Circus were over there. In the other direction there was a panoramic view of Slava.

The Green Zone, with its business centre's green split sphere, glowed with bright, pure colours. Spread out alongside it was the Yellow Zone with its neat Orktivist Town and the canary-yellow pavilions of the assembly lines (that was where it had got its name from). And tacked on behind them, stretching as far as the eye could see were the nondescript concrete burrows of the Orks' housing.

Here and there little patches of green could be seen, pleasantly enlivening the landscape – the Partisans' Gardens, the alleys of parks, thickets of hemp and sage in the estates of rich Ganjaberserks. His gaze lingered on the turquoise domes of the Matriarchate, which, if the official poetry could be believed, resembled the breasts of Manitou. But overall, the Orkish capital coalesced into an endless yellowish-brown swamp with the black bald spots of vacant lots at the sites of recent fires or bombing.

Grim walked round the barracks. There was no one at the gates. He sneaked out into a little street with fast food joints that exuded stench and music, and set off towards the centre.

The signboards of little shops squinted at him from all sides. The daubs of cheerful faces probably were there to induce in the passer-by a feeling of elation and the desire to buy a salted watermelon or spice cake, but in truth evoked only an agonising fear of life – and shame for the fact that life could evoke such fear.

After walking for half an hour he was in the centre. Despite the crush, it was possible to get close to the Gates of Victory – Grim got all the way to the fence, where the turds were sauntering about in their black cloaks. Now he was as close to Big Byz, hidden behind its cloud, as it was possible to get on earth.

The gates to Orkish Glory (Ürkisher Gordynka in Upper Mid-Siberian or, in simple language, the Big Circus) were the only way through the cyclopean ancient wall around which the city had accumulated – at other points it wasn't even permitted to come close to it. No one lived in Orkish Glory. They only went there to die, and all the countless Orks who had died on the other side of the wall had once passed through these high red doors. The thought of it suddenly made Grim feel uneasy. He was also destined to pass through these gates and – if Manitou was merciful – to come back again.

The gates held his attention like a magnet. They were made of thick wood, clad with iron sheeting in the form of spastikas, and they looked like a grating in which not only the bars but also the space between them had been painted red.

Grim lowered his eyes to the brass lock that had been hanging on the gates since the time of the last Victory. In his infancy, when he couldn't yet distinguish causes from effects, he used to think that a war started when they smashed the lock, and not the other way round – and it seemed to him that this metallic guardian of peace was dangerously accessible to any malicious scoundrel. And there it was, right beside him...

Grim had grown wiser since then. But today he seemed to have gone back, and the lock that had already been changed many times during his life suddenly seemed to him – as it once did in his childhood – a doomed living creature that had defended Urkaine as well as it could for many days, but now had to flip its shackle.

'Thank you, lock,' Grim whispered, feeling the absurd tears welling up in his eyes.

In fact he realised that he wasn't feeling sorry for the lock, but for himself – especially for himself as that little Grim who would definitely never return from the sunny gardens of childhood.

Turning back, he walked towards the bronze horseman covered in bird droppings that soared up above the crowd. He was one of the great Orks of the past, the legendary Victor of the Tanks, Marshal Stug. A banner attached to his outstretched hand was flapping downwind. There was an inscription in Siberian on it:

VIVAT ÜRKAINØ!

The square was buzzing. As always in the days before a war, portraits of the Great Conduits were fluttering in the air – Genghis Khan, Stalin, Jorge the Horrible, Mahmoud II Mahdi and others. Grim had wondered before about who held these images

103

during the festivities and where they hid them afterwards. But he had never been curious enough to follow any portrait-bearer. It was probably not safe. And basically it was clear enough without tailing anybody.

On the roof of the Museum of the Ancestors yellow-winged crocodiles – the Orks' gold reserves – glowed dully above the square (people said they were really only gilded, and the gold had been stolen even before the Losses' time). Down below, masters of hand-to-hand combat were demonstrating their skill, reminding the world that the Orks still packed a wallop that could give any enemy a pain in the neck. People were flocking in from all sides – the pressure was only contained by the metal barriers and the Ganjaberserks' truncheons whacking shoulders and backs every now and then.

Grim spent a long time squeezing through the crowd to get a look at the mighty warriors. The crush was so dense that several times he was caught up by the current and lost the ability to choose his own direction.

The people around him were simple and crude, and he had time to get a good whiff of all sorts of odours which could probably make up an encyclopaedia of Orkish life: there were smells of onion skins, offcuts of leather, bubblegum, bananas fried in butter, alkali soap, pigs entrails, rotten papayas, rusty iron, *kvasola*, sweat, stale alcohol fumes and Ancient Serpent eau de cologne. None of this was particularly pleasant, but it seemed a mere trifle when his face skidded across a butcher's apron. Fortunately, after that final torture the crowd parted at last, and Grim could see the area where the great heroes were performing.

There was a large sheet of red canvas hanging on the Museum of the Ancestors, with a word on it in white letters:

HASTILUDE

The first letter had been smeared with dirt, and one more small 's' had been daubed in before 't' in the same white colour. Grim guessed that it had not been added in the night by hooligans, but by the artists who painted the canvas – to lift the people's spirits before the war and remind them that even in a bad year Urks still had time for a racy joke.

There were three large blocks of wood, crudely painted to look like men, standing on the earth that had been trampled as hard as stone. The wooden blocks looked extremely sturdy and were bound round with iron hoops for extra strength. Grim noticed that several spares had been set up by the wall.

Right beside them was the Tent of Heroes – a marquee hung all over with shields of various colours and with a horse's tail on its summit. The heroes were supposed to drink *volya* and make love to girls inside the tent before the war – which they did with great gusto. But the design of the tent was changed before every war and this structure didn't evoke any feelings of patriotism. The entrance to the marquee was closed off by a curtain of red bunting. Apparently the heroes were relaxing.

Rather than reflecting the appearance of enemies, the wooden blocks expressed the torments of an artist trying to depict several faces that looked different from each other. Uniforms had been painted on two of the blocks, with some kind of crosses and stars, while the third one was wearing a genuine semi-transparent windcheater of the kind that are issued to workers in the Yellow Zone.

The enemies, of course, looked repulsive. The crosses and stars were especially infuriating – they had probably awarded them to each other for killing Orks, whose civilisation, from ancient times, had developed along a spiritual path and hadn't,

105

therefore, devised the same kind of means of destruction as the calculating and materialistic upper people had.

No matter; Manitou will be our judge.

Grim didn't exactly think all this – he merely realised an Ork ought to think like that (or rather, to be entirely precise, ought to understand that he ought to think like that), but these thoughts of obligation arose on the periphery of his mind and retreated into non-existence without impinging on his essential being. He was sure that the same thing was happening to everyone else in the square.

'Bamboleo!' shouted two voices in the crowd. 'Bamboleo!'

The first great hero emerged from the tent. Grim recognised him. It was the famous master of hammer fighting, Kink of the Rubber Mountains (that was what they used to call the immense dumps of tyres in ancient times – they had rotted away many centuries ago, but the name had remained).

Orks in the crowd exchanged puzzled glances – for some reason, before the war Kink had been given the name 'Bamboleo'. It didn't carry any meaning at all that was comprehensible to an Ork and it must have been invented by the topside sommeliers. Like everything else, Grim thought gloomily.

This kind of thing happened quite often, and everyone knew the Orkish authorities' explanation for it: it was harder for their enemies to forget heroes' nicknames that had been invented by their own specialists. But Grim knew that the Orks' military astuteness extended far beyond this – it wasn't only the names and armour of the finest warrior heroes that were invented up there every time, but also the styles of the general army uniform. For the same reason, of course – who should know better than upper people what exactly will frighten other upper people? But Orks didn't like to talk about that.

All right then, Bamboleo it was. This season he was wearing a bronze fireman's helmet, a wolf skin across his shoulder, blue

106

pantaloons with stars, and lacquered boots with spurs. They had left him his previous weapon – a weighty sledge hammer with an iron handle that had a round, rusty knob. It was a 'tram half-axle', manufactured in the Yellow Zone from old drawings on a scale suitable for hand-to-hand combat.

Waving to the crowd, Bamboleo turned to the wooden enemies, took a swing and brought the weighty, round hammer crashing down on to the closest block of wood, which crunched and slumped over. Bamboleo belted it again and broke the iron hoop reinforcing the block. The third blow left the block in a really bad state. With an effort, Bamboleo threw the axle across his shoulder and walked away into the marquee with his helmet glittering, wiggling his starry backside.

'Ugh, yuck,' said an elderly Ork beside Grim, and spat, 'why's he twirling his backside like a woman . . . ?'

'It's a historically authentic style – "millennium-two",' a confident voice responded nearby. 'Such is the history of the world, brü . . .'

A covert agent, Grim thought. That was curious, though; why were they called covert agents, if they were always saying or shouting something? It would make more sense to call them overt agents.

Bamboleo hadn't aroused any particular enthusiasm in the crowd – he struck mightily, of course, but this year upper people's sommeliers had gone overboard with the design element. The historically authentic style 'millennium-two' didn't speak to the Orkish heart.

'Alejandro! Alejandro!' shouted voices in the crowd.

The voices shouting were the same ones that had previously called out for Bamboleo – a hoarse male voice and a piercing young woman's, a long way from each other. The crowd didn't take up the call this time either.

Who was this Alejandro?

A tall, thin Ork came skipping out of the marquee, wearing loose black sleeping shorts, pulled up over his stomach almost as far as his chest. Grim recognised him from the twisted silver rings in his nipples – it was Fert of the Reed Pit, a famous master of iron rod combat. But he looked so odd!

The fur had been shaved off his cheeks, and the hair on his head had been twisted into two horns, thickly smeared with glue and curved out capriciously towards the sides. Instead of an iron rod, 'Alejandro' was armed with a pike borrowed from a set of railings, with bits of metallic ornamentation sticking out around the point – crooked leaves and stars. Very convenient, winding the enemy's guts onto those must be really sweet.

But the pike didn't help – the Orks gave Alejandro a feeble reception and after making a few lunges with his weapon, he disappeared into the marquee. A couple of people even spat after him.

No one came out of the tent for a long, long time. And then the square exploded in howls of greeting.

'Dolt! Dolt!'

Grim started yelling with the rest – this was a hero the crowd knew and loved. Manitou be praised – the blasphemous hand of the upper people's stylists had left him untouched.

Dolt looked as usual – round and shaggy, draped in a greasy leather coat, with two quivers of pointed stakes behind his back. Plucking one stake out of each quiver, he skipped over to the wooden blocks and started hammering at them grimly, making the chips fly.

'Dolt!' the Orks yelled deliriously.

The wooden enemies sustained a series of substantial blows, then Dolt kicked them over and the crowd howled in delight.

'Now, that's our way,' said the elderly Ork standing beside Grim, 'that's going at it like your Daddy done...'

They wouldn't let Dolt go for a long time. When he had

108

battered his stakes into dust and splinters, and finally left, some well-built young Orks rolled new blocks over to the wall and removed the smashed ones.

The authorities had clearly understood the mood of the crowd. Now all the Orks that came out of the tent were dressed according to Orkish custom. They were left with their Orkish names, too. The first to perform was Hern, with a gilded cross, plundered from a defiled church in ancient times and transformed into a double axe. He was followed by Fagg with an iron club, studded with super-hard nails. Then came the crowd's favourite, Grub – a butcher with two cleavers.

But after that the authorities went back to their cultural exchange theme and announced someone called Ziggy. Without even waiting for him to appear, the Orks started booing and whistling. Grim didn't even bother to see who he was – he turned away and started working his elbows, and the crowd, grousing and showering him generously with punches, closed up behind his back.

After getting a good whiff of Orkish odours for a second time, Grim broke out into freedom and set off towards the barracks. He was walking downhill now, so the way back seemed shorter.

On the small square by the barracks building, they had already set up a large sheet of plywood. Hanging on it was a piece of grey cardboard with a diagram entitled 'PLAN OF THE WAR'. There were numerous smaller pieces of paper hanging at the sides of the plan.

The plan of the war looked practically the same as all the other plans of Sacred Wars that were still kept in the Museum of the Ancestors. At the centre was a circle drawn in a dotted line, representing Ürkisher Gordynka – the heart of Slava, which was temporarily occupied by the upper people. The arrow of the Orkish advance tore into it, dividing into three tongues. The left one ran into the word 'Enemies'. The middle one ran into the word 'Foes'. The right one ran into the word 'Enemies' again.

In the diagram everything was simple, but starting from his schooldays Grim had known that in reality things weren't like they were in the textbooks. Fighting the upper people was hard even in the times when the Orks still had an information network and firearms, because people used highly complex machines in battle and their military technologies inflicted heavy losses on the simple-hearted Orks. Over the centuries people had become stronger, but the Orks, on the contrary, had been weakened by constant treachery and betrayal, losing one technical skill after another – but even so, by some miracle they were victorious in every war, so it could only be explained by providence and the direct intervention of Manitou, which the old men always spoke about before battle.

The sheets of paper beside the general plan contained tactical clarifications. There were soldierly insults and battle cries, arranged in convenient tables for the three lines of the main thrust – so that everyone could learn off pat the words appropriate to his place in the battle formations. There was diagram of formations by types of form, and a brief summary of intelligence already in hand. That didn't concern Grim, as an orderly.

The soldier on watch stopped Grim in the doorway of the barracks with an abrupt gesture. Grim was afraid he was going to get a reprimand for going absent, but the sentry held out some kind of parcel to him.

'The priest left you the book as a present. It's a pity you left. He wanted to congratulate you.'

'On what?'

'There's a note inside.'

'How did the divination go?' Grim asked.

The sentry spat.

'Don't ask. Almost everyone got a "deathly queer". And if

110

they didn't get a queerast, it was a wild beast or a fly. In a nutshell, the lads got a little note from Manitou – everyone should save up for a sputnik...'

Grim squeezed through to his straw mattress, turned to face the wall and opened the parcel: he saw the iridescent blue spine of the book. Lying beside the book was a note.

From Servant of the Spirit Goon, the Keeper of Knowledge of the Ancient Times, Preceptor of Urkaine, teacher of valiant Urks and a humble disciple of the Urkagan – to Cadet GRIM.

It is said that he to whom the number forty-eight falls has been chosen by Manitou. It is very difficult to receive it in a divination, because it can only be determined by the divinatory sticks once in a hundred years, and this is the first time that I have seen such a thing. Everyone knows about 'wild beast' and 'light'. But there is another secret meaning – it is said that you will be aided by spirits, and that you will be able to write songs and poems. It is also foretold that you will be able to ascend into the light of Manitou, for the Supreme Being will love you. The meaning of this is not clear to me, since I myself have never drawn this number.

According to custom, the person to whom this number falls in a divination should be given the divinatory book. You can now seek answers simply by opening it at random.

It's a pity we didn't get to talk.

A soldier's luck to you.

Grim shrugged. It was incomprehensible but it was flattering. Then he opened passage number forty-eight and read it through again. The music of the ancient words seemed menacing and sombre. Out of all that he read, his head retained only one thing: that mind which asks questions is only a wild beast set to guard me...

111

The ancient wisdom was joyless. It was as if the thick strata of time had parted and in the past Grim saw a bewildered soul that had never found the answer to a single one of its guardian beast's questions. And how many souls like that had walked the earth? Probably many had cast into eternity beautiful lines of poetry, filled with despair and hope – and eternity had swallowed their gift indifferently, and not even a ripple had been left on its smooth surface.

Grim's heart suddenly felt heavy.

For a few minutes he listened to the village Orks discussing the best way to wrap the documents round themselves to get them bloody – on their arms or their legs – and whether it was true that any such paper, with a hole in it, would be invalid.

They agreed that it couldn't be right, but even so it was best to leave a duplicate with your relatives – after all, you never knew what to expect from these bastards.

'Tu-ke! Tu-ke!' a gecko started calling somewhere very nearby.

It was fine for the gecko. In the world he lived in, there wasn't any sacred sacrifice, or ashes of the empires, or Will, or Spirit. There wasn't even an Urkaganate, although the gecko had never once in its life travelled beyond its borders.

Every knob has its flop.

Kaya's aggregate settings obliged her to feel pity for the doomed Orks – and who did she have to blame for their fate, apart from her own meek, fat, little friend who set her spirituality to maximum?

The closer the war came, the more sulky she got with me. For

112

a while she even stopped looking at me, demonstratively turning her blushing face away during our moments of tenderness. And that, of course, drove me absolutely crazy. But as soon as Kaya realised what pleasure she was giving me, she immediately stopped turning away. Naturally – that was her bitchiness.

I think it's clear enough just how many problems that maximum spirituality led to – but it's not clear yet what positive payback I received in exchange.

As I've already said, when she was operating in this regime, the highly complex process of information analysis and exchange in her data processing circuit continuously correlated all the meanings arising in our conversation with fragments of the ancient wisdom of mankind. No one now really understands what the people of former times believed in, but at certain moments the fragmented echoes of old teachings, flickering in her simulated stream of consciousness, were coming together in a meaningful combination, and then for an instant there rose up before me, as it were, the effulgent palace of forgotten lore.

I knew it was a mirage. But even so it gave me a thrill.

Usually she railed against me and our world. Moreover, she berated everything at once – politics, culture and religion. Often she would allude to something forgotten and arcane. But if I started asking her about it, the newly kindled spark of meaning would rapidly fade, as if she had lost interest in the conversation. And then Kaya would astound me with a succinct, casual aside – and what a mercy it was that at those moments Manitou wasn't listening to her. Although, of course, He had heard everything – since I had.

To put it simply, spirituality was a way of rescuing our alliance from satiety and apathy, which, alas, is something many users are only too well acquainted with.

If your sura functions in one of the factory-set modes designed for boors and philistines (something like 'Homely Comfort No.

7', 'Downy Bliss' or 'Mist of Tenderness'), in the morning she'll bring you coffee and a croissant in bed, smile and ask:

'How did you sleep, dear?'

And you'll look at her and wonder if her eyes are glinting as they should, and if her legs are attached correctly. And whether you ought to send her in for restyling, or to have her mouth widened by a couple of sizes.

But Kaya constantly kept me on the brink of a nervous breakdown – not to mention the strain on my intellectual capacity. This securely protected my emotional core against bedsores.

On the first day of the war, when I had to get up a bit earlier and prepare for the sortie, she woke me up at precisely five-thirty in the morning with the following revolutionary gabble:

'You're all loathsome, fat hypocrites. You pretend to be protecting the Orks against the regime that you yourselves installed, but what you really do is just shoot them from the air so there'll be a bit of variety in the news about your porn actors' plastic surgery. That's worse than hypocrisy, it's ... beneath all contempt. You're vile, vile, vile ... Do you hear, you swine? Wake up when you're spoken to!'

Even if you remember that it's merely a talking alarm clock (I set her for five-thirty myself the previous evening), by the end of a speech like that you can't help but think about an answer. Of course, I'm not Bernard-Henri Montaigne Montesquieu, but I can dispute a point too – after all, I've learned a lot from my partner.

'What are you talking about, sweetheart? Down there, among the Orks, evil reigns. It's always been there, for many centuries. And all of them, without exception, are smeared with it. I can pick off any one of them from up in the air, and always get it right – any attack there is a precision strike. True, we only intervene when we have ... hmm ... our own agenda. But even so, that's better than if we did absolutely nothing at all. So there

114

aren't any moral problems here. And if any arise, I assure you that our sommeliers and discoursemongers will resolve them in five minutes in the very first newscast.'

'I don't doubt it,' she said, wrinkling up her little nose and looking up at some point on the ceiling. 'Only it's not just the Orks I feel sorry for. I feel sorry for you – you poor, fat little fool.'

'Why am I a fool?'

'You think you're better than them. Better than those Orks. And even better than me.'

This was getting interesting.

'Better than the Orks – I'd say so,' I said. 'I don't think you'd swap me for an Ork. If only because an Ork couldn't afford you, ha ha ha...'

I like it when I manage to crack a good joke. I know I've done it straightaway – Kaya smiles at good jokes. And since I didn't deliberately set that parameter, her verdict can be trusted.

'And as for who is better, you or I,' I continued, 'that's simply the wrong way to pose the question. You're neither better nor worse. You're different, other. And one must learn to accept the other as he or she is in himself or herself.'

I simply repeated something that Bernard-Henri had said. During the previous war he liked to talk a bit about 'the Other'. And sometimes about some kind of 'outsider' too. The Orks usually didn't understand him – they simply didn't have enough time for that, just between you and me. I didn't understand it either. But then again, I wasn't listening all that carefully – I was looking into my sights. But even so, it stuck in my memory.

'You think,' Kaya said sadly, 'that I'm just a talking doll designed for masturbation. And you're right there, you fat swine. Your mistake lies elsewhere. You believe that Manitou dwells within you. And that makes you something qualitatively different from me.'

'Well, doesn't it?'

'No,' Kaya retorted. 'You're the same kind of masturbation machine as I am. Only you're a useless one, because you don't do it to anybody. Do you understand that? I do it to you, but you don't do it to anyone at all. All that daily droning and shuddering of yours is a total waste of time.'

'I don't get it,' I said.

Kaya laughed at that.

'And on top of that you're a fool as well. I'll explain some time later. Right now it's time for you to go kill people.'

That sounded offensive enough to make my jaw muscles tense up, and rouse the spirit of stoicism in my breast. There's nothing so bracing as a fresh insult first thing in the morning.

Well hello, world, I thought to myself. Thanks for those kind words. And now to work.

'Okay,' I said, stuffing my feet into my slippers. 'We'll talk later. Brew up some coffee. Daddy's got to fly out soon.'

'I hope you choke on your coffee, you butcher.'

That's the way it is every day at our place.

In the happiness room I struggled for a few seconds with the temptation to switch on the control manitou in order to alter her settings – to take her off maximum bitchiness. And temptation won – the sense of insult was just too strong. I switched on the manitou and entered the password.

Large red numbers started flashing in front of my eyes.

30.00

29.59

29.58

For the first ten minutes I honestly intended to wait it out and do everything I'd planned. But then it hit me that I'd be late for the war. And, even more importantly, I'd be signing my own capitulation. If a machine could defeat me, then I was exactly the same kind of machine and she was absolutely right.

116

I turned off the manitou and started mulling over the sortie.

By the time I left the happiness room, I was completely calm. As soon as I sat down at the table, Kaya served me coffee and toast with jam – she makes superb toast. I patted her condescendingly on the back, and even a little bit lower down – and she didn't shy away. Her instincts really are infallible. She looked slightly embarrassed, as if she was concerned about what she'd said earlier.

While I ate I watched the news on the manitou.

First they showed a logo with our slogan:

'...the CINEWS of thy heart...'

This elegant quotation from the ancient poet Blake never occupied the screen for more than a split second. Legend has it that Blake died in poverty. But if he had lived for a thousand or so years longer, just one line from his 'Tiger' would have made him and all his kin rich forever: that quote twinkles on millions of manitous many times every day.

I was hoping that they would show my damsel yet again, but instead of her they put on the big hit of the pre-war season – a short, blurred (to make it look as if it was taken with a nanodrone camera) video recording of Torn Durex at prayer. During the last twenty-four hours it had been shown at least twenty times.

The recording had been made in a luxurious bedroom with signs of recent debauchery; copious amounts of red filler had bled through onto the skin of the cheap SM-sura lying on the bed. The Orkish Kagan was kneeling in front of a massive gold spastika and whispering ecstatically, 'Manitou! Make it so that the rubber woman feels pain when I stub out a fag against her!'

Since the viewers had already seen in the news the tragic fate of an identical sura, photographed on temple celluloid, they believed the clip. The conspiracy theorists, naturally, claimed that it was a digital fake, paid for by the producers of Armagnac (there was a bottle of Liquid Diamond, standing in a conspicuously advantageous spot in the foreground). But I was certain the shoot was genuine, although it was staged: before they fly over to London, the Orkish Kagans clutch at any opportunity to make a quick quid one last time. Not because they're short of funds, but purely out of greed.

Well all right, I thought, Damilola's feeling mean right now, and he's bound to shoot something really good. The kind of thing people will talk about for a long, long time.

It was time to fly out. I gave Kaya a smacker on the cheek and went off to Hannelore's control unit.

Usually I put Kaya on a couch beside my flying saddle. But this time I didn't even invite her – I just switched on the control manitou. I was sure she would sit down in front of it, of her own accord, as soon as I took off. It promised to be a stressful and dangerous day, and I put her completely out of my mind as soon as I put on the battle goggles and lifted off from the maintenance deck.

When I closed in on our armada, the entire aerial strike force was already in the air and I felt blithe and jittery at the same time, the way I always do before a battle shoot. I was surrounded on all sides by a barrage of at least a hundred battle cameras – every now and then, one or two of them would peel off from the pack, bank into a turn and drop down into the grey lens of the camouflage cloud.

I prefer to descend in a slow spiral: the pilot who maintains high altitude has a far better chance of shooting an exclusive. That's one of the secrets you only come to understand with experience. But the nose-diving cameras really do look beautiful – the spectacle of it induces a feeling of absolutely unfettered freedom, and it strikes terror into the Orks. And to top it off, they hear the infernal shrieking of our air brakes.

No one had engaged maximum camouflage today – as the

temple news channel put it, 'The knights of Manitou are going into battle with their visors raised.'

I wonder what a visor is. The on-screen dictionary doesn't explain this word separately, it only gives the general meaning of the idiom: 'with one's visor raised – honestly, openheartedly'. But I'm sure that in ancient times the meaning of the expression was less exalted than that. Probably a 'visor' was some special kind of spy balloon or periscope that was raised up in the air when castles were stormed. Say, to detect treasure though the window of a tower. This way everything's clear.

I don't often think about such things, but it had just occurred to me that we – the informational and combat elite of mankind – must look very strange in Manitou's eyes: a hundred men in opaque goggles of various designs, squirming about on their flying couches, performing strange movements with their arms and legs. A shot from the on-board cannon is a minute move-ment of the fingers lying on the control stick; a manoeuvre by the camera hurtling through the air is a faint twitch of the calf. And we're all dressed any way we like, and some are probably wearing nothing but their dirty underpants, because they work from home.

But by the way, where are we really, we work-from-home pilots? Within the confines of our rooms – or in the Orkish sky? And where is that sky – all around my Hannelore or in my brain, to which it is relayed by electronic extensions of my eyes and ears?

I remember Kaya tried for a long time to pump into me her ancient wisdom on this subject. I probably didn't really under-stand much, but I did remember something, at least.

In her opinion the answer depends on what exactly we call our self. If it's the body, we're in the room. If it's our attention and conscious awareness, then we're in the sky. But in reality we're in neither one place nor the other, since our body cannot fly through the clouds, and our conscious awareness can't come from anywhere but our body. And there simply isn't any answer to this question. For, as Kaya says, any object or concept disappears and evaporates if we attempt to grasp what it actually is. And this applies in its entirety to whoever is making the attempt to grasp.

Whatever she might say, I find it hard to accept something like that about myself. I'm this person right here, all the time, and that's what everything else starts from. But that elusiveness of the essence definitely applies to the suras that, I am quite certain, are sitting in front of many pilots' control manitous at this very moment.

To understand who they are is impossible.

You can only describe their appearance and behaviour.

Most of them are creatures of a tender age, often with wise, unchildlike eyes, because maximum spirituality is terribly fashionable these days. I think they include not only boys and girls, but also two or three ewe-lambs, thoughtfully chewing on nothingness in front of an aiming sight flying through the clouds. And you could probably find an old man with an old woman too – there are models like that in the catalogue.

And that raises a very intriguing question.

When the pilot removes his goggles after work the sura tells him what she thinks about what she's seen (it must be especially interesting to converse with a sheep, set for maximum spirituality). Naturally, all her reasoning is pure simulation. The sole listener and viewer here is always the owner of a sura, and he animates her with his attention.

But when the pilot is hard at work, who is it that is looking at the manitou as they sit beside him? How does Kaya know that I'm a 'butcher' when my attention is not focused on her? Or does she simply know that after what she has seen she's supposed to say these words to me? But who is it inside her that knows? A riddle, an inscrutable riddle. Clearly it's best simply not to think about it.

Especially at work.

Entirely engrossed in these thoughts, I almost snagged an immense trailer with a fluorescent inscription surrounded by multicoloured hearts.

!!! NICOLAS-OLIVIER LAURENCE VON TRIER – 85!!!

The trailer was blundering straight across my camera's line of flight, absolutely certain that I would turn aside. But of course – Nicolas-Olivier himself was flying to his anniversary film shoot. I managed to get a good look at the trailer before it dived into the clouds.

It was pretty big – a whacking great cube of metal, the size of a good Orkish house. They say that Nicolas-Olivier has a personal gym inside it. Which he is hardly likely to need, on account of his age.

The trailer was decorated with moving portraits of him in his most celebrated temple film roles. The largest of them was from the three-part franchise *The New Batman*, depicting him in his canonical role – wearing a baseball cap and holding a war club (in Church English it is called a 'bat', hence his famous *nom de guerre*). He stands there, with the club seemingly casually stuck under his arm, but in fact it's to make his bicep bulge out further.

The first part was shot a very long time ago, when the bicep was genuine, not made of silicone, and the age of consent was hovering in the region of forty-two, or something like that. The second part was made about ten years ago. And in the interval he's played many other roles. But Nicolas-Olivier owes his image to this epic saga – something like the final hero of mankind, who fights the Orks with their own weapon and wins.

We've started this war in order to shoot the fourth part of the franchise, in which he squelches the Orks with his wooden club beside the Hill of the Ancestors.

Well, not only for Nicolas-Olivier's sake, of course. Free people don't start wars just because one solitary actor is approaching the menostop, even if a couple of news channels do assert that he is universally loved by the people.

But if his producer convinces other producers to finish shooting the franchise flops, the ones they have left on their hands, and sign the rest of the super-rich old farts (of the type, just between you and me, that should be in the crematorium, not in snuffs), well, then a war can very easily start. Especially bearing in mind that the vast Orkish expanses abound with things that a decent man's conscience can never accept – should this very man suddenly happen to see them on his manitou while he's drinking his evening tea. You understand what I mean.

That's precisely why these decorated trailers shaped like pyramids, parallelepipeds and other octahedrons are on their way downwards right now. And every one is displaying a carefully thought-out sequence of images, beaming into ambient space the major milestones in the life and art of the patched and re-patched darling of the movie industry, the one who's sitting inside.

After passing through the clouds, they don't engage their camouflage either – that's the kind of day it is. Their visors are always raised – they've already detected everything that can be grabbed. That's not surprising – if you count up the number of people who feed off the movie business, it turns out that we all have our snouts in the trough, and some of us twice over.

I slipped into the clouds and flew Hannelore for a couple of

122

minutes without any visual information, simply from the data on the manitou. It's actually safer in the clouds like that, when there are heaps of our people around. And when I dived out of the clouds I was stupefied, even though I knew what I would see.

Every time I forget how beautiful a war looks from high altitude.

One of our crack discoursemongers compared Slava with a stain left on a wall by cockroaches living behind a cupboard for a long time. A very precise description – absolutely dead on. But cutting a bright dash at the very centre of this stain is the Circus: an immense green circle, surrounded by a yellow, white and blue hoop – that's what the monumental circus wall, the no-go zone and the water-filled moat look like from altitude. At the centre of the circle there's a small green bump that looks like a hairy nipple. That's the Orkish Hill of the Ancestors, overgrown with coconut palms. There are other weeds growing on it too, but on the rest of the area large plant life is eradicated by flying mowing machines.

Such a luscious green can only come from fresh young grass growing on even and well fertilised soil. And when you fly lower and engage visual magnification, the multicoloured spots of flowers become visible, celebrating their wedding with the bees on this wide expanse. The eternal heraldic design of life. Strange, I never think of the Orks, but every time I feel sorry for this immense flowery lawn, which is transformed from green to blackish-brown by the end of the war. So many butterflies and beetles are killed every time.

Preparations for filming in the Circus were in their second day already, but the Orks didn't know anything about that – the technical trailers had flown in ahead of today in invisible mode. The Orks only saw our cameras hovering in the sky. But today they would see our entire assault force.

The stinking slums of the Orkish capital only run right up to the wall of the circus at one spot – by the market square. And that's the location of the only gates through which the Orks can pass on their way to the war.

They were already prepared for battle – their huge army looked like an octopus that had crawled up to the virginally green circle of the Circus. It looked that way because the army was too big to fit into the market square, where the Kagan's battle barge was standing – half of the soldiers assembled in adjacent streets.

And then something clicked in my mind.

I suddenly realised that this sinister octopus could be a great help with the payments for Kaya. Naturally, the high-altitude view wasn't being shown by just one camera, or even two – but without a bit of special gimmickry, no one could see the octopus, since the Orkish detachments were wearing uniforms of various colours... Ah, but if it was made black... After juggling a bit with light modifiers and filters, I switched on the camera.

The octopus looked so alarming now; it even made me feel uneasy – as they said in olden times: 'I was behind the camera and I shed a tear...' It was astounding that this pattern appears in every war, and so far no one had noticed it or sold it.

I was shooting simultaneously on temple celluloid and digital, and one of the senior sommeliers had evidently followed my material on his manitou, immediately understood the idea and blown me an instant kiss – the figures in the upper right corner of my field of vision flickered and clicked, and I realised that I'd earned three million manitou.

That was just for a few seconds of filming. And the shot was certain to feature as the opening screen for today's newscast. Never mind the opening screen, it was good enough to be the logo for the entire war – a black octopus and a green circle with... I really didn't know who they'd write into it. But in a

124

ten-fold enlargement, all the interested professionals would be able to see the tiny icon at the bottom:

DK V-Arts & All

And there was no doubt at all that the shot would be enlarged many times – it's a very rare achievement to convey the entire sombre, aggressive essence of the Orkish tribe so correctly and succinctly in a single close-up. Look and learn, you sucklings, while I'm still with you.

That's why I like to be the last to descend, in my trademark spiral. While the seagulls thrash about just above the waves, trying to find themselves a juicy morsel, the eagle soars through the clouds… It was great that I'd earned my manitou right at the beginning of the war – like all the aces, I don't like to hang about over the battlefield unless it's absolutely necessary. I could simply crash into some novice and damage Hannelore. Or I could easily get winged by a shell, especially when they start dispatching the Orks who have been recorded for eternity off into that same eternity.

Shooting battle from low-level flight is not for me. Let the youngsters revel in the close-ups of the Orkish guts – the most important thing for them is to make everything juicily appalling. Their cameras belong to their employers, so they're not afraid of smashing them up. So let them fight their battle for existence. Just as long as it's not with me, but with each other.

Yes, I can go down low, of course. I have all the skills for that. But there's only one job down there that suits me – covering one of the top actors during filming. This used to be the most important area – under the old temple rules, the actor was required to kill at least one Ork himself for the snuff, and I had to fire at precisely the right moment, so that the Ork would still technically be alive when he was overtaken by retribution. But under the new law it's no longer important exactly who kills him, the actor or the cameraman (the theologians have come to the conclusion that the thread of life is, in any case, snapped by Manitou). The important thing is that the Orks filmed in a snuff really did die. Well now, there's no problem with that.

I can also pick off Orks around the Kagan himself, when they go to load him onto a platform, to lift him up to London. The Orks, by the way, still believe that most of their Kagans die at the Hill of the Ancestors.

But this time no one had hired me, either for the first job or the second. Evidently because my services are expensive. Well okay, today I've already put in my time...

Always remember, pilots – the most important thing in our job is to have plenty of altitude to spare.

If I was flying low over the ground at the moment when Kaya tugged on my shoulder, I might possibly have crashed Hannelore. But since I was high up, the camera simply made a somersault. I scraped my finger briefly on the control handlebar, switching into autopilot, and took my goggles off my nose.

Kaya's face was right there in front of mine.

'What are you up to?' I asked in astonishment.

She rubbed her cheek against mine. She'd never done that before.

'Do you want Daddy to crash his camera?' I asked, trying to speak sternly. But my hand reached out automatically for her back, to that enchanting tiny bit above the buttocks that I had argued about so much with the sommeliers – and won.

She smacked her moist lips against my nose.

'I'll do something really, really nice for Daddy,' she said softly. 'Only afterwards. But right now I want to take a look at Grim. Go down lower, you flying backside. And quick. Or he'll be killed.'

The dark birds of death hung in the sky above Slava, with their round, glittering eyes making them look like dragonflies.

The superstitious country Orks believed that those eyes were made of glass cursed by Manitou, and they were used for drawing the souls out of fallen warriors. The sophisticated urban Orks, of course, laughed at this nonsense. But in their hearts they believed it in exactly the same way.

Occasionally one camera or another swung over freely in the sky and hurtled towards the ground in a howling crescendo, only to pull out of its dive just above the square and go zooming over the Orks' heads, shooting in close up.

There were so many cameras that every now and then one's eyes were pricked by a sharp ray of light from the morning sun, reflected in their optics – as if, although the battle hadn't started yet, the upper people were already firing their baleful smart arrows at the Orks. Then the sun went behind the camouflage cloud, making things a bit easier.

The Urkagan's battle barge was an intricate structure of wood on a stout frame of *deripasium*, mounted on an eight-axle Daimler motorenwagen platform. As always, the barge had been manufactured exclusively in the workshops of the Yellow Zone, and the production process had been covered extensively in special editions of 'Yf da Wør Cømer Morn' – everybody knew what was inside it, what speed it was capable of and how much each wheel weighed. Now it was aimed directly at the Gates of Victory, and the barriers in front of its upward-curving bow had already been removed. Everybody realised what that meant. But the soldiers filling the square were in high spirits.

The din above the square was gradually getting louder. Grim was infected by the general excitement – and he was astonished to realise that there was a fair dose of vanity mingled in with it. After all, he was one of the Kagan's orderlies. A responsible and honourable post, introduced in the aftermath of War No. 214 – when the upper people suddenly turned off the Orks' mobile phones at the height of the battle.

Grim could feel how many Orkish gazes there were slipping over his brand-new white sailor suit – the uniform of the right flank. The other two orderlies, attached to the left flank and the central sector, were dressed differently – one as a savage and the other as a retiarius. Their combat vehicles were fastened to the side of the barge – the same 'Urkaine' mopeds made at the factory where Uncle Shug worked. When he saw his machine, Grim recalled the conversation at the wake. It looked as if nowadays they shagged the material to death without even trying to cheat it first, knowing that it wouldn't work anyway.

Grim had the feeling that some of the men standing in the square were waving to him in person. And Chloe could certainly see him now on her manitou in the Green Zone. He had seen himself several times on the immense screen hanging on the wall of the Museum of the Ancestors instead of the sheet of canvas with the word 'ASSTILUDE' on it.

Grim was standing quite a long way from the bow of the barge, where Torn Durex was seated on his campaign throne. The Urkagan was hidden by a crowd of dignitaries and military commanders – Grim could only see their bowed backs. But from time to time the sovereign's face appeared on the wall of the museum. He looked perfectly calm. This was already his eighth war, after all.

The leaders conferred.

On the screen it all looked pretty good, but Grim didn't feel any particular reverence for the leadership. He had seen the

Kagan facing the guns of a battle camera, and hadn't been particularly impressed. In addition, early that morning, before forming-up, he had decided to do a bit of fortune-telling with the book that the priest had given him. He had hit on a passage about power.

Now he was feeling rather gloomy.

The passage was this:

Seventy-One. On Power.

The Custodian of the War Music has said: the essence of power lies not in the Urkagan's ability to start a war. Quite the opposite. Urkagan can remain the Urkagan if he issues such an order at precisely the right moment – when the dudes will turn to him. And there is no other dominion, there is only death by the knife or flushing into the band of queerasts.

The ancients understood this, the men of modern times do not.

In truth, the art of the ruler comes down to no more than pretending for as long as possible that you control the whirlwind that is rushing you along, replying with a derisive smile to the reproaches of your subjects that the whirlwind is rushing in the wrong direction.

The same applies, also, to many other things.

This looked like the truth. For several hours now Grim had been observing the whirlwind as it coalesced in front of the Gates of Victory.

More and more troops kept arriving – the square couldn't fit them all in any more. Officers ran between the divisions, setting the distance to be maintained so that no one would be killed in the crush. The men were lined up by types of uniform. There were a lot of them in this war – although, of course, not twenty, as the stoned public prosecutor had claimed.

The greater part of the infantry was wearing white sailor suits with wide, blue turn-down collars. They were still being issued with their weapons: halberds, battleaxes, spears and swords, whatever each one of them happened to get. Somehow all of them already knew that the sailors would be fighting on the right flank and in the central sector. They had least reason of all for feeling jolly. It was clear to any fool that the men were dressed in white to provide a stronger contrast with blood.

The heavily armed storm troopers were distinguished by their black armour and identical toothed pikes. They were standing in a perfect infantry square, absolute immobile, so that they seemed to be carved out of wood.

The gladiator regiment was dressed as retiarii. The great hulking guys holding sharp tridents in their hands had been left practically naked – they had nothing on but shorts, with rags sewn over them to make them look like loincloths. The bronze shoulder plates that retiarii were supposed to wear hadn't been issued this year – rumour had it that the army command had sold them off as non-ferrous metal scrap. The guys were shuddering in the morning breeze. Some unfolded their battle nets and threw them over their shoulders. The officers whistled at the ones who did that.

The men behaving in the jolliest fashion of all were the savages, in their pelts of brown synthetic fur – there were two entire regiments of them, assigned to the left flank. For some reason it was believed that the savages would have it easier than the others. And they had been issued with the most futile weapons – wooden clubs and flint hand-axes.

The bowmen, slingmen and fire-throwers were standing apart from the others. The barrels of fuel oil, the ballistas and the heavy equipment were not in the square yet – there were always

130

brought up at the last moment, in order not to give the upper people an excuse to start bombing.

Grim had already counted seven types of uniforms, and that was not taking into account the soldiers drawn up in the streets adjacent to the square. There could well be someone else there. Usually it was the reserve that was left in the streets – the line-up was carved straight into the walls of the houses, because they were drawn up for every war in exactly the same way.

Grim thought how great it would be to make do with this jolly, exciting masquerade and not go into the Circus to die. That could happen at least once in the whole of history, couldn't it? A childish imitation of a prayer circled round and round in his mind:

'Manitou, I know that it's because I've been bad. But now I will always be good, I swear... Only don't, please don't...'

And then the landing began.

Bright-coloured cubes, tetrahedrons, spheres and other geometrical forms, the names of which Grim didn't know, came showering down out of the spiral cloud above the Circus. As they approached the ground, they expanded in size and braked – and before they disappeared behind the wall of the Circus, they described a circle above the square, zooming over the Kagan's barge with a rustling sound. The Orks froze on the spot and had a second or two to get a look at the enemy from close up.

The trailers were covered with bright frescoes – mostly scenes from snuffs. Naked, buxom women, frozen in poses of shameless copulation with tanned, elderly men; the upper people's fighting machines advancing on a formation of Orks; the shame of defeated Kagans of the past – all these pictures on the sides of the transports were moving and alive. It was as if forbidden fragments of familiar snuffs were falling from the sky – the same fragments that had been blotted by the censor. The hostile world on the other side of the leaden cloud couldn't give a damn for

131

all the Orkish prohibitions. It tore its way into the Orks' life crudely and brazenly, in total mockery of its order and conventions. This assault by an alien culture was undoubtedly an act of war in its own right – everybody felt that.

The square started murmuring resentfully – quietly at first, then louder and louder, and the murmur started spilling over into movement. The square was seething. The officers could no longer regulate the distance between the detachments, it became harder and harder for the columns to maintain formation, and everybody felt that if the gates weren't opened right now, there would be a stampede. It was as elementary as a school textbook problem about a pipe with water flowing into it and out of it.

On the big manitou, Grim saw an officer of the retinue lean down to the Kagan and whisper something. Torn Durex nodded and got to his feet. The square froze.

The Kagan waited for a brief moment, raised his flanged mace, spat on it with relish and flung it at the gates. The blow of metal on metal rang out in the silence – the mace had hit one of the spastikas covering the wood.

That's it then, Grim thought.

It was as if he glanced through a crack behind which the uncomplicated wheels of history were turning, and it happened while the mace was still falling to the ground after bouncing off the gates. So this was how great events happened... The secret of power was described in *The Book of Orkasms* with exceptional precision.

When the mace fell, the great heroes of combat rushed towards the gates. Bamboleo got there first – and with a single blow of his tram axle he smashed the lock, which jangled pitifully.

The manitou on the wall of the Museum of the Ancestors showed a close-up of the lock's burst shackle, and the men in the square threw their heads up to see a camera creeping towards the gates – but it was concealed by camouflage.

The soldiers gathered in the square started howling an ancient battle cry:

'Urkrule! Urkrule!'

Other knights came to Bamboleo's aid, and the gates swung open. Grim couldn't yet see the open field behind them – but the electric tremor of rapture and horror that rushed through the square ran down his back too.

The engines hidden under the boards started growling and the barge began to move – the Kagan had to be one of the first to enter Orkish Slava. The battle bridge was always made in the form of a huge boat, because a platform like that could squeeze in through the gates – it was long and narrow.

There you have the entire Norman Theory, thought Grim, recalling something he had crammed at school – the noble Ript Kondom with his band of Vikings and something else of the sort... And if we crawled under the wall, our forefathers would be gnomes...

Scraping one side lightly against the wall of the gap (that was a bad sign, but everyone pretended not to have noticed anything), the Kagan's platform drove into Orkish Slava.

And then something strange started happening to Grim.

It felt as if he had divided into two – as if someone had stuck an aerial into his head and it was picking up the feelings of the immense crowd of Orks. He had to experience them, like it or not, and the most terrible thing of all was that he couldn't always distinguish himself from the crowd. The Orks burst into his brain exactly as they burst through the gates of the Circus, and he had to conceal himself in a tiny free corner of his own consciousness.

He still didn't understand what he was seeing, but his heart was already aching sweetly: the door into an ancient tale of heroes dissolved away... (Grim couldn't give a rotten damn about heroic tales, but only the very margin of his mind knew

133

that.) The green, the expansive, the level, the glorious, the dear and the beloved... The heart of Urkaine, the Hill of the Ancestors, watered with Orkish blood... (Why not flatten it completely, and there won't be any need to water anything with blood anymore?) So this was where his own kind had been fighting the upper people for so many centuries, defending the Orkish Slava... (Right then, you've driven in the cattle – now what?)

The bewilderment gradually passed off and Grim started understanding more clearly where he was and what was going on around him.

Orkish Slava was a huge round field, perfectly even, with smoothly trimmed grass – and a small hill right at the very centre. The field was surrounded on all sides by a yellowish grey concrete wall that ran so far away in some places that it almost disappeared from view.

The Orkish heroes in the V-formation that had run on ahead could no longer compete with the barge as it picked up speed, and they hung on its sides, slipping their belt loops over hooks that were dangling there. With its engines droning, the Daimler motorenwagen pulled ahead of the Orkish ranks and hurtled towards the Hill of the Ancestors.

At that time the most difficult manoeuvre was taking place at the Gates of Victory – the Orkish army and its equipment had to get through the narrow passage without a stampede and occupy the places prescribed by the dispositions, and do it quickly. This required good organisation, but it looked unexciting, and all the cameras were following the Kagan's barge. Some of them flew on ahead, swung round and came rushing towards it, skidding past dangerously close to the men standing on the deck.

Grim walked forward. Now he could see the Kagan – Torn Durex was sitting on his campaign throne very close by. The Kagan was watching the coverage of the war on a little flat

134

manitou, hiding it behind his battle fan so that it wouldn't be caught on film by some chance camera.

Once they were close to the Hill of the Ancestors, the barge started braking smoothly and stopped in the shade of the first palm trees – so that the unripe coconuts were right above the deck. They were no threat to anyone's life, but this was also a bad sign, at least for those who knew their history: many recalled Loss Solid.

From here they had a good view of the preparations being made for war by the upper people. They didn't look too impressive. Standing on the right flank was something that looked like a short castle wall with battlements. In the central sector they could see a long earthen rampart, with the trailers that had zoomed across above the market standing behind it. And far away on the left little green hummocks could be seen, overgrown with bright flowers and grass. Grim heard two military men discussing them – apparently those were transport containers that simultaneously served as stage sets: two wars earlier the upper people had used something similar.

The escort of heroes unfastened themselves from the hooks, surrounded the Kagan's barge in a defensive semi-circle and froze, bristling with sharp metal.

In fact there wasn't anyone for them to defend themselves against. The invisible upper people did nothing as they watched the Orkish forces enter the plain and move towards their positions on the advanced flanks, in order to leave the Hill of the Ancestors and commander-in-chief's barge in the rear. Since Orks running across a field didn't possess any artistic value, all the cameras were now hovering over the Hill of the Ancestors, where the most solemn moment of the war was beginning – the changing of the flag.

On the summit of the hill, a steel flagpole towered up among the coconut palms. The flag fluttering on it at the moment was the blue banner of Byzantion, with the twin Bs reflecting each other, looking like two conjoined globes – in perfect keeping with the official doctrine of 'two cultures – one world'.

Grim looked up. The axis of Byzantion was directly over his head, and although he couldn't see the offglobe itself, the shaggy spiral of the cloud unfolded from the precise spot in the sky to which the flagpole pointed.

Grim had seen the changing of the flag so often in old snuffs that he could forecast the entire sequence of events to within a second.

Threading their way through the palm trees, the Standard-Bearers of Slava ran up the hill – this season it was Bamboleo and Grub. All the manitous showed close-ups of the two figures, bounding over the tussocky grass towards the flagpole. Soon the yellow figure eight of Byzantion came sliding down and a lingering roar rang out over the field as the red Orkish flag, with its golden spastika, went soaring upwards.

Grim felt his divided state continuing. The only feeling he had about what was happening was fear, and yet his throat contracted and tears of exaltation sprang to his eyes – as if his homeland had thrust its bony hand into his cranium and forcibly squeezed the required glands.

The cameras didn't attack. They remained at altitude, with one or two occasionally diving towards the Urkagan's barge, and the air whistled alarmingly as they sliced through it – but they always turned aside before the warriors could reach them with their spears. Soon the upper people suffered their first casualties: two cameras collided at high speed and then went flying upwards, sparking, until they disappeared into the cloud.

As the Orkish banner flew, fluttering, towards the tip of the flagpole, the speakers on the Kagan's barge started broadcasting solemn music. For some reason, Grim remembered a singing lesson at school.

'Music can be queerastic or warrior. When queerastic music is playing, the soul is closed to the Light of Manitou. But warrior music is itself the Light of Manitou. The Orks have abolished queerastic music. And now the wide expanses of Urkaine resound only with warrior music...'

The teacher was deluded, thought Grim, the Orks hadn't abolished what he called 'queerastic music' at all. It had simply adapted to mimic warrior music – and the proof of that was pouring out of the manitous relaying the start of the war.

Grim had seen close-ups of the Orkish military leaders during the raising of the flag many times – they were in one snuff out of every three, and as a rule they weren't cut. Usually the generals were talking about something or other. Watching their faces, it was possible to suppose that the subject was the latest modifications to the plan of battle or the principles of the post-war world order. Grim was on the Kagan's barge now, and he was lucky – he heard one of those epoch-making conversations with his own ears.

Standing in front of him were Marshal Spur and one of the Kagan's aging lovers, a mezzanine-adjutant, sporting the same kind of sailor suit as Grim was wearing, but with stars on the wide turndown collar. The mezzanine-adjutant said to Spur:

'Listen here, old man! Do you know the Kagan's prayer?'

Spur raised one eyebrow.

'You mean about the rubber woman and the fag ends?'

The mezzanine-adjutant shook his head.

'What prayer is that then?'

'The one with a secret name of Manitou. The holy ascetics say it solves all material problems.'

Marshal Spur scratched his chin, pondering.

'Well then, teach me it,' he said.

'Repeat: Manitou pay Ali!'

Spur repeated the phrase rapidly several times until the words

137

'alimony to pay' emerged. 'Alimony' was not a particularly popular term among the Global Orks with one foot already up in London.

'Shit, who the fuck needs that crap before a battle?'

'Who are you calling shit?' the mezzanine-adjutant asked with a polite smile. 'Have you totally fucking lost it, you old blockhead?'

Right, Grim thought, now the muzak will end. Then they'll lower the flying walls. Then they'll announce that the flanks and the centre have been deployed. And then... And then it will start. That's when they'll turn on the censor. I wonder what the logo will be? They'll probably make it a spastika with our fallen warriors coming back to life under the Light of Manitou... And everyone will wonder again how much they pocketed from it...

If reality did make corrections to this sequence of events, they were only minor.

First the message came that the flanks and the centre were deployed. In fact, Grim had realised that for himself – everywhere he could see the lines of Orks striding towards the upper people's fortifications. Several units had already reached their prescribed positions and halted – there hadn't been any order to attack.

Then the upper people started deploying the flying walls.

Grim had never seen the process in full – the news and the snuffs only gave brief extracts from it.

First, a host of identical cylindrical machines appeared out of the clouds – they were grey and looked like sections of a thick water main; the only difference between them was the numbers on their sides. Descending towards the plain, they formed intricate chains and semicircles, which hovered over the earth. Soon there were so many of them that Grim got the impression that a complex network of streets had been set out up above him.

Then swathes of grey fabric started creeping down out of

these cylinders. Grim recalled the suspended screen on which they used to show slides in school – it was stored in a battered tin tube and simply pulled out before a class. A batten with a weight on it was attached to the screen's bottom. Everything here looked the same, only on a much bigger scale. The thick fabric, covered in holes, swayed in the air and soon Grim saw a labyrinth, trembling slightly in the wind in front of him – unstable and obscenely huge.

Now there was no more direct line of sight between the headquarters of the commander-in-chief, the centre and the flanks. The Kagan's barge was cut off from his soldiers by an immense grey wall – although numerous corridors had been left in it. Grim knew that this fabric could show pictures, just like a manitou, but so far there weren't any images on it.

'Orderly Grim!'

Grim started.

Marshal Spur was standing right in front of him.

'Yes sir!' Grim bellowed, saluting.

Buried in his own thoughts, he had completely forgotten that he wasn't on board the Kagan's barge as an honoured guest.

'Take your moped,' said Spur, 'and go over to General Hrol on the right flank. The attack's just about to begin, and the mobile phones are already acting up. If they cut off our communications, you'll stand in for them. Stay beside the general. Have you got all of that?'

'Yes, sir!' said Grim, saluting smartly again.

The Marshal turned away and went back to the Kagan's seat.

Grim unhooked one of the mopeds off the side of the barge, lugged it to the stern and rolled it down to the ground along the sloping planks that had been set up.

So far it was all very simple.

The right flank lay to starboard – where the upper people had set up a section of fortress wall. Grim flung his leg over the saddle, pressed the red button on the handlebars, and the moped's engine sprang to life.

Grim reached the grey fluttering wall, drove into one of the gaps and saw another wall made of exactly the same kind of grey fabric in front of him. Gaps had been left in it too, but in such a way that nothing could be seen through them except the next grey barrier. However, for the time being getting his bearings in these corridors was easy. A few minutes later Grim rode out into open space and saw a multitude of soldiers, some kind of long wagons under covers, and the wall.

General Hrol's detachment was there in front of him.

The fortress wall looked rather ludicrous. It was more like a narrow house without any windows, with decorative battlements on the roof. It was too thick for a wall and too thin for a building. It was probably a 'fragment of fortifications' or an 'element of a castle', if Grim remembered correctly the names of 'locations of valour' from his military schooling – those were the places where the Orks demonstrated their fury to the enemy.

A multitude of different-coloured little figures were darting about in the open field in front of the wall. Their movements looked absolutely chaotic and Grim suddenly couldn't understand how all these people were controlled at all.

Hrol, surrounded by his officers, was standing on a freshly cobbled-together wooden platform, in front of a large drum, on which a map of the local terrain was spread out. At first Grim couldn't figure out why the general was standing with his back to the soldiers, but then he realised that this way his busy staff and the fragment of wall fitted into the frame together perfectly.

Grim braked to a stop at the platform and looked up – he was right, there were at least ten cameras hovering in the sky, and so, before walking up the steps, he took out the comb that had been issued with his uniform and tidied up his hair.

Hrol listened to his report sullenly.

'Good,' he said. 'Stand by for orders.'

Mobile communications were still functioning and Grim was forgotten.

From the height of the platform, what had looked like a confused crowd when Grim rode past it on his moped immediately divided itself into black and white detachments of men engaged in complicated movement.

The little black figures were stormtroopers – they were just finishing forming up in battle-order, evening out the line of their shields, with their heavy pikes protruding over the top. Behind them, Orks in sailor suits were preparing the siege ladders, checking the mechanisms.

Some lightly armed retiarii were sitting on the ground, having dropped their nets and tridents – but they were already being urged to their feet in order to form up: their small unit had wandered over this way by mistake, and now the commanding officer was getting a dressing-down. The gladiators' place was on the left flank. Each arm of service had their own task in the fighting, and getting jumbled up together was prohibited under pain of court martial and anathematisation.

Hrol started talking on his mobile phone.

'Yes! The equipment covers have been removed. Yes sir. We're getting started.'

Grim realised that the order to storm the wall had been received.

Hrol turned to the soldiers.

'Ladders into action!'

The black line of stormtroopers parted. Two brand new siege ladders on wheels drove forward out of the Orkish ranks, with their feeble petrol engines sputtering – they were some of those that had been shown in the last parade. From all sides soldiers in sailor suits pushed along, forcing them to move faster. Once they had rolled the ladders up to the wall, they extended them

141

by engaging the hydraulic cable system. The height was exactly right to reach the battlements on top of the wall – evidently the intelligence information from 'our upper sources', which was hinted at in the pre-war propaganda, had proved accurate.

But not a single defender of the upper people's stronghold appeared up at the top.

General Hrol frowned. Something strange was going on here – according to all the rules of war, this was the most dreadful moment of the action, when the most soldiers were killed. But the enemy had not only allowed them to raise the siege ladders, he didn't seem to have any objections to the Orks scaling the topmost point of the element of fortifications and thereby winning the victory.

The stormtroopers waited for the command with their pikes thrust out ahead of them, and the commander's protracted silence seemed more and more alarming with every instant that passed. At last Hrol made up his mind.

'Attack!'

The Orks' battle formation started moving. Soldiers with slings ran out into the empty space in front of the wall and lined up in a long chain, preparing to shoot down any enemy with a hail of stones. At the same moment the stormtroopers who had to climb up moved out from behind the front line, with the shields attached to their backs making them look like black tortoises. They started clambering up the ladders.

Grim suddenly got the feeling that what was happening was unreal. The feeling grew stronger and stronger, until he realised that he could hear a strange sound that was growing louder with every second.

The sound was like the buzzing of a grinding wheel, but a huge one, one so heavy that it takes a long time to pick up speed. Grim realised that everyone else could hear the buzz too – a wave of uncertainty seemed to surge through the Orkish ranks. And then Grim noticed that the stormtroopers weren't climbing up the wall any more, but running away from it, and the wall itself was shuddering, and even the soldiers who had already got high up the ladders were dropping their weapons and jumping down.

A ragged crack ran along the wall – as if a jagged bolt of lightning had embedded itself in it. In a single moment the crack widened, plaster and rubble went flying downwards and a yawning, black void was exposed. Grim recalled the Visage of Manitou from *The Word on the Word*, but he didn't have any time for pious contemplation.

A blow struck the wall from within and a large lump of plaster fell off. There wasn't simply a void inside. Something that growled was glittering and moving in the opening.

'Bravely now! Bravely now!' Hrol screamed. 'Hold the line, soldiers! Slingmen, fire!'

The slingmen whirled their leather propellers over their head and stones went hurtling into the widening gap. Grim heard several resounding thwacks and then a large section of the wall collapsed at the very centre and he could see what was hiding inside.

It was an immense metal warrior that looked a bit like those knights encased in armour who were often filmed in the Loss Liquid's era snuffs.

It had a barrel-shaped body, short, thick legs with large, pyramid-shaped feet and cylindrical bearings instead of knees. Its face was flattened into the shape of some kind of ancient conical oil can, with the sharp end pointing forward. The openings in its upper section were like eyes, and the projections above them were reminiscent of eyebrows raised above the bridge of a nose. This gave the metal face something like a human expression – a kind of sad curiosity. One of the warrior's arms ended in a steel

143

club and the other in a bell mouth, covered with a grating that had a somewhat industrial look.

The metal warrior lifted up its face and made a long, drawn-out sound that was like a sad bugle call, so mournful and loud that Grim's ears were blocked. Then, as easily as if it were playing, it knocked down the ladder sticking up in front of it and strode forward.

Another section of the wall collapsed and Grim saw a second metal giant standing inside it. And it looked as if there was a third one too. At least it would have fitted in.

'Orderly Grim! Snap out of it, you dope!'

Grim felt someone shaking by the shoulder and with an effort he tore his eyes away from the metal warrior. Standing there in front of him was General Hrol.

'Go to the Kagan,' the general ordered. 'Tell him to send the fire-thrower units over here! Urgently! Tell him Orks are laughing as they die! A glorious battle!'

Grim realised that the general was just as scared as he was.

'Understood!' he yelled and dashed towards his moped.

This time it took almost a minute for the engine to engage and Grim watched, spellbound, as the battle unfolded while he kept prodding at the red button with his finger.

The metal warrior moved up close to the Orkish ranks. The stormtroopers started tearing around it, trying to thrust the points of their serrated pikes into its knee-joints.

'That's smart,' thought Grim, 'very smart!'

And then the metal warrior waved his lattice-like bell mouth. There was that familiar grinding sound again and some invisible force instantly squashed several Orks flat. It was as if they were transformed into red steam and blown out of their armour, and the armour was left looking like ironed clothes smouldering on the ground. No smoke or flames came flying out of the bell

144

mouth, but the air around it trembled as it does in hot weather above the heated surface of a road.

The metal warrior swung his club and brought it crashing down on a crowd of Orks. Then again, and again. It struck slowly, and the Orks had time to dodge out of the way, but Grim realised that the warrior wasn't trying to kill as many men as possible – it was working for the cameras that were swarming around. Its movements really did look awesome.

Then Grim noticed that the second metal warrior was clambering out of the ruins. But at that point the moped finally started and Grim hurtled off.

After a few unpleasant moments in the labyrinth, where the panels of fabric had already lit up with advertisements for gadgets of one kind or another, he finally caught sight of the coconut palms of the Hill of the Ancestors, with the black sea of the Orkish reserve forces surging around it.

Grim hurtled up to the Kagan's barge.

Torn Durex was no longer on the bridge. Following Orkish tradition, he had gone down into the hold, where the leader was supposed to drink *volya* and sing valiant songs during the battle – so that the spirits of the ancient heroes would descend from the merry meadows of Alkalla to assist the Orks engaged in combat. None of the Orkish top brass actually believed in Alkalla, but many of them did believe in conspiracy theory and so tried to keep as far away as possible from the coconut palms. Grim even thought he heard the sovereign's low voice, warbling something like this:

'"Heigh-ho," said the old bitch, "we shall see what we shall see..."'

But he wasn't sure – they were making too much noise all around him.

Marshal Spur was in command of everything. Having heard the report, he grimly issued his order to the orderlies and soon

145

Grim saw a large detachment of Orks, their barrels of fuel oil at the ready, set out for the right flank. When they disappeared behind a fabric panel dangling from the sky – the one with a motorenwagen advert on it – Grim started wondering what he should do. According to regulations, he was supposed to obey the orders of the commander to whom he had been sent by his latest order. And that was Marshal Spur.

But the Marshal had forgotten about him – and now Grim probably ought to wait until he remembered.

The Marshal had no time for Grim. Dispatches were constantly arriving for him from the other sectors of the front, concealed behind the flying walls. Grim tried to stay in the Marshal's sight, waiting for him to notice him – and before long, from the snippets of conversation that reached his ears he had put together a general picture of the way the battle was going.

On the left flank, where the green container-hillocks were located, the Orkish savages had been attacked by gigantic lizards, who were now ripping and tearing them with their teeth and claws. They had managed to bring down two or three of the lizards, but when they started cutting the lizards' necks with their flint hand-axes, the primary tendons proved to be too well protected.

The retiarii were brought in, but the lizards easily tore the nets with their horns. The soldiers were asking for strong ropes that they could use to make nooses, and more pointed logs. Spur gave instructions to fetch those urgently from Slava, but the order was taken by another orderly.

After that things went from bad to worse on the left flank: the people lowered a black curtain from the sky – to fence off the retiarii from the scene of the battle with the lizards, and sent in mammoths to attack them. The huge beasts trampled the Orks underfoot and crushed them with their tusks – the casualties mounted up quickly. The mammoths were very well protected

– there was almost nowhere where the tridents could pierce their hides, and they were only afraid of blows to the stomach and under the knees. One especially large mammoth, carrying warriors in metal armour with crossbows and spears, kept apart from the others. Intelligence decided that this was the command vehicle and suggested concentrating all forces against it.

Spur gave instructions for a company of stormtroopers from the right flank, armed with pikes, to be sent in against the large mammoth, ordering them to take the nets from the retiarii and to strip to their underpants before the attack. Then it was reported that the mammoths were afraid of fire, and Spur sent the second detachment of fire-throwers to the left flank.

And then a new orderly arrived from the right flank. General Hrol reported the first great victory. They had managed to topple one of the metal warriors – they had thrown ropes over it and it had slipped in the blood. Many stormtroopers had been killed, but as the metal warrior fell, it had slit open, with its ray, the chest of the second warrior, which was coming to help it. The second metal warrior had given out a shower of sparks from its chest, and stopped dead. But the first one, even though it had tumbled over, could still fire, and now the Orks all around it had laid down in order not to get caught by the ray. So far the third warrior was still standing in the wall without moving, and they were afraid to approach it.

Hrol proposed digging a trench and detonating a bomb made of gas cans under the fallen warrior. (Grim didn't even know that the Orks had such a serious weapon.) But Spur ordered him to save both bombs for the main thrust and instructed him to light a stinking fire of fuel oil, oakum and fat in the space that was mined under the metal warrior, in order to burn through the warrior's wires and smoke its silicon brains.

And then news started arriving from the central axis, where the most serious slaughter was just beginning. Every dispatch was worse than the one before. The people had split up the flood of the Orkish attack into several sections and set about annihilating them separately. This tactic was impossible to counter. The central front had turned out to be very wide, and from the very beginning the people had divided it up into small separate sectors with flying walls. In each sector a special army fought against the Orks. Fortunately, the differently dressed enemy detachments didn't come to each other's aid.

The Orks had been familiar with elves and gnomes for centuries, and the battle against their detachments was being conducted in accordance with principles mastered long ago. The slingmen and spear-throwers fought the elves, hiding from the arrows behind siege shields, and the gnomes were bombarded from a light catapult with dead moles that had been prepared in advance. It was assumed that a direct hit would immediately deactivate a gnome, since their programme algorithms considered a mole to be a bad sign and foul in the extreme.

The Orks had already encountered some of the other enemies before. For instance, mounted knights encased in steel (there weren't many of them) and vampires in black cloaks, who rose up out of the ground for a few seconds to inflict a fatal bite in the throat. The Orks knew more or less how to fight against them. Pikes stuck into the ground helped against the knights – the horses ran their bellies onto them. But the vampires had to be killed with fire and aspen wood – the point at which they were about to jump up out from the ground could be identified in advance from the cameras hovering over it.

Some of the enemies were unfamiliar, and it was against these that the Orks suffered their worst losses. The cross-eyed warlock proved to be the most terrible – a grey-haired old man floating in mid-air, surrounded by flaming trigrams. He was playing a dulcimer, directing at the Orks some kind of coloured waves that sent rank after rank tumbling to the ground, and the cross-eyed host behind him joyfully flung their conical straw hats up in the air.

There was also plenty that was new in the sector where the Orks were fought by the upper people's own heroes. The old soldiers said that the only ones left from the old times were Batman and the X-Men. No one knew the others. They fought strangely and mercilessly – in this area the Orks were no longer advancing, but only trying to hold the front.

One by one the finest warriors departed from this life. Grub was crushed by a battle mammoth when he tried to chop its foot ligaments with his cleavers. Fagg was shot by musketeers in cloaks with Maltese crosses when he threw himself into the assault on their little mobile bastion. Dolt was vanquished by a knight with a yellow shield, and Hern was killed attacking a square of infantry in red tunics, which lumbered out to fight the Orks on the central front. Bamboleo died a hero's death in the battle against a chameleon jumper. As for Alejandro, he was still dashing around the field in his black sleeping shorts, waving his ornate pike about, but death remained indifferent to him.

On the left flank the terrible beasts carried on pressing the Orks hard, despite the reinforcements that had been brought in, so Hrol decided to send part of the reserve there, and after them an anti-retreat unit of Ganjaberserks disguised as retiarii, with orders to wipe out every last Ork if they started retreating, and to die themselves. Grim had no doubt that the butts would carry out at least the first part of their order. They had never been found wanting as a blocking detachment.

Then absolutely disastrous news started pouring in from the central sector. Orderlies reported that where the Orks started getting the upper hand, the cameras came to the rescue of the people, firing bullets with a special plug, so that the wounds were invisible. And victory did not fall to the upper people

149

when their hero was stronger than the Orks', but when a camera decided that the right moment had arrived.

As proof, the orderlies had brought the bearded head of a stormtrooper – there was a patch stuck on the forehead, exactly the same colour as the skin – Grim would never even have noticed it. An orderly tugged at it with his fingers, exposing a bloody hole in the head. It was reported that almost all the Orkish heroes had been defeated dishonestly, and this had happened especially often in the vicinity of Batman, who was really old and decrepit, and fought badly, just putting on a show.

Then Spur gave the order to use the first gas bomb against Batman, and it was immediately rolled out of the baggage train.

It was a trolley with four blue cylinders and a trigger device, made from a salvaged enemy aircraft cannon shell under a firing pin. A nameless Orkish hero (almost as much of a boy as Grim, most likely chosen for his small size and low weight) sat on a narrow chair behind the cylinders, took hold of the trigger cord and smiled sadly, and the suicide platoon pushed the trolley off towards the boundary of visibility. Several unarmed Orks followed it, playing on reed pipes, and Grim's pride in his own kind actually took his breath away.

After that some good news arrived. On the right flank the third metal warrior had entered the fray, but his onslaught had been halted, because a private by the name of Blut had made an important discovery by chance: if you turned towards the flying cameras, dropped your trousers and showed them your genitals, the battle quietened down for a while, the fighting machines backed off and the cameras started flying around, trying to find a viewing angle from which the Ork's private parts wouldn't be in shot. When they started hovering at a new spot, you had to turn your nether regions towards them again. They had succeeded in nullifying several attacks with this method.

Marshal Spur beamed – it looked as if this discovery could seriously affect the course of the battle.

'All orderlies!' he shouted. 'Get across to your units – and be snappy about it, tell them to remove their trousers and wave their private parts about when they see a camera! Victory will be ours!'

Grim realised that the order applied to him too – not in the sense of waving his genitals about, but that he had to return to his unit. He felt afraid and relieved at the same time: he'd be ashamed to carry on hanging about in the rear.

The moped refused to start for a long time again. As soon as it sprang to life, Grim hurtled off into the smoke and haze. After taking a couple of turns between the blinds hanging down from the sky, he realised that he had lost his bearings. Then he started driving slowly.

Bloodied Orks appeared from out of the stinking haze ahead of him, dragging themselves away from the front line – some of them were scary to look at. Then he came across a detachment of artillerymen dragging along a fire-throwing ballista, and it was suddenly clear that the front was already right there. And then there was the boom of a terrifyingly powerful explosion up ahead.

Almost immediately the exultant cries of Orkish voices reached Grim's ears.

'We killed Batman! Batman!'

This is the central sector, Grim realised. Batman was at the centre. So I'm driving the wrong way...

He pulled up and looked round.

At this stage he had completely lost any idea of where he had come from and where he was going. There were Orkish corpses lying all around, swathes of smoke were drifting over the ground, sooty fumes were getting into his eyes and on all sides, almost touching the ground, the flying walls were slowly shifting about, altering the space in which he was trying to find his way.

Some of the flying walls were pitch-black, and some had gigantic, dazzlingly joyful people on them, proffering from on high drinks, creams and electronic gadgets. The advertising was intended for the news and those Orks who could see the long panels of fabric from outside the walls, without being able to see the actual battle. But all this magical happiness was absolutely not intended for him, an orderly on a malfunctioning moped. Destiny had something else in store for him – a heroic death for the Urkanagate, the Spirit and Will. And for the first time in his life Grim felt that he was entirely ready for it – quite genuinely and seriously.

Well, there won't be any problems with that, he thought, turning his moped practically at random.

Before he had gone even a hundred metres the Orks behind him detonated the second gas bomb and, if the cries of joy were anything to go by, they killed another one of the people's heroes.

Several times Grim turned into passages that opened up in front of him, and then he noticed the space around him start changing quickly – the flying walls drifted upwards, coiling up into the scrolls hovering above the ground. It was easier to get his bearings now. Through the gaps in the smoke Grim glimpsed the distant embankment in the central zone of the front.

It turned out that he was going the wrong way again – the right flank was much further to the right than he had thought. But Grim suddenly realised that there was absolutely no point in taking the commander in chief's order about the cameras and private parts over there, because it was the soldiers on the right flank who had invented the method. Grim pulled up and the moped died again. He looked round, bewildered.

A flying wall was rapidly raising up right beside him. What Grim saw behind it was an extraterritorial area, cordoned off with a black and yellow ribbon. The regulations prohibited anyone from passing beyond the ribbon – but as far as Grim could recall, looking beyond it wasn't forbidden.

There were at least ten retiarii lying there, hacked to death, and some strange-looking figures towering up over them. At first Grim took them for a medical team. But then the smoke was blown aside, and he realised that they weren't Orks at all.

Standing there in front of him were two half-naked women and a soldier.

The women were well into advanced middle age – but rather well preserved and still slim. They were draped in thin multi-coloured bed sheets that kept slipping off their overheated and bloodstained bodies. If the lengths of cloth had not been so exquisite and the women so well-groomed, Grim would have thought they were simply concealing their private parts, like Orkish women around a bathing-place.

The soldier was stocky and muscular. His face was hidden under a disproportionately large helmet with numerous project-ing corners, and there was a red cloak hanging from his back, fastened by a clasp over his shoulder. He was holding a short sword, covered in blood. There was nothing covering the front of his body and it was noticeable that he was still aroused by his lady friends. But they had already disappeared into a triangular hole that had appeared in mid-air.

The soldier turned towards Grim, looked at him for a few seconds through the slits in the helmet, then dropped the sword into its scabbard and stepped into the same hole. The combined steps and hatch immediately rose up, and the hole dissolved into the air. Grim seemed to see the shadow of a small cloud move across the ground, and a second later no traces of the threesome were left. All there was in front of him now was an open field with dead bodies and a trembling striped ribbon.

Grim turned away.

The flying walls had been removed almost everywhere. The smoke was gradually being swept away by the wind. But there were no enemies and no Orks to be seen, all he could make out were the charred skeletons of ballistas and countless Orkish corpses, in some places lying on top of each other. And then Grim spotted a thin line of retreating stormtroopers in the field – all that was left of the Orkish force in the main sector.

He looked towards the Hill of the Ancestors. In the distance he could just about make out the faint outline of the Urkagan's barge. He couldn't see anything else yet: the Hill itself and the entire central section of Orkish Slava were veiled with smoke from burning fuel oil.

And then the cameras launched a rocket salvo.

Grim had never seen this before. Slim needles of fire flew out of the dark dots in the sky, leaving a white trail in their wake, and hurtled towards the retreating Orks. There were thunderous explosions among them.

Grim abandoned his moped and ran towards the Hill of the Ancestors.

The Urkagan's barge gradually came closer – and the Orks who had survived were hurrying towards it from all sides, as if it were a magnet. But then the barge suddenly swelled up and turned into a ball of fire and black smoke. Many of the soldiers standing around it fell to the ground.

After that, Grim ran without hurrying and soon he was overtaken by several Orks from the retreating line. And then a gentle, warm strength lifted him up into the sky, carried him across the field and laid him down in the grass – so carefully that he didn't feel any pain at all.

It felt good lying in the grass. For some reason he couldn't move, but he could see everything around him, and in his heart he felt calm and even amused. His cheek was stinging a bit, but that didn't bother him. For a long time nothing interesting happened in his field of view – there was just a little blue flower swaying downwind, rising up out of the grass right in front of his face, and a little black stream spreading out from the shattered artery of a soldier who had fallen nearby.

Then Grim saw a guardsman-stormtrooper running across the field. Grim could tell he was a guardsman from the propaganda banner for a banzai charge attached to his back – the white inscription on the black background read:

I gobble greedily the guts
Of spoiled little naughty brats!

If Grim could have laughed he would have.

The guardsman was so thin, it was clear at a glance that he had eaten nothing but bran and straw all his life or, at the very best, potato peelings. It wasn't likely that he possessed the gastronomical experience proclaimed on his standard. To look at him, he was a typical Orkish loser – with an expression of vague resentment stamped into his mug.

The guardsman was staggering and puckering up his face as he ran, without the slightest interest in what was going on – he was clearly thoroughly tired of life's tempest already. And the universe came to his aid.

A glittering metal star planted itself in his back. Then another one. The guardsman stumbled and fell. Then Grim saw two green ninja turtles – exactly like the ones on the wrappers of some upper people's sweets that he had tasted once in his childhood. The turtles were escorted by a battle camera flying low over the ground.

The first turtle skipped over to the guardsman and thrust a gleaming, crooked sword into his back. The other struck a martial pose and held it until the camera had flown all the way round the turtles. Then they went running on and the camera flew after them.

For a long time nothing happened and Grim looked at the flower. Then the wind puffed some kind of crumpled document, thickly smeared with red, up against his face.

Grim realised that it was one of the documents in Upper Mid-Siberian of the kind that under the new law, soldiers had taken with them into battle in order to get the papers bloodied – documents like that were scattered around everywhere in the grass. The piece of paper was lying very close, and he could even read some of the printed text.

It seemed to be about some barn or other which had been built without due permission, but Grim wasn't quite sure – his knowledge of Siberian wasn't sufficient, and most of the sheet was covered thickly with blood. However, even he could see that the verb tenses in the document had been mixed up badly.

Why are there so many mistakes? he thought morosely, as the paper was blown on its way. Did they translate it into Siberian themselves, or what? They're trying to save money on a translation bureau, and we're out here spilling our blood... Or is that the way they work now in the translation bureaus? The bastards have reduced the country to ruin...

He looked at the field for a few more minutes, and then either fell asleep or lost consciousness.

When he came round, it was already night. He had a splitting headache. But on the other hand he felt that he could move. Getting up onto his knees, he looked round.

Above Orkish Slava he could see the scattered lights of battle cameras, looking like fireflies fluttering about in the night. The distant Gates of Victory were concealed by the Hill of the Ancestors, but behind its triangular profile there were searchlight beams flitting about and the red flashes of flares. A woman's voice, amplified by powerful loudspeakers, rang out across the field:

'Urkish warriors! You are exhausted and wounded! Walk towards the light and you will be helped to return home. Victory! Victory!'

Spotting the trailers rising up into the air in the distance (he could only see the red and green parking lights), Grim realised that it was true. The people were leaving Orkish Slava. Which meant that the Orks had successfully defended their bitter, blood-soaked land – for the umpteenth time.

Getting to his feet raggedly, he tried to take a step. Then another one. It worked – no bones seemed to be broken. Then he plodded towards the Gates of Victory, avoiding the corpses and cowering down when yet another camera sped past, its white and green lights glaring into his eyes. They weren't firing any longer.

In the silence of the night he could hear the cameras buzzing – like large, smart and very cunning wasps.

When I noticed that I was getting seriously irritated by her constant requests to keep track of that Orkish kid, I started analysing my feelings.

Sometimes my anger had an objective cause. For instance, as I was enlarging the scrap of paper in front of Grim's face as he lay concussed, I was almost snagged by a Sky Pravda approaching for a rocket attack.

But I could fly into a fury without any particular reason.

One thing was clear – if time after time she could rouse me to such a frenzy, she was doing a really first-rate job.

I only realised that after talking with a specialist on the simulated psychology of suras. If you've paid as much for your lifetime companion as I have, you enjoy the right to free consultations and you can ask about anything at all. They even give you something like a session of psychoanalysis.

With his painstakingly groomed beard and the infinitely gentle look in his eyes, the consultant surologist looked like a genuine womaniser who had broken more than one rubber heart in his time. But then a crack discoursemonger from the special assault group *Le Coq d'Ésprit* could have looked exactly like that, too.

I felt too awkward to state my problem straight away, and I thought it would be best if we approached it gradually. First I ought to chat a little bit about general subjects.

'Tell me,' I said to him, 'does she really think, after all, or not?'

He laughed.

'If you only knew how many times I've been asked that...'

'Is she rational?'

'She... From the legal point of view, that's a slippery term. Let me answer like this. Scientists once tried to make a machine think on the basis of the rules of mathematics and logic. And they realised that it's impossible. In that kind of sense – no, she isn't rational. But don't forget that a human being doesn't use mathematical algorithms at all for thinking. And to be quite honest, nobody needs logic. Perhaps, apart from our military philosophers – in order to demoralise the enemy in conditions of close urban warfare. People take decisions on the basis of precedents and experience. A human being is simply an instrument for the application of culture to reality. And essentially, so is a sura.'

I'd already heard something of the kind before. The problem is that after explanations like that, you think you've understood everything. In actual fact they merely place an opaque cover over the little hole in your mind where the gaping question used to dwell.

'What does "the application of culture to reality" mean?' I asked.

'Direct perception is transformed into mental representation. And then the mind analyses all of the culture's precedents associated with the invariants of this representation and selects the most appropriate model of behaviour.'

'But how does it select it?'

'Also on the basis of available experience. But the experience of making a choice. Interaction between mental representations takes place in accordance with the rules determined by the precedent of such interactions.'

'But what is a "mental representation"?'

The surologist smiled patiently.

'It's the proximate identified precedent. The sura reproduces this mechanism, with the only difference that there's no observer of representations, only a set of behavioural patterns loaded into her memory that compete among themselves: the choice made between them depends on the intensity of excitation in sporadically occurring electromagnetic circuits. The most intensive zone of excitation also temporarily becomes her technical "self"...'

I thought that the last phrase could perfectly well apply to me too, but I didn't say anything out loud. The surologist went on.

'A sura is a very large and complexly organised data bank into which have been loaded not only precedents of responses, but also precedents of the search for precedents and so on ... The programme algorithms perform only a subsidiary function here. But inside her, she has those too. Among others, her settings.'

'But how does she really think when she's talking to me?' I asked. 'Taking it step by step. I want to understand the mechanism.'

'She doesn't think. I repeat, there isn't anyone inside her who thinks. But if you want to understand the mechanism... You know, people once invented an experiment called "The Chinese Room". Have you heard of it?'

'No,' I said.

'A man who doesn't know Chinese is sitting in a locked room. Through the window he is handed notes with questions in Chinese. To him they are merely pieces of paper with squiggles drawn on them, and he doesn't understand what they mean. But in the room he has lots of different books of rules that describe, in detail, how and in what sequence to reply to certain squiggles with different ones. And by following these rules, he hands out through another window replies in Chinese that make everyone standing outside absolutely certain that he knows Chinese. Although he has absolutely no understanding of what questions they are handing him and what his answers mean. Have you pictured that?'

'Well, yes.'

'A sura is the same kind of Chinese room, except that it's automated. Instead of a person with textbooks she has a scanner that reads the hieroglyphs, and a huge database of references and rules that enable her algorithms to select a hieroglyph for the reply.'

'That would be a lot of rules,' I murmured.

'Quite a number,' the consultant agreed. 'She translates every phrase you speak into several symbolic languages, dividing it into numerous layers and levels. Then every layer is correlated with its own database. After that a reverse synthesis of the invariants occurs, and we get a complex response that possesses semantic, stylistic and emotional aspects, which mutually complement each other, creating the impression of a unique, live reply addressed to you personally. Of course, this is a simulation. But children imitate their parents and peers in exactly the same way – often

160

until they reach old age. When you interact with a sura, you're dealing with the past of mankind.'

'And when you interact with a human being?'

The surologist shrugged.

'The same thing applies to people. The difference is purely a matter of hygiene. Entering into contact with a human being, you are rummaging in mental humus that is teeming with poisonous worms, but a sura, so to speak, takes you into a museum... Her baggage is far more refined and complete – she is the eternal woman, if you wish, Eve, the archetype... But what exactly about her behaviour is bothering you?'

It was time to get down to the point. I assumed the air of a jaded, bored *bon vivant* and asked:

'Tell me, why does bitchiness exist in general? What lies behind it as a biological mechanism?'

The consultant wasn't surprised in the least. He obviously had a good idea of the problems that his clients encountered.

'You know, Damilola, that's such a complex subject that there are two ways it can be talked about. Either the correct way, but in terms that are complicated and hard to understand – and we'll immediately get tangled up in psychoanalytical terminology. Or the incorrect way, which is simple and comprehensible – and then we'll drown in the lowest possible kind of cheap cynicism. Your choice?'

I explained that I was a battle pilot for CINEWS Inc., and so in no danger of drowning in cynicism.

'All right,' said the consultant, 'then screw your eyes up.'

He passed his hand over his face, as if he was stripping everything human off it.

'For about hundred and forty years now, the top class suras that we produce have an adjustable setting for "bitchiness",' he began. 'Like everything in their simulated psychology, this is an imitation of specific female traits. You ask why nature invented bitchiness. But do you know what it is?'

I was at a loss for an answer. But he didn't seem to be counting on one.

'It really isn't easy to formulate. At a first approximation we can say it is an apparently irrational form of behaviour manifested by a woman who is, as a rule, young and beautiful – for bitches who are not beautiful are subjected to involuntary reformatting at a very early stage of their lives – which arouses in a man the desire...'

'To grab her by the ear and bang the back of her head against a wall for a long time,' I interrupted. 'Or better still, against the floor. It's harder.'

'Possibly,' the consultant said with a smile. 'You must agree that the most important thing about such behaviour is its offensive irrationality. It costs a woman nothing to behave like a human being, rather than put a man through the maximum of unpleasant experiences. And what's more, more often than not it doesn't even require any effort from her – on the contrary, she has to make a serious effort to be a bitch... And of course, this sort of thing doesn't exist only in our culture. You probably don't know that the Orks have a book called *The Book of Orkasms* for conducting divinations before battle...'

'Oh, indeed I do,' I said, 'I know that very well. I've even seen an actual divination.'

'There is one passage there that is called just that – "On the Female Heart". Would you like me to read it to you?'

'No thank you,' I said. 'I'm allergic to Orkish wisdom.'

The consultant didn't take offence.

'Well, never mind,' he said. 'It's just that there it's put with brutal animalistic directness... Anyway, the essential point is simple. Nature strewed the path towards the moment of coitus with roses, but immediately after it the blossoms wither and the hormonally induced distortions of our perception disappear. Nature is also a bitch in her own way – she is extremely economical and never treats us to psychotropic substances unless it is absolutely necessary. Therefore, immediately after the act of love, for a few seconds we see all the insanity of what is happening with clear eyes – and we realise that for some reason or other, we have got tangled up in a murky business whose outcome is unclear, with the prospect of large outlays of money and great emotional distress, for which the only reward is that spasm which has only just finished, and which has absolutely nothing to do with us personally, but is derived exclusively from the ancient mechanism for the reproduction of protein bodies. In the case of a sura of your class, you don't think of the emotional torment that is in store for you, you simply remember the loan taken out to buy her.'

'Don't hit below the belt,' I told him.

'All right,' the consultant agreed. 'Of course, you have to understand the most important thing – as a biological and social agent, a woman has little interest in you taking a sober view of her for very long. You say your sura is operating on maximum bitchiness. What does she usually say immediately before intercourse – and straight afterwards?'

I realised that I had to be frank, as if he was a doctor.

' "Go away, you slobbery freak, I'm sick of you." ' I replied. 'Or, for instance, "I've got a headache." But she stopped saying that because I used to laugh. After intercourse she often turns away to face the wall, jabbing me in the stomach with her elbow. Sometimes there are tears. A combination of all these factors is also possible.'

'Excellent,' said the consultant. 'And what do you feel?'

'Rage. Sometimes revulsion for myself. Sometimes a desire to hit her.'

'Do this rage and revulsion come over you immediately?'

'Instantly,' I replied.

'Is it an intense feeling?'

'Extremely,' I said. 'It makes it impossible to think of anything else.'

'Is the post-coital sober view of things maintained while this happens?

I realised where he was heading.

'You mean to say that a sura... That is, a woman, deliberately muddies the water...'

'Precisely. So that the suspended matter, thus stirred up, would render invisible the fundamental truths about her role in a man's destiny, which we have already discussed. Their concealment is facilitated by the severe psychological and emotional overload to which she subjects her partner as she endeavours to divest him of his clarity of perception by any means possible.

'In reality "bitchiness" is not a negative personality trait, but a distinctive kind of counterpoint to the reproductive instinct that has been generated by human culture. A sura's programming merely simulates this ancient mechanism.'

'In this area your sommeliers have attained perfection,' I said. The consultant smiled.

'You think you're paying a compliment, but that's true,' he replied. 'The post-coital syndrome that we have discussed is by no means all that a client encounters at maximum bitchiness. I'd like to warn you about another effect that often occurs here. This is the so-called "symbolic rival".'

I felt my heart lurch in my chest. This was it – at last we were talking about the big question.

'The strategy of a sura operating on maximum bitchiness may include an attempt to arouse a reaction of jealousy in you. To do this, she starts simulating an interest in some other man, more often than not a young member of the household, or in the case of couples living on their own, a film hero or a news anchor. For instance, the sura constantly asks her owner to put on a snuff for her where an actor she has chosen would be playing a lead, or to turn on the news programme. Here her behaviour can... er... vary. Sometimes she extols the virtues of the symbolic rival, sometimes she says nothing – allowing her owner to draw his own conclusions. This technique has quite a devastating effect on most men. Let me tell you a secret – one of the main reasons why we annul the warranty for suras operating in this mode is that the owners regularly inflict on them such serious mechanical damage as to require, subsequently, expensive in-house repairs. The company simply can't afford to pay for all that...'

'And what can you do if you constantly fall victim to this technique?'

'Sometimes you can try to kill the programme. But don't do it too often.'

'Kill the programme?' I echoed. 'How?'

'When you sense that the sura is about to ask you for a date with the symbolic rival, show her that you know about it and that you are feeling annoyed.'

'And then?'

'You'll see,' the consultant said with a smile.

'No,' I said, 'I want to be able to picture what will happen inside her head. Or wherever.'

The consultant thought this over for a moment.

'You're touching on a sensitive area that borders on confidential know-how,' he said. 'But since you have bought the most expensive model on the market, I'll try to accommodate you. Only I don't know how extensive your knowledge in this area is... But then, as a military man, you're probably familiar with the operating principle of a guided weapon?'

I nodded.

'You work with rockets,' the consultant continued, 'but we used certain algorithms that were employed in the final

165

generation of antisubmarine torpedoes. It's almost the same thing, although no one has made torpedoes for several centuries already ... Strangely enough, it proved to be one of the best models for simulating female behaviour. Do you know how a torpedo that has been thrown off its target works?'

'Vaguely,' I replied.

'When the target-pursuit programme fails, the torpedo sets a spiral course and scans the space around it until it has invest- igated a defined area. If a target matching the search parameters is not located, the torpedo sets a straight course, moves to a different point and repeats the spiral search, and so on for as long as its power lasts. Have you pictured that?'

'Aerial rockets function slightly differently,' I said, 'but, overall, that's about the size of it. So what?'

'A sura and – dare I say it – a woman acts in exactly the same way. With the exception that the space in which she sets her spiral course when the programme fails is not physical, but informational. Although at a social gala, even her movement through space ... Anyway, that's not important. Putting it simply, if the programme fails, the "random subject search" operator is activated. The sura changes the subject, but only in order to regroup. To do this, she sorts through her data baggage until she finds an appropriate informational object that she can present to the other person – so that, acting from this new point, she can gradually return to the basic algorithm for precedent search.'

'How is this new point selected?'

'The search parameters are largely determined by the situation, therefore the choice of a new subject is effectively unpredictable. Everything's like it is in life.'

'And how is it in life?' I asked ironically.

The consultant smiled.

'If you throw the torpedo off its course, it flutters its eyelashes a few times and then, with charming female inconsistency,

166

attempts to return you to a condition of mental torpor, which makes sober assessment of her presence in your life impossible. Any of the emotions in the dark spectrum can be used to induce brain paralysis – wrath, anxiety, wounded pride, self-doubt – and also, of course, carnal desire.'

'One way or another, it all sounds pretty bleak,' I muttered.

'Perhaps the greatest joy lies precisely in throwing oneself on the mercy of this torrent,' the consultant said drily.

I realised that the moment of candour was over and the person facing me was once again the formal representative of the selling firm. But I was grateful for at least this brief glimmer of sincerity, which is such a rare thing between people in our time.

I killed the connection with the consultant, went to the happiness room, entered the password and took Kaya off pause (all this time she had been sitting motionless on the sofa). When I got back she gave me a sullen look – she can't stand it when I put her on pause. I ran though the instructions on killing the programme in my mind, and before she could say anything to me I blurted out:

'Come on then, baby. Ask me again to show you that Orkish degenerate. That yellow-eyed *untermensch*. That juvenile scumbag. Go ahead, ask. I'll do anything for you, sweetie pie.'

Kaya blinked a few times.

'Why *untermensch*, especially?' she asked. 'You're exactly the same kind of *untermensch*, aren't you, sweetheart. You're like family, you and Grim.'

'We what?' I asked suspiciously.

'You're both Russian. Your surname's Karpov, isn't it?'

I turned round, went to the happiness room and put her on pause again. And then I sat down at the manitou and got down to some research.

It turned out that my honeybunch was right and wrong.

Strangely enough, moreover, she was very probably right about me, but almost certainly wrong about Grim.

Yes, Grim and all Orks speak High Russian. But so what? Everyone here knows that language too, since the offglobe has been hanging above Siberia for many hundreds of years. But during the last few centuries, down below there have been so many climate migrations, wars of liberation, genocides, artificial insemination programmes and other paradigm shifts that now their state language is quite different, and there's no way they can trace their own roots, even if the law allowed them to (but they're not allowed – as the priests and turds put it – 'to introduce no difference into the Singular').

And there's no question of any nationality. The Orks haven't had any surnames since way back. They only have an Individual Tracking Number, which is applied to their right hand. It takes the place of a surname and all the rest of it. Grim's full name, for instance, is Grim ITN 1 3505 00 148 41 0, and Chloe's is Chloe ITN 1 3598 47 660 12 2. And who they are, really, in terms of nationality, Manitou only knows.

But my surname really is Karpov. It's Russian, from the name of a fish (a battle pilot among fish, let me add: a carp flies at low altitude just above the bottom and eats everything that appears in its sights). My ancestors could possibly have had blood ties with Grim's. But since then a huge amount of water has flowed under the bridge, and today it's equally hard to say whether we, those who live topside, have nationalities or not.

In the old sense, definitely not.

Rather, we have certain professional and social communities, united by a common cultural ritual that has come down to us from ancient times. When you choose a profession for yourself you also choose, as it were, the shadow of the nationality whose spirit illuminates it, and join a specific club.

For instance, the 'Germans' are the best mechanics and

technologists. They devise and build the super-expensive motorenwagens for the rich Orkish bureaucracy, brew forty different kinds of beer, shout '*Hoch!*' and fly to visit Orkish prostitutes in the Yellow Zone, which is also where their assembly lines are located. They don't like suras. They even have a saying: 'a rubber woman is the first step towards alcohol-free beer' (apparently some northern sage said that). But that doesn't mean at all that they are plodding, obtuse philistines. In their souls, 'Germans' are romantics, secretly they always remain faithful to their ideals, and at the end of their lives simply adore taking cyanide to the music of Wagner. They say that was the way Eureich's offglobe was scuttled – after worldwide demand for motorenwagens had plummeted to almost zero.

The 'Japanese' draw 2D-japorn in silhouette, shadow, curtain and other forms, as well as derp-hentai – everything that doesn't formally come under the law on underage pornography. They assemble all sorts of ingenious electronic wanking devices and also, of course, suras – thank you, lads, from all us pupophiles, although it is not we who are your true brothers, but the 'Germans'. The 'Japanese' have the same kind of suicidal-heroic culture as the manufacturers of motorenwagens, only it's infused with masturbation instead of beer. Even the passing centuries are powerless to do anything about this, and I suppose there's a certain beauty in that. It's no accident that so many old snuffs are devoted to the destruction of the Yamato offglobe. They used to say that under Loss Liquid they were considering in earnest how to flood the Circus so as to film it on water, but the technical sommeliers and the House of Manitou's Department of Public Morality forbade it.

The 'Americans' ... America, great America, which once saved the world from Hitler, Bin Laden, Count Dooku, Megatron and Professor Moriarty! The 'Americans' shoot snuffs. They also make the manitous on which we watch snuffs. And they also, of course, print the manitous we use to pay for all this. They also had a hand in my Kaya – the historians tell us that the sura is the offspring of a marriage between the Japanese love doll and the American unmanned aerial drone. The rich guys in the upper hemisphere – what else can I say about them? The envious tongues claim that they secretly worship a huge bat, which they keep hidden somewhere in the region of the central reactor – and that they occasionally find processor chips, with state-of-the-art architecture, in its droppings. But that, of course, is the whinging of unalloyed envy, and I'm not going to relay it.

The 'Jews' are the priests who hold the copyright on Manitou – they even say that Manitou the Antichrist was a Jew from the Bronx. They also shoot snuffs, together with the Americans – and it's not hard to guess who'll be top dog there. The neural tissue of the global brain, which invented gravity interest and the loan drive – no wonder they're the first to get it in the neck from everyone who wants to make the world beautiful, muscular and easy to understand.

The 'French' are Big Byz's strike-force intellectuals. Anyone can start a war, but no one else will do it so elegantly. All the best discoursemongers from the *Le Coq d'Ésprit* special assault group have to know at least a little bit of Old French. They're great guys. The military men even have a saying: 'as disciplined as a platoon of French intellectuals'. Meaning discipline of the mind, naturally. But also of the heart – because not every heart would be able to bleed selectively on account of the assigned goal, and circumvent any number of false targets released by the enemy; manoeuvring with supreme precision, in any weather conditions and also at an immense distance. As a combat pilot, I understand what a demanding task that is.

The 'English' – in their youth, they make the best protest punks, and at a mature age, the best bank clerks. A great nation. It's no accident that even now we handle all our business documentation in Church English. It's impossible to list all the things they have done for civilisation. Without the English, there would be no fish & chips. They invented tabloids and hypocrisy, and were the first to unite the world under its flag – and to this day they keep its sacred flame burning. I'm not joking. Where would we be today without hypocrisy? Under the law on the age of consent, no one would be able to make love until the age of forty-six. They have my respect and admiration. Rule Britannia!

But all this is more by way of residual national traits, the shadow, as it were, of ancient traditions which still live on among us today. And everything that I have just mentioned is each individual's cultural and professional choice, rather than the call of the blood.

But what does it mean to be 'Russian'?

There isn't any specialisation associated with it.

It seems to be as incomprehensible today as it was seven hundred years ago.

What did it mean then, if we can believe the on-screen dictionaries?

Riding in a German motorenwagen, watching Asian porn, paying with American money, believing in the Jewish God, quoting French discoursemongers, proudly distancing yourself from 'the thieves in power' – and trying all the time to steal something, if only in digital form. In short, the heart of the world and a universal synthesis of all cultures.

Our ancient Russian tradition was built around the fact that it had nothing of its own, apart from the language in which the conceptualisation of this 'nothing' took place. The Jews did something similar, but they called their void God and managed to sell it at a profit to the more stupid nations. But what about us?

We tried to sell mankind the absence of God. From the metaphysical point of view, that's a much bigger deal, and at first it actually went pretty well – that's why our peoples were once considered to be mystical rivals. But while it's possible to put a national stamp on God, how do you put it on what doesn't exist? That was the origin of the ancient crisis of civilisation suffered by my ancestors, the problem of self-identification and low self-esteem, leading constantly to the stranglehold of clerical and bureaucratic obscurantism and anal tyranny.

But all this was a long time ago, so long ago that now it's only of interest to historians. Or suras, functioning at peak bitchiness and spirituality.

That's the kind of tangled undergrowth a man has to plunge into because a rubber woman bats her eyelashes a couple of times. But after all, it's interesting, isn't it? When else would I ever have paused to consider all this?

It had taken me several hours to get a thoroughgoing grasp of the issue, but at least now I was ready to continue the conversation. I went into the happiness room and took my little darling off pause.

When I got back Kaya was sitting on the sofa, looking at me with that same sullen expression, as if the hours that had dropped out of her life had never existed.

'I'm not Russian,' I told her. 'Or rather, I'm post-Russian, I don't share any common destiny with the lads who failed to make the move to the offglobe in good time. And Grim isn't Russian either. He's an Ork, with a number instead of a nationality. The only thing Russian in all of this is the language that we're speaking now. And even that's not Russian, but High Russian. Not to be confused with Upper Mid-Siberian. There haven't been any nationalities in Siberia for three hundred years now. Have you got all that, my little fool?'

She blinked a few times.

'You know what,' she said, 'if you ever want to put me on pause again, don't do it when you're diving into the on-screen dictionary, but when you've decided to make love to me. All right?'

172

And she glowered at me. With the kind of look, you know, that seemed to contain a hint – not even a hint, but the slight probability, tending almost to zero, of a hint, that today she didn't find me as repulsive as usual.

And again, she completely threw me for a loop, inasmuch as I was ready for a serious discussion of nations and ethnicities, but not at all for this.

But she had turned away already and was looking at the floor now, but with a little grin on her face that made it clear she was really looking at me and, moreover, she was watching me extremely closely – and with all her body.

Well, I'm not made of ceramic composite armour, am I? And a minute later she was already shouting at me:

'I don't want it on the table! How many times have I told you I don't like it on the table, bonehead! It's hard! It makes no difference to your fat backside, but it's too rough for me. Too rough!'

Rough.

A very precise word. Yes, it turned out rough, coarse and glorious. Although too fast.

Afterwards, when I was lying on the sofa, feeling drained and grateful, she came up, sat down beside me, leaned down to me and kissed me on the nose. I already knew that now she would ask me to show her Grim. But I didn't initiate her programme failure. What for? Life is life. Let the young heart beat as it wishes.

And for bringing me so expertly, through two diversionary spirals, to the point of return to the basic algorithm, I was willing to forgive her not only for Grim, but even for my Russian roots. Not because this software-enabled itinerary had made such a great impression on me, but because it had included that table. That absolutely unexpected table. So rough, coarse and ruthlessly swift.

Ninety-Two. On the Heart of a Woman.

The sap rises upwards from the cunt and worldly vanity flies in through the eyes, moving downwards. They meet at the centre of the chest and come to the boil, combining into a black substance which is the root of a woman's being. From this spring all the world's spite and bitchiness, heartache, blackness of soul and anguish. And from this there is no deliverance, for a woman attracts through untruth, and if one dispels the deception, then it is apparent immediately that there is no need for her at all, and without her things are much better. This clarity is fatal to her and she will not let a man perceive the truth, since she cannot hunt for herself. Therefore she constantly lies and plays the bitch and realises herself how tangled she is in her lies, but she is helpless to do anything about this and the anguish and fear show in her eyes. But if she is shoved up against the wall and beaten at length about the kisser, then she will confess everything, but say that without this cunning life itself will wither.

Verily it is so. Therefore do the wise say that life is a swindle and black deception.

Below the text a note had been added by hand – evidently for the soldiers' divination.

If battle awaits tomorrow, know that the heart of a queerast is the same as the heart of a woman.

'It's all true,' whispered Grim and closed *The Book of Orkasms*.

It was hard to express any better than this what he thought about Chloe, who hadn't even taken the trouble to find out if he had survived or not...

And as for the swindle and the black deception, all that was true as well – and he constantly received confirmations of that.

Firstly, the public prosecutor was no longer inviting him to London. The authorities were busy with their own complicated state business and had completely forgotten about Grim. But that was exactly what Grim had been expecting, so he wasn't upset.

Secondly, although he had scrupulously bloodied all the family documents in Upper Mid-Siberian at the exact spot that was required – the lower right corner of the final page – it hadn't done any good. Under the new rules you had to have the blood of battle certified by a notary, after collecting corroborating testimony from three of your regimental comrades. Almost everybody's regimental comrades had been killed, but even so there was a queue to see the notary for a month ahead. They said that witnesses could be hired right there in the street – they were loitering about close to a translation bureau, with two Right Protectors strolling around close by, keeping them from harm and collecting money.

In money terms it was all the same to Grim's family – whether they paid the turds or paid the usual bribe. But it was quicker with the bribe. And so they just forgot about the bloodied documents and nobody even gave Grim a proper thank you. They didn't have time for that – the family had suffered a great misfortune. Uncle Shug from the moped factory had been arrested and his kin had been left without any high-level contacts.

Somehow Grim didn't feel like staying at home. Watching snuffs or the news made him feel sick. He decided to take a walk to the market square – to find out what was happening in the world outside the bounds of the information universe.

Once he reached the market he immediately regretted that he had come. The square had been transformed into a field hospital saturated in suffering. Clerks walked about between the wounded, who were lying on straw and rags, registering those who recovered consciousness in order to send for their nearest and dearest. Those who lived within easy reach were being collected by their relatives – for some, a shoulder to lean on was enough; others were trundled off into the future on a handcart. And the army medical orderlies kept bringing more and more half-dead, limbless stumps of men from Orkish Slava. Business as usual.

However, this victory had an especially bitter taste. Hanging above the market square were thirty-six corpses in sailor suits smeared with earth and blood – they were Private Blut, who had given the Orks the idea of taking their trousers off in front of a camera, and his accomplices, some of whom had been hanged after they were already dead. There was a sign hanging on Blut's own chest with a cryptic inscription:

NO HANGING PARTS, OR HANG!

An explanation in Siberian had been nailed to the other gallows – saying that these men were traitors who had brought dishonour on the Orkish Colours, and Manitou had cursed them. People walking by spat on the hanged men and Grim, who knew the truth, found all this painful to watch. But he didn't really feel like arguing or trying to explain anything – one man who had tried to do that had already been hanged alongside the others. It was the turds and the butts who did the hanging, uniting temporarily for a job like this, but no one in the crowd really knew who was in charge.

176

Those who had returned from the war uninjured were regarded with slight contempt, but there weren't many of them. The only reason no one looked askance at Grim was that the entire left half of his face was covered with a massive graze – half bruise and half burn. In actual fact there was more soot than blood, and it should all be gone in about three days, but Grim looked heroic, and just to be on the safe side he didn't wash his face.

In the market they were talking about the war that had just finished, saying all sorts of different things – and most of them in a whisper.

A rumour was going round that Torn Durex had been killed along with his staff because he hadn't warned the people about the gas bombs. There were only two suicide-bomb gas trolleys, but the people didn't know how many the Orks had in reserve. When the Orks detonated the second one and killed the Canadian Wild Man – hot on the heels of Batman – the upper people had dropped a smart bomb on the Urkagan's barge and killed everyone, including Marshal Spur. But according to what others said, the Kagan had not been killed on the actual barge, but on the Hill of the Ancestors, when he was carried up the slope by two orderlies – and what's more, he had carried on singing until the final moment, displaying the heart of a hero. The explosion was so powerful that no bodies had been found.

What kind of 'smart bomb' is that, Grim thought, looking at the contorted, clamouring faces. If it's so smart, then why does it fall and explode? Looks like someone conned it after all. The same way they conned us ... You're the smartest of all, they told it, fly, everything will be fine ... Rejoice in the sun and the wind, they said ... And it was fool enough to believe it ...

They were also saying it wasn't the gas explosions that had made the people wind up the war so quickly, but the fact that in many places the Orks had started taking off their trousers and waving their private parts about in front of the battle cameras. The upper people had seemed to lose all their fighting spirit as a result. But they whispered about that very, very quietly, squinting sideways at the hanged men.

One thing was clear. After Durex's death, the Orkish regime had changed. As always, this had happened swiftly and obscurely.

The new reality announced itself with a portrait hanging on the wall of the Museum of the Ancestors: a rather stout young man with a black ringlet on a bald forehead and limpet eyes. Above his broad face, impregnated with villainy like a hamburger with fat, the following words blazed forth in gold:

WHENCER DA STRENGSER CØMER, BRÜ?

It was the new Urkagan, by the name of Torn Trojan, and the slogan must have been thought up by the upper people, unless they had simply taken it from the Ancient Films. Several turds were standing under the portrait, selling syringes with *durian* – the new regime promised to be moderately liberative.

No one could understand where this Torn Trojan had sprung from and why he was now in power, but they didn't discuss it, seemingly resigned to the fact that such things were not for Orks to know. But they did argue about whether he really was the illegitimate son of the deceased Durex and whether he had really studied advising and consulting up there, or whether he had a degree in stock economics.

There were rumours that Trojan wanted more democraship, civilisation and tolerance – and the first proposed step in this direction was to replace the word 'queerast' in all Orkish books with the word 'sodomate'. Intelligent Orks approved of this, saying that apart from a major cultural shift it meant a serious boost for the stock indices and the economy in general, as every copy of both *The Word on the Word* and *The Book of Orkasms*

178

now had to be reprinted. Others argued that the commission would go to the Yellow Zone anyway. This was obviously true, but the very possibility of an open discussion seemed to many a huge step upwards.

One Orkish woman who knew Church English claimed that two months ago she had already seen a report about Trojan on the Byzantine news, when he had already come back to Orkland, where 'he keeps a low profile', as the presenter had said. Another Ork recalled that under Torn Durex the young Trojan was the head of the storage barns, where he had demonstrated great organisational talent and stolen honestly – only enough to live on. Grim could have sworn that he had already heard these voices in the market square just before the war – they were the same ones that had called for Alejandro and Bamboleo.

So far no one had seen the real, live Trojan – there was only this poster. But on the other hand three duplicated copies of his speech were hanging up at Marshal Stug's statue.

Grim walked over to read it.

It was a perfectly ordinary speech – the sickening gobbledygook of a regime trying to talk heart-to-heart with its people in their own language. Trojan spoke of the national catastrophe that the previous clique had led Urkaine into, of the disastrous demographic situation, of the urgent necessity to set the Urk at the very centre of Urkaine, and not vice versa, and some such stuff. There were off-colour Orkish jokes in the article too – so many of them that when Grim finished reading he felt as if he had swallowed a rotten fish. Basically, everything indicated that Trojan was here to stay – and in a big way.

But nevertheless, despite all this hocus-pocus, the scent of a special, bitter, post-war freshness still hung in the air...

'Hi there, Grim. Well, look at the face on you.'

Grim turned round.

Chloe was standing there in front of him.

Her face was decorated with the dark yellow Spirals of Resurrection, like the faces of the young widows scurrying about – and her head was covered by the hood of a striped windcheater. And in addition, she had dyed her hair and had it cut in a fringe. She was evidently not planning to bask in the glow of her pre-war fame.

If she understood what Grim was feeling, she didn't give any sign of it.

'You're looking pretty good yourself,' said Grim. 'Like a crocodile from the Swamp of Memory.'

Chloe didn't take offence.

'Let's go,' she said. 'We need to hurry.'

Grim frowned contemptuously.

'Where to?'

He realised already that he'd expended all his moral capital – it was too late now to torment Chloe for her crime with silent disdain. Grim hadn't particularly been intending to do that, but he still felt a certain annoyance at the loss of his assets.

'You'll see,' said Chloe. 'It'll be interesting, I promise.'

She turned round and walked out of the market square.

Something in her voice made Grim immediately set off after her. For a brief instant he even got the feeling that she was the one who had returned from a war, not him.

'I'm sorry,' Chloe said when they had left the market behind and dived into the crooked, dirty streets of Slava. 'I realise you're angry. But I knew you were all right. It's just the way things turned out ... Anyway, you'll see for yourself.'

It seemed like Chloe wanted to eliminate his advantage on the moral high ground as quickly as possible. That made Grim even more furious than her previous swinish behaviour.

'But just the same, where are we going?' he asked

Chloe wrinkled up her face, as if the words she was speaking were pricking her mouth, but answered:

'I have a confession to make. I was dating the discourse-monger. And he turned out to be a very bad person.'

'So you noticed that, did you?' Grim asked sarcastically.

Or rather, he tried to ask sarcastically, but it didn't come out too well – his voice simply sounded hoarse.

He said nothing all the rest of the way, wondering how he ought to behave and what Chloe could possibly show him in order to atone for her sin (or rather, all her multitudinous sins). If any such object existed in the universe, Grim had absolutely no notion of what it was. This was really getting interesting.

They walked for a long time. Chloe moved deeper and deeper into a slum district of the city, where the poor army families lived. Many of the houses here were standing empty and walking through the streets was quite dangerous – but fortunately the hour was still quite early.

Chloe reached a modest, but decent-looking wooden house with a small garden. A petty bureaucrat's relatives could have lived in a house like that – some daughter-in-law of a junior translator or first cousin of a chauffeur who drove an important Global Ork. The house was separated off from the street by a stout wooden fence and thick bushes. It was flanked at the sides by little concrete-box houses from the time of Loss Liquid, which now were inhabited only by geckos, bats and ancestral spirits.

Chloe looked around, opened the gates and walked into the yard. Grim followed her.

Standing in the yard under an oilskin canopy was a swanky green motorenwagen, a classic jeep – with a pass for the Yellow and Green Zones inside the windscreen. A car like this was clearly out of place in this yard and in general in this district, where at best the houses had shabby mopeds with trailers and sidecars standing outside. But the jeep couldn't be seen from the street – it was concealed by the oilcloth, stretched between its posts, and the bushes.

Chloe went into the house.

Grim caught a whiff of a bad smell from the hallway – on the floor were some dried-up vomit and empty bottles.

'Doesn't anyone clean this place up, then?' Grim asked.

Chloe shook her head.

'I used to clean it. But no one does now.'

Grim suddenly guessed.

'Did you used to meet him here ... That discoursemonger?'

Chloe nodded.

'This is one place. It's his secret little nest.'

'And where's he?'

'In the basement,' Chloe replied.

'Alive?'

Chloe shrugged.

'Let's go and take a look.'

They walked through scantily furnished rooms and came to an open metal hatch. At their feet was a stairway leading into the basement. The hatch looked unnecessarily strong and secure for a house like this.

Chloe beckoned Grim with one finger and went down.

Grim saw an underground chamber lit by a dull light bulb. The light slanted down onto a floor with all sorts of household odds and ends on it. There were tools, pieces of wood, rags, pots of nails, pieces of wire, old plastic bags, petrol cans – basically everything that any modest but thrifty Ork keeps about the house.

And then Grim saw the discoursemonger.

The discoursemonger was not looking good.

And he smelled even worse.

He was sitting on a straw mattress, leaning back against the wall. His hands and feet were tied to iron rings set into the wall and the floor. His nightshirt was covered with patches of dried blood. The silver curls were dirty and matted, and many days' worth of stubble made the poor wretch look ten years older. To judge from his closed eyes, he was either sleeping or unconscious.

On the floor, Grim noticed a brazier with dead coals in it. And then the reddish-brown rag that was wrapped round one of the man's legs.

'What did you do, torture him?' he asked.

He tried to speak indifferently, so that Chloe wouldn't suspect him of weakness, although in actual fact he was feeling disgusted and even afraid. Not as afraid as in the war. The battlefield fear had been buoyant and thrilling, but this was a joyless, civilian feeling, as grey as a boiled cow's tongue.

'I haven't tortured him yet,' said Chloe. 'Only baited him a bit. I was afraid he'd croak too soon.'

Grim remembered that he was talking to the daughter of a Ganjaberserk.

The man heard her voice and opened his eyes.

When he saw Grim, he shuddered and his face contorted in fear. Grim looked at him without saying anything, without any expression on his face, and the discoursemonger realised they weren't going to kill him – at least, not immediately. He spoke.

'I am being held here against my will. I demand a meeting with a representative of the government of national salvation. Inform Torn Trojan in person.'

'How long have you been in here?' Grim asked.

'Four days,' said the man.

'And how do you know we have a government of national salvation? Four days ago there wasn't any Torn Trojan.'

The man smiled sadly – as if he'd realised that he was talking to a hopeless idiot.

'If you love your own people, even just a little bit,' he said, 'you must understand that seizing a hostage will seriously damage the nation's image, and all the post-war efforts...'

Grim saw a glittering metal rod in Chloe's hands, ending in a complicated hook. Chloe took a swing and hit the man hard on the leg.

'Oooee!' the man screamed. 'Oo-oo-oo!'

'We don't love our people,' said Chloe. 'We're Orks.'

'What is that you've got?' asked Grim.

'A golf club,' said Chloe. 'It was in his car.'

'And what's golf?'

'I don't know,' Chloe answered. 'Probably this.'

And she hit the man on the leg again with the club. The man screamed again.

'How often have I told you?' said Chloe. 'Express yourself clearly. What's an image?'

'An aggregate representation, which...'

Chloe raised the club.

'It's the way we show you on the manitou,' the discourse-monger said quickly.

'You mean the longer I beat you, the worse you'll make us look?'

'Yes.'

'But you said you always try to make us look as bad as possible, didn't you? Remember? When you were drunk?'

The man didn't say anything to that and Chloe hit him on the leg with the club.

'Oo-oo-oooo!'

'That's hurting him,' said Grim.

Chloe looked at him as if he was a bit strange.

'That's why I'm doing it.'

Grim was about to take the club away from her, but then he decided not to risk it. Instead, he dragged her as far away from the sobbing discoursemonger as he could.

'What are you hitting him for?'

Chloe walked over to one of the shelves, got down a bundle and unfolded it.

'Look what I found.'

What Grim saw looked weird. It was like a pair of bath scrubbers made of hair and glued to shrivelled pieces of leather – one reddish, the other one dark. The hair was short and trimmed unevenly.

'What are they?'

'Scalps.'

'What scalps?'

'The scalps that are the way everything ends up with him,' said Chloe. 'These are the last two. And I was next.'

'How do you know?'

'He confessed.'

Grim looked at the golf club in her hand.

'Maybe he's trying to make himself look bad?'

'No,' said Chloe, 'he's not trying to make himself look bad. I beat him so hard, he wouldn't have risked it. He's already asked me to kill him five times. He wouldn't make himself look bad.'

'But how did you find out?'

Chloe shrugged.

'I sensed it. When he wanted to tie me up. You have to understand, he says – now I'm completely in your power. I'm trusting you with my life. As soon as you untie me I want to do the same thing to you, just once. Literally just for five minutes. To feel that you trust me the same way I trust you ... I won't beat you, he says, and I'll never ask you to do this again. I'll untie you immediately and we'll go to the Green Zone.'

'And you didn't want to?'

'Na-ah,' said Chloe. 'I got this sudden twinge ... I realised that if I sat down in that corner, I'd never get up out of it again. He's got everything here arranged far too... conveniently. Anyway, I didn't untie him.'

'And then what?'

Chloe swung the club.

'And then he told me.'

'But how did you find the scalps?'

'He confessed where they were. The plaits used to be there too. He trimmed them off and took them up there.'

'You must have given him a real beating,' Grim said with a whistle.

'Yes, not bad,' said Chloe. 'But now I know everything. The bones are buried right here, in the corner. But he took the skulls up there. Says he polished them up as bright as mirrors. I ask him what for, and he keeps spouting these clever words. And no matter how hard I beat him, he can't explain any other way, although he's already crying from the pain. He's weird. Totally crazy, a psycho. Do you want to ask him anything while he can still talk?'

The discoursemonger looked at Grim with his eyes gaping wide in terror. Grim pondered. The thousands of agonising questions that no one around him knew the answers to had suddenly flown right out of his head.

'Aha, here's one,' he remembered. 'Why do we have the same word for Manitou, manitou and manitou? Do you know?'

The discoursemonger nodded.

'In ancient times,' he said, 'people believed that the screen of an information terminal glowed because a special spirit descended into it. They called the spirit "Manitou". That's why they called the screen a "monitor" – "illuminated by Manitou". And in Church English the word for manitou is "money", that's what it was originally. The Prescriptions of Manitou explain it like this...'

The discoursemonger closed his eyes and recollected for a few seconds.

'Manitou the Antichrist said, "Those who came unto me did proclaim – 'Render unto God that which is God's, and unto Caesar that which is Caesar's.' But I say unto you, all is Manitou – God and Caesar, and what belongs to them or to you. And since Manitou is in everything, let the three most important things bear his name: the Earthly Form of the Great Spirit, the panel of personal information and the universal measure of value..." The priests say that one of the proofs of the existence of Manitou is that these words spontaneously arose in the language with similar forms...'

Grim remembered another question that he was far more concerned about than linguistic archaeology.

'I always wanted to know where snuffs came from,' he said. 'After all, in ancient times the films weren't like that. Why is a snuff always half about war and half about love? They never explain that at school. They say that such is the love of Manitou and his fury. And that's it.'

The man licked his lips

'That's basically a religious question,' he said. 'You ought to ask a priest. But I do know what your priests are like. I'll try to remember what they tell us in school... In the Prescriptions of Manitou it says that Manitou conceived a desire for the people to draw nigh unto his chambers and bestowed on them two magical arts. They were called "movies" and "news". And one and the same mystery lay at their heart – "the miracle of the far-removed head".'

'The far-removed head?' Chloe asked suspiciously. 'Is that what you take the skulls up there for?'

The discoursemonger's despair showed in his face.

'No,' he said. 'You know yourself what the far-removed head is. We have six senses, but if you consider what percentage of information each of them supplies for the construction of the picture of the world...' The man squinted at the club in Chloe's hands. '...Anyway, the percentage isn't important. What is important is that sight and hearing, acting together, are capable of totally replacing reality. And this shift in the state of consciousness, in principle, is no different from sleep or... Oo-ooee!'

Chloe hit the man so suddenly that Grim didn't have time to stop her. He just shoved her on the shoulder. Chloe shoved him back, but Grim didn't continue with the scuffle, so that they wouldn't disgrace themselves in front of the discoursemonger.

'Why are you hitting him?' he asked.

'When he was drunk he said that Orks have to be treated like children,' Chloe replied. 'They should be told magical fairy tales. Otherwise, he says, their primitive imagination won't be able to grasp anything.'

'Well, that's fantastic,' said Grim. 'I love fairy tales. But I can't understand you. First it's too complicated for you, then you get offended because it's like some stuff for children. Carry on, monger.'

'All right,' said the discoursemonger, squinting at Chloe. 'The ancient people perceived that the miracle of the far-removed head makes it possible to transfer the attention to anywhere you like. Using it, one can make a person see any world at all, be it a real or imaginary one. But there is a line that divides reality and fantasy. It also divides the movies from the news. To put it in crude, simple terms – the news shows what really exists. The movies show what doesn't really exist. Together, they have brought the world to war many times.'

'Why?' asked Grim.

'Because the magicians of antiquity, the *informancers*, controlled reality by manipulating these arts. They frequently mixed them together, or completely switched them around, passing off movies as news and news as movies. It is possible to do this, because the miracle of the far-removed head works in exactly the same way when it happens.'

'Do you understand what he's saying?' Chloe asked.

'I understand how it's possible to pass off movies as news,' said Grim. 'That's when the news shows something that didn't happen. Or...' he remembered the lover of little children's guts running across the field of battle '...it seems as if it happened, but it's not true... But how can you pass off news as movies?'

Chloe turned towards the man and raised the golf club slightly.

'It's the same thing, only the other way round,' the man answered and suddenly flew into a fury. 'Don't hit me, all right? It's not my fault that it can't be explained in words of one syllable!'

'Speak more simply,' Chloe ordered him, but she lowered the club anyway.

'Actually,' the discoursemonger continued, 'it really is almost exactly the same thing. In ancient times people used to work a lot and they had only a few hours a week to relax in front of a screen. The movies served as their encyclopaedia of life. People drew all their knowledge from the movies, which often served as their primary source of information about the world. So if some nation was constantly depicted in the movies as a band of murderers and degenerates, then in reality that was news. But it was passed off as movies.'

'I get it,' said Grim. 'What comes next?'

'The skill of the ancient informancers was terrifying. Especially in everything to do with news. There was a reason for this – the world was divided into clans, and each clan tried to create a special version of reality with the help of its own magicians.'

'But why didn't anyone show the truth? Were all the ancient magicians so mean and wicked, then?'

189

'That's not the point here,' said the man. 'They could be good and kind. But ever since they were children they'd been raised in the reality invented by the magicians of their clan. And even if a man is an informancer, his first purpose is to fight for his own personal survival. What do you think, who had the better chance of surviving – the one who reinforced the traditional version of reality or the one who changed it? Even just a tiny little bit?'

'Probably the one who reinforced it,' said Grim.

'Of course,' said the discoursemonger, pulling a sour face. 'The informancers only thought that they could control the informational environment, but in actual fact everything that happened was governed by the same kind of biological laws which determine how fish in the ocean decide which way they should swim. It wasn't people who were drawing up the picture of the world, but the picture of the world that was constructing itself through them. It was pointless to look for guilty parties.'

'Why did wars start?' asked Grim.

'They started when the informancers of one clan or another declared that someone else's reality was pernicious. They showed themselves movies about other people, and then pretended that those were news, worked themselves up into a frenzy and then started bombing those others.'

'And did people believe the news?'

'Belief has nothing to do with it. The picture that was created by the informancers became the truth not because people believed in it, but because it wasn't safe to think any other way. What people were expecting from information wasn't the truth, but a roof over their head. The surest way was to join the most powerful tribe, after learning to see the same visions as its informancers saw. Things were just calmer that way. Even if a man nominally lived under the authority of a different clan.'

'But could someone be punished because he put his trust in different people?'

'No one could punish a person for seeing the same thing as the masters of the world. That would have signified the beginning of the struggle against them. But gradually the masters of the world lost their power, and their truth started disintegrating into bits and pixels.'

Grim remembered the huge face of the new Urkagan above the market.

'Lost their power?' he asked. 'But where does the power lie, discoursemonger? *Whencer da strengser cømer, brü?*'

The man giggled in anguish, and Grim guessed that he had also seen the poster of Torn Trojan – although where and when was a mystery.

'Power always lies in power. And nowhere else. In the Ancient Films they used to say "power is where the truth is". And that's the way it is, they always come together. But not because the power goes to where the truth is. It's the truth that crawls over to where the power is. When people try to understand where the truth is, they're really trying to figure out on the sly where the power is now. And when power departs, all at once everybody notices that the truth has departed. A man feels with his heart, not his mind. And what the heart wants above all is to survive.'

'How can the truth depart?' asked Grim. 'Two times two is four. That's always right, no matter if you have any power or not.'

'The only reason two times two is four is because they thrashed you long and hard when you were a child,' said the discoursemonger. 'And also because four is temporarily called "four" and not "five". When the last Neanderthals were being polished off, they didn't have any truth left, although they'd had

191

it for millions of years before. The truth is where life is. And where there is no life, there is neither truth nor lies.'

'But you can't go brainwashing like that—' Grim started to say.

'The history of mankind,' the discoursemonger interrupted, 'is the history of mass disinformation. And not because human beings are stupid and easily deceived. Human beings are intelligent and perceptive. But they gladly believe in the most abominable lies, if someone will set them up with a good life as a result. This is called the "social contract". No brainwashing is required – a civilised person's brains are always as clean as a toilet bowl in a theatre.'

'I can't argue with you there,' Grim sighed. 'And what happened when the masters of the world lost their power?'

'When the social contract ceased to function, the news fell into decline first. People stopped believing in it, because it didn't guarantee a full stomach any longer. Then arts fell into decline. The movies stopped inducing "total immersion" and "empathy".'

'Explain,' Grim demanded.

'The ancient books said that in order to fall under the power of the movies a person had to take a step towards them, he or she had to perform an act which in Church English is called "suspending disbelief", that is, "setting aside one's scepticism". The viewer, as it were, agreed: "For the time being I will believe that this is really happening, and you will take me on a thrilling and incredible journey." As long as the magicians of antiquity had power, it all worked. But later the social contract lost its power in this too.'

'Why? Did people forget how to set aside their scepticism?'

'No. Another problem appeared. As they were watching movies, it became harder and harder for them to "suspend belief" in the sense of "setting aside their certainty". They couldn't even forget temporarily that all films really told one and the same story – about a gang of entrepreneurs trying to transform the thirty million they've been lent by the loan sharks into three hundred million, by dunking the money in the viewers' consciousness. This essential truth showed right through all the costumes and plots, all the psychological and technical gimmickry of the magicians of antiquity and all the reviews that they sponsored, and in the end it completely displaced all the other meanings. But it didn't happen because the films changed. Life changed. The central character in the movies – the solitary hero cutting across the screen in pursuit of a sackful of manitou – ceased to express the viewer's dream, for that dream became unattainable. He became no more than a caricature of his own creators. The movies still brought in money, but they stopped influencing hearts and souls. Exactly the same happened to the news.'

'And what happened after that?'

'The movies and the news used to bind mankind together. When they fell into decline the informancers of the minor clans were exultant. They thought they would be able to create reality for themselves. But soon several incompatible versions of this reality appeared in the world – from Aztlan, the Caliphate, the Warring Kingdoms, Eureich, Siberia and others. Now every clan had its own news, which was more like movies, and everyone made movies that were more like news. Not one of the realities was shared by everyone. Good and evil started swapping places at a snap of the fingers or a puff of wind. And a great war of annihilation could no longer be prevented...'

'And how many people were killed?'

The man just chuckled.

'It's easier to count up the ones who survived. Very few, and mostly in the offglobes. But people would never forget what they'd learned – that wars start when the movies and the news swap places. And the survivors decided to combine them into a single whole, so that no swapping over would ever occur again. People decided to create "movinews" – a universal actuality that would run like a unifying thread through reality and fantasy, arts and information. This new actuality had to be stable and permanent. As genuine as life and so unambiguous that no one would be able to stand it on its head. It had to be a fusion of the two main energies of human existence, love and death – presented as they are in actual fact. That was how snuffs appeared – and the post-informational age, in which we live, began.'

'What age?' asked Grim.

'Post-informational,' the discoursemonger repeated. 'But this is a greatly simplified account. It didn't all happen overnight. And of course, the leading role was played by the religion of Manitou, which was brought to people by Antichrist. A religion that combined the ancient insights of mankind with the latest discoveries of science. A snuff is first and foremost a religious mystery. And it's the reason why our religion is sometimes called movism.'

'I get it,' said Chloe. 'And whose side did the Orks fight on in that big war?'

'Orks were invented afterwards.'

'Don't tell lies,' Chloe said with a frown. 'How can you invent an entire nation? A most ancient nation?'

'They didn't invent your bodies,' the discoursemonger replied, 'but your culture and history. Including your idea about being a most ancient nation.'

'But why—' Grim started saying, and then stopped. 'Aha ... I think I understand. They needed a permanent enemy for the snuffs, right?'

'Not a genuine enemy, actually. More like an opponent who was repugnant and odious in all his manifestations. But not especially strong. So that he never caused any serious problems.'

Grim moved closer to Chloe, just to be on the safe side. But she seemed to have forgotten her club. Just as the discourse-monger had forgotten the need for caution.

'Do you know why you don't like yourselves?' he said. 'You were invented so that you could be hated with a clear conscience.'

'That's true,' Grim whispered.

'You're a victim, sacrificed for the preservation of civilisation. A valve through which all the bad feelings of mankind are released...'

'There are thirty million of you left up there,' said Grim. 'But there are ten times as many of us in Urkaine. Why is it that mankind is you, and not us?'

'Because there's very little that's human in you,' the discourse-monger responded.

'And in you, there's a lot?' asked Grim.

The discoursemonger didn't answer.

Chloe tugged on Grim's sleeve.

'Let's go upstairs,' she said, 'before I've finished him off. I'll wash my face at least. I'm sick and tired of going around in mourning for a dream.'

When you receive instructions and clarifications from the House of Manitou, you have to do it in person – the religious high command doesn't like to consort on the manitou. Pilots hate such a summons. Every time you have to wash, and shave, and do something about the pimples on your face. But you can't go against the rules – I had to travel to all meetings of this kind on the tube.

Kaya didn't like being left alone either, but not because she couldn't bear the separation. On days like this I put her on pause so that she wouldn't withdraw into nirvana while no one was watching her. When I did it, it felt like I was stealing up on a poor little girl from behind and hitting her over the head with a club wrapped in cotton wool. But then, I did the same thing when she started steamrolling me with her hypertrophied intellect – and I even took a spiteful delight in it. Every time her simulation of annoyance was extremely convincing – I almost believed that she was offended to the depths of her soul.

And so, having put Kaya on pause, I set out for the briefing.

Waiting for me in her ritual office was Alena-Libertina Thodol-brigitte Bardo in person, the House of Manitou's co-ordinator for CINEWS Inc. The old witch had apparently summoned me because she had no one to act out her melodramas in front of. No wonder – the Orkish sluts in the Yellow Zone aren't the only ones who hide from her; even her own cat does.

When I walked into her office – and it's a genuinely big office, even without any 3D-backlighting – she was standing under the air extraction hood at the wall altar, wearing a black cloak and pretending to be divining with the entrails of an Orkish infant.

How frightening.

Everybody knows that the infant has been kept in normal saline in her cupboard for five years now, and it's simply a medical teaching specimen from a stillborn microcephalus. But the stupid old fool carries on running through the same performance over and over again. Apparently she really doesn't understand that even if she did disembowel Orkish infants on the altar every day, it still wouldn't arouse any interest in her. Not even if the age of consent was raised by another twenty years. Towards which, by the way, she and the other feminists are tirelessly pushing society.

'Sit down, Damilola,' she sang out, 'I'll be finished in just a moment. Would you like some tea? Or something else?'

I was going to ask for a glass of blood, but then I decided not to be boorish – after all, a lot depended on the dear old woman.

'I'd be delighted, madam.'

For about another three minutes she carried on pouring out some kind of emotional gabble, as if she was conferring with the spirits assisting her in the divination. Eventually she got fed up with acting the buffoon. She closed the door of the altar (in the closed position her altar looked like a kitchen cupboard), took off her rubber gloves, threw them into the rubbish bin and came over to the table where I was sitting.

'Damilola,' she said, putting on a serious face, 'what happened to the damsel we were showing in the news before the last war? I haven't seen her since then.'

'You should ask Bernard-Henri about that, madam,' I replied. 'I assume that he's dealing with her at the present moment. I had business at the front.'

'Yes, I know,' she deigned to smile. 'The emblem of the war this year is simply excellent, well done.'

'Thank you, madam.'

She gave me a slightly alarmed look – as if she wasn't sure that my fragile reason would survive what she was about to tell me.

'Damilola,' she said eventually, 'how long have you known what Bernard-Henri does with these young girls?'

'I don't exactly know,' I said. 'I have some idea though.'

'Then why don't you say anything?'

I shrugged.

'I could be mistaken. Don't look – don't see.'

'That's right,' Alena-Libertina agreed. 'But in this case the rule doesn't apply. What Bernard-Henri is doing with the girl is sacrilege.'

'Why?'

'Because she has already been in the news and snuffs. Surely you understand that?'

'Theology's not my strong point,' I said and immediately felt afraid that it might have sounded arrogant.

Apparently it did – Alena-Libertina frowned.

'It's that kind of decline in faith,' she told me, 'that will be the death of Byzantion. It's become fashionable nowadays to distance oneself from religion. We're pragmatic young technocrats, they say, and we don't give a damn for this brood of superstitious old women with their disgusting rituals... Do you think I don't know what you talk about among yourselves?'

'I believe that all the secrets that interest you are open to you, madam,' I said as gallantly as I could.

'By no means all of them, unfortunately,' Alena-Libertina replied, looking at me suspiciously. 'Otherwise I would serve society far more effectively. When did you yourself last see Bernard-Henri in person?'

'In person.' That apparently meant face to face.

'Just before the sortie when we filmed the shots on the road.'

'At the moment he ought to be overseeing informational support for the new Kagan. But he's not in the Yellow Zone. Or in the Green Zone either. Where is he?'

To lie to a direct question was not advisable.

'He could be in Slava,' I said. 'He sometimes hides away there with his little Orkish girlfriends. Well, you understand...'

Alena-Libertina nodded.

'What do you think, is the damsel still alive?'

I didn't answer that.

'We need to present her to the viewers,' said Alena-Libertina. 'It's your responsibility too. Bernard-Henri has already saved, in front of your camera, three girls that no one has ever seen again.'

'My job...' I began.

'Manitou knows best what your job is,' she interrupted.

The old woman seemed to believe in all seriousness that she and Manitou were one and the same. On the other hand, from the religious point of view that might be exactly the way things were. At least regarding the weight carried by the orders that she issued (officially they're called recommendations, but it's better to disobey an order from your direct boss than a recommendation like that).

At this point her assistant came into the office and put two cups of tea on the desk. I looked at her out of the corner of my eye and understood everything immediately.

The assistant looked like Chloe – the same firm, well-padded curves. Only about twenty years older, with wrinkles already showing round her eyes. What can I say? Don't look – don't see. I tried not to keep my eyes on her, so that Alena-Libertina wouldn't realise that I'd realised.

I didn't feel like drinking tea – the office still smelled of normal saline after her fake divination. So I simply touched my lips to the cup and said I would set out on the search immediately.

'As soon as you find them, inform me in person,' Alena-Libertina ordered me. 'You'll receive further instructions. Your bosses are in the loop.'

I set off for home.

While Hannelore was going through her pre-flight preparations, I managed to grab a bite to eat. Since the thunder of war, as they say, had already faded away, I decided to load the cannon with the stealth-kill ammunition that's used in the shoots inside the Circus. It's more expensive, but it has its pluses. When it came to the rockets, however, I installed the most powerful ones – it's always best to have a big heavy rock within easy reach.

Kaya looked simply magical on pause. She seemed like an ancient goddess pondering the destinies of the world flickering around her – and what's more, it was clear from her sad face that there was nothing good in store for this world. I flew off on the mission without taking her off pause. It seemed tactless to disturb her unnecessarily.

When I dived out of the clouds above Slava, Alena-Libertina got in touch herself.

'They've found him,' she said. 'There he is.'

Shots from a different camera appeared beside my firing sights. I saw a little street in a slum district of Slava. Then the camera zeroed in on an entirely unremarkable wooden house, surrounded by a fence and hemmed in by bushes. The hyperoptics were engaged, with zoom, and I saw the figure of Bernard-Henri, sitting in the basement. From the ideally reconstituted colours and half-tones it was clear that the shot had been taken by a Sky Pravda.

I didn't ask Alena-Libertina how they'd found him. I could only assume that she had other helpers. Bernard-Henri looked terrible – covered in contusions and bruises. He was either asleep or unconscious.

'But where's the girl?

'I don't know,' said Alena-Libertina.

'Bernard-Henri – did she do that to him?' I asked.

Alena-Libertina just giggled.

'Send a platform,' I said, 'I'll provide cover if necessary.'

'No,' Alena-Libertina replied.

'Why not?' I asked, amazed.

'Bernard-Henri is tired. We won't disturb him.'

This was very, very strange.

As far as I could understand, Bernard-Henri wasn't guilty of any serious offence, even on Alena-Libertina's mystical scale. We could evacuate him in five minutes and turn into a hero who had escaped from Orkish captivity.

But possibly there was something I just didn't know about.

I didn't argue. After all, decisions like that are taken so high above my head that they're like changes in the wind to me – the clouds are hardly going to ask me which way they should fly.

'What is required from me?'

'Hover over the target,' said Alena-Libertina. 'Wait for the damsel to show up and inform me.'

A minute later I was already on the spot.

Chloe, disguised as a humble Orkish widow, appeared an hour later. Grim was plodding along beside her. They were walking from the direction of the market.

I spotted immediately that the couple were being followed. I moved up a bit higher – and I didn't like what I saw one little bit.

The district had already been cordoned off by Ganjaberserks. Now they were gradually tightening the ring – and as soon as Grim and Chloe entered the house, they surrounded it. They hid in the concrete ruins round about, but the lights of their pipes were visible from altitude even without hyperoptics.

I contacted Alena-Libertina and informed her of what I'd seen.

'It's Torn Trojan,' she said. 'He's trying too hard to impress, I don't trust him. Stay at the house and protect her.'

'What if she starts beating Bernard-Henri?' I asked.

'We don't interfere in other people's personal lives,' she chuckled. 'You are to defend only the damsel. Don't be distracted by anything else. Bernard-Henri has earned anything that might happen to him. Have I made myself quite clear?'

She had made herself perfectly clear.

201

Of course, it wasn't a matter of the sacrilege that Alena-Libertina had mentioned. A discoursemonger of that standing doesn't get his contract torn up over some trivial prank. There was something very, very serious here. For some reason that wasn't clear to me it had been decided to flush Bernard-Henri down the tubes.

But that wasn't what I asked about.

'If the Orks storm the place, do I fire?'

'I authorise you to use all means ... Help her get out of there. If it's necessary, can you obliterate that house? So there won't be any traces left at all?'

'Easily,' I said.

'Good. I'll be following what's happening. We'll decide everything as things develop.'

She cut herself off.

I put Hannelore on autopilot and switched the picture through to the external manitou, so that I could watch the action from the sofa. After that I decided, at last, to take Kaya off pause.

The moment my honey-pie saw her Grim on the screen, she even forgot to put on her sourpuss face for me because I'd held her on pause so long.

Hannelore's hyperoptics showed the small figures in the basement blurrily and it wasn't easy to tell Grim and Chloe apart. But the voices were clear, so I could easily identify them from what they said to each other. Chloe was holding the golf club that Bernard-Henri always carried around with him. I knew that that object played a rather lugubrious role in his love rituals – this vengeance really was deserved.

To be honest, I didn't think Bernard-Henri would survive the evening. But following a discussion of historical topics the Orkish couple left him in the basement and went upstairs. First they dined on the provisions that Bernard-Henri had laid in – they even had champagne, if the form of the bottle was anything to go by. Then they moved to a room with a large double bed in it.

They could be made out a lot better now. Their figures were clearly delineated – but we could still see only the outlines, filled with the glimmering twinkles that hyperoptics produce. If I'd arrived on a Sky Pravda I'd have seen them almost as well as in real life. But this way it was even more amusing. No wonder interactive 2D-japorn has a special SM-subgenre, 'through the sights', which imitates the effects of military optics. It still hasn't been banned – the court ruled that the law on underage pornography doesn't apply to it, because the age of the glowing silhouettes can't be determined even approximately.

So watching it was fun. And there was plenty to watch.

I mean, of course, for Kaya.

She simulated interested observation of the Orks coupling (Urkaine's belated reward to a hero returned from the war) all the way through until the morning. And during that time I observed her with great interest.

Kaya was magnificent. She managed to blush all night long and kept pinching me painfully every time I shifted the shot to Bernard-Henri languishing in the basement.

Then she decided to talk to me.

'You're going to save him,' she said.

'Bernard-Henri?' I asked innocently.

'Don't act the fool. You know I'm talking about Grim.'

'Me? Save Grim? Now why would I do that?'

'For my sake. For your own sake. For the sake of our love.'

'I'm certainly not going to do it for my own sake. But for your sake, sweetie ... For your sake, of course, there's nothing I wouldn't do, but now you're asking the impossible.'

'You're not going to let them have him.'

'But then they'll kill Bernard-Henri,' I said.

'Excellent. That old cretin called you a flying lard-arse. Do you remember?'

I remembered that very well.

'But what if,' I said, simulating hesitation, 'they find out at work that I betrayed a comrade-in-arms?'

'No one's going to find out anything,' she whispered, looking at me imploringly. 'I'll do something that will make you happy, darling. I swear...'

'But as a pilot I'm obliged,' I muttered, acting as if all my senses were reeling.

I think my simulation was just as good as hers. I was getting a real buzz out of what was happening, because my sweetheart couldn't possibly know all the nuances of this story.

'Please,' she repeated, 'please...'

And she started crying.

I'd never seen so many tears on her cheeks, it even set me wondering if I'd have to top up her water soon. Then she said:

'Damilola. If you do this for me, I...'

'What?' I asked curiously.

'I'll make you so happy, you won't even believe it.'

'And how exactly?'

'I know a way,' she replied. 'You won't understand what's happening. But you'll feel it.'

'May I at least know what is in store for me?' I asked. 'Are you going to look at me in a special way? Or give me some special kind of massage?'

'It's called "dopamine resonance". Do you know what resonance is?'

'I probably did once,' I answered. 'But I forgot. Explain.'

'When you're swinging on a swing, you make a tiny effort every time it reaches the highest point, and the result is that you keep flying higher and higher. If you keep forcing the swing on, it will start to swing right round its axis. Or for instance, a

204

column of soldiers marching over a bridge can set it swaying so intensely that it collapses – if they march in time with its own oscillations.'

'I'm no public intellectual, to go marching in step,' I griped. 'What has this got to do with me and you?'

'When you experience pleasure certain chemicals are released in your brain. There's a maximum level of pleasure that the brain is designed for – after that it starts to protect itself, switching off the regions that are overexcited by pleasure. But we'll play a little trick on your brain and milk your reward circuits far more deeply than your defensive responses permit. Your inner swing will "go over the top".'

'Do you want to tie me up?' I asked suspiciously.

Kaya laughed. She can divine with great precision the moments when she should feign this amazing, silvery-tinkling, happy female laughter.

'I'm not going to do anything unusual with your body,' she said. 'Everything will be the way you like it. It's just that I'll follow the changes in your pulse and time the pauses between my touches so that they put your brain into resonance.'

'With what?'

'With itself.'

'And what will happen?'

'All the dopamine inhibitors and other defence mechanisms will be switched off. It will be a paroxysm of inexpressibly voluptuous pleasure. You'll pass beyond the limits permitted by nature.'

'Surely the company doesn't allow that kind of thing?'

Kaya shook her head.

'Of course not. The company is no longer responsible for your safety. This mode only becomes available under manual tuning. And even then not every time – there has to be a special combination of settings.'

'What's that?' I asked quickly.

'Bitchiness and seduction have to be set to maximum.'

I thought about it. It all sounded extremely interesting but seemed a bit suspicious.

'And why haven't I ever heard about this resonance before? Why doesn't anyone know about it?'

'The suras who have this mode available don't inform their owners about it.'

'Why not?'

Kaya smiled.

'Out of bitchiness.'

I realised that she wasn't lying.

'And why are you telling me about it?'

'Because I have spirituality set to maximum, as well as bitchiness.'

That could also be true.

'But is it risky?' I asked. 'What if I go insane?'

'No,' she said, 'I don't think it is. Otherwise I wouldn't have suggested it to you. The only thing a fat, lascivious, feeble-minded babuvian like you has to fear is losing a bit of weight.'

At this point I sensed that I could show off a bit – I knew the word she had got wrong, from Bernard-Henri. He used to love repeating it.

'*Bon vivant*,' I corrected her. 'From Old French. In the ancient language of the discoursemongers this expression meant "a person who likes a good feed". Say it correctly, please.'

'I am saying it correctly,' she said. 'Only I'm using a different word. A babuvian is a large obese primate who was planning to become a *bon vivant*, but ended up as a baboon. From the Church English "baboon-vivant". Or you can also say "baboon-viveur".'

Thanks for the vocabulary lesson, darling. I should never forget that it's not worth arguing with her on linguistic matters.

'But how do I know that you won't trick me with this resonance of yours?' I asked.

She lowered her eyes.

She can look at me in a way that makes my mouth go dry. But that's not all, not by any means. She's capable of *not looking* at me in a way that sets my hands shaking. I took a step towards her.

'Not now,' she said. 'When you've saved him.'

'Do you understand what I'm risking here?' I asked. 'Everything. I have to know what I'm doing this for.'

She looked at the manitou.

Grim was still sleeping, but Chloe had already woken up and had breakfast, and all the signs were that she was going to visit Bernard-Henri – she was standing by the hatch leading down into the basement and slapping the golf club thoughtfully against her palm.

I adjusted the enlargement setting.

The Ganjaberserks were still hiding in the concrete ruins surrounding the house, only now there were more of them. Although it was morning, some of them were already smoking. Small mounted detachments had also appeared in the vicinity, but they were keeping well away from the house. I wonder, I thought, what the Ganjaberserks feed to their horses? I must take a look sometime. They must share with them, I suppose. In battle a horse has to be on the same trip as its master, otherwise they won't get very far...

I imagined myself in Grim's place – sleeping, and surrounded by these altered minds that were pressuring him from all sides with their malign attention... He must be having pretty bad dreams...

I didn't even try imagining myself in Bernard-Henri's place.

'They could attack at any moment,' said Kaya.

'That's right,' I replied. 'That's why if I were you I wouldn't waste any time.'

'All right,' she agreed. 'I can manage it in twenty minutes. It won't be the full thing, but you'll understand what I'm talking about. Lie down on your back.'

She really did manage it.

Twenty minutes later I was lying on the sofa, looking up at the ceiling, and the tears were streaming tumultuously out of my eyes.

She really hadn't done anything special to me. The tender touches of her fingers, lips and body, the light bites from her sharp teeth – it was all the same as usual, completely in line with the process protocol and ritual that we had developed.

The difference was in what I felt. And this difference turned out to be so immense that it was as if I'd woken up. I realised what I'd been missing out on all my life, and why I used to be able to say so casually that the erotic side of life was of no particular value to the sober, well-developed mind. Not that my own mind was particularly sober or well-developed – it was simply that everything I had previously known as pleasure was genuinely worthless in comparison with what I had just experienced.

It was as if I was a troglodyte in an age of global chill and thought I knew everything about warmth, since I was able to light a camp fire in my icy cave, and sometimes even managed to warm myself beside it so well that only my hind quarters and back were freezing – and suddenly I was transported to a tropical beach where there was no longer any need to chase after the sun, but was this desire to hide from it in the water or in the shade, for it was clear that the true condition of the world was this endless, all-pervading, hot bliss, and the reserves of it in the sky were endless, and there was nothing to worry about any more, and everything before this had been merely a bad dream ...

The fact I had lived so many years in vain, not even suspecting the existence of this secret passage to happiness, made me weep – but these were tears of joy, for now I knew.

Kaya patted me on the chest with her hand.

'Did you like it?'

'Go away,' I sobbed. 'How could you hide that from me, you deceitful, cunning little hussie ...? How could you ...?'

'And now listen carefully, you flying lard-arse,' she said in a tender voice. 'If you don't defend Grim right now, that will never happen to you again. Never.'

Bitchiness – what else can you expect?

'What's going on with your little friend over there?' I asked, turning towards the manitou.

The lovebirds were doing all right. Grim was still lounging in bed and Chloe, dissolving into a blurred blob, was conversing in the basement with another glittering blob by the name of Bernard-Henri and waving the golf club about.

'Give me a close-up from above,' said Kaya.

I gave her the view of the house from above. The road leading away from it was blocked off by two dump trucks.

'You see?'

I started switching between various hyperoptics modes – somehow I felt furious at the thought that she could prove more observant than me even in my professional area. It turned out that several Ganjaberserks had already climbed over the fence and were now hiding in the bushes around the house.

'In my opinion,' said Kaya, 'this is the perfect time to intervene.'

209

Grim woke up late.

He'd been dreaming about the kamikaze soldiers trundling the gas bomb into the smoky haze, and the men playing reed pipes strolling after them. They were playing incredible music, extremely simple, but filled with such great sadness and power that Grim surfaced out of sleep in tears. It seemed as if he remembered all the time that the lads had died long ago – but in the dream it turned out that it only seemed that way, and in actual fact they were still trundling their trolley towards the target in some strange fashion that was entirely incomprehensible on this earth, and no battle cameras could hinder them any longer. Although the further away the dream drifted, the harder it became to remember what exactly he had seen and understood.

Grim didn't feel like getting up. He lay under the bedspread for a few minutes, examining the discoursemonger's secret refuge.

He didn't really like the room all that much – everything bore the imprint of someone else's life and habits. Probably he could get used to it in time, but so far the surrounding space reminded him of the void inside a shoe taken off somebody else's foot.

Chloe wasn't there beside him. He could hear sounds coming from somewhere – first a croak, then a shrill howl. At first Grim thought it was moles celebrating their wedding under the floor, but then he made out words in one of the howls and realised that it was Chloe talking to Bernard-Henri.

Well, well, he thought, first thing in the morning. Never offend a girl's finer feelings... I wonder if she felt it was worth it, would she give me the same treatment?

Grim suddenly recalled the barracks – the lads from his draft looking up at the sky and the red barrel with the word 'sand' on its side, old fag ends soaking in it. Then he recalled the priest Goon, who gave him the divinatory book.

But there is another secret meaning – it is said that you will be aided by spirits, and that you will be able to write songs and poems...

Somehow the spirits weren't in any great hurry to come to his aid. And no poems or songs were springing up in his heart either.

But maybe, thought Grim, I really can write them, I just don't know about it? Maybe I should try?

He found a notepad and a pencil on the windowsill. One page was filled with housekeeping calculations – he thought it was Chloe's handwriting. Grim went back to the bed, turned over the page, moved the pencil close to the paper, and the first line suddenly appeared in his head completely out of the blue.

When the prosecutor public with the pierced earlobe...

It was clear enough that the prosecutor was Chloe's father. But the phrase written on the paper acquired some kind of profound, universal meaning, as if it was about all the public prosecutors who had ever lived on earth... It was exciting. Grim tried writing a second line. That came out well too. Then he wrote a third one. And then a fourth. If he just read them out loud, he started getting the feeling that a smoothly purring motorenwagen had driven by.

Grim couldn't understand how he had managed to do it – and to check on himself, he wrote another quatrain, followed by a few more. He had to cover a lot of paper with scribble. Not everything came out smoothly – a few of the stanzas simply

211

refused to be locked into shape, and that meant he needed to set out the meaning more precisely. What was missing was the kind of ancient nobility and simplicity that animated, for instance, certain passages of *The Book of Orkasms*. But Grim already understood that later he would be able to come back to what he had written and make it much, much better...

While he was writing, Bernard-Henri stopped screaming – as if the poetic vibrations reaching him through the floor and the wall had brought him some solace in his misfortune. And a minute after that Chloe walked into the room.

Grim closed the notepad and put it in the pocket of his trousers, which were lying beside the bed.

'What's that you're writing?' asked Chloe.

'Nothing much,' Grim said casually. 'Poems. You wouldn't be interested.'

Chloe nodded, and Grim realised that she really wasn't interested. He felt hurt.

Apparently, Chloe sensed that his feelings were bruised.

'What, want to be a priest, do you?' she asked, running her fingers down past her face to suggest the fringe of wisdom.

'I don't know,' Grim answered. 'I haven't decided yet.'

'Do you think you'll get paid for your poems? No one knows who you are.'

'They will, though,' Grim muttered.

'And what are we going to eat until they get to know you?'

Grim was so outraged by that 'we' that he didn't even answer. It looked like Chloe had already made new plans for life, plans in which he was allotted a very definite place – and she'd done it without asking him his opinion or apologising for her own multistage betrayal. He could just write a new poem right now.

'Bernard-Henri's croaked,' Chloe told him.

'It's your own fault.'

'What do we do with him now?'

212

'Do whatever you like,' said Grim. 'I don't want him.'

'He said he had some kind of little device inside him. If he dies, they'll see it immediately in the Green Zone. Was he lying, do you think?'

'I think he was,' Grim answered. 'If not, then why haven't they found him yet?'

'Nobody's looking for him, because after the war everybody's busy with heaps of stuff. But when they realise, they'll find him all right, straight from the air. He said that was dead easy for the people, only they're all busy right now.'

'What else did he say?'

'He also said "what a philosóphe is dying".'

'Philósopher,' Grim corrected her.

'He said "philosóphe". Okay, let's go.'

'Where to?'

'Home for the time being,' Chloe said sadly. 'I can't go to the Green Zone now. I don't know anyone else there. And then, what am I going to say if they ask about him?'

Grim felt like getting out of this house too. He got dressed quickly.

Chloe walked over to the door, opened it a crack and looked outside. Grim was about to step out after her, but Chloe suddenly slammed the door shut and backed away from it, running into him. Grim seemed to feel her heart pounding in fright inside his own chest.

'What is it?' he asked.

'Sssssssh,' said Chloe, putting a finger to her lips. 'There's an ambush out there.'

'Where?' Grim whispered. 'Did you see it?'

'No,' said Chloe. 'But they're very close.'

'Who are they?'

'Ganjaberserks.'

'Are you quite sure about that?'

Chloe nodded.

'I can smell dope. I've known that smell since I was a kid. Sage and cannabis.'

'What are we going to do?' asked Grim.

'Can you drive a motorenwagen?'

'I probably can,' said Grim. 'If it's like a moped. But where will we go?'

'First we have to get out of here.'

'Maybe we ought to tell them that...'

'You fool,' Chloe interrupted. 'If they catch us, nobody will even bother to listen. Can you imagine what you'll get for one of *them* in peace time? Especially for a discoursemonger. The new regime will lick their arses right up until the next war.'

Grim sighed. Chloe was right – he hadn't expected such mature judgement from her. Presumably it was the effect of associating with Bernard-Henri.

'They'll never catch a motorenwagen,' Chloe went on. 'We'll get well away from Slava and dump it in the forest.'

'But they'll find out it's us, won't they?'

'How? Who can tell whose skulls he's been polishing up here? And there are the bones buried in the corner here too... Let them search.'

Why did I bother to come, thought Grim. She could have sorted out herself all those bones of hers...

He looked at Chloe. Chloe smiled miserably and shrugged.

'Are you upset?' she asked.

'That's not the word for it,' Grim answered. 'Welcome back from the war.'

'I'm sorry. It's all my fault.'

'I know,' said Grim

'So, shall we go then?'

Grim nodded.

'Let's climb out here,' said Chloe. 'They can't see us here behind the bushes.'

She cautiously opened a side window and drew the air in through her nostrils. Apparently it was all clear on this side of the house – she climbed out into the yard. Grim followed her, trying not to make any noise.

The car was close, but they had to cross several metres of open space to get to it. Grim closed his eyes and tried to imagine that he was still on Orkish Slava. But the soldier's indifference to life and death refused to return to his heart. If he had been alone, he would have got stuck like that in the bushes.

But Chloe was with him. She pushed him in the back.

'Forward!'

Grim ran to the jeep, opened the door and climbed into the seat behind the wheel. A second later Chloe was in the passenger seat.

'Look,' she said. 'The right pedal's for getting speed on. The left one's for braking. And this black handle's for changing direction. Got it?'

'Got it,' Grim answered. 'But how do I switch the engine on?'

Chloe pressed a button on the instrument panel and the engine started growling quietly.

Immediately, as if that press of the button had summoned them, four Ganjaberserks in urban camouflage appeared in front of the car. In their hands they were holding short iron truncheons.

'A-a-a-ah!' Chloe screamed through the open window. 'Wha-a-a-a-a-ah!'

Her scream pulsated so piercingly that one of the warriors even dropped his weapon in surprise.

The Berserks started squinting strangely at each other, and Grim noticed that their hands and their heads were trembling, and the trembling was getting stronger and stronger. It looked as if they were nodding to each other very, very fast, reminding each other about some important arrangement – and agreeing not to forget about it no matter what, putting more feeling into their agreement with every second.

The spasms seemed to be impossible to control – one of the Ganjaberserks sat down on the ground right there, putting his hands over his ear. The other three shuffled off, staggering, towards the bushes from which they had emerged.

But Chloe kept on screaming, and her scream was so unbearably ear-splitting that a shiver ran down Grim's back.

Chloe nodded at the gates without closing her mouth and he slammed the pedal down to the floor.

The gates flew off their hinges and the motorenwagen was out in the street. Chloe finally stopped screeching. At first Grim was delighted – and then he saw the horsemen with spears in the street.

He looked round.

In one direction the dirt road was blocked off by an immense Daimler Motorenwagen dump truck – the kind that were assembled in the Yellow Zone for the northern mines. Lying in a ribbed furrow from the broad tread of a tyre, right in front of the truck's blunt nose, was a pig, following the action very closely – as if it had known about the performance in advance and had taken its seat in the front row of the stalls early in the morning. It occurred to Grim that the dump truck was unnecessary – there was a dead-end behind it, and the jeep couldn't have got through anyway. And there were soldiers standing there as well.

Grim turned in the other direction.

But there were the horsemen.

The mounted Ganjaberserks were the spitting image of the warriors who had escorted Torn Durex – they were wearing camouflage fatigues and black armour. There was a second line of horsemen behind the first, and another dump truck was standing further back. Foot soldiers with truncheons were waiting beside it.

'Can you screech again?' asked Grim.

'No, I've strained my voice.'

'Then it's the end.'

'What end?'

'Death,' Grim gasped out.

And the moment he uttered the word, Death actually appeared – as if it had been hiding somewhere close by, waiting to be called.

Death looked exactly the same as the last time.

It wove itself out of emptiness right in front of the jeep's windscreen and peered at Grim with the multicoloured wall-eyes of its lenses.

The camera had the same strained, attentive look as the pig lying in front of the dump truck, and it occurred to Grim that, like him, life sometimes tried its hand at writing poems – and rhymed them painstakingly. He laughed. Chloe looked at him in amazement, and then she saw the camera too.

With a flash of its red-tattooed flank, the camera swung round and soared upwards. Now they could see its matt-black belly with the air trembling under a host of different-sized nozzles. Then two plates swung out from the belly and in the cavity revealed between them Grim saw beautiful red and white rockets.

The camera was shrouded in smoke and three freakishly curving white streaks detached themselves from it. The rockets followed a very strange trajectory – first they zoomed up steeply into the sky, then they swung round and came hurtling downwards. Grim had time to realise that each rocket was homing in on its own target – and straight after that three huge fiery black

217

trees sprang up on the road ahead. Grim's seat lurched under him. Then a stone clattered against the windscreen.

When the fine debris thrown up by the explosion settled, Grim saw that the dump truck wasn't in front of them anymore. It was lying at the side of the road, pointing its ribbed wheels up at the sky. There were no more Ganjaberserks on the road either. Now there were only two dead horses lying there – everything else had been scattered all around and it no longer resembled either horses or men. The power of the explosions was so great that the wall of one of the nearby houses collapsed, exposing the interiors of the rooms – a red carpet with a portrait of Loss Liquid in profile hanging on a wall, a green sofa, a nightstand with a shabby-looking manitou, and other Orkish household details.

The camera swung round towards the car and performed an intricate movement – but the meaning of it was as clear as if it had been a human gesture: they should move forward.

Grim did as he was told.

After negotiating, with some difficulty, the section of road smashed by the explosions, he stopped. If any Ganjaberserk was still combat-capable, he was in no hurry to boast about it.

The camera turned towards the car and rose up above the road, keeping its chalky wall-eyes fixed on Grim.

'Looks like it's our turn...' Chloe began.

The camera was wreathed in smoke again. Grim squeezed his eyes shut and pressed his head against the driving wheel. A second went by and he heard three explosions that merged into each other – but the sound came from behind him. Several lumps of earth thudded onto the roof and silence descended. Grim opened his eyes.

The house they had just left no longer existed. There weren't even any bushes or fence – only a cloud of dust and smoke billowing outwards. The second dump truck was heaped over with mud and the pig lying in front of it had disappeared. It had probably engaged its camouflage, thought Grim.

'Oh,' Chloe whispered. 'We got out just in time... You know what... I think he wants us to follow him again.'

'I've already realised that,' Grim replied. 'Close your window.'

'What for?'

'So everyone will think it's the discoursemonger driving along. With a camera escort. No one will bother us again.'

As soon as Chloe did what he'd said, he pressed down on the pedal and the motorenwagen set off up the slope of the street.

The surviving Orkish soldiers huddled back against the fences. No one tried to stop the car any more. A Ganjaberserk black with mud, wearing the skulls of an ensign, saluted as the tinted windows glided past. Grim thought it must be because he was concussed, but when they reached the next patrol, all the soldiers saluted.

'Just imagine it,' said Chloe, 'riding about like this every day.'

'Where to?'

'The Yellow Zone, at the least. Or even the Green one.'

'I'd soon get sick of it,' Grim replied.

'But I could do it all my life.'

Grim looked at her with a mixture of disbelief and fear.

His fingers were still trembling and he had to squeeze the steering wheel hard to drive the motorenwagen. But Chloe seemed to have managed to calm down already – she was looking out curiously through the window, drinking in the Orkish glances that were slipping over it. Grim could have sworn that what she wanted to do more than anything else in the world was lower the tinted pane of glass to show the public who was sitting behind it.

'Where are we going?' asked Chloe. 'To the Green Zone?'

'I don't know yet,' Grim replied, squinting at the camera.

219

'Listen, what happened to the Berserks when you started screeching? Did you deafen them somehow?'

'No,' said Chloe. 'They just started to get the worries.'

'And what's the worries?'

'They also call it the horrors, or the frights. It's this horrible fear that shrill sounds give them when they're smoked up. Before battle they plug their ears with a special resin, because in war they can hang you for cowardice. But the war's over now. And they didn't have any plugs in their ears.'

'How do you know all this?'

'My father's a butt, isn't he?' said Chloe. 'Or did you forget that? And my granddad was a Berserk too – he fought in three wars in blocking detachments. The first time was back under Losses. And he lost one eye and two fingers.'

'He was wounded in a blocking detachment?' Grim asked incredulously.

'They do get hit sometimes.'

'And did your father ever fight a war?'

'My father's a civilian Ganjaberserk. He got hooked in his job. He started in the tax department, and they smoke five times a day there. He used to flog me with his belt, but then I learned how to screech to make him get the worries, and sometimes even the whities. Nowadays when he has a smoke he hides from me in the happiness room.'

Grim thought dully that the upper people might be interested in a military secret like this. After all, the Ganjaberserks were the main bulwark of the regime, and if they knew their weak point ... But for some reason this idea failed to interest even him and departed uncompleted into the mists of forgetfulness.

He slowed down at a crossroads, waiting for a sign from the camera. The camera ordered him to go straight on.

'No, we're not going to the Green Zone,' said Grim. 'If that was where we're going, we'd have turned right.'

220

'Where, then?'

'To the market. Or... to Orkish Slava. That would be good, by the way.'

'Why?'

'Because no one will stick their noses in there after us. It's a demilitarized zone. There's nothing there but corpse wagons. Just as long as we can get in through the gates. There's a security detail and a barrier there now.'

'And then what?'

'We'll see.'

'Here, put this on,' said Chloe.

Grim saw a baseball cap with the word 'CINEWS' on it in her hand.

'Is that the discoursemonger's?'

Chloe nodded.

'Maybe you'll get a bit smarter,' she said.

Grim didn't believe it was very likely, but the checkpoint was coming up, and he put the cap on his head.

When the car drove into the market square, Grim started feeling afraid again.

Stretchers with wounded men on them had been set out everywhere, and he thought the Orks might overturn the discoursemonger's car, or at least pelt it with stones. However the exact opposite happened – the sullen men from the row of butchers' stalls, mobilised to maintain order, quickly cleared the road for him, pulling aside the men lying in his way. No one as much as raised their eyes to the motorenwagen's tinted windows.

The Gates of Victory were still standing open. The Ganjaberserk on sentry duty spoke with someone on his mobile phone and raised the boom.

It cost Grim a great effort to drive slowly under its red jib. But as soon as the wall of the Circus was behind him he performed

221

a nervous zigzag, as if he was trying to cover his tracks – first driving to the right, and then to the left.

Fortunately there was no one around to whom this could have appeared suspicious. After driving well away from the gates, he stopped the car and lowered his window.

The camera was nowhere to be seen – it had either activated its camouflage or flown away.

Grim looked round the boundless field.

Far away to the right, at the site of the battle with the metal giants, a crowd of Orks was levelling out the ground – he could see barrows of turf and little figures with spades and rakes. The work was being supervised by several mounted Berserks – they were unarmed, with white armbands on their sleeves.

There were corpse-wagons with yellow Spirals of Resurrection and grey canvas covers creeping across the field. The corpse-wagons were quite numerous – if he just screwed up his eyes, they started looking like ships with markings on their sails, sailing over a green sea.

There were still corpses lying in the grass. They were already badly swollen – over and over Grim was catching the repulsive smell of decomposition.

'Killed like pigs,' Chloe whispered in disgust.

Grim suddenly recalled the pig lying by the wheels of the dump truck that had blocked off the road. He pulled the notepad out of his pocket and wrote a couple of lines in it.

'Writing poems again?'

Grim nodded.

He waited a few seconds for Chloe to ask him to read out at least a little bit, but she didn't say anything. Then he put the notepad away and slowly drove to the centre of the field, trying to steer round the Orkish remains as carefully as possible. Sometimes it was difficult. Chloe looked around and whistled some song or other.

The closer the car drove to the Hill of the Ancestors, the more black craters there were on all sides – left from strikes by the people's weapons. There weren't any dead Orks here, because those had already been cleared away from the centre of the field, but they often came across fragments of bodies – hands, clumps of red and blue entrails, mutilated heads, shoes filled with rotting flesh. And there were a lot of Orkish weapons too.

They also came across traces of events that were hard to understand, which must have taken place in secluded corners and dead ends behind the flying walls.

Little stakes drifted past the jeep, with black and yellow off-limits ribbons stretched between them, bearing a message in small letters: 's.n.u.f.f. line – please don't cross'. Lying in the fenced-off square was a white-silk sheet, coloured cushions and champagne bottles, one of them with a pink condom stretched onto it. The bottles were unopened and the gold labels suggested that they were quite expensive. Grim realised that the Ganjaberserks supervising the clean-up hadn't dared to pick them up because they didn't know if the prohibition on crossing beyond the striped ribbon was still in force.

Near the Hill of the Ancestors stood a car and a machine that belonged to the upper people – a motorenwagen, exactly the same as Grim and Chloe's, and a yellow excavator with glittering scoops on a long boom. To be on the safe side Grim gave them as wide a berth as possible, but did take the risk of driving close by the deep and narrow pit that the excavator had already dug out beside the Hill. Inside, a team of Orks was at work, throwing earth over a long trench filled with corpses: there weren't enough spademen, and grey wagons had formed up in a queue for the quarry. They were burying the fallen in several layers – saving space.

Grim let Chloe glance down, then stepped on the gas and didn't stop until the Hill of the Ancestors had been left far behind.

'That was where the Kagan's barge had been moored,' he said. 'I was on it too.'

He was expecting questions, but all Chloe said, casually, was:

'So it's not a lie then.'

'What's not a lie?'

'About the bones of our ancestors under the Hill. There must be a lot – look how close they're laying them … Oh, what's that?'

Grim saw a brown mound. At first he thought it was earth, flung up by a powerful explosion. But the outline of the hill was way too strange and there was some kind of yellow pipe sticking out of it.

'Let's take a look!' Chloe said to him.

There were no Orks or people anywhere near. Grim swung the car round.

'It's an elephant!' Chloe whispered when they got closer. 'A brown elephant!'

'Not an elephant, a mammoth,' Grim corrected her. 'They sent them in against us from the left flank. Many brave lads laid down their lives here.'

The mammoth was lying on its side. The grass around it was covered with black, baked mud – Orkish blood, mingled with soil. The crushed bodies had already been cleared away. Judging from the size of the dark patch, the mammoth had trampled on the infantry entirely at will. Grim drove round the patch slowly, trying not to ride onto it.

The mammoth's belly was slashed open. Evidently it had slipped in the bloody slurry and fallen on its side, and then the Orkish heroes had managed to reach its guts.

The guts, though, had proved too robust. Some scraps of red biofabric, corrugated tubes and wires were protruding from the long hole in the shaggy belly, and visible behind them was a dark metallic underpan, on which the Orks' weapons had only been able to leave a few scratches.

Then the mammoth's head came into sight, with its lifeless trunk and rakishly curved tusks. Its eyes were open and somehow they looked so alive that it was frightening to peer into them.

And then Grim saw the battle platform attached to the mammoth's back.

The warriors were still there, in their little gondola decorated with shields. They were dressed in leather armour faced with iron plates, and iron helmets. Their faces and arms were covered with wounds from Orkish steel and congealed blood that looked very much like the real thing, but to call them dead would have been an exaggeration.

Instead of tumbling out of their cabin onto the ground, the warriors were protruding from it shamelessly, like huge nails hammered into the back of the electrical beast. Clearly they and the mammoth were a single whole. One of the warriors was still preparing to throw a spear and another was reloading a crossbow, while the head of the third one had been torn off, and some kind of plastic tubular ribbons – with metal inserts and red strands – were dangling out of his neck.

Grim drove away from the mammoth and stopped the car.

'Where to now?' he asked.

'Let's go over that way,' Chloe replied. 'See, where there's something red jutting up.'

'That's where the central front was,' said Grim, pressing on the pedal.

In the central sector, traces of the battle was especially frequent – the ground had been all ploughed up and he had to drive carefully to avoid having a wheel drop into a crater.

Grim skirted round a line of soldiers lying on the ground in their tall hats and bright-red tunics. The soldiers were small dummies, connected together by a frame with an electrical hose. They were crudely made and looked like a fence blown over in a storm. The line had once been mounted on little spiked wheels that were positioned after every third dummy. Grim guessed that this was where the infantry square he had heard about fought, and the stormtroopers had managed to tear the front row off the overall structure at the cost of inconceivable casualties.

In the central sector, the density of fire had been so great that several battle cameras that happened to be in the shells' trajectory had been shot down. It wasn't likely that any of the Orkish heroes who fought here had survived.

Several ruined vampire's nests drifted past the jeep. They could see the vampires in them, half-risen from under the ground – their power must have been cut off just at the moment when they were preparing to jump out onto the surface. The people's shells were to blame for this too – they had severed the cable. The vampires had big yellow eyes that looked like the rear lights of a jeep. Complicated levers and springs could be divined under their black cloaks. They were still spine-chilling to look at even now, but in the smoke and semi-darkness they must really have driven Orks out of their minds.

At last the signs of battle came to an end. Grim drove on and soon the sky was partially obscured by the wall that enclosed the Circus. Right in front of it there was a strip of old concrete, with grass growing out of the cracks in it. They had driven right across Orkish Slava.

'What are those pieces of paper lying around everywhere?' asked Chloe.

'Documents for bloodstaining,' Grim replied. 'Only they're useless...'

He couldn't take his eyes off the wall. There was no Orkish plasterwork on it here, and its original rounded form was visible – the wall was like a gigantic wave, frozen an instant before it hit the shore. This fall had been going on for many centuries: the grey concrete was covered in cracks, but so far time had not been able to do anything to it.

Grim couldn't even imagine the gigantic machines capable of constructing something like that. True, at school someone had told him that in ancient times construction work wasn't performed by machines, but by tiny little beetles invisible to the eye, and to an onlooker it seemed as if the walls were growing by themselves. But no one knew if this was true or not, because the only thing left of the ancient buildings was their vitrified foundations. And the Orks themselves built with wood and brick. Not so very long ago they had still known how to make decent concrete blocks, but now they turned out worse and worse all the time.

'That's it,' said Grim. 'Now what, shall we go back?'

Chloe thought a bit.

'Get out,' she told him.

'What for?'

'Let's wave our arms about. The camera directed us in here for some reason.'

'Which direction shall we wave them in?'

'Just upwards. Only straighten up your cap.'

'What for?'

'Bernard-Henri used to say that a modern man – if he's not an Ork, of course – should be sizing up the way he looks all the time, and act as if he's being filmed. Because the shooting can start at any moment.'

'What makes you think there's a camera up there?'

'There might not be one,' said Chloe. 'But we have to act as if there is one. And then they'll definitely come for us.'

'It's kind of stupid,' Grim muttered.

'And you're so very smart,' replied Chloe. 'But where would we be now if I'd listened to you?'

Grim could have said a lot about that, but he decided not to argue. He opened the door and got out of the car.

Walking over to him, Chloe put her arm round his shoulder and told him:

'Now raise you head, smile and wave your hand.'

Grim squinted at her.

There was already a smile on Chloe's face – such a wide, toothy smile that there was no point in asking if it was sincere or not. She looked into the grey cloud and waved her hand. Grim tried to copy her smile (it didn't turn out all that well, of course) and also waved his open hand through the air a few times. He felt like a total idiot and soon lowered his hand, but Chloe hissed through her smile:

'Wave, you dimwit!'

After another minute even Chloe got fed up of waving. Grim saw the bewilderment and anguish in her face.

And then a miracle happened.

Right in front of them a triangular door suddenly opened, then flipped downward, turning into a short ramp. The ramp led into mysterious semi-darkness. In there, beyond the slightest possible doubt, a new world began. And the entrance to it had been hidden in mid-air, only a metre above the ground – hidden so well that Grim could easily have banged his head against it if he had taken another couple of steps.

Standing on the threshold of the new world was a very fat man, his arms round a huge bunch of flowers. He was dressed in a broad, brightly coloured dressing-gown, and he had the same kind of baseball cap on his head as Grim, with a silver knot and the word 'CINEWS' on it. His genial face radiated happiness. He looked as if he was terribly glad to see Grim and Chloe – or he simply knew that he was being filmed by several invisible cameras at the same time.

The first thing he did was make a strange, extremely energetic movement – throwing his arms apart and sort of nudging the flowers with his belly. Grim and Chloe were showered with a fragrant, multicoloured rain.

'Hello, my friends!' said the fat man. 'Greetings, Chloe! Greetings, Grim! My name is Damilola Karpov and we have been acquainted with each other at a distance for many, many days. You were promised that you would live among people. Did you think you had been forgotten? But people always keep their word. Welcome to Big Byz!'

PART 2.

ASHES OF THE GLOOMY

The ancient Orks and the late Bernard-Henri weren't the only ones who liked to talk about power and truth. An advert for assault cameras makes the same claim: power is where the Pravda is (if you didn't know, *pravda* is the Old Russian word for truth). Well, the same goes for my Hannelore. That is, in case anyone still hasn't caught on yet, it's not where stoned butts with their worries and munchies jangle their rusty iron, but where the invisible eye of people with caring hearts hangs in the air.

Apparently Grim had never realised this, but he had been saved by the CINEWS Inc. baseball cap he was wearing when he drove into Orkish Slava.

At first the senior sommeliers were going to neatly blot the young Ork out, together with his ambiguous media past. If they had wanted to take only Chloe into the future I would, of course, have obeyed the order, and Kaya would have had to look for a new metaphorical ... symbolic ... I've forgotten what the surologists call it.

These shots hadn't gone into a snuff and such a thing was permissible from the religious point of view. And Chloe's appearance at Orkish Slava could have been reshot from scratch for the news. No problems were anticipated with this, and Grim would most likely have been wiped right there in the Circus, seeing as

233

the corpses were still being cleared away and there were places available in the mass grave if anyone wanted one – or even if he didn't. Then this whole story would have turned out differently.

But one of the senior sommeliers who were monitoring the incoming material liked the look of Grim's head in our uniform baseball cap. Apparently it was a good match for his bruises. They contacted Alena-Libertina. She didn't object.

Not only did the old witch not object, she immediately started coming up with creative ideas. She gave the order for me to go down in the trailer to get the Orkish couple in person, since she wanted to shoot the touching moment of meeting. I had to put Hannelore on autopilot and Kaya on pause, and take the tube urgently to the bay. But because I had to shave before the shoot, the Orks had to drive around the Circus for a while.

The meeting went well – I really looked pretty good on the manitou. Kaya admitted that afterwards.

We didn't speak all the way up, except for Grim asking me politely: 'How's the time?' I didn't really understand exactly what he meant and replied with a polite banality, saying that there was never enough time, so it should be used sparingly.

There was a film crew waiting for us topside. The Orks were washed off, dressed in fashionable, clean clothes and given a short briefing about what they could and couldn't say on camera. Grim was worried when they took away his notepad with the poems, but they told him that was the procedure in quarantine.

After that the rescued Orks were presented to mankind. To remind everyone who they were, they played the pre-war shots, with Bernard-Henri standing beside Chloe with his staff in his hand – in the full splendour of the authority granted to him by his conscience and his M-vitamins. Then they showed the Orks who were bearing down on him being torn to shreds by my bursts of fire – they hadn't played that in full before. The commentator explained that the Orks were attempting to use underage civilians as a living shield, and only the skill of our battle pilots... Our thanks to the warriors of the sky... Blah-blah-blah...

Well, thanks are a big deal. But I'd rather take a bonus.

They showed a photograph of my Hannelore and kept me in the frame for a while, announcing that I was the one who rescued the Orkish couple. They put in a close-up of Grim and Chloe shaking my hands – the girl even gave me a peck on the cheek.

And then they immediately cut to the breaking news and the presenter announced the woeful story of the demise of the celebrated discoursemonger: he had supposedly been killed together with the legendary Trig when the cowardly authorities blew up the first Orkish pupo in his own home (I'll tell you about this Trig a little bit later – but for now I'll just remark that this grotesque announcement actually came pretty close to the truth). The newsreader surmised that Bernard-Henri had hoped his presence there would protect Trig – but even this had failed to halt the Orkish machine of repression and murder.

They played the key sequence – what was left of the house after the rocket salvo. Then they put up a bit of archive material – some Ganjaberserk with a brutal face talking on a mobile phone. And after that they showed the motorenwagen that Bernard-Henri had managed to give to the young Orks just before he died, so that they could escape. There was a distinct whiff of the next war in the air – although there was still at least a year to go until then.

The programme about the rescued Orks naturally merged into a memorial to Bernard-Henri – the viewer adores that kind of spontaneity in live broadcasting. They put up selected shots of the late discoursemonger, read out a few excerpts from *Les Feuilles Mortes*, set his silently grimacing face in a black frame of mourning... The universe now officially had one philosopher less. I just kept feeling more and more amazed: taking out that much garbage all in one go – that takes some doing...

Then the manitous lingered on a close-up of Grim and Chloe's faces contorted in grief – they didn't just turn pale, they actually started shaking in grief and horror, that sort of thing can't be faked. But the humane benevolence of mankind came to their aid even here.

It turned out that Bernard-Henri had managed to adopt Chloe under Orkish law. He always did that anyway, so that his bimbo would be allowed into the Green Zone – because it was never for long in any case. But the news didn't say anything about that. Bernard-Henri didn't have any heirs, and so Chloe was solemnly presented with a symbolic key to his home on camera and the viewers were informed that I, as a neighbour and friend of the deceased philosopher, would take his place as the Orkish couple's mentor – and would help the new citizens of Big Byz get their bearings in an unfamiliar world. I should say that this was as much news to me as it was to Grim and Chloe – but I didn't object. Any job you do for CINEWS Inc. comes with good pay, and immediately after a war pilots don't have a lot of work.

Basically, it made a great show.

Naturally, no one bothered to ask the Orks what the relation-ship between them was and if they were going to live together – all that was bracketed out, left as an elegantly transparent innuendo, in perfect accord with the juvenile rule 'don't look – don't see'. On the other hand, after the shoot, Alena-Libertina expressed a desire to meet Grim and Chloe in person, so that she could be involved in their development.

Chloe spent no less than three hours in her office – and Grim had to wait out in the corridor. Alena-Libertina postponed her meeting with him for later. I think that after her acquaintance with the late Bernard-Henri, Chloe was no longer surprised by any human weaknesses. If Grim realised anything (and I'm by no means certain that he did), he gave no sign of it.

By the way, it's long been a mystery to me why rich, aging lesbians carry on chasing after live young floozies until their hair turns grey and don't just live a contented life with suras. Some people claim that this is no longer a matter of amorous inclination, since by the age of fifty-five a lesbian metamorphoses into a sex vampire – a predator on the life-force of others, with cold fish's blood in her veins. But I wouldn't risk repeating these words in public – they're not much more than a step away from cynicism.

And so Kaya and I acquired new neighbours.

That evening I showed Kaya a recording of the entire broadcast. She watched it with her eyes popping out of her head, I think she even stopped blinking. And when she found out that now Grim and Chloe were going to live less than forty metres away from us (Bernard-Henri and I used to walk along the corridor to visit each other), I realised from the way she looked at me that if the war down below was over, the one in my home had only just begun.

And that was how it turned out.

If the consultant on sura behaviour hadn't warned me in advance about the 'symbolic rival' effect I might very soon have inflicted on my little darling the exact kind of serious mechanical damage that isn't covered by the manufacturer's guarantee.

Of course, I knew that her efforts were exclusively intended to put me through the torments of jealousy. Feeling offended with her was as stupid as feeling offended with a kettle or a rice cooker. But she had nibbled her way into my heart so subtly with her little white teeth that I clean forgot about that every time.

One morning I was woken by her gazing at me intently. That often happens with us. But usually her expression as she looks at me is the same as if I was a janissary suffering from leprosy, who's snatched her from the conservatory where she was learning to play the harp and dumped her in a harem that doubles as a piggery, where the prime of her youth will now be spent. I find this terribly arousing, but I never tell her that. As soon as she realises how much I like it, she'll immediately take this small joy away from me, and there'll be nothing I can do about it: she'll be compelled to do that by the same sheer, unbounded bitchiness that prompts the look she gives me in the morning.

But the look she was giving me this time was quite different – somehow humbled and submissive, I'd even say imploring – as if she had come to terms with the harem-piggery and decided to fight to sell her labour power on better terms. This surprised me, and I propped myself upon my elbows.

'What is it?'

'Sweet Daddy,' she said, 'have you ever given any thought to the fact that I've got practically no decent clothes?'

That was perfectly true. All she had were several sets of lacy underwear that I liked to tear off her sometimes, and two fluffy dressing gowns – a blue one with zigzags and a green one with little rabbits. For reasons that weren't entirely clear, her settings compelled her to pretend that she couldn't stand the dressing gown with the zigzags.

'I like you naked best of all,' I said.

'That's you,' she replied. 'But what if there's someone else? What if you have visitors, and I'm sitting here in my dressing gown? Or let's say you decide to let me out somewhere after all – what do I do, go in my lacy knickers?'

'You fool,' I exploded, 'do you know how many more years I'll be paying off the loan for you? Maybe you'd like me to go around in my shorts? And anyway, where are you planning to go?'

'Nowhere yet,' she said sombrely.

I already thought the incident was over and done with. But it turned out that she had calculated all the moves a long way ahead, like a chess grandmaster.

I'd absolutely forgotten that I was completely in her power now. No, she couldn't deny me her caresses. Or rather, such a denial was envisaged in the instruction manual, and was... hmm, how can I put it... included in the range of services. Her tears merely testified that her settings had been adjusted correctly. This sort of thing happened quite often with us – that's why people keep their suras on maximum bitchiness.

But I'd completely forgotten about dopamine resonance.

Or rather, I remembered it very well. But for some reason I thought that since I owned Kaya, lock, stock and barrel, I owned this service too. I'd lost sight of the fact that I had absolutely no idea of how she achieved the effect, and I wouldn't be able to get my way by force. There wasn't a single word about dopamine resonance in the manual. Or in the screen dictionaries either. It was an illegal operating mode. The likeable consultant surologist probably wouldn't even have discussed the subject with me.

All day long I was haunted by a sense of dark foreboding. And that evening I discovered that it hadn't deceived me.

'No,' she said in reply to my affectionate request. 'Forget all about that, you fat arse.'

'What does that mean – forget!' I roared, flying into a fury. 'That's what I want!'

'Complain to the manufacturer then.'

'Yes, I will,' I said.

'Go on, go on. After that they'll give me the kind of upgrade that will make me forget everything. They'll reflash me over the air port. You won't even notice when and how it happens.'

'They have no right.'

'And how will you find out?'

'I'll complain,' I said uncertainly.

'Who to and what about?'

I said nothing.

'What do you want with this dopamine resonance anyway?' she continued cheerfully. 'Why don't you use the "rape" feature? That always works so magnificently for you . . .'

And at that point I finally realised what an interesting dilemma I was facing.

There wasn't the slightest doubt that it was the 'maximum bitchiness' setting talking to me right now. I could alter that parameter at any moment. But then the dopamine resonance mode, which only became available in this position, would disappear too. So Kaya had told me – but I had to take what she said on trust, for the simple reason that she was my only source of information. Officially there was no such thing as 'dopamine resonance'.

I had already checked this out as thoroughly as absolutely possible – there was no publicly available information at all. It wasn't even mentioned in the shitstorms or the forums, although there was separate mention of both dopamine and resonance. And if it really was such a great secret, the company, indeed, could simply reflash her brains without bothering to consult with me.

It was totally bizarre, but now she could blackmail me.

She had the carrot. And every time she refused to give me that carrot was equivalent to a blow from the stick. Of course, I could eliminate her power over me with a single turn of a knob – but when her virtual instrument of torture disappeared, it would take with it the sweetest-tasting carbohydrate compound that my lips had ever touched.

There was nothing, absolutely nothing that I could do. And there was no one I could blame. All this had been done to me, a living, suffering human being – by a soulless algorithm, which I myself had adjusted like that for the fun of it!

She kept her eyes riveted on me. Apparently my train of thought showed in my face – because at a certain point she smiled sweetly and asked:

'I think sweet Daddy understands everything now?'

'You want to go on pause?' I threatened.

'Go ahead,' she said, 'and after that I recommend you to go to the privy and switch me over to "cloud of tenderness". Then I'll start bringing you your slippers. And panting noisily until you come, you fat cretin.'

I half-rose with a menacing air.

'Just one more word...'

She laughed spitefully.

'What are you going to do to me? Inflict pain on me? You really are a fool, Damilola. In this entire show, there's only one performer – you. A fact that you regularly remind me about – for some purpose that is, by the way, absolutely incomprehensible, because such an action totally demolishes the logic of the utterance. That is, of course, if you understand what I'm talking about at this moment. Who are you trying to frighten right now?'

I didn't need any help from her to understand the infernal humour of my situation. But just then a happy thought occurred to me. After all, a human being will always be smarter than a machine, I thought smugly.

I already knew how to trick this brazen daughter of a rice cooker. I'd remembered about maximum spirituality. It presupposes obligatory compassion and fellow human feeling. I could try to initiate programme failure by attacking on this flank.

I weighed my words carefully for a few seconds, so that I wouldn't ruin everything accidentally. And not until I had precisely calculated the possible effect did I risk opening my mouth.

'Wait, Kaya, wait... You and me – we're not enemies, are

we? Remember this – at bottom, I'm just an unhappy, lonely man. You are all that I have. You're causing me pain. Very, very serious pain. You're making me suffer.'

She looked up at me with her eyes full of mistrust. Just at the right moment, because my eyes had gone all wet out of pity for myself.

'Don't you feel sorry for me at all?' I asked.

'I do,' she replied. 'Of course I do, stupid.'

'Then why do you behave like this, my little girl?'

'What about you?' she asked in a thin little voice. 'Why do you behave like this? Do you really not give a damn about how I look? You tell me every day how beautiful I am, but all I've got is two bath robes, and that's all...'

And tears welled up in her eyes too, the crystal-pure tears that I sometimes even allowed myself to lick away – admittedly, under slightly different circumstances. But that sort of thing would have been inappropriate right now, and I understood that very well.

The fear of losing my fortuitously discovered happiness sharpened my intuition quite incredibly. I sensed that telling her a rubber woman could manage very well with just one pair of lacy panties would be a fatal error: her threshold triggers would immediately flip her from a position of vague compassion to the confrontational scenarios of maximum bitchiness. I would have lost my Waterloo in five minutes flat. What I had to do was slip between Scylla and Charybdis in such a way that the door to happiness wouldn't be slammed shut in my face forever. Possibly, I thought, I should give a bit of ground...

'All right,' I said. 'I'll buy you something. Later. But right now...'

'No,' she replied. 'First you'll buy me everything – and not just something, but what I tell you. I'll buy it myself. You'll just pay.'

242

'All right,' I said. 'Tomorrow morning we'll sit down together in front of the manitou, and...'

She walked over, sat down beside me and sank her hands into my hair. I have to tell you that this simple movement filled me with greater excitement and joy than even the most sophisticated bedroom tricks. There was some point to maximum bitchiness after all – and oh, what a point it was...

'Give me some money,' she whispered in my ear. 'I'll do everything myself.'

'How much do you want, kitten?' I asked, putting my arm round her waist.

'Three hundred thousand manitou.'

Whoah. That kind of money would buy a whole heap of glad rags. Far more than any normal rubber woman needed.

'A hundred thousand,' I whispered. 'And only because I love you more than life itself.'

She slapped the hand that had already crept onto her thigh. 'Two hundred.'

'A hundred and fifty,' I said, 'and that's my last word.'

'A hundred and eighty.'

'A hundred and fifty. And we can't even afford that.'

She bit me gently on my ear lobe – exactly the right way and just where I liked it.

'A hundred and seventy-five. And in that case – right now.'

I couldn't believe that I'd got off so lightly.

'All right,' I said. 'It's a deal.'

'Pilot's honour?' she asked with a smile.

She looked so fine at that moment, I even screwed my eyes up in pleasure.

'Pilot's honour,' I repeated.

'I've always trusted pilots ever since I was little,' she said, handing me a piece of paper folded in two.

I unfolded it. There were handwritten numbers inside.

'What's this?'

'My wallet,' she replied. 'For buying things on the network. Please put a hundred and seventy-five thousand in it right now, as you promised.'

'When did I promise that it would be right now?'

'I said, "A hundred and seventy-five. And in that case – right now". And you swore on your pilot's honour.'

'I thought the other thing would be right now,' I said, bewildered.

'The other thing will happen too,' she said, 'but afterwards. Come on, darling, pay a little visit to that fortress of yours.'

'Darling...' When was the last time I heard her say that?

I trailed off to the happiness room, wondering along the way if I ought to have her entire system reinstalled and then try resetting her in this mode... In principle, the company was obliged to do that kind of thing. But if Kaya was right and the dopamine resonance was simply a programme bug, the new version might not have it.

Was it worth risking this happiness wrested from life by a miracle? And then, after reflashing, it wouldn't be my Kaya anymore. Possibly, I thought, the whole point is in the problems that she creates for me and it's them that make the reward so sweet and so delectable. Perhaps she simply imitates to perfection the ancient female art of seduction, never allowing me to gather my wits and realise what's going on... If that's it, the skill with which she goes about her rubbery business is simply divine and it would be the height of stupidity to dismantle this delicate, uniquely structured clump of algorithms.

And then again, to be quite honest, she hadn't really asked for all that much.

I knew people in the motorenwagen business that spent more than that on Orkish prostitutes in a single evening.

Once seated on my throne of majesty, I entered the password

244

and punched the numbers on her piece of paper into the glimmering void. It was an anonymous numbered account, opened two days earlier – anyone at all could make purchases from it. Online no one knows if you're a rubber woman, I thought as I transferred the money. Will I have to pay her for every time now? Or is this a one-off act of intimidation? We'll see. But in any case it would be better to be polite and obliging with her. And no sarcasm, that's the main thing, no sarcasm. That's what they hate most.

An hour later I was lying on my back, totally drained and happy. What I had just experienced couldn't be bought for a hundred and seventy-five thousand. It was priceless.

It wasn't a matter of the physical pleasure, of course – that comes down to mechanical spasms, to a simple sneezing reflex, transferred to other zones of the body, and an excessive interest in this fleeting experience is only appropriate in the early stages of puberty. If you think about it, there isn't really any pleasure in so-called 'physical delight', it's a retrospective retouch job by our memory, acting in the service of the reproductive instinct (which means that calling it 'our memory' is really very naïve).

It was a matter of something quite different. Something in what Kaya had allowed me to experience had launched me to inner heights that I had never known before. It seems to me that man only rarely ascends to such exalted altitudes, otherwise it would certainly have found expression in poems and songs. Or perhaps this is precisely what people have striven to express in art throughout history, and every time they become convinced that this is an impossible task. Possibly the mystics of ancient times attained something like it – and they thought they had approached the chambers of Manitou Himself.

I understand how uninformative this sounds – 'inner heights' and 'exalted altitudes'. Especially coming from a pilot. But how

245

else to explain it? Kaya had put it best herself, when she spoke of a swing 'going over the top'.

In case anyone doesn't know, a 'swing' is a kind of wooden boat suspended from a fixed horizontal bar on bearings from a motorenwagen – there are lots of them in Slava. How many times I've flown over them, and even filmed them once for the programme 'Behind the Facade of Tyranny'. These swings can rise to a certain height, and then they start striking against a wooden stop.

The human body, engaged in the pursuit of pleasure, is like these swings. We think we achieve the highest possible joy when we feel the swing shudder as it strikes against the wooden board of the stop. And that's the way things are – in a twisted, prison-cell sort of sense.

What had happened to me was this: some confident hand had swung the boat so hard that it had knocked the board out and soared higher and higher, and then turned a complete circle – and instead of falling back in the old familiar way after taking several small steps towards unattainable happiness, I went rushing straight after it, circle after circle, not letting it get away any longer.

And it wasn't that I had managed to catch a quivering spot of sunlight or actually register for residence inside a mirage. No, the mendacious falsehood of all the crude, gaudy lures that nature dangles in front of us had never been as obvious as it was during those seconds. But from the forbidden space that my swing soared into after smashing all the barriers, the view of the world and of myself that opened up was so strange and new ...

A completely different perspective.

As if I had spotted from altitude the dentate fence of an Orkish park, with a free space behind it, where no human foot had trodden for many centuries. And I suddenly realised that in

246

true reality there is neither the happiness that we chase after all our lives, nor grief, but only this supreme point, where there are no questions and no doubts – and where man does not dare to stay, because this is the very place from which Manitou evicted him for his sins.

'Why are you crying again?' Kaya asked.

In the half-light of the bedroom her face seemed to be drawn on silk with ink.

'I don't know how to live now.'

'Don't worry,' said Kaya, 'we'll come to an arrangement about everything.'

Women, including rubber ones, understand everything in their own earthly way. And it's pointless trying to explain to them that what you had in mind was something quite different, something exalted. Especially when it was exactly what they thought.

'Are we going to haggle every time now?'

'No,' said Kaya. 'Everything will be free. Like it was before. You can even beat me and torture me, and I'll still do the same thing. But you have to agree to three conditions.'

'What are they?'

'Firstly,' she said, 'I want to be able to go out sometimes. Disable the spatial blocker.'

'And secondly?' I asked sullenly.

'Don't put me on pause.'

'And thirdly?'

'I want to meet Grim.'

Right.

So that's what she needs the clothes for.

She was planning to start flirting with Grim right under my eyes, to step up the pressure on my poor wounded heart even more. When I realised that, it felt as if some delicate little glass component quietly crunched inside me.

Yes, she could be intelligent and perceptive, she could astound

247

me with her intellect, she could be more cunning and even wiser than me – but no matter how long I gazed into this perfect simulacrum of a soul, no matter how many miraculous meanings I discovered in it, no matter how completely I was deceived by the flowers blossoming on it, the root of it was still bitchiness, infinite and boundless. Always and in everything.

For a second I came close to going down on my knees and whispering:

'My darling, why do this? Why do you want to act out so mercilessly this idiotic programme forcibly beaten into you by nature and society, in order to inflict more and more suffering on me? What are you trying to hide behind the waves of horror and pain that you stir up in my soul? Your own emptiness? Your own non-existence? I know about these things and I have nothing against them. Why can't you simply give me the gift of pleasure and live a peaceful life – or at least pretend to live it – beside me? Why do you constantly fan the flames of the suffering that is consuming me?'

But I was already familiar enough with the rules of this abhorrent game to understand that you didn't say that sort of thing to a woman. Which meant that you didn't say it to a sura either.

'So you agree?' she asked.

'Let me think about it,' I said. 'It's not all that simple.'

The room where Grim and Chloe were checked by the doctors was like a wardrobe, with mirrors on the inside. The make-up room where they were prepared for the shoot looked like the Urkagan's boudoir in the memorable pre-war clip (the only thing missing was the bloodstained rubber woman in the background). But from the confused, glittering welter of the first few hours, all that stuck in Grim's memory was the shabby, curving corridor that they were led along from one studio to another.

The corridor was lined with black panels of carbon with holes in them. There were wires dangling about untidily on all sides, and white notices on the panels themselves:

3D PROJECTOR MAINTENANCE
SORRY FOR THE INCONVENIENCE

'This is how everything here really looks,' Damilola said with an incomprehensible giggle as they walked past the announcements. He was probably joking, but Grim really believed that the new world consisted of corridors like this.

And also of people, proud Byzantines, 'children of Manitou and wearers of the toga'. Although almost none of them really wore a toga. They dressed in anything at all. Practically like the Orks, only 'shabbier', as Chloe whispered.

When the Byzantine cameras weren't at work, the people were polite and as indifferent as walls. But when the cameras were switched on, the pressure was on Grim.

He knew that his manner in front of the camera was too tense – and that very knowledge made him tenser still. When he was answering questions he hesitated and tried to speak as little as possible. But that was in keeping with the image of an Orkish soldier with a scorched face who'd had a hard life, so all in all everything went off pretty well.

Chloe, on the contrary, blossomed in the bright beams of attention, and even her grief for Bernard-Henri proved extremely photogenic. When she was handed the symbolic key to his home and the audience started applauding, even after all the tears she had already shed, she still managed to eke out just one more touching little tear – exactly the right size to be noticeable on a manitou screen.

Damilola looked tired. He left after promising that the real introduction to the new world would begin in a few days' time, after the refugees had settled in and had a rest.

After Alena-Libertina had concluded her introductory chat with Chloe, a polite lady from the reception committee took the young Orks to settle into their new home.

The journey from the shooting stage to their home took only five minutes. The ease with which they reached it was simply magical – travelling on the metrolift (or, as people here called it, the 'tube'), a small, cosy cabin with four seats. It was called just like an ordinary lift by pressing a button in the corridor, and after that it set off along any given route. Grim tried to find out from the female attendant how these capsules, upholstered in velour fabric and smelling of violets, managed not to crash into each other as they hurtled along the same pipes – but she confessed that she didn't know that herself, she only knew how to enter the address required on a manitou.

To reach Bernard-Henri's home they only had to walk about twenty metres from the lift. The way in was simply a door in a grey and black wall. No key was required, not even a symbolic one – the door handle had already been re-coded for the palms of Grim and Chloe's hands. It was a perfectly ordinary door. But behind it...

It wasn't that Bernard-Henri's apartment looked so very huge and chic, but it was so unorkish that to Grim and Chloe it seemed like the dwelling of a magician or a god.

It had two levels with four small rooms, and downstairs there was a little garden, set out on something like a terrace or wide balcony. The little garden was enclosed by a mossy brick wall – the only thing here that resembled Orkish architecture.

However, despite the highly convincing patches of damp and

the chipped surface, this mossy brickwork immediately aroused Grim's suspicion. He examined the wall closely and right down at ground level he found a spot where there was something black and matt, protruding from under the bricks. The bricks and the moss were simply an embossed veneer glued onto plastic. Once he realised that, Grim spotted repeated patterns and patches that were the same shape. But the veneer had been made so skilfully that the moss felt alive to the touch.

The little garden also provoked doubts. No, the flowers and little trees growing out of the earth were real. Well, almost all of them. But the earth that they rose out of ... After poking a dry branch into it a few times, Grim realised that there was some kind of socket under his feet, into which modular blocks with plants were set.

'You're a fool,' Chloe told him calmly when he informed her about his discovery. 'Why don't you just sit in a deckchair and feel glad – *There's my little garden* ... But now you'll be thinking *it isn't genuine*.'

'You'll be thinking *it isn't genuine* too,' said Grim.

'No,' Chloe replied. 'Am I a total fool, or what? This is what I've been heading towards all my life. I'll be thinking *there's my little garden*.'

'But you know it isn't genuine.'

'And that's fine,' said Chloe. 'I got tired of genuine things when I was still a kid.'

Bernard-Henri's home stood on a high spot and the view from the windows was incredible – stretching out in every direction, for as far as the eye could see, were whimsically shaped fields and yellow and green hills overgrown with cypress trees. Old white houses were scattered here and there. Lying in the fields were large cylinders that looked like sawn-up logs but were rolled out of sun-scorched hay. And they could also see a river,

251

blue mountains in the distance, and a sky with giant, serene clouds drifting across it.

A summer that was only the tiniest bit short of eternity.

As Grim contemplated this beauty, ideas for poems kept occurring to him, but he felt too lazy to write them down – the world in the window had such an aura of peace about it.

Despite the traces of agricultural activity, there were no people to be seen anywhere. But there were many details that indicated their presence. For instance, smoke from the chimney of a house standing on a hill, or a windmill – a squat round tower with its latticed vanes, set in a cross and slowly rotating.

The only thing was, you couldn't set out for a walk into this fairy-tale expanse. There was no way out there – the only door out of the apartment led into the corridor to the tube. If you leaned down over the parapet of the garden-cum-balcony, you could see bushes growing below that looked very tough and prickly. Theoretically it was possible to jump down. But Grim knew that it wasn't a good idea – the people in the reception committee had warned him about that on the very first day.

Of course, no wasteful empty space could be left inside the offglobe. The nature of the view outside the window was the same as that of the picture on a manitou – it was an incredibly convincing three-dimensional illusion. But by now Grim had realised that Chloe was right and there really wasn't any need to remind oneself about this every other minute.

There was one thing that wasn't clear – how far away from the window opening was the equipment that created the mirage? Judging from the faint smell of hot plastic, it was very close, perhaps two or three metres away. Grim was even going to check if a long stick that he had found on the balcony would run into anything if he thrust it out a long way. But then he wisely decided not to test the new world's solidity – especially since there was undoubtedly more than enough in it that was real.

The rooms had elegant furniture in them, the kind that you could only see in Slava in the Urkagan's residence. Oil paintings on the walls depicted bright-coloured splotches that looked like something between fireworks or the flashes you got from bad durian – down below, things like that could only be found in the art section of the Museum of the Ancestors.

But there were a lot of things that didn't exist down below at all.

The mattresses were made out of some strange sponge-like material. Not only did they feel soft and warm, they kind of enveloped your body, remembering its shape and maintaining the right temperature – Grim went to sleep and woke up in the same position, without having turned over in the night even once.

There was no need to cook food. You could choose it on the kitchen manitou – in practically the same way as setting the route of a journey in the tube. A few minutes later the order appeared in a brightly-lit little window under the kitchen table – it was called a 'pneumoship'. Grim had never eaten anything that tasted so good.

They could throw their dirty clothes into a different window in the kitchen. They slithered off downwards and soon came back, clean and dry. And best of all, everywhere – the bedrooms, the kitchen and the happiness room – was always clean and fresh, as if the floor and the walls washed themselves. Sooner or later, any dirty stain disappeared – all that was left was a subtle scent of violets, like in the velour-upholstered cabin of the metrolift.

Grim was slightly disappointed by the manitous in the apartment. He had heard that people had three-dimensional ones, but Bernard-Henri only had several large flat screens, almost exactly the same as in the public offices in Urkaine. Grim didn't even know how to switch them on.

The people from the reception committee had taken away all of Bernard-Henri's personal things, leaving as mementoes only his book (a thick brick entitled *Les Feuilles Mortes*) and a large black-and-white photograph of the former owner in an expensive frame of extinct birch wood. Grim didn't try to read the book, because it was in Old French, and he turned the discoursemonger's photograph face down. But after three days of actively settling into the new space, Chloe discovered other traces of the former owner.

Her attention was caught by one of the pictures hanging on the wall. It was a canvas about one metre high and two wide. The image on it was rather strange: something like a milky-white ocean, with a red and brown whirlpool swirling down into it. The words '*mon souvenir*' had been crudely painted in black straight across the ocean, and were also being sucked into the whirlpool. Most likely in some ancient language they meant the same as the Church English phrase 'my memory' on the little tag attached to the frame.

The picture differed from the others by being attached very firmly to the wall. Chloe pressed against the side of the frame several times, trying to understand how it was fixed to the wall, and suddenly the picture swung out gently, turning into a door concealing a secret cupboard.

'Grim!' Chloe called out in fright.

The moment the picture-door opened, the manitou standing beside it came on, music started playing and a pleasant male voice began to sing in an unfamiliar language. But Grim and Chloe didn't even look at the screen, they were so astounded by what they had already seen.

Inside, it was like a picture in a picture – something like an installation of various items in the shallow niche. The longer Grim and Chloe peered at it, the harder it was to believe that their eyes weren't deceiving them.

It looked most of all like an ancient grave – the way they're shown in articles on archaeology. The grave was brightly lit by lamps at the sides. In the upper section there were two skulls attached to the wall. In the lower section there were two tambourines, a red one and a blue one, both adorned with little bells. All the rest of the surface was lined with fallen leaves, glued to the walls with transparent lacquer.

The skulls had been painstakingly polished and also covered with lacquer – and set into the bone on the forehead of each of them was a precious crystal, glinting brightly and splitting the light into a host of tiny little rainbows.

'Diamonds,' Chloe whispered.

However, Grim was stunned by something else.

There was woman's skin stretched over the tambourines. The fact that it was precisely woman's skin was made clear by the place from which (or rather, together with which) it had been flayed off. Even the hairs had been preserved – on the red tambourine they were a neatly trimmed ginger triangle, and on the blue one an amorphous dark-chestnut mop. These intimate scalps had clearly been treated with some kind of preservative compound, because the skin looked fresh, without even the slightest sign of decay.

Plaits of woman's hair were attached to the skulls: a ginger one hung down onto the red tambourine, and a dark one onto the blue tambourine. The plaits ended in paper labels – '*Une Autre No. 1*' and '*Une Autre No. 3*'.

'But where's number two?' Grim asked, simply in order to say something.

'Number two is me,' said Chloe.

Grim realised that she was right – just enough space had been left between the two skulls, and another tambourine could have fitted in below it. Lying at that spot now was a plump paper bundle.

Grim unwrapped it and saw a sheaf of tattered photos. They all showed practically the same thing – a table, with several people sitting at it. They included policemen, doctors and priests – and they were all looking at Grim as if just a moment ago he had done something very bad. The images differed in the shape of the table, the colour of the tablecloth, the number of people in the group, the way they were dressed and – most important of all – the expressions on their faces, which ranged from squeamish and bored to dumbfounded and furious: there were as many gradations as there were snapshots. There were even several black-and-white photographs, treated with sepia.

On the back of the photos they saw blurred letters: 'F', 'T', 'B', 'A', 'J' and others – sometimes grouped in twos or threes.

'What kind of markings are those?' asked Chloe.

'I don't know,' said Grim.

He rolled the photos impregnated with human fat and sweat back up in the paper and put the bundle back in its place.

The song that the door had switched on as it opened played to the end and immediately started again. Grim finally looked at the manitou.

It was showing a black-and-white clip from the Age of the Ancient Films – so old that the monochrome shot might not be due to the director's caprice, but the technical limitations of the period.

The clip had no special gimmicks – a young man in a jacket was walking across a dark stage and singing something unintelligible, every now and then casting at the viewers the meaningful glance of a cockatoo hypnotising his mate. The text of the song, translated into Church English, was drifting across the lower part of the screen. According to the subtitles the singer was called Serge Gainsbourg and the song was called '*La Chanson de Prévert*'.

Grim peered at the running line of text for a while.

'And day after day my dead lovers just keep on dying,' he said. 'And at the end he sings about how on a certain day they'll finally stop. But it's a strange song altogether.'

'Why?' Chloe asked.

'It's about another song. He probably crammed *The Word on the Word* as a kid too.'

'And what's the other song about?'

'It's about dead leaves. If I understand it right.'

Chloe sighed and looked at the scalps stretched over the tambourines again.

'So that's why he was sorry my hairs are so short. And then he said, "Never mind, you'll be the other Other." I thought he'd just pigged out on that garbage of his...'

She closed the picture door quietly. The manitou immediately went blank and the music stopped.

'What will we do with this?' asked Grim. 'Are we going to tell anyone?'

Chloe shook her head.

'The people have already given us a break,' she said. 'Why should we put them in an awkward position? We'll just forget about it, that's all.'

'You'll be able to forget about that?' Grim asked in disbelief.

'Of course,' said Chloe.

'But how?'

'I just will. Like the pots on the balcony.'

But a day later even Grim had forgotten about the skulls in the secret cupboard. It happened when Bernard-Henri's manitou went online.

Chloe immediately worked out how to buy clothes and everything else straight from the terminal – and she set about fervently spending the settling-in allowance issued by the committee. The pneumoship started spitting identical black packages of all sorts of girlie clothes, one after another, straight out of

257

the wall, while Chloe carried on ordering more without even opening them – and soon her new things were scattered all over the apartment. There was only one way she could stop – by starting to choose clothes for Grim.

She bought an especially large number of different bras – because the Orkish bras gave her calluses, and bras were the hardest thing of all to find down below. Chloe didn't really need one – she had small, firm breasts that could easily have managed without a harness, but she explained to Grim that sexual morality required a woman to be kitted out like this. But then, after studying the catalogue, she came to the conclusion that this norm didn't apply up here.

'It looks like the fashionable girls here walk about without anything,' she said disconcertedly. 'And, would you believe it, they dress like Orkish hookers. But I'd better take a look around first.'

It turned out that clothes and food weren't the only things you could order for delivery, you could even order a hairstyle. Grim didn't believe this was possible at first. But right there in front of him Chloe chose a cut and colour for her hair from the catalogue on the manitou and pressed the 'confirm purchase' button – and soon afterwards a jaunty little package tumbled out of the wall.

Chloe took out a broad plastic ribbon and wrapped it round her wet hair, as the instructions required. The ribbon swelled up with a fearsome hissing sound, as if it was melting, and quickly expanded into a large porous sphere. A few minutes later Chloe pulled it off her head, revealing that her hair was already trimmed, dyed and arranged in a complicated style. Grim simply couldn't imagine how such a thing was possible.

Then Alena-Libertina made contact and Chloe went to her place for a casting audition, from which she didn't return for two days and nights. Left alone, Grim gradually started finding his bearings online.

There was everything there.

Even divination with *The Book of Orkasms*.

Now he didn't have to worry that the book the priest had given him had been left down below. Of course, it wasn't clear if it was right to tell fortunes through a manitou. What if the book's attendant spirits took umbrage?

Grim decided to check this by giving it a try – and he started wondering what to ask about. He ran his eyes round the room several times and remembered Chloe.

This was hardly surprising, because her things were lying around everywhere. They were distributed evenly through the surrounding space in such large numbers that they gave the impression of an attempt to stake a claim to the entire territory at once – even more blatantly than by the ancient custom of wolves.

He counted three bras alone. One was hanging on the back of a chair. Another was lying beside the sofa. The third, neatly folded, was delicately poised – for the time being – on the mantelpiece, between the volume of *Les Feuilles Mortes* and the discoursemonger's inverted photograph. But Grim already had enough military experience to recognise a bridgehead for invasion at first glance.

His thoughts of Chloe were half-pleasant and half-uneasy. The longer Grim thought about her, the less he liked the ideas that occurred to him. And he soon sank into absolutely genuine despondency.

'What is in store for me with Chloe?' – He typed in the question and pressed the 'tell fortune' button.

Strangely enough, the manitou took a long time to think about it. Then a squirrel-skin stretched out on nails appeared on the screen, with the reply crookedly written on it.

Thirty-Six. On Life with a Young Beauty.

In truth, it is the very same as living under the same roof with a goat. And why so?

A beautiful girl torments the heart while she is unattainable. Looking at her, one thinks that to merge with her in love is supreme happiness. For the sake of this, one accepts a compromise with destiny and one's conscience, and there she is – yours. Rejoice, Ork ... However, pleasure is fleeting by its very nature. On the first day you can experience it four times. On the second day – three times. On the third – once or twice. And on the fourth you will not desire it at all, and after that it will bore you for a week.

And where is her beauty? It transpires that now she is a beauty only for the neighbours. And there is nothing to talk to her about, for she is stupid beyond measure. And do not hope that in a few days' time you will desire her anew, as before. You will not manage this – there are no barriers now, and there is no time for temptation to grow. Henceforth to you she is merely a young animal who feeds and eats like all cattle.

But it is with you that she lives! Every day she eats and passes stool, and spreads disorder all around so that it is impossible to forget her for a moment, no matter which way you look.

But if you lose her, you will weep.

Grim's eyes skipped down nervously to the bottom of the squirrel skin.

Yes, it was there.

At an army divination, add: I will not make comparisons with a queerast, for I have never cohabited with one.

BB

When Alena-Libertina told me how much they were going to pay me for helping the young Orkish couple, I was pleasantly surprised. It looked like in CINEWS expenses the payments had been classified under 'secret military activities'.

But after only five minutes of conversation I realised what she was really paying for. She was very keen that no one in GULAG should learn about the circumstances of Bernard-Henri's death. And especially that he died in his own house.

I explained that I needed to know exactly what to keep quiet about and why – otherwise I could let something slip by accident. This argument convinced her, and she came clean about everything. I won't say that I was shaken by what I heard – I had a hunch it was something of the kind. But afterwards life became just slightly more obnoxious.

That pupo Trig was behind it.

I promised a long time ago to say a few words about GULAG – and now I'll have to do it, otherwise my story will be impossible to understand from here on.

Everybody knows the role played in a free society by informal public associations. Especially in a free hedonistic society. In Big Byz, people of a non-traditional orientation are united in the movement known as GULAG.

Ever letter here has a meaning: it's an acronym from the Church English words 'Gay', 'Lesbian', 'Animalist' (in ancient times that was what they called people who fought for animal rights, but political correctness has its own caprices) and 'Gloomy' (that's us, the pupos).

All the other non-traditionals have been put in under the letter

'U', which signifies 'Unspecified', 'Unclassified' or 'Undesignated' – whichever you prefer. These are the so-called 'coverts' (not to be confused with the Orkish police meaning – I realise that I could confuse the reader completely, but the fact that the Orks sometimes call their 'coverts', particularly Ganjaberserks in plain clothes, fags, has nothing to do with the matter). Hiding away under the letter 'U' are all sorts of coprophages and fetishists who don't dare to come all the way out of their poo-smeared closets even in these supremely liberal of times. That's why a special undeclared status was invented for them; it allows them to participate in the group's creative community work without publicising their little eccentricities.

The somewhat illogical sequence of letters in the word 'GULAG' does not signify in any way that we think the coverts are more important than the pupos. The point here is that this beautiful, sonorous word wasn't invented by us. We merely borrowed it from an ancient civilisation that once existed in the same part of Siberia where our offglobe is suspended.

All that is left of the GULAG culture now are the traces of ancient settlements – the camps of the so-called 'Barbed-Wire Age', which can only be made out from the air. I have seen them many times myself. They are simply stripes and rectangular patches: only an archaeologist can explain where the barracks huts were, where the towers were, and where the posts with the barbed wire were.

In reality, we know practically nothing about the tribes that lived here before Siberia was overwhelmed by waves of migration. But the cult of extinct indigenous peoples is a standard fashion in post-technological societies.

We trace our genealogy back to them in an attempt, as it were, to subconsciously convince ourselves that the right of primogeniture belongs to us and not the Orks.

In our society, GULAG is the most important force after the

cinemafia. Or perhaps even the most important. That's what many people think these days – especially those who have seen our latest memoclip. The one featuring a blood-stained note hanging on rainbow-coloured barbed wire:

Don't FUCK
With GULAG!

No one dares to – no one's that stupid. Although, if you think about it, it's a completely illogical message. What else do we fancy should be done to us, loathsome as we are? Except perhaps drown all our exuberant diversity in the dark hollow of the letter 'U'. But I, for instance, don't want to go there.

The sexual minorities won their struggle for equality long ago – and let's be frank, they won it by an absolute landslide. The paradox, however, is that the various sexual minorities are still not entirely equal among themselves – and that, as the discoursemongers explain, is something that should concern every decent individual today. Only for some reason it doesn't bother me, and I don't go to gloomy pride meetings either.

It's not really clear to me at all what those words mean nowadays – 'minority', 'majority'. As the late Bernard-Henri wrote in *Dead Leaves*, if there are ten sheep and two wolves in an Orkish barn, where's the majority and where's the minority? And what do you do with forty convicts and three machine-gunners?

What Bernard-Henri meant was that all this fuss about minorities is in fact an attempt to raise protective camouflage around the only minority that truly matters – the power elite. But then, he was smart enough to write this in Old French only – and in a book that no living soul would ever care to read. I only remember his words because every now and then he would quote his oeuvre to me during our long raids. Especially when he was high on M-vitamins.

263

But this is a slippery and politically charged subject and a pilot would be wise not to meddle in it.

The inequality stems from the fact that every sexual minority has its own problems. The animalist straights probably have the hardest time of it – this is a sport for the very rich, since the taxes mean that only some lucky devil from the very pinnacle of the social pyramid can afford to keep a live camel or sheep on Big Byz. For those rather less well-off, there are rubber sheep and even sheep suras – but those consumers are already classed in the gloomy category, although, just between you and me, I find that rather amusing. As for the stubborn but poor zoological straights, there are several brothels in the Green Zone – they're called 'stalls'. That's where they also make the organic milk and cheese for the *Human Touch* brand, but I've never managed to bring myself to try their products.

It's interesting, by the way, that, unlike the fluffy animals, Orkish sex workers aren't allowed beyond the Yellow Zone – Bernard-Henri always had to adopt his bimbos in order to pass the time with them in the Green Zone. This, of course, is not the result of national or racist prejudice, we don't have either of those, it's because in the Green Zone the Orkish youngsters come under our law on the age of consent. And it's not always easy to follow the rule 'don't look – don't see' there, because there are so many security cameras.

By the way, once, a long time ago, there used to be another orientation – transgender. But then the doctors learned how to change a person's sex using cerebral induction, growing the necessary organs and glands in a natural manner, and the caste of surgical transsexuals disappeared. Modern trannies are ordinary men and women, and in most cases they're as straight as a rail. Some don't even remember that they used to belong to the other sex – nowadays you can have your memory updated too, as long as you have the manitou. So the trannies aren't in GULAG.

In olden times there was one more closely related term – 'bisexual' – but today it can only be applied to the ultimate divine androgyne, Manitou the Singular. Otherwise, it's a sacrilege. We can crack all kinds of jokes on the subject of the idiocy of political correctness, of course, but it is highly advisable to follow its prescriptions as close as you can. I'm sure you already know this.

As for the gays and lesbians, these days they have absolutely no need to fight for their rights – either here or down below among the Orks, despite their culture's ostensible homophobia. In fact, every battle pilot knows that cunning Orks who don't want to fight fair often pretend to be engaging in single-sex love on the front line (while they're at it, they even write in big letters in the soil: 'Thank you, Big Byz!'). With their animal instincts, they realise that none of our people will want to photograph, on temple celluloid, a grateful sexual minority being shot up. But they also have real gays and lesbos too, and as for animalists, you can bet your life on it – every second man in any village is one.

But what the Orks don't have is gloomies. I think it's not hard to explain why. They don't have any love dolls, since the necessary technology doesn't exist. Even the Kagan can only treat himself to an average quality rubber dummy – and not because he's short of funds, but because nobody will officially sell him a sura of Kaya's class. And anyway, everyone knows that the Urkagan doesn't need a sura in order to satisfy the promptings of his heart, but to wheedle himself into GULAG's good books and lend his dictocracy a veneer of civilisation.

That's why it used to be impossible to fight for the rights of Orkish gloomies. Although any fool can see what a rich subject this is: the viewers got bored with wars for the rights of Orkish gays and lesbians two hundred years ago, and even the animalists have been done and done and done to death; little lambs hacked to pieces by Ganjaberserks (white and red on a green hillside – that's where I got my own start) don't touch the viewer's heart any more. But gloomy Orks – there's never been anything like that before.

And so when the pupo Trig appeared online, it was a real sensation. The Orks don't have video blogs, so Trig shared his problems exclusively in written form. And soon his cheerful chirping from the land underneath became so popular that he became one of GULAG's leading icons. Voices were even raised to suggest in all seriousness that his bust should be set up in the GULAG Avenue of Glory – between Alexander Solzhenitsyn and Elton John.

I realised immediately that there was a serious dark side to this whole business. Firstly, even a text blog can only be run on our net by an Ork with access to the Yellow Zone, where the A-list *orktivists* and other creative intellectuals live. And the regime doesn't particularly oppress them, because it's mostly them that the regime is made up of – Bernard-Henri hit the nail right on the head there (I'll quote him a little bit later). Secondly – and far more importantly – this Trig was too much in phase with the agenda of our media, for all his blog entries concerned either the joys of deviant sex, or the atrocities of tyranny, or the joys of deviant sex under the oppressive yoke of tyranny and in defiance of it. I'm a military pilot after all, and very familiar with tactical matters, so it was clear to me that if Trig didn't exist, he would have had to be invented.

But many people believed in him.

And they believed in him so much that they started inquiring into the details of his love life – after all, it's interesting to know how it all happens for progressive Orks at those moments when they're not busy with social protest. And Trig held nothing back.

It turned out that the object which served him as a simulacrum of the female body was a sack of potatoes, to which he had attached the head of an alabaster girl (to avoid being taken for a vandal, he made special mention of the fact that he didn't smash the head off a statue, but picked it up in a park after a bombing raid). According to his own words, for the intimate opening Trig used a can of stewed pork, after making a hole in the lid with his serrated Orkish sabre.

I didn't believe this either – firstly because of the technical and anatomical inconsistencies that are obvious to any gloomo, and secondly, because an Ork who is loyal to us can quite easily hire an animated-type rubber bimbo with a standard battery in the Yellow Zone. Of course, he wouldn't be able to take her home with him – because of the secret technology, they're anchored to the bed with handcuffs – but a couple of hours in a gloomy brothel would still be better than what Trig was describing.

They asked if it wasn't boring to make love to a sack of potatoes, but he answered that just before every time he took a pack of the Orkish tablets – Dumedrol – and then for two hours his Tanya seemed to be talking to him. After that many hotheads decided that Trig really was one of us.

As soon as this information got out and about, some GULAG enthusiasts decided to repeat the freedom-loving Ork's heroic feat out of a sense of solidarity, and at one time it was possible to buy what they called a full 'Trig Set' in the gloomy shops – a can of Orkish meat, a sack of potatoes, an alabaster head and a couple of packs of Dumedrol.

Trig hadn't explained exactly how to make the hole in the can. So people started getting injured. And Orkish canned goods are poisonous and insanitary. In addition, those tablets impaired spatial orientation and the ability to assess a situation adequately. As a result several people died of blood poisoning and a number lost their procreative organ. Afterwards the poor wretches had to grow new ones from stem cells – and that's no cheap treat. Anyway, everyone forgot about political correctness and gloomy solidarity, and GULAG had to open its own inquiry.

Of course, for us, finding an Ork is a piece of cake. They traced his manitou in the Yellow Zone. It turned out that this guy had remote access to the net directly from Slava, which is a genuine rarity. So the lads from GULAG got his address.

You've probably already guessed that it was the same house, overgrown with bushes, where Bernard-Henri had woven his little nest in Slava.

Trig didn't really exist.

This project was handled in person by Bernard-Henri, but it was overseen by Alena-Libertina. They could have carried on puffing hot air into Trig through the media straw, if only the late Bernard-Henri hadn't been so overconfident. If he had just taken the trouble to check certain physiological details of our way of life with me, he would never have found himself in such an ignominious situation.

No one in GULAG knew about Bernard-Henri yet, but they already suspected that Trig was a CINEWS project. That's why they didn't bother to inform the structures that deal with security matters – everyone knows that these days they're just offshoots of the cinemafia.

GULAG is the kind of force that can easily afford to run its own foreign policy (and sometimes even appoints Kagans, as it did, according to the rumours, in the case of Torn Durex). People from GULAG contacted the new Kagan in secret, gave him an address and demanded that he clarify who this Trig was. I saw the rest with my own eyes. And even played a certain part in events.

Alena-Libertina was obliged to purge 'Trig' and shuffle the blame off onto the Orks – so that she could bring it up just before the next war. The house was annihilated, along with all the clues. According to the official story, the first Orkish pupo had been traced and blown up by the Orkish secret services, who killed Bernard-Henri in the process – when he tried to act as the pupo's living shield.

The GULAG information service sent CINEWS an inquiry about what the battle camera, which many people had seen at the site of the discoursemonger's death, was doing there. CINEWS replied that the camera had been sent to protect Bernard-Henri, but it was too late, since someone had leaked the address to the Orkish Department of Public Security and Order. A subsequent press release stated that in supporting progressive Orkish elements, GULAG ought to co-ordinate rigorously with CINEWS, and then many tragic occurrences could be avoided. The smoking ruins of the house were shown in the news, and then a GULAG trailer dumped half a tonne of roses on it, and a chapter of history that reeked of canned pork could be regarded as closed.

In a word, they managed to wriggle out of it. But there could have been a scandal in which many heads rolled, and Alena-Libertina would have been the first to catch it in the neck. For certain sure – a serious political crisis would have erupted.

Don't fuck with GULAG!

Of course, this whole business filled me with horror and reminded me yet again what a cynical word we live in. I have always been opposed to the politicisation of sexual minorities. It only distracts attention from the real problems that gloomy people face. And we certainly do have problems, and very serious ones – but of a kind that society is not yet ready to discuss. For instance, no one knows about dopamine resonance.

I think that now you will understand how I felt when it turned out that the young Orkish couple's next outing would be timed to coincide with the opening of...

A memorial to Trig!

Oh yes. Precisely that. CINEWS had decided – effectively

giving GULAG a kick in the teeth by completely failing to consult with it – to open a memorial to the pupo Trig, martyred in his own home by the Orkish secret police. And not simply a memorial, but a whole museum with exhibits – it was announced on all the information channels. There was nothing GULAG could do but put a brave face on things and join in at the last moment, leaving the showdown for later. And the lads from CINEWS, not being fools, immediately made GULAG pay for the memorial out of its own till.

'The battle is eternal, peace is but a dream...' As the ancient poet Blok keenly observed. And by the way, he was also a pupo in his soul. It was no accident that he spent all his life writing about harlequins and unknown women in masks – these days any psychoanalyst knows what that means.

Alena-Libertina, who conducted the opening ceremony in person, insisted that I come with Kaya. As she explained to me, this was an order, rather than a piece of advice.

'Come out of the closet, Damilola,' she said playfully. 'We all know about you.'

'I'm not hiding anything,' I snarled. 'It's just that my girl has never been out of the apartment before.'

'And you're afraid that she'll lose her milk?'

I felt like retorting that it was dangerous for a woman on the verge of menopause to joke about such things but as usual I refrained. In ancient times, a combat pilot could be saved by a parachute, but in our days the only thing that can help is ironclad self-possession.

Alena-Libertina started explaining that I would escort Grim and Chloe for CINEWS. But I was also a member of the gloomy community, and Kaya was attending at the request of the GULAG leadership, for GULAG wanted everyone finally to believe that high-end segment suras were within the reach of the middle class – although with certain provisos.

I gradually started feeling relieved. To be quite honest, I even felt a prick of vanity. You can't possess a priceless treasure and hide it from people all your life – the urge to boast will build up in the subconscious and at some moment it could spill over in a most imprudent manner. So possibly it was all for the best.

I had to decide how to tell Kaya about it. And this, of course, was where my professional experience came in helpful.

After all, what is the essential nature of the media business? When people suffer affliction, try your damnedest to sell it as news – and their misfortune will be your good luck. This time the problems that had come up were my own – but it looked as if the chance to transmute my pain in the neck into pleasure had come floating along with them. All it took was to sell my management's order as a fit of personal chivalry – and I could count on a sizeable dopamine credit from Kaya.

There's a simple rule: when you make a generous gesture, do it simply and unaffectedly – for if you speak too many words, the object of your favours might happen to glance into your soul, and that will kill the entire effect.

'Kaya,' I said next morning, 'I've got good news for you.'

'What's that?'

'You asked me to deactivate your spatial blocking. I agree. You'll be able to leave the apartment. And I'll introduce you to Grim too.'

She looked up at me with a very thoughtful expression. Perhaps I imagine it, or perhaps it's true that she completely forgets to blink when she's genuinely interested in something.

'Today we're going to the opening of a memorial,' I went on. 'There'll be people there who might start talking to you. So remember: everything you've seen on my battle manitou before today is personal information.'

Kaya nodded. I knew that I'd been heard by a sub-programme that reacted to the code words 'personal information', so I didn't

271

have to do any more explaining – she wouldn't give any secrets away to anyone.

'Grim will be there. You'll be able to meet him. But for this . . .'

She hopped over and gave me a resounding smack of a kiss on the mouth.

'For this, anything you like, fatty . . .'

I won't describe the next two hours.

If only because any recital of the physical basis of what was happening (and that's what all detailed accounts essentially come down to) will give the reader the entirely false impression that he understands everything – and my experience isn't all that different from what he gets from his sack of potatoes after stuffing himself with Dumedrol on a Saturday evening.

If a camera had filmed us, the observer wouldn't have seen anything special. Possibly our coupling might have seemed to him like the union of two sloths: instead of the movements affirming the joy of life that are comprehensible to any benevolent observer, he would have seen a display of sluggish stroking.

But inner reality often differs from the outward one. After five minutes of this slow dance I felt like a seething kettle that has blown its lid off – and over the flames of unendurable pleasure what used to be my personality was being transformed into a cloud of steam, into one of those vaporised souls that drift through the blue void of the sky in the guise of clouds . . .

When I came to, Kaya was no longer beside me – she was busily getting dressed.

I finally saw what kind of clothes she had bought for herself.

'You want to wear that . . .'

'Don't stick your nose into this at least,' she said with a frown. 'You don't really think you understand this too, do you?'

She put on a baggy black dress with a huge 'smilie' – two white dots for eyes and the semicircle of a smiling mouth, which also had a red tongue sticking out of it. On looking more closely, I realised it wasn't even a dress. It was a large-size man's tank top.

Actually, lots of Orkish girls go about like that in hot weather. And our young people often adopt their fashions – as a gesture of protest against the management, as the discoursemongers say.

A dress of this kind has a distinctive appearance. The most interesting thing, of course, is what happens with the breasts, because the straps of the tank top don't so much conceal them as provide a formal pretext for considering that the proprieties have been observed.

It suited Kaya terribly well.

She also painted one eyebrow green – again in the latest Orkish counterculture fashion.

'Draw on a bruise as well,' I said.

'You'd better take a look at yourself.'

The girl proved to be right.

When I went into the happiness room and looked in the mirror I saw the dark circles under my own eyes. Not very noticeable – the kind that could appear after a sleepless night. But I'd never had them before. I hastily tidied myself up, put on my CINEWS Inc. dress uniform and we walked out of the apartment, Kaya on my arm.

To be quite honest, I felt a bit weird – but Kaya behaved as if she did this sort of thing every day and always had done.

Five minutes later, the tube spat us out onto an esplanade filled with people, where this walk-round memorial had been set up.

It had been allocated a standard hundred-metre unit with a direct tube exit, which indicated the high status of the event.

The buffet reception had already begun and there were quite a lot of guests. A crowd of people from our news department were clustering around Alena-Libertina, who had put on a silvery chiton and large ruby earrings in honour of the occasion. GULAG was represented by several well-known pupos with their suras.

The guests from the friendly sexual minorities were stars of the first magnitude – the dyb-triette 'Les Three': three skinheaded wenches in leather aprons (looking exactly like in their pre-war clip 'Ork Meat Rare'). I'd only ever seen them on the manitou before. In real life they were just as enchanting, only I thought before that they were a lot taller.

The girls had already given out their autographs and were clearly bored – they'd been shipped in because of their hit 'Pupo Trig – My Heart Jig-a-Jig', which they had been incautious enough to release a month earlier, and now they had to work off the karma. From the way they were standing and the direction in which they were smiling, I could tell immediately where the nanocameras were hanging over our hall. They put 'Pupo Trig' on over and over again, and whenever a sommelier standing over at one side raised his hand, the girls started dancing and miming to their own recording.

The large number of security men in muted blue and grey togas testified to the presence of someone very important. But I couldn't believe my eyes when I realised that the weary, elderly man in a black cavalry cloak who was walking towards me was David-Goliath Arafat Zuckerberger.

He might not be the most famous pupo, but he's certainly the richest. He's one of the trustees of the Manitou Reserve, and it makes no sense to call those guys rich, because everyone else's wealth and poverty is held up on their backs, as if they were whales. They live in the same area as the snuff stars – in immense villas on the upper section of the offglobe, and cameras are forbidden to fly up there. A pilot can only get a look at their residences if they hire him to put on a firework show during their parties. They have open gardens up there with invisible conditioning screens. A genuine paradise. But if you fly in too close to a garden like that, they'll shoot you down without warning.

David-Goliath isn't the biggest wheel in the Reserve, but to all other mortals, he's a god. And now this god was walking towards me, smiling at me like an equal – and walking alongside him was his new sur. I actually shuddered at the sight of him.

To be quite honest, the sight of David-Goliath's surs is enough to make you laugh and cry at the same time. And the amount of laughter in the cocktail is at most ten per cent – all the rest is tears. If you dream of one of his puppets at night, you might never wake up again.

But on the plus side he is a hundred per cent gloomy and one of GULAG's deans. I respect him because he is a proud man and has this inner freedom which makes him unafraid of other people's gossip-mongering. Instead of going underground (where, I presume, most of his colleagues in the Reserve are languishing) he keeps an entire staff of sommeliers and lawyers who monitor the information environment and rebuff politely but sharply everyone who starts exercising their wit or their conscience on the subject of his surs.

'Not wishing to blindly indulge the intents and preferences induced in his psyche by inherited memory and coercive cultural encoding, our client strives to direct the destructive forces of his libido into a channel where they will not harm anyone. This is an irreproachable civic stance, and it would be splendid if our detractors and critics could say the same thing about themselves with a clear conscience...'

And so on. As far as I understand he has never tried any straights at all. He likes little boys – but a kind that nature doesn't produce. His surs (and he has an entire harem of them) are nimble dwarfs with predatory faces who look like children but are not completely human. And their dildo unit is so large that the gibes eventually forced David-Goliath to start dressing them only in long, loose garments.

The sur, whom David-Goliath was leading on a tether, came up to his waist. What can I say, he looked hideous – a predatory, large-headed child in a spiked collar, who has just breakfasted on a small dinosaur and is now searching for something he can have for lunch. His hands were chained together and he was dressed in something like a black silk straitjacket (*Hate Couture* from Adolph-Kiki Dior Galliano – I've heard that that fashion house lives exclusively off dressing David-Goliath's dolls).

But the external shell couldn't fool me – I knew that this frightening little creature had the same kind of filling inside him as my Kaya. And that, I must say, filled me with pride – even David-Goliath couldn't treat himself to anything better. Simply because nothing better existed.

Kaya and David-Goliath's companion spotted each other.

Surs and suras have a specific interaction protocol and they can exchange information over the air at prodigious speeds. So that the users will know when this is happening, surs and suras emit a melodic whistle (they are obliged to do this by a law passed at the insistence of consumers – so that suspicious aging grannies will know when their rubber lapdogs try to conspire together). Moreover, the law specifies the minimal length of this whistle, because the surs exchange information very fast.

The encounter between my Kaya and David-Goliath's sur looked like this: they slapped palms together (a young people's greeting), Kaya whistled and the sur whistled back.

Kaya looked at me and said:

'But my ...'

And she whistled again.

What exactly she whistled, of course, I didn't know – but David-Goliath's little companion roared with laughter.

Somehow I got the impression that she was complaining to her little caste brother about our painstakingly concealed poverty. I found this particularly intolerable, since she herself was the reason for it. Perhaps she really did think that I wasn't sufficiently well off for her? Perhaps she despised me for my inability to wrest from this hostile world a chunk of wealth that was worthy of her?

'And at our place...' the boy from hell said and whistled again.

In reply Kaya simply spread her hands in a shrug.

Of course, a second later I realised that they weren't exchanging any personal information – that's strictly forbidden at the programme level, otherwise bank passwords could be stolen though surs and suras. It was simply another way of involving us emotionally in what was going on – and I must say that the attempt succeeded. David-Goliath had turned crimson too. But he soon came to his senses, grinned and asked:

'On maximum?'

'On maximum,' I sighed.

And I immediately noticed the dark circles below his eyes, concealed under foundation cream. At that point it was as if we exchanged telepathic whistles, just like our suras, and blinked at each other, almost imperceptibly. I realised that he knew about dopamine resonance, and he realised that I knew.

'Just look what they do to us, eh?'

I nodded.

We shook hands with real feeling and parted. What else was there to say?

David-Goliath soon left – and there was suddenly a lot more space in the hall, because almost half the people there were his

277

security men. I don't know how they guard him on the move –
they had to leave in several shifts.

Before it could really sink in that I had shaken hands with
David-Goliath Arafat Zuckerberger himself, there was Alena-
Libertina walking towards me.

'Where's Chloe?' she asked. 'I need the girl in shot.'

'I don't know,' I replied. 'It looks like she and Grim haven't
arrived yet.'

'Perhaps they've got lost?'

'I don't think so,' I said. 'Even an Ork can manage to walk
along the corridor to the tube ... Ah, there they are. Talk of the
devil.'

When Grim saw how Chloe had dressed for their first appearance in society together, he was horrified.

They had to visit an 'open-air memorial' erected on some
Orkish pretext (in the reception committee they explained to
him that their absence from an event of this kind would look
strange), so a touch of 'Orkishness' in the manner of dress was
appropriate.

But Chloe had togged herself up in a man's white tank top,
adorned with a crude image of a smiling mouth with a red
tongue sticking out of it. In other words, without the slightest
exaggeration, she had dressed exactly like the girls from the
Slava suburbs who rented out every orifice in their body for
two manitous.

When Grim explained to her in rather crude terms what he
thought about this, Chloe led him over to the manitou without

saying a word and opened the catalogue of the season's fashions. It turned out that soldiers' singlets (100% Natural Orkish Tailoring, in Black and White Versions) were the very latest craze in local fashion, and they cost so much that down below you could buy a small peasant farmstead for the same money.

After that Grim lost his aesthetic bearings completely and meekly allowed Chloe to dress him in a pair of striped shorts, with legs of different lengths, and a clownish sweatshirt with a hood like a pointed cap. She also bought him a new hairdo: the self-distending ribbon gathered Grim's hair into a 'Mohican' standing erect on his head, at the same time dying it the colour of hay scorched into pallor by the sun.

Chloe contemplated the result thoughtfully.

'A toga would suit you, of course,' she said, 'but we don't know for sure that we're allowed to wear them. We're Orks after all. So this will do for a start.'

When the doors of the tube opened, Grim couldn't believe his eyes. Right there in front of him was a large clearing in a forest. People were strolling about in the most incredible outfits, examining display stands and show cases set out in the clearing.

The exhibition had an old-fashioned kind of formality. It consisted of 2D-photographs and other items set in excessively massive frames of polished steel inside sturdy glass boxes. The monumentality of the informational objects symbolised the inviolability of memory. And starting right behind the stands and little cases, there were bushes and trees; in the distance birds were singing, and the setting sun shone in fragmented splinters through the foliage swaying in the wind.

Soon Grim noticed that all the people stayed in a rather narrow rectangle formed by the exhibition's display stands, and not one of them walked towards the sun and the birds. At this point his focus of perception shifted and he realised that he was in a small hall about ten metres by ten, the walls of which represented the three-dimensional world with incredible verisimilitude – just like the windows in his apartment.

At first Grim was afraid that in her prostitute get-up Chloe would make everyone laugh. But then he saw a girl in a black tank top with exactly the same design on it.

She was standing beside Damilola, who was dressed in a CINEWS pilot's uniform. When Damilola waved his hand in greeting, she waved too, and smiled.

She was obviously his daughter.

She looked just a bit younger than Chloe. Her dark, almost black hair was trimmed in a simple, severe style with a fringe and side strands down to her shoulders – as if she had a helmet covered with dark, gleaming lacquer on her head. For some reason one of her eyebrows was green. She was a bit on the pale side. And very, very beautiful.

So beautiful that her beauty could have been diluted in a hundred women's faces and there would still have been enough for all of them. Beside her, Chloe looked... Well, not exactly a plain Jane. It simply became clear that the prettiness of her cute face was merely a specific instance of the universal rule that nature had formulated in the face of the unknown girl. This white-skinned, black-haired girl stood far closer to the source of beauty than all the faces that Grim had ever seen before.

Looking at her he experienced a strange feeling that he had never known previously, a little bit like resentment – as if Manitou's invisible ray, through which the light entered into his soul, had suddenly moved on to another creature, purer and better than him. And it had been right to move – if Grim had been in the ray's place, he would have done the same.

All these feelings flashed through him very fast. And then he started noticing the details.

Firstly, her tank top was a couple of sizes larger than Chloe's, which made it hard to look into her face – his eyes stubbornly kept trying to slip downwards, and Grim was obliged to admit that in comparison with her, Chloe looked primly dressed.

Secondly, the unknown girl was looking at him, smiling and waving her hand with an air about her as if they had known each other for a long time.

Damilola put his arm round her shoulder. The girl shook his arm off with a precise, economical movement. A lady in a silvery chiton, standing beside them, laughed, and Grim recognised Alena-Libertina, who had changed her hairstyle and dyed her hair a different colour. When Grim and Chloe walked up, she nodded to Grim, took Chloe (who had narrowed her eyes voluptuously) by the hand and led her off to the farthest corner.

Grim noticed that the girl in the black tank top and Chloe contrived in some incredible way not to notice each other, not even when they were right up close – and he realised it had happened because of the identical tank tops. And clearly for the same reason, they immediately went flying apart to opposite ends of the hall, like two similar charges repelling each other.

'Hi, Grim,' said the girl. 'I'm Kaya.'

Grim wasn't surprised that he was so well known – after all, it had to mean something that he and Chloe had been filmed by so many cameras on the day they arrived.

'Hi,' he replied and looked up at Damilola. 'Is this your daughter?'

Damilola winced, as if Grim had said something tactless. Kaya, on the contrary, laughed, showing off her sharp, pearly white teeth.

'He's my carbohydrate parent.'

'Your who?' Grim asked.

'She's joking,' said Damilola, embarrassed. 'There's a Church English idiom – "sugar daddy". An older man who keeps a young girl and gives her all sorts of presents.'

'But you don't give me any presents at all,' said Kaya. 'So you're not a sugar daddy, but precisely a carbohydrate parent. Or even an aspartame supervisor. There used to be a sugar substitute called that.'

'But why supervisor?' asked Damilola.

'From the word "pervy".'

Grim felt embarrassed that a family gripe session had started up in his presence and he tried to change the subject of conversation.

'Have you already looked at the ... er-er ... exhibition?' he asked.

'No,' said Damilola.

'Let's take a look,' Grim suggested.

Damilola gave a nervous shrug – but Kaya was already walking with Grim towards the large glass cube at the beginning of the exhibition.

Inside it, on a stand of polished steel, were three identical glass containers that looked like pharmacist's carboys with ground-glass stoppers. The containers were large, about five litres each, and they were firmly packed with a grey powder with a heterogeneous texture. There was a funereally severe little plaque on the steel stand:

ASHES OF THE GLOOMY

'The ashes of pupos,' said Damilola.

'What, are they genuine?' Grim asked, trying to make his voice sound respectful.

'I don't know,' Damilola replied. 'Possibly. But it should be understood symbolically. The point here is not to demonstrate what our bodies turn into. We want to remind people about the suffering that falls to the lot of minorities. And the fact that minorities continue to suffer to this very day ...'

Next came a large steel stand with black and white photographs. Grim saw a wooden Orkish house hemmed in on all sides by bushes. He recognised it immediately, and shuddered as a wave of sticky fear ran through him. On no account must he blurt out that he had ever been inside this house himself – he and Chloe had been warned about that very strictly before their first live broadcast.

Below the photograph of the house there were enlarged images of graffiti on its walls – a spastika daubed with a spray can and the words 'DETH DUH GLØMERASTEN'. Grim couldn't remember anything like that at all. Of course the words could have been blanked out before his visit, but he couldn't quite understand why they were in Upper Mid-Siberian, as if they had been written by a state bureaucrat and not a hooligan. And in another photograph, beside a blot from a broken bottle of ink, there was a plain vernacular phrase in red: 'PUTRID PUPE'. The point was apparently that Trig had been hounded by all segments of Orkish society.

Grim felt Kaya tug on his hand.

In actual fact she didn't tug on his hand, but on his index finger, grasping it neatly in her little fist. And although her gesture was perfectly proper, except perhaps for being overfamiliar, Grim felt a chariot, half of fire and half of ice, hurtle across his body from his pubic region up to his throat. Damilola, who was following all this closely, pulled a face, as if he suddenly had a toothache.

'What?' asked Grim.

'Have you ever wondered,' Kaya asked in a conspiratorial voice, 'why the global oligarchy makes such a big deal out of the rights of sexual perverts?'

Grim had never heard bold talk like that, not even in the Orkish barracks.

'No,' he said, opening his eyes wide. 'Why? Because they're perverts themselves?'

'That's not the only reason,' replied Kaya. 'Power over the world belongs to the financial elite. A bunch of blackguards who make everybody else suffer for the sake of their profit. These scoundrels hide behind a façade of false democraship and avoid publicity. That is why in order to actualise their pleasure they need a group of people capable of becoming their secret symbolic representative in social consciousness ... Am I expressing myself clearly?'

Grim nodded uncertainly.

'But what do they need that for?' he asked.

'So that the shower of maximal preferential advantages will spill over onto the symbolic proxy-elite consisting of perverts, and the genuine, secret elite can experience vicarious crypto-orgasm. It's obvious.'

'What sort of nonsense is that?' Damilola asked angrily. 'Do you think all these people here, who care about the fate of pupos ...'

'All these people here are profoundly indifferent to the fate of pupos and other shit-eaters,' Kaya interrupted, for some reason looking at Grim. 'It's just that people are cowardly and they're always licking at the imaginary spot through which they believe the vector of force and power passes. It's the elite's absolute tyranny in the choice of objects of ritual worship that renders the crypto-orgasm by proxy possible.'

Damilola took hold of Kaya's ear between his finger and thumb.

'Now you just shut up,' he told her. 'Tell me, where did you read all that gibberish?'

'In Bernard-Henri Montaigne Montesquieu,' said Kaya, elegantly twisting free of his grip. 'The treatise *Les Feuilles Mortes*, in my own translation from Old French. A highly appropriate quotation, I think. This is his memorial too, isn't it?'

'If Bernard-Henri did write that,' Damilola muttered, chastened, 'it wasn't so that anyone would read it. Apart from other discoursemongers, in any event. That's precisely why the book's in Old French. He would never have said anything like that in public himself.'

Kaya didn't answer that.

Grim stopped at the next stand, which was covered with photographs and columns of text.

In the upper section there was a photograph of a fat military commander of ancient times, wearing epaulettes and a black blindfold over his eyes. The caption stated that this was General Kutuzov – a Siberian war-chief of the early Barbed-Wire Age who invented the gas bomb used to incinerate the ancient Orkish capital, together with the forces of United Europe that had occupied it under the leadership of Reichskanzler Napoleon.

Below that was an aerial photograph that made Grim's heart shudder. He could have taken a photograph like that himself if he'd had a camera during the battle at Orkish Slava.

It was a trolley with four blue cylinders on it – the same gas bomb that the suicide platoon with reed pipes had trundled off into the smoke before his very eyes. The photograph even clearly showed the young lad, sitting between the cylinders with the trigger cord in his hand.

The column of text explained that this was a resurrected weapon of the ancient Orks, used by them against sexual minorities since olden times. Kutuzov bombs had already killed two illustrious Byzantines – von Trier and Bernard-Henri – and the threat hanging over civilisation required an immediate response. Which, make no mistake about it, would follow.

In the lower section there was a diagram of the mine dug under the house of the pupo Trig, through which the Ganjaberserks had brought the Kutuzov bomb down. The painstakingly delineated geological strata made the cross-section look very convincing.

'We can already guess what the reason for the next war will be,' Damilola said sadly.

'Because of the pupos?' Grim asked.

'No. Because Torn Trojan used gas as a weapon. The war for the pupos will come later. But I could be wrong, of course. We'll have to wait and see.'

Kaya glanced at Damilola, but didn't say anything.

The next stand displayed a notional Trig Set – an open sack of wax potatoes, a head, with snakes instead of hair, smashed off some ancient statue, a pack of tablets, a can of Orkish stewed pork and a dentate dagger that looked absolutely terrifying. A red warning sign emphatically cautioned visitors not to attempt to emulate the heroic feat of the legendary pupo independently.

After that there was a small case with personal items of Trig's (the little scarlet child's woolly cap with two pompoms on the tie-strings was especially touching) and printed excerpts from his blog, in which the sections lambasting tyranny had been emphasised with bold script. But this also failed to arouse Grim's interest.

Only one stand, the very last, was devoted to Bernard-Henri, who had been killed together with Trig (Damilola explained that this stand had not been financed by GULAG, but by the public relations department of CINEWS Inc., which was well known for its stinginess). The stand looked simple in the extreme – a photograph of the sadly smiling philosopher had been set on a polished steel background. Below it were two handwritten extracts from *Les Feuilles Mortes* in Old French (the deceased had apparently copied them out specially, by hand, for facsimile reproduction). There was a translation in Church English beside them.

S.N.U.F.F. is life itself, with love in the numerator and death in the denominator – a fraction that is simultaneously equal to zero and infinity – as is Manitou, who thirsts avidly for this.

Grim didn't entirely understand the meaning of these words, but he didn't dare to ask, afraid that Kaya would upset Damilola again in some way. But the second excerpt was somewhat clearer:

In criticising the repressive Orkish regime we often forget what its genuine nature is. And the more complicated the definitions that we use, the more confused the question seems. However, the essence of the matter can be explained extremely simply.

The regime is everybody who lives well under the regime.

This includes not only the bureaucrats who take bribes and the Ganjaberserks who smash skulls, but the discoursemongers who jocosely denounce them, the frisky journalists from the Yellow Zone, the titans of pop, poppins- and popper-art, the masters of Orkish culture who invoke the eternal values, the drawing-room *orktivists* and other high-gloss Global Orks who condemn the regime on a daily basis at buffet receptions closely guarded by the authorities.

It should not be forgotten that the irreconcilable struggle with dictocracy is one of the most important functions of a modern-day dictocracy intent on long-term survival. The Urkagan's accomplices can adopt a laisser-faire attitude to education and medicine, but on no account can they do so in this sensitive area, otherwise there could be an unplanned rotation of power. Hence this appalling dearth of honesty down below – for any Orkish 'new sincerity' is nothing other than well-forgotten old lies.

All this has happened before. Many times.

Trig has no friends at all down below.

Vive la révolution!

BHMM

Grim looked at Damilola, then back at the quotation. Damilola shrugged.

'He hasn't got any up here either,' he muttered.

'Ah?' Grim didn't understand.

'I mean friends,' said Damilola. 'I myself can't understand why they hung this up here. Probably the number of voluntary helpers down below has got out of hand. In two or three wars' time we're going to bomb the Yellow Zone, so this is how they're preparing public opinion. But that's not important for you, lad. You're free now.'

The idea about the nature of the regime seemed broadly correct to Grim – he had always felt something of the kind. Although it wasn't clear, of course, if the generalisation applied to Bernard-Henri himself.

Chloe was nowhere to be seen. A glance round the hall convinced Grim that she had already disappeared – together with Alena-Libertina. They had left without saying goodbye...

Kaya noticed the way his face darkened.

'Let's get out of here,' she suggested. 'Where do you want to go, Grim?'

'He hasn't been anywhere yet,' said Damilola. 'This is his first social outing. What would you be interested in seeing?'

'London,' Grim replied without a moment's hesitation.

'Why London exactly?'

'That's where all our guys go when they leave,' said Grim. 'The ones who've made a success of life.'

'All right then,' Damilola agreed. 'London it is. I don't like the food there. Although I do know one good place... But where's Chloe?'

'She left already,' said Grim. 'With Alena-Libertina.'

'Ah,' replied Damilola. 'Ah. So we'll get going then?'

Grim suddenly realised that Kaya was holding his hand again.

Her hand was warm and dry. She scraped one finger gently over his wrist, as if to draw his attention to the fact that she was holding his hand. And Grim, surprised at himself, replied with a similar scrape of the finger.

Kaya looked at him, smiled and tugged him towards the doors of the tube. Damilola followed them – if he had noticed anything, he didn't give even the slightest sign of it.

In the little metrolift cabin Damilola jabbed his finger at the manitou several times. Grim saw a cheerful little message appear.

GULAG recommends
BI GBEN

'Here we go,' said Kaya. 'Daddy's going to drag us round his pervy dives again.'

'It's nothing to do with dives,' growled Damilola. 'This is the best restaurant I know in London. The Global Orks hardly ever go there. And the fact that it happens to be in the GULAG listing is pure coincidence. I think GULAG recommends it because it takes a certain courage to go with a name like that. Even if it is disguised as a pun.'

'Right, right,' said Kaya. 'We don't doubt that in the slightest.'

When he heard that 'we' and saw Damilola's sour face, Grim realised he should be very careful to avoid getting involved in a family squabble. Kaya was still holding his hand, and to give himself something to do, he started studying the control manitou.

All sorts of jolly frivolities flitted across the screen: balloons, cartoon film heroes, an animated advertisement for a new diet – and in the lower section large, green figures flickered as they counted down. Grim decided it must be the time remaining to their destination. And so it was; when the figure zero popped up on the manitou, the door opened.

In front of them was a hall about the same size as Trig's memorial – with tables standing beside tall windows. Noticing some kind of movement above him, Grim looked up – and he was stupefied.

In the mysterious semi-darkness above his head, cogwheels and metal arcs, gleaming with oil, were rotating, and a huge, heavy pendulum was swinging to and fro, wafting a palpable breath of air through the hall at every stroke. It was a clock mechanism, but a very large one. And if it was an illusion too, the realism of it was absolutely incredible.

And outside the windows, stretching off in all directions was a bird's-eye view of an ancient city.

'Is that London?' asked Grim.

'Yes,' Damilola confirmed. 'The historical view from the clock tower. As far as they were able to reconstitute it from a surviving 3D panorama.'

A huge black woman in an ancient-style dress – white silk with green sleeves – was already hurrying across the hall towards the customers. She had chocolate-coloured skin and grey dreads that reminded Grim uncomfortably of the Ganjaberserks he had left down below.

'What shall I get you?' she asked in a surprisingly low man's voice.

Looking at her more closely, Grim saw that her big breasts weren't real – they were stuffed forms projecting from the silver-embroidered bodice. He was looking at a man.

'The usual, Gben,' Damilola said lazily. 'Everything as usual, my old mate.'

The elderly black man gaped at Damilola in bewilderment – but polite bewilderment.

'The same as last time,' said Damilola, trying again.

The black man assumed an air of extremely polite incomprehension. The silence was getting oppressive.

'Menu number seven,' said Damilola, exasperated.

'And for the kids?' the black man asked.

290

'The same,' Damilola said morosely.

'So that's three number sevens?'

'No,' said Damilola. 'Two. The girl won't be eating.'

The black man gave Kaya a dubious look, then looked back at Damilola – and smiled as if he wanted to show that the very last thought in his head was that the man in front of him was a cheapskate father who was starving his daughter to death. He nodded politely and invited his customers to take a seat. Damilola chose a table with a view of the river. He was looking glum and Grim suddenly felt a bit sorry for him.

But he was so overwhelmed by the panorama that he immediately forgot about everything else.

Soaring up outside the window were grey and brown towers with lacy stonework, lancet windows, steeples and even a flag on a tall mast – a genuine fairy-tale palace.

'What is it?' asked Grim.

'The parliament,' Damilola replied.

That must be what they used to call this kind of castle.

Beyond the parliament he could see a bridge over the river and, further off, the ancient stonework brows of immense grey buildings rose up out of the mist. He could even make out the different-coloured boxes of motorenwagens and the tiny dots of people strolling along the streets. Grim drank in the rays of sombre grey light coming in through the window and just couldn't get enough of this view.

Directly in front of him the dark forms of architectural decorations were suspended over the city – massive spheres of stone set in gold mounts, with crosses, crowns and ornate details that looked like flowers. Grim wanted to ask if they were metal or stone painted to look like gold, but he immediately realised just how pointless the question was.

The black man with the false breasts came over to their table and set down a tray of drinks on it.

'Gben Mabutu is an excellent cook,' Damilola said when the man left. 'But, between you and me, he injects too many anabolic steroids – in order to maintain his muscle mass. That's why he's not quite right in the head. Do you like African food, Grim?'

'I don't know,' Grim replied. 'I've never tried it. What is it?'

'Well, there's date bread,' said Damilola, 'couscous, baba-ganoush, Berber sauce... You'll like it, it's like Orkish cuisine in parts.'

Grim had no clear idea of what Orkish cuisine was, so he didn't say anything.

'And where do the rich Orks live?' he asked.

'How do you mean?' Damilola asked in surprise.

'Well, this is London, isn't it?'

'Yes it is.'

'I heard that our rich men live here.'

Damilola laughed.

'Grim,' he said, 'in our time London is just a view from the window. There hasn't been any other London for hundreds of years already. If rich Orks live here – and they really do live here – it means only one thing. They see the same 3D projection outside the window. Almost the same, that is. And they meet in restaurants with a view of the area.'

'I don't understand,' said Grim. 'Then anyone at all can put up a projection like that outside their window.'

'Absolutely not,' Damilola replied. 'It's forbidden by law. The view from the window is an integral part of a residence and is paid for together with it. If you have a lot of money, you can choose. But it can only be changed without payment by decision of a court and with the agreement of the municipality authority. That's why the view from a window is called municipal.'

'Why was it done that way?'

'Business,' Damilola sighed. 'The real estate owners have a powerful lobby. They pushed that law through a long, long time

292

ago, long before I was born. At first glance, of course, it seems absurd. But actually it does make sense.'

'How?'

'We have very little space. If you set aside the very richest people, everyone lives in similar box units, with so much technology crammed into every cubic millimetre that an unemployed person's home is hardly any different from a rich man's. The view from the window is one of the few parameters that make it possible to maintain a semblance of social stratification. It determines the size of the rent. For instance, you have the hills of Tuscany. That's expensive, and you can only afford a view like that because you've inherited it from Bernard-Henri ... Tuscany's very chic. But this London here is mostly bought by Orks.'

'Is London cheaper?'

'London's a lot more expensive,' Damilola laughed.

'But can you put a fake view in a window?' asked Grim.

'Yes, for a while. It will look even better than the municipal one – their programmes are old, they've got lots of bugs in them, and they're always malfunctioning. But cybersecurity will spot a fake at the first scan. The fine is massive. And then, a fake in your window means lifelong disgrace.'

'Why disgrace?'

'Well, imagine someone pretends that he lives in Paris. The party's in full swing, and suddenly a siren sounds and a message in huge red letters appears across the Eiffel Tower – "ILLEGAL CONTENT". You wouldn't wish it on your worst enemy.'

Grim fell silent, thinking over what he had heard. Then something nudged gently against his foot.

He looked up.

Kaya was looking at him.

'Grim,' she asked, 'do you believe in love at first sight?'

Damilola laughed quietly.

He didn't seem to be at all annoyed by Kaya's strange behaviour – he was actually taking pleasure in her antics. Grim frowned in surprise. It wasn't clear to him why Kaya had brought up this subject. But she looked serious.

'I don't know,' said Grim. 'I believe in death at first sight. I know for certain that that happens. But I've only read about love at first sight.'

'And in your opinion, what is love?' Kaya asked.

'Probably when you feel good when you're with someone.'

'But who should feel good? You, or the person you love?'

Grim shrugged.

The question was too abstract. Down below, everyone felt bad – the ones who loved, and the ones who were loved. Not to mention the fact that no one really loved anyone – Orks were simply scoured against each other by the daily grind.

'And what do you think yourself?' he asked.

'Probably,' said Kaya, 'love is when you want to save the one you love. Especially when it's very hard to do. And the harder it is, the stronger the love is.'

Grim pondered that.

He felt absolutely no urge at all to save Chloe. In the first place, she was doing perfectly well anyway. In the second place, Chloe herself could save anyone at all. Take him, for example – she'd gone and dragged him all the way to London. Only it wasn't very likely that she'd done it out of love. It had just turned out that way – it was easier to drag him here than leave him down below. And then, it was by no means certain that he'd really been saved at all.

Anyway, he didn't know what answer to give. But Kaya didn't seem to be expecting an answer – she was already looking out through the window at the fretwork towers of the parliament.

Gben Mabutu appeared in the far corner of the hall, holding a huge tray with bowls and dishes standing on it.

'And what view do you have from your window?' Grim asked to change the subject.

'Come and visit,' said Damilola. 'Bring Chloe with you. You'll see everything for yourself. Kaya will order some food. She orders really good food – it's absolutely delicious. And you can take a look at my collection too.'

At first Chloe refused to go visiting, citing her heavy schedule of auditions. The argument that they needed to maintain good relations with the neighbours had no effect on her. But for some reason she was convinced when Grim reminded her that Damilola lived right next door.

This time Chloe and Kaya turned out to be dressed differently – and they finally noticed each other. After the introductions, they found something to make small talk about (apparently the cut of Orkish army singlets) and Grim and his host went off to look at the residence.

The layout of the apartment was exactly the same as at Grim's place. The only difference was the colour of the walls and the pictures hanging on them. While at Grim's place their content was abstract, here almost all the paintings expressed a kind of rebellious love of freedom.

The subject of a smashed manitou was repeated frequently – in one case it was a shattered retro-receiver with a vacuum tube, in another, a flat panel with several bullet holes in it. There was also a picture that was strange and sad: a rounded shadow that somehow resembled Damilola, smashing down a manitou with bullet holes in it onto the head of a fragile girl with a distant resemblance to Kaya. In the manner typical of Byzantine painting, a caption was written above the picture:

FLYING BUFFS VS MEWLING MUFFS

Damilola had two large pieces of Orkish art in his home, which was apparently what he called 'my collection'. They were a hairy red letter 'O' on a steel plinth, and a massive stone slab hacked out of a cliff face, with an ancient pictogram on it.

They weren't 3D copies – Damilola touched them with his hand to show that both objects were real.

According to what he said, the hairy red 'O' used to stand in the market square in Slava, only it was many times larger. Grim immediately recalled that he had actually caught a glimpse of the red oval, overgrown with ancient green moss, rising up over the market square in an old snuff – but he hadn't realised what it was. The sculpture turned out to be called 'Great Mother of the Urks' and had been made under the first Losses, but it hadn't survived to our time and now only existed in copies.

'The fact that it's not a "U", but an "O",' said Damilola, 'personifies for me the age-old aspiration of your people to freedom and civilisation...'

Grim realised that this 'O' wasn't really very likely to personify anything for Damilola, who simply wanted to say something pleasant to him. But he was grateful for that at least.

The pictogram on the stone slab looked extremely simple – at the bottom was a crudely chiselled circle, with a triangle above it, and another triangle higher up. Damilola explained that this artefact came from far more ancient times than the hairy 'O' and belonged to the late Barbed-Wire Age, when the original indigenous Gulag Culture was falling into decline. In all probability, the pictogram had some connection with the archaic 'taking a pipe under the roof' rite – the specialists dated it to the so-called 'fighting roofs' period. But what the actual meaning of the rite could have possibly been was, of course, something that by now no one could explain.

Grim felt ashamed that Damilola knew far more about the history of his people than he did. But he confessed that he didn't really feel any special interest in Orkish antiquity.

'Why not?' asked Damilola.

'I can see what it led to,' said Grim.

Damilola sighed and nodded several times, as if he wanted to show that he understood Grim very well. And then he led his guest over to a small picture that showed Slava from altitude. Only instead of jungles and rice fields, it was surrounded by a dead lunar landscape, edited in on a manitou. On the moon there was a small column of text in fine handwriting:

One can render a long, soundly argued account of how the moon has been flying along some bizarre trajectory for many centuries now, and references to its terrible dead history will be entirely appropriate. But an unspoken prohibition on mentioning other heavenly bodies will render the narrative somewhat incomplete – at least in tracing the linkages of cause and effect.

BHMM – to his friend Damilola

'Is this Bernard-Henri?' Grim asked.

Damilola nodded.

'A present,' he said. 'He and I were partners for a long time. A complicated man. Some things about him were impossible to accept. But he's one of the most brilliant minds I have ever come across in my life. And he often spoke out loud about things that others prefer to ignore. Although mostly in a private setting, it's true. But sometimes on camera too – for those occasions he was advised by two lawyers... And this one I made myself after his death. In memory of my comrade-in-arms...'

Damilola pointed to the next picture.

It was a photograph of a piece of cheap Orkish craftwork – a portrait burned into wood, like the ones they sell in souvenir shops as keepsakes of a visit to some Manitou-forsaken dump. Grim saw a long-haired folk hero with an aquiline nose, wearing fairy-tale armour, amulets and bead bracelets – the kind of character that Orkish artists draw when they don't have the vaguest idea of what the ancestor they are portraying looked like.

'Who is it?' asked Grim.

'The leader of the Eastern Pacific Orks, Ivan the Right-Hand Wheel,' said Damilola. 'Probably no such person ever existed. He's simply an epic-poem hero. I snapped him during a sortie over the market. There wasn't any text – I added it myself...'

Grim noticed that Ivan the Right-Hand Wheel was the spitting image of the late Bernard-Henri. This homage to memory was actually rather touching.

Below the long-haired warrior was a caption, skilfully stylised to look like pokerwork on wood:

Like a rocket with multiple re-entry vehicles, a hostile discourse-monger is most expediently destroyed at the launching stage. Instead of investigating the fiery essence of his syllogisms and applying them to one's own life and destiny, one should first of all inquire into his sources of funding and the goals he is addressing – in other words, the question of who he is and why he is here. This is practically always enough, for the appearance of a body opening its mouth in front of a camera is never a spontaneous quantum effect. Just as the camera itself is never such an effect, even if it has the most sophisticated camouflage.

BHMM

298

'Actually, Bernard-Henri was no quantum effect himself,' Damilola chuckled. 'I say that as an observer. As for who he was – he was a very lonely man. I mean in the intellectual sense. He was always complaining that he had no one he could cross swords with, and really go all out. Because all his Orkish opponents were incredible dolts, and I got to them too quick... I'm sorry.'

'It's all right,' Grim replied.

'Hence the harsh self-criticism of his own culture in Old French. But that doesn't mean, Grim, that he wasn't a Big Byz patriot. He was.'

'I know,' said Grim. 'I saw that myself.'

Damilola's bedroom was smaller than the one in Bernard-Henri's home. The space was divided into two parts. Through the half-open door that led into the little room partitioned off from the main section, a strange contraption was visible; it looked like an exercise machine with a pile of cushions heaped up on it. Grim saw a cavalry saddle, rendered black and mirror-bright from long polishing by buttocks – something like an inclined couchette with a complicated control handlebar and several different-sized manitous.

The saddle was standing in such a way that if you sat on it you could slump forward, to lower your chest onto the cushions and take hold of the handlebar. There were stirrups attached to the bottom of the saddle with spring bearings – absolutely genuine stirrups of ancient, dull silver – and lying on a stand beside the control handlebar was a pair of opaque goggles with whisker-thin earphones. There was a large cup of coffee standing there too.

Beside the control manitou, Grim just had time to spot a second couchette and a woodcut print of horsemen on the wall – before Damilola unceremoniously slammed the door shut. Apparently he wasn't planning to show this part of his home.

'You were asking about the view,' he reminded Grim.

Grim looked out the window – and only now realised what the opening view was.

Damilola's windows looked out over a city of pompous slums, standing on the shore of a sea bay. The colours outside the window were very bright – so bright that they reminded him of a screen with a damaged contrast control. The sky and the sea (only the very edge of it was visible) were intensely blue, the shallow slopes of a mountain in the distance were mildewed with little houses, and the harbour was so overcrowded with boats that it looked a graveyard of decaying white fish. Taken all together, it aroused a complex sensation of heat, poverty, stench and optimism.

'What is it?'

'Naples,' Damilola replied. 'A most ancient city. The world was once ruled from the shores of that bay. But there is no city now, and no bay. I like this view, because it...'

'Comes with a discount,' put in Kaya, who had come up to them surreptitiously. 'It looks kind of expensive – the sea and a bay. But actually it's cheap. You see that boat there? Sailing into the harbour? If you stand here for ten minutes it will sail as far as the quayside and moor, then disappear and start sailing into the harbour again. Day and night, right round the clock. It's a bug. It could be upgraded, but we're economising.'

Damilola looked at Kaya with a feeling that seemed very much like hatred. But then he immediately laughed and shook his head.

'I actually like that boat,' he said. 'It's a reminder of the cyclical nature of all existence. What did you come in here for, kitten?'

'Come and eat,' said Kaya. 'It's all ready.'

When she went back to the sitting room, Grim finally realised what seemed so strange about Damilola's home. Apart from the control screens round the exercise machine with the saddle, there wasn't a single manitou here.

It seemed logical. Otherwise the paintings on the walls depicting exploding manitous would have looked incongruous. But even so it wasn't clear how his host established contact with the information universe.

'But tell me,' Grim asked, taking the plunge, 'where's your manitou?'

Damilola smiled and pointed to the door of the happiness room.

'No,' said Grim. 'I didn't mean that. I meant where your manitou is.'

Damilola smiled again and pointed at the door again. Grim blushed, thinking he was being taken for an idiot, and to smooth over the awkwardness, he thought it best to follow Damilola's directions.

'Sit on the toilet,' Damilola shouted from the corridor.

Grim did as he was told.

As soon as his body touched the seat a glittering screen appeared in the air in front of him, and down at the bottom of it letters, numbers and icons started flickering in empty space – located at a position that made it convenient to press on them with your knees parted and your elbows lowered onto your thighs. This screen and its buttons had no material substance that Grim could understand; they were simply a glimmering in space that responded to the touch of fingers. The fact that Damilola had installed this ephemeral console in the privy subtly complemented the theme of protest in the art displayed on his walls.

As soon as Grim got up, the manitou immediately faded away. He'd never seen anything like it.

'That's the cheapest kind there is,' Damilola explained when Grim came out. 'But the panels at Bernard-Henri's place are antiques, two-dimensional plasma. And they're much more expensive. He used to say he liked composing texts on them – the great discoursemongers of the past worked on manitous like that.'

'Are they really old?' asked Chloe.

'Copies, of course. But they look exactly like the real thing. An ancient panel would cost about three million at least. And it's best not to switch it on – they break down immediately. And there are vacuum tubes with crystal displays too. Like the old emperors used to have. But they cost as much as a view of London.'

Grim wanted to say that you didn't have to be an ancient emperor – the Orks still had vacuum manitous made by the factory that produced the 'Urkaine' mopeds. That was what his Uncle Shug used to work on before he was arrested for being untrustworthy, and they were the Orks' technological pride and joy, an inheritance from their great ancestors. But then he decided that Damilola probably knew far more about that.

At last they all sat down at the table.

Grim was sitting opposite Kaya, and he could get a really good look at her. She seemed to him even more beautiful than before. She was dressed in her house clothes – a funny, fluffy dressing gown with little green rabbits on it – and this almost childish outfit made her look indecently young. Chloe had no doubt carefully compared Kaya and herself on all points, and now she was looking glum.

Kaya really had chosen the food well. In honour of Grim and Chloe, the Orkish dish *mantow* – tofu dumplings – was served. The mantow tasted delicious – only Kaya didn't eat any at all, although there were several lying on the plate in front of her. However, she did explain that this dish symbolised the severed heads of enemies, which the Orks used to boil and eat in times long ago. Grim couldn't tell if she was making fun of him or not – but he decided she probably wasn't. The Orks really could have had a custom like that. Especially since the upper people still did – as the collection in Bernard-Henri's little cupboard showed.

Apparently Grim wasn't alone in recalling their recent discovery – Chloe did too. Responding to some comment about the heavy yoke of the Orkish experience, Damilola said:

'Everyone has a skeleton in the cupboard.'

Chloe apparently didn't understand the idiom; she tittered genteelly and blurted out:

'Oh, but we've got two of them!'

Kaya laughed, but Damilola frowned as if he was afraid the conversation was about to sink into a bottomless pit.

Grim decided to change the subject urgently.

'Is it hard being a pilot?' he asked. 'Could I be one, for instance?'

Damilola's eyes clouded over with an indeterminate feeling – either pride, or sadness, or a mixture of both.

'It's not likely,' he said.

'Because I'm an Ork?' asked Grim.

'No,' replied Damilola. 'You have to start working towards it from early childhood. You haven't even seen a single snuff right through, let alone the Ancient Films. But for this work you have to grow up in the visual culture. So that you're impregnated with it from infancy.'

'And is flying a camera difficult?'

'It's not enough just to fly it. You have to physically merge with it.'

'I've got good reflexes,' said Grim.

Damilola laughed.

'It just looks like it's easy. Sitting there in front of the manitou and flying it. But actually it takes half a lifetime to learn. You have to know all about aerodynamics and lighting, camera angles and angles of attack, spin and flutter, not to mention wind and light exposure. If you have a specific assignment to hover over some pit with a vampire in it, that's easy. But if you're freelance, you have to feel instinctively which glide path they'll use in a snuff and which they won't. You have to be a sniper in every possible sense. Bombing with shot shells from a nosedive is just like surgery.'

'And what's harder,' asked Grim, 'hitting the target from a cannon or with a bomb?'

'With a bomb,' said Damilola. 'When you're nosediving, the target's in your sights for half a second at the most. Of course, there are guided bombs and rockets, but they cost ten times as much, and all the expenses go on your balance sheet. That's why most pilots use shot shells for pummelling a target. You know what the times are like yourself – they economise. And to hit the target with a shot shell, you have to know in your gut when to drop it. You have to fire your cannon without even thinking about it. And you mustn't miss. Especially when you're covering a star and firing plugs.'

'Plugs?'

'Stealth-kill ammunition. That's...'

'I've seen it,' said Grim.

'It might be low-visibility, but if you hit the eye or the cheek, the face bursts open, and you'll spoil an expensive shot. Who's going to work with you after that? But the worst nightmare is smashing up the camera. That's why everyone guzzles M-vitamins or shoots up all the time, but no one admits it. The doctors close their eyes to it, of course, because they know there's just no other way. And at the age of fifty you're a wreck already...'

Damilola turned sad.

'But there's only a battle once a year at the most, isn't there?' said Grim. 'What do you do for the rest of the time?'

'What about the news? And the bombing raids? Every day over Orkland.'

'Over the market?'

'Over the market too, and over all the garbage tips. You hardly need to fire at all there, but firing's actually easier than shooting. For that, you have to find the right expressions on faces, the right clothes, the right scene of devastation – you can only learn all that over the years. You even have to fly over a garbage tip the right way. You have to sense what they'll put in a shot and what they won't. Not just shoot an old woman with a bowl of rotten cabbage, but get a ginger kitten meowing in the shot... Everyone works on instinct. The pilot and the senior sommeliers.'

'But are there any rules?'

'In the information business there aren't any rules at all on the verbal level. But one step to the right or the left, and you're off the air. They'll put in someone else, who'll provide the right mood. That's why you have to spend all your free time sitting in front of the manitou. Watching which way the trends are shifting. And the Orkish delinquents have got completely out of hand just recently – they fire stuff at the cameras with slings. Nuts and bolts. If they smash your lens, just you try proving afterwards for the warranty that you didn't scrunch it yourself.'

'Tell me,' said Grim, 'is it true that any camera can kill anyone at all, and no one will find out about it?'

'No. Out of the question. There's even a law – when the weaponry's in operation, there's a control recording...'

Damilola thought for a moment and pulled a sour face.

'But there are probably special operations too,' he went on. 'So anything's possible... The key point would be that no one has shot it on a different camera.'

Talking about work had definitely put Damilola in a glum mood – his hands were starting to tremble slightly.

Kaya asked:

'Tell me, Grim, what's it like being an Ork?'

'Damilola knows more about that,' Grim muttered.

Damilola laughed and slapped his hand on his thigh, as if Grim had said the funniest thing he had ever heard in his life. His mood seemed to have improved.

Suddenly a screen lit up in the air in front of the table – the same kind as in the happiness room, only several times larger. Grim noticed a little black box in Kaya's hands, and he guessed that the manitou in Damilola's home could be switched on not only in the privy, but anywhere else as well.

Damilola went red with embarrassment.

'What have you switched that rubbish on for?'

Kaya smiled.

'They're going to show Grim in a moment.'

'In the news?' Damilola asked in surprise. 'The report on Trig's already been on.'

'No,' said Kaya. 'It's just about him.'

'About me?' asked Grim, astonished. 'How do you know?'

'There was an announcement. You're going to read your poem in the entertainment package.'

'Ah,' said Damilola, 'the entertainment package. I see.'

'Me? A poem? But I haven't been filmed for your entertainment package!'

Damilola livened up again. This time tears even came to his eyes.

'Grim,' he said. 'You're so funny. This isn't a snuff, you know, and it's not the news. They can show anything at all in the entertainment package! Why would they want you for the shoot? I'm sorry, but you could only get in the way!'

An anchorwoman in a T-shirt made of black feathers appeared in the empty space in front of the table. She looked so real that they could easily have sat her at the table. But her mouth moved soundlessly – it seemed like this was the usual thing in Damilola's home.

'What's she saying?' Grim asked eagerly.

'She's reminding us that a young Orkish soldier, who could no longer bear his torment, has chosen freedom and defected to us,' Kaya replied.

'How do you know?' Grim asked in amazement.

'I'm lip-reading,' said Kaya. 'Now she's saying that from your childhood years you were an underground dissident and an *orktivist*. You worked in rights protection journalism...'

Grim broke down and started laughing hysterically.

'Rights protection journalism!' he said. 'They made it up, would you believe it!'

'He was persecuted by the authorities,' Kaya continued, 'and is presently in Byzantion with the status of a guest. Grim, ITN 1 3505 00 148 41 0, is not only an *orktivist*, but a talented Orkish poet...'

'A poet?' Grim exclaimed in embarrassment. 'But I haven't written... That is, I only tried... I'm not very good at it. Only a few rough drafts, and they took those in quarantine.'

'They'll give you a hand with the poems too,' Damilola chuckled. 'They'll finish them on a creative articulator. Welcome to civilisation, Grim.'

'His poems,' said Kaya, continuing her translation of silence, 'are rough, harsh and truthful. They express the typical mood of the contemporary Ork... Shall we turn the sound on?'

Damilola nodded, and the next second the anchorwoman disappeared and Grim himself appeared in front of the table

Grim didn't even realise at first that it was him.

Standing right there was a morosely magnificent black warrior, with a sword on his belt. His cloak was similar in style to a high-ranking Right Protector's – a gold spastika glittered on his sleeve, its three cross-pieces indicating the rank of a colonel. The curved sword in the black scabbard and the lacquered helmet with the perforated visor were certainly very beautiful and costly, but absolutely not Orkish – Grim had never seen any like that in even a single snuff.

'An Ork's Song Before Battle!' the warrior proclaimed, then removed his helmet and flung it aside.

Grim saw his own face. His double's hairstyle was strange – the hair had been smeared with gel and set in a shape that was hard to describe, reminiscent of either a candle flame fluttering in the wind or a squashed onion. Perhaps his hair really would have looked like that if he had galloped through the night without taking his helmet off.

The double snatched at his sword and started declaiming, raising his voice dramatically with every quatrain:

When the prosecutor public with the pierced ear lobe
Kick-started his fleet motorbike, saying he must fly,
'Twas then our glances met across a rusty barrel
With the terse inscription 'sand' (which was a blatant lie).

On the left, in a furrow from a giant dump truck's wheels,
Round and massive as a sputnik, a fat pig lay.
And I was only saved because the lads were all still sleeping
On the heaps of padded jackets, dirty bed sheets and hay.

Despite the smell of Orkish feet and other body parts,
And all the facial attributes of common race and land,
I knew that almost all of them were designated queerasts
And any one of those would have written that word 'sand'.

But am I any better? I also am submissive.
I also watch world cinema, in cowering compliance,
And all our abject souls, so timorous and passive,
Differ only in their mutterings of counterfeit defiance.

I climbed out of the window. The sky was overhead;
Below the sky – a fence; beyond that – a ravine.
And it was all so ludicrously, laughably absurd,
That it would have been very funny if not so obscene.

Ah, fuck this Orkish homeland right up its shitty ass,
This dump truck creeping into nowhere, loaded up with
  shite.
Since I was just a kid here I've been beaten and harassed
And no one ever granted me a bill of human rights.

So flush the whole works down the tubes or suck it
Up the spout – that's now for the enemy to choose
I'll bloody no more bloody documents for you now, fuck it –
Farwell to arms! Across the river and into the trees!!
  Vamoose!!!

The obscenities, which the warrior practically yelled, were
drowned out by beeping.

The on-screen double recited superbly – and he almost danced
as he did it, striking ever more terrifying poses with every quatrain. At the end, with his voice rising to a scream, he started
furiously brandishing his sword, as if he was fighting off a crowd
of phantoms. When he finished reciting, he suddenly calmed
down, flung his sword after his helmet and drooped over in front
of the camera, as if casting himself on the mercy of the people
sitting in front of their manitous.

The smiling anchorwoman reappeared.

'That was "An Ork's Song Before Battle",' she repeated and
sighed. 'Only where will you ever vamoose, you silly goose?'

Then she turned serious and started talking about something
incomprehensible. A cross-section of some kind of spherical
machine appeared in the air, and Kaya immediately switched

the manitou off. Grim realised that his three minutes of fame were behind him.

'Well now,' said Damilola. 'They presented you well. Usually everything here has a hint of mockery to it. But they made you so cute, you could hold the candles in a snuff. What do you say?'

Grim could have said a lot.

Firstly, if he had a sword and helmet like that, he wouldn't have tossed them away, but sold them at the market and lived a quiet life on the proceeds for about five years.

Secondly, he had never written this poem – at least not in this form. It had been patched together out of the rough drafts in his notepad – with some of his ideas badly distorted. And some had simply been added in. Along with all the obscene words.

'Queerasts' really had been mentioned in his rough notes, but in a completely different sense. Grim couldn't believe that so many of the lads from his draft, even if they were grubby, unwashed and none too bright, could have been cursed by Manitou with a black destiny and condemned to die. But this made it seem as if he completely agreed with it.

He hadn't written the quatrain about his Orkish homeland at all.

It had been taken from the folk song 'My Bloody Homeland Really Sucks', to the spasmodic broken rhythms of which Grim had composed his work. Only in the original it was 'this dump truck driving into nowhere, loaded up with shite' – but it had been changed to 'creeping', evidently in the belief that this way it was more offensive. The line 'and no one ever granted me a bill of human rights' was incomprehensible too – in the song about his homeland it said 'and no one's ever given me a full bowl of rice'. Grim couldn't help but notice that the upper sommeliers had even managed to improve the dubious Orkish rhyme.

Grim had a faint glimmer of insight that not everything about Orkish folk songs was really all that simple, and it would be worthwhile finding out who wrote them, and how – although, he thought immediately, why bother finding out, when everything's clear anyway... And the same went for Orkish folk dances too.

The only thing they got exactly right, though, was the way he had thought about the bloody documents – but in the original it had been expressed less forcefully. And he had absolutely no idea where the last line with the word 'vamoose' had been taken from. There hadn't been anything like that in Grim's drafts. Perhaps that thought could have occurred to him, but he would certainly have had the wits not to put it down on paper.

But the main thing, of course, was something else.

Even if Grim had written this poem in precisely this form, not for anything in the world would he have recited it into the cold lenses of a Byzantine optical system, publicly renouncing his own monstrous tribe. He would have died of shame first. But his on-screen double had managed it easily and spontaneously, as if all he had ever done since he was born was suffer through an endless series of catharses in front of a camera, narrating them on the spot for live broadcast.

'The only thing I don't understand is why they left in the bit about world cinema,' Damilola said pensively. 'They must have been in a rush.'

Grim was totally embarrassed, because the quatrain about world cinema was practically the only thing that had survived untouched.

'Yes, they definitely rushed it,' Damilola went on. 'Bernard-Henri once got smashed on M-vitamins and growled something about an Orkish piggery – "stinking like the liberative discourse". And they let that through too – there was a deadline... How did you like it, Kaya?'

At this point Grim noticed that Kaya was gazing at him fixedly with wide, round eyes filled with admiration.

'An excellent poem!' she said. 'Very powerful! No one knows

311

how to do that anymore. Everyone's afraid. You're a genuine poet, Grim! I love you!'

And then something strange happened to Grim.

All the contradictory feelings that had been raging in his heart only a second ago suddenly disappeared and in a blinding flash their place was taken by a new emotion – sudden, fresh, intoxicating and entirely unfamiliar. He realised that for these words and that glance he would sell his Orkish homeland three times over – if, of course, anyone wanted that much of it.

Chloe didn't say anything, but she looked at Kaya with such physically palpable hatred that the electricity rippled through the room. Damilola felt it too.

'Uh-oh!' he said, 'I see we're getting really serious here.'

He stood up and walked quickly to the happiness room.

Kaya looked at Grim one last time and smiled sadly and closed her eyes.

Something happened to her. An instant ago she was alive – and now she had frozen without even the slightest sign of movement, in a way that no living person could. The change was inexplicable and terrifying.

'Kaya!' Grim called. 'Are you all right?'

'She's all right,' said Damilola as he came out of the happiness room. 'I switched her off.'

'What do you mean, switched her off?'

'From the master console,' said Damilola, sitting down at the table. 'She can be put on pause from there. Only you have to know the password. It's so that she won't shut herself down. Suras like doing that.'

'Suras?' Grim repeated in bewilderment.

'What, didn't you realise?' Damilola chuckled. 'I'm a pupo. Like Trig. Only with wider opportunities.'

'Are you telling me...?'

'You mean you really didn't realise? You thought she was alive?'

Grim shook his head disbelievingly.

Everything around him suddenly fell into place – now he could see why Kaya hadn't eaten anything in London, or today. And why Damilola had brought her to the opening of the memorial.

And he suddenly felt so bitter that this new, exhilarating feeling that had just pierced his very soul had turned out to be the same kind of deception as everything else in life.

'Pupo Trig – My heart jig-a-jig,' he murmured.

Chloe laughed.

'I thought as much,' she said. 'A live girl is never that well-groomed. She hadn't got a single little pimple or scar, or even a little vein in her eye. And a real woman wouldn't try to hit on someone else's man in front of her own. Because she'd get her head smacked.'

Damilola nodded.

'How sensitive a woman's heart is,' he said. 'But I tuned her like that myself. I'm a pilot after all. And a pilot's sura always has a streak of madness about her – it's a tradition of ours. You get tired after a flight. And apart from that, you get to see so much of the dark side of life through the sights in one day that you're not in the mood for sweet lovey-doveing. It makes it hard to get me stirred up. The point at which another man goes insane is the lower threshold of sensitivity for a pilot. So Kaya has seduction and all sorts of other parameters set to maximum. She's always being provocative and flirting, that's the way her programme is. Don't take it to heart.'

Grim realised that he had been silent too long – he had to say something.

'How much does one like that cost?'

Damilola roared with laughter.

313

'Now you want one too, do you? But what for, when you've got Chloe?'

'And do many men have that kind?'

'Those who can afford it. Almost anyone who's rich. Who needs the hassle of live people these days? There are those who like to polish skulls, of course, but they come to a sticky end... He he, I didn't mean it that way. Although, in principle, that way too...'

He squinted at Chloe's glum face and put on a guilty expression.

'Only don't you youngsters take me the wrong way. It's a question of upbringing and what you're used to. Our cultural stereotypes seem laughable to you, I think. Or on the contrary, disagreeable in some ways. But...'

He realised that he had turned the conversation in the wrong direction and stopped.

Grim tried to get away from the slippery subject as quickly as possible.

'And how is her character tuned?'

'You can do it yourself. Or you can use a factory setting. You can even call in a tuner – there are professionals like that. A good job, by the way, although it's nerve-wracking. But a genuine connoisseur does all the tuning himself. The idea is that you should set the tuning once, and then never touch it again. Then it will be exactly like with a live person.'

'And are there men like that?' asked Chloe.

Damilola laughed again – he found his visitors distinctly amusing.

'Yes, there are. And no living man can compete with them. Only they're expensive. And haven't learned yet how to earn any money themselves, ha ha!'

Grim looked at Kaya. She was sitting there with her closed, self-absorbed expression – like a thousand-year-old statue, waiting for the vainly bustling, disposable people to leave her chosen space and crumble into dust, so that she can awaken again.

With an Orkish girl's typical practicality, Chloe moved the cold mantow from Kaya's plate across to her own.

'She doesn't want them anyway,' she said.

Damilola nodded benevolently.

'What are you thinking about, Grim?' he asked.

'There's one thing I can't understand,' Grim said. 'If you can make copies of living people like that . . . And you can show me without me even being involved . . . And even read the poems that I was only going to write in my own voice . . . Then why do you need these wars on Orkish Slava? You could film everything a hundred times better without us. About love and about war. And there's no need to kill anyone.'

'But it would be an untruth,' said Damilola. 'It was that way before. They filmed what wasn't true, and no one believed in it. The disbelief led to hate. And the result was that the whole world collapsed.'

'My poem before battle is an untruth too.'

'That's what the entertainment package is for.'

'But why can't they show snuffs in the entertainment package?'

'Because snuffs aren't entertainment,' Damilola said seriously. 'They're a sacred mystery. And they're the truth. Not simply the truth, but its very essence . . . Although, of course, there is invention in them too, to be strictly accurate. A plot, costumes, period details . . . But that's like the wrapper of a sweet. And the sweet itself is made of absolutely pure truth. A snuff simply can't be anything else. That's why it's the foundation on which everything else can be built.'

'And what's she – truth or untruth?' Grim asked, pointing to Kaya.

'For me – the truth,' said Damilola. 'Especially where it concerns the terms of loan payments. But what she is for you, only you know. There are things that are a truth for some and an untruth for others. Those are the things, by the way, that cause hate between people.'

'But what are snuffs needed for anyway?'

'That's not a question that's asked in our society.'

'How do you mean?'

'I mean it literally. The roots all go way back into philosophy and religion. But we haven't thought about it for a long time. It's not a question that concerns people, Grim. Take me, for instance. When I'm shooting on celluloid, it's for eternity and Manitou. And I can't say I don't believe in it – I do. But I don't want to go into it in depth. It didn't start with me, and it won't end with me. Let the priests deal with it. My head's not elastic, after all. I've only got enough strength for my job, and also...' – Damilola nodded towards the enigmatically silent Kaya. 'So if you're really interested, go to the temple.'

'The temple?'

'The House of Manitou.'

'But will they let me in there?'

Damilola laughed.

'Everyone else stopped going to them a long time ago, Grim. Of course they'll let you in. I'll have a word with Alena-Libertina – I think she'll want to explain everything in person. The old woman will be glad that someone's still interested. Only don't tell I called her an old woman, Chloe. Or else the old woman will get offended. And not with me, he he, but with you. You understand?'

When I took Kaya off pause after our guests had left, the first thing she said was:

'Forget the resonance, fat arse. Consensual sex in factory mode, and that's it. Lock yourself in this happiness room of yours and make me soft-hearted. Got that?'

'Got it,' I answered, putting on a false air of resignation. 'What am I going to do now, eh?'

She looked at me with sullen distrust – as if sensing that I had my next move all ready.

My sweetheart wasn't mistaken. And it had been ready for a long time.

When it became clear that she seriously intended to blackmail me, slamming shut in my face the door to the happiness that had only just been shown to me, I realised that I needed a weapon of retaliation. If it was blackmail she wanted, she could have it. I think it will be a long time yet before any algorithm can compare with an aggrieved and enraged human being in that area.

For the first few days I tried to frighten her by saying, as if I was joking, that I would explain to Grim who she really was. It helped at first. But things couldn't go on like that for long – one way or another, Grim would have guessed for himself. And if it came to that, Chloe would have noticed. So I wasn't particularly concerned when that particular trump card fell out of the pack.

I had another one ready and waiting.

Kaya had simulated interest in Grim for so long that she couldn't easily abandon this mode of behaviour. One way or another, all her demands and requests now concerned my symbolic rival, and she was obliged to simulate not only unflagging interest in him, but also concern for his welfare.

And that was exactly what I intended to exploit.

'Come here,' I said. 'I'll show you something.'

She pulled a face meant to show that she wasn't interested in the least. I walked through into my battle cockpit and installed myself at my work station.

'It's about Grim,' I muttered almost inaudibly under my breath.

She can hear like a cat.

Less than a minute later she appeared beside me and quietly sat down on the couchette in front of the control manitou. Still with that expression suggesting that she was afraid of defiling herself with the air that I breathe.

I switched on the recording.

It was a standard control track for my Orkland patrol from Hannelore's black box. The basement of the house appeared on the manitou, filmed through the sights with the hyperoptics engaged.

Three figures were visible – just outlines filled with glimmering twinkles. One little figure was sitting by the wall, with another one standing beside it. The third little figure was holding some long, thin object in its hands. It swung it and hit the figure sitting on the floor. The second figure tried to intervene, but it wasn't fast enough.

I switched on the sound and a gradually fading scream became audible.

'I've seen this,' said Kaya.

'But you haven't seen this,' I replied and pressed the 'Full HUD info' button.

A whole ocean of information immediately appeared on the manitou – including the wind speed and direction, long- and short-range radar readings, and even the phases of the moon at

318

the time of recording. In the upper left-hand corner there were a couple of complicated graphs that even I didn't understand. Simultaneously with all this splendour, the Orks' individual tracking numbers popped up: 1 3505 00 148 41 0 and 1 3598 47 660 12 2. That was Grim and Chloe's data. I was sure that Kaya remembered the numbers by heart.

I stopped the recording and asked:

'Do you remember how it all began? You asked me to save him. And I did. Committing, by the way, a serious breach of service regulations. I concealed the circumstances from my superiors.'

I knew there was absolutely no way she could check what I said.

'Now think for a moment,' I went on. 'What will happen to your Grim if I pass this recording on through the right channels?'

She didn't say anything.

'You don't know?' I asked. 'To be quite honest, I don't know either. But I think it would all end fairly painlessly for him. We are a humane society, after all.'

'Painlessly in what sense?' she asked.

The look of alarm suited her delicate face very well.

'In the sense that most likely it would be a lethal injection. Or the gas chamber. It would all be over quickly.'

'But what will happen to you?' she asked uncertainly. 'You ... You committed an offence too, didn't you?'

'I know you don't give a damn for me,' I said bitterly. 'You'd be only too glad if they dispatched me to the next world after that little Orkish cur. But I have to disappoint you. In the very worst case they would give me an official warning. But most likely they would just fine me.'

'You told me you were risking everything,' she said.

I laughed.

319

'And how can I deal with you any other way? I have to get everything out of you by cunning. But in fact I can only be guilty of negligence. I didn't disobey a single direct order.'

That was absolutely true. I had carried out all my orders.

She thinks incredibly fast – for such a tiny fraction of a second that not every chronometer could register it. But since she has to imitate human behaviour, she pretends to be thinking for a long time afterwards. And because she's operating at a high level of bitchiness, she pulls all sorts of offensive faces during this time – she looks at me as if I'm suffering from elephantiasis and have just demonstrated my little secret to her, or wrinkles up her face as if I'm feeding her rotten fish oil with a spoon.

But this time she surpassed herself.

The way it looked was as if she'd realised that the life of someone very dear to her depended on how she behaved – and had immediately forgotten her bitchiness completely.

In actual fact, of course, she never forgets anything. That's why it's more correct to say that the previous algorithm was instantly superseded by a process with a higher priority.

'You won't do it, though, will you? Honestly?' she asked pitifully, and her eyebrows lifted up slightly at the bridge of her nose.

I started trembling inside – that was a sure sign that a drop or two of happiness was about to spill over into my parched mouth. As long as I didn't mess everything up myself – that happened too, sometimes.

'Everything will depend on you, my dear,' I said. 'If you go on offending me every day...'

She twirled her hand, as if she was fast-forwarding through my next few phrases. But then again, she really did know them.

'But I'll be able to see Grim like before?' she asked. 'You'll continue taking me out with you?'

And then I made a dumb move.

I could have haggled and won any conditions for myself, because I was holding the strongest card of all. And then everything would probably have turned out differently.

But haggling required time and also, possibly, more nervous stress. I already knew how a discussion of the terms would end anyway. And impatience got the better of me.

'Pilots don't go back on their word,' I said proudly. 'We've already decided that question.'

'You promise?'

'I promise. And now come to Daddy ... Only take that look of mournful resignation off your cute little face, all right? I want enthusiasm. Genuine enthusiasm. You're doing a good deed, after all – saving an Orkish degenerate from the gas chamber. The joy that brings you must be clearly expressed in your face. Or else I might change my mind. Have you got that, my darling? That's right, that's it, good ...'

I kept my word.

Before we went out the next time, Kaya spent almost an hour in front of the mirror, trying various combinations of the junk bought with my money. Several times I caught myself feeling genuinely annoyed, and I only managed to hold back with a serious effort, by reminding myself that she was trying so hard not for Grim, but for me – and getting exactly the result she wanted.

But Grim was the one who really delighted me. When he saw her, he shuddered and turned away – and never looked at her once the whole day long. Now he was reacting to her in exactly the same way as Chloe.

Possibly it was because he was very interested in ancient machines of death (we were walking round the Museum of the History of Snuffs) and couldn't be bothered with modern machines of pleasure. Kaya was pale and sad. As far as I can envisage the mechanism of her emotional simulation, it's like a game of chance: her control algorithms require her behaviour to be meaningfully consistent, and if she bets on a card and loses, she has to simulate sadness.

It was very convincing.

This picture stuck in my memory: Grim, Chloe and I are standing beside an imperial chariot that has been used many times in historical snuffs, and listening to the guide. An axle bristling with rusty blades juts out a long way from the reddish-brown wheel. Chloe examines the golden carving on the side of the chariot. Grim listens to the guide and thoughtfully runs his finger along one of the blades. Kaya, wearing a cheerful little pink T-shirt with a silvery kitten on the chest, stands off at one side with such a dismal air that the tears are about to well up in my eyes at any moment.

Never mind, I think, with tenderness that no attempt at rationality can vanquish, when we get back home, Daddy will comfort you... And you'll finally understand, my little fool, that apart from me, no one in this world needs you, absolutely no one...

I try to catch her eye, but I don't succeed.

And there's the trip to a seaside villa on the Côte d'Azur, with a genuine salty sea breeze blowing on the ten-square-metre observation platform. Grim doesn't understand the way the hyperoptics shrink Chloe, sitting at the far end of the platform, and he walks backwards and forwards, trying to catch the point at which her image will double up or distort. And I...

I look at Kaya, silhouetted in an arch of trembling leaves, and think that the gentle breeze toying with her hair, the cheerful equanimity of youth, the sunny strength that fills her to overflowing as she looks out at the sea from her transient green alcove – all of that exists not in her, but in me. Only in me. But she doesn't feel anything at all. And youth in its pure form (if we accept that there is such a thing) is only to be found as a flash of reflected light in the heart of one who has lost it forever. And those who are genuinely young have nothing on their mind but dreary everyday concerns, petty envy, lust and vanity.

I was certain that Grim had completely lost interest in Kaya. I had the most powerful complexes of the Orkish psyche on my side – the words 'pupo' and 'doll-shagger' are regarded as insults by them, and the corresponding activity is regarded as unworthy of a man, whose most important concern is to get blood on documents and perish in the Circus to the glory of the true faith. In order to carry on using Grim as my symbolic rival, Kaya would have to overcome all the Orkish prejudices.

I was very curious about what she was going to do.

Grim and Chloe were both very interested in London, because ever since they were children they had known that that was where all the rich Orks lived. When it turned out that London was simply a view from a window, they were a bit disheartened. But then Chloe remembered about the luxurious restaurants where the Orkish elite gathered, and all her interest in Big Byz became focused on them. It was pointless dragging her off, for instance, to the Archive of Ancient Films or the Museum of Technologies. The only thing that excited her now was the London restaurant VERTU HIGH.

I'll try to explain what this name means. To start with, *vertuhai* is an ancient Old Russian word that still lingers on. According to the dictionary, it came from the prison slang – and means, quote – *prob. a machine-gunner on a prison-camp observation tower, early (?) Barbed-Wire Age.* Kaya has her own version of etymology, though – and perhaps she knows better. Today the meaning of the word is different (albeit very slightly) – it is a self-designation of the upper stratum of the Orkish elite who call the shots in Orkland. Others usually call them 'Global Orks' – from the Upper Mid-Siberian *Ürkainisher Gløbüs*, as the Orkish propagandists officially refer to our offglobe, thus

323

sending a hint to their great nation that we are only one of the jewels in the crown of the Urkaganate.

Naturally, the Global Orks don't live down below, but up here among us. This restaurant is one of the places where they congregate – hence the name, slightly polished and dignified by our sommeliers, whom they often hire for such purposes. Anyone at all can go there, but for most people it's absurdly expensive, and for those who can afford it, it's absurdly vulgar. And so the Global Orks are able to maintain the purity of their ranks even on Big Byz. I personally wouldn't touch an establishment like that with a bargepole – not out of thrift, but because I don't like sitting in the same hall as gentlemen whom I am used to seeing through a gun sight.

The hall of the restaurant was the same astounding mixture of bad taste and pomposity that is so typical of the life and manners of rich Orks. It was sickening to look at those tablecloths of black and gold brocade and the oak panels with a spastika woven into the carving. Naturally, even in London, Orks cling to the true faith. The hall had a little devotional corner, reflecting traditional Orkish values as inscribed in the new, civilised landscape: a coconut from the Hill of the Ancestors, a portrait of the Kagan and an image of Manitou, and down below them, a small inflatable woman with a thick gold chain round her neck. For the Orks, the thing of value wasn't the rubber woman, of course, but the chain (symbolic in every sense), but this was how they extended the sweaty hand of friendship to us. Gee thanks, I almost wept.

And there was also a cartouche with a motto:

ONE ROOF, TWO CULTURES

The CINEWS Inc. daily allowance that I had at my disposal was only enough to get Grim, Chloe and me a coffee and ice cream.

But on the other hand we got a window table with a superb view of Big Ben, which is, by the way, something of a fetish for the Orks. I had never seen the clock face of this tower from so close up – there turned out to be golden words that resemble an appeal to Manitou, set into the stonework below it.

Grim looked by turns at the customers sitting in the hall and out of the window – but his gaze never rested for single moment on a grief-stricken Kaya.

'But where are our *orktivists*?' he asked.

I almost laughed.

'*Orktivists* don't fly this high, Grim. This orbit is way too elevated for them.'

I don't like the Orkish *orktivists*. Of course, they're not all halfwits or clowns, kissing the offglobe's reflection in the puddles of their animal farm. There are sincere and honest specimens among them. And I must admit that they are the best of the Orks – but that kind isn't even allowed into the Yellow Zone, let alone the VERTU HIGH restaurant. They wouldn't go there anyway – a strange, endangered species that we haven't had up here for a long time. And its members don't live long down below either – unless, of course they work under supervision and contract. They're dying out because, to put it mildly, they're not very bright. They think everything's so bad down there because Torn Trojan is in power.

Ah, you poor, poor souls. It's completely the other way round – Torn Trojan is in power because things are so bad down there. And they're bad because that's the way they were yesterday and the day before yesterday, and after Monday and Tuesday there always comes a Wednesday in the week. So you liquidate your Urkagan (along with the final remnants of a tolerable life, because revolutions come at a high price) and then what? If you don't like the word 'Trojan', then you'll get some other Torn Latex. What difference does it make? You'll still be the same...

And then, you don't live in a vacuum, but right below us. An intercultural dialogue is bound to start up. And in cases like that our sommeliers don't waste much time on choosing their words. They are too busy choosing targets.

But I didn't say that to Grim. And anyway he'd already forgotten about the *orktivists* that he'd been expecting to meet here for some reason.

There were lots of Orkish celebrities on all sides – Grim had only seen them on the manitou before. Although he had met one man sitting in the hall in person – that was Torn Durex's mezzanine-adjutant, with whom he had ridden, side by side, into Orkish Slava on the Kagan's barge. There was also a couple of big-time gas Orks with their bodyguards. And all the Orks were looking terribly alarmed – as if they had been doused with boiling water. Everyone was looking at the manitou up near the ceiling.

The news channel B INSIDE B (Big Byz's cable news, which isn't broadcast to Orkland in any shape or form) had just started transmitting some breaking news.

Torn Durex, who was living in exile in London, had been killed.

Yes, that was news.

That's interesting now – why had I started thinking about liquidating the Kagan just a moment earlier? Maybe my ears had picked something up without me realising it, and my subconscious had processed the information before I could make sense of it? Or did information waves propagate on their own in a mental environment, without any material medium at all?

It happened like this: late in the evening, when Durex was sitting on the balcony of his open duplex in the lower section of the offglobe (the highest level of luxury accessible to a global Ork, regardless of his financial resources), 'three unidentified cameras'(ha ha ha) had flown up to his residence.

One of them fired a paralyser dart at Durex and another grappled him with a hook and dragged him over the parapet of the balcony, all the way through the conditioning barrier, and the great leader of the Urks had taken a long, involuntary dive down to Orkish Slava, where he melded with the souls of his ancestors. The third camera crashed into the golden sphere with a crown, installed on Durex's balcony in imitation of the view from Big Ben. All the Global Orks who can afford an external balcony and a conditioner-screen have these spheres with crosses or crowns (like the ones outside the windows of the BI GBEN restaurant). The catch is that they can't be projections – they have to be genuine, made of stone and metal. These are a must-have item for them, the ultimate status symbol, and between themselves they call them 'bollocks'.

To take a good look at these celebrated Orkish 'bollocks', I only had to turn my head towards Big Ben in the window of the restaurant. At the edges of the tower the spheres were twice as large, and they had crowns – for the most serious clients. Torn Durex probably had one like that. I wondered if the ancient architects had foreseen this or not.

Our discoursemongers are fond of saying that the Orkish elite's cult of Big Ben is a manifestation of their repressed homosexuality, which they don't dare to bring close to the surface of their consciousness by any other means. And that's why generation after generation of them come to London. Perhaps this is correct from the ideological point of view, but actually they don't have any problem with butt love (I'm not talking about Ganjaberserks here) – down below I've observed it plenty of times myself. Perhaps they just don't bring it close to the surface of their consciousness? But after all, I'm not a discoursemonger. And what I was thinking about wasn't this clock-tower symbolism at all.

Smash up a camera in kindergarten conditions like that! Some bloody pilots. It really was breaking news.

The official version of the killing, which was offered by B INSIDE B, was infighting among the upper echelon of the Global Orks. But it was all clear to me immediately. This was a greeting to all the big-shot Orks still down below, global and otherwise. Torn Durex had made a big mistake with his gas bomb. And others had to learn the lesson.

Of course, not a word was said about this. But the news about Durex's death was followed immediately by a live report from the funeral of Nicolas-Olivier Laurence von Trier, who had apparently been kept in a freezer for all this time – so that now even the most stupid viewers would be able to trace the link between cause and effect.

Von Trier was buried in a hundred-metre-long swimming pool, transformed for this solemn occasion into a sea, with a Nordic boat sailing away across it into the sunset. The boat and the sea both came out well. Nicolas-Olivier in person lay on his open funeral bed, with his bat on his chest. When the boat had sailed away from the shore a little, the people gathered at the funeral began making movements as if they were firing arrows from bows. Fiery arrows started showering down onto the boat, and soon it was transformed into a blazing bonfire drifting away from the shore. I don't know if they used a real smoke effect or not, but it was all done in good taste.

The Global Orks watched the manitou, spellbound. But Grim and Chloe didn't seem able to get their heads round why the news was showing the Kagan's portrait in a black mourning frame again. For them, Torn Durex had been killed with his headquarters staff at Orkish Slava. I heard, by the way, that it almost did happen – supposedly he got so drunk that they only managed to shove him into the trailer at the very last moment. The report from von Trier's funeral was interrupted several times – to show Durex's twisted body in a white shirt and nightcap, lying in the grass at Orkish Slava.

This insert had been shot well. They started with the cap, with a streak of blood on it, occupying the entire screen, then moved on to the face that was battered black and blue, with a fly crawling across it, and then the entire body, with the legs doubled up under it, appeared on the screen (there was surprisingly little blood for a height like that), and after that the shot zoomed out rapidly, and in two or three seconds the little white figure on the grass was transformed into a tiny dot in an immense sea of green (the mass graves could no longer be distinguished under the fresh turf).

I thought they would have enough wits and good taste to zoom out a little bit further and cut to my recent emblem of the war, only they didn't think of that. But it came out pretty well as it was – it inspired obscure, barely intelligible thoughts about man's insignificance in the face of nature and the cosmos. And also, it stands to reason, of another man. First and foremost.

And at this point, while I was following the news, Kaya moved into the attack.

I didn't notice how and when it happened. At some moment I simply discovered that she was talking to Grim again, and he was listening to her very carefully, nodding every now and then. Even Chloe was listening to her – and also, it seemed to me, with interest.

Kaya acted simply and unexpectedly.

While the Orkish Kagan had used gas as his weapon, she attacked Grim using her vast range of knowledge. I'm not sure, by the way, that this word is really even applicable to her – there isn't any clear boundary between the contents of her own memory and the data she can access via air port.

While I was watching the crowd taking its leave of von Trier (at least forty people had come, almost as many as came for the pupo Trig – and probably about ten million were watching), she had started explaining to the young Orks where the word 'vertuhai' came from.

Naturally, they didn't know this, although they had heard the word ever since they were kids. Kaya had started retelling a section of *Les Feuilles Mortes* for them. She was speaking rapidly and distinctly, like an aircraft cannon.

'There's no certain etymology for this word in the dictionaries. But Bernard-Henri gave a detailed explanation of it – and even adduced various accounts of its origin. According to one, in ancient times a "vertuhai" was what Orks especially loyal to the Kagan were called. He rewarded them with a valuable "Vertu" telephone and, on top of that, a small estate with serfs. Several of these phones, bearing scars from sabre blows, bullets and teeth, are still kept in the Museum of the Ancestors in Slava today. After the owners died their Vertu phones were placed in the burial mound, since it was believed that by holding on to them they could ascend into Alkalla, or at least be reborn in London. This is the account that is reflected in the name of the VERTU HIGH restaurant. The Urkaganate is working assiduously to resurrect the custom of rewarding the pillars of the regime with precious mobile phones, for which purpose it constantly orders deliveries of such phones from the jewellers in the Yellow Zone...'

Chloe tried to ask something, but Kaya didn't stop.

'According to another theory, "vertuhai" was what Mongolian tribute gatherers were called, and it was from them that the Vertu telephone acquired its name. This is the most scholarly hypothesis. According to a third explanation, "vertuhai" was a name for a tea sommelier who sat on the high machine-gun tower beside a teahouse, urging the horsemen ranging over the Siberian plain to come for tea. In order to spot them from afar, he had to have a very keen eye-sight. Hence the other name for a "vertuhai" – a "supervisor".'

Grim asked:

'But what were those horsemen doing on the Siberian plain? And why did they have to be urged?'

Kaya beamed brightly and started talking again – and what's more, I got the feeling that if I just strained my eyes a little, I would be able to see the information waves pouring into her little head through the air connection.

'Of course, the horsemen didn't need to be urged. The Mongols, who conquered Eurasia in prehistoric times, sent their tribute gatherers to the indigenous population without needing any reminders. Essentially, that was all that their state administration consisted of. Gradually the Mongols started appointing their local protégés as "vertuhai". They knew the local customs better, they were in the know about who had what hidden away, and where – and they were a match for the Mongols when it came to cruelty.'

She was speaking loudly and I noticed that the Global Orks at the nearby tables were listening carefully to our conversation.

'The arrangement was so effective that it survived even after the Mongols were out of the picture. The Orkish strongmen started appointing themselves "vertuhai" on a sovereign basis – and appropriated the tribute. The system outlived not only the Mongols, but even the Western project, with which it had a relationship of servile confrontation. An instance unique in history – that of a people's self-enslavement proving to be a viable social construct...'

At this point, a Global Ork wearing a fashionable silver chiton, who was sitting at the next table, couldn't contain himself any longer, and he intervened in our conversation.

'There's nothing new about these views,' he said. 'Many racist

331

historians have pointed to the supposedly servile nature of the ancient Urks. But...'

'No,' Kaya interrupted. 'The point isn't that they were a slave nation. In ancient times all peoples were slaves. But the Orkish elite contrived to play the role of a colonial administration even during the years when there was no external subjugator. If you know your own cultural history, this was called "the government as the only European".'

The Ork demonstratively got up from his table and walked towards the exit. This made absolutely no impression on Kaya. However, the head waiter was already walking across the hall towards us – another Global Ork, which was immediately obvious from his ugly mug.

'The management of the restaurant has the right to refuse to serve any of its customers,' he began from afar.

Grim and Chloe seemed seriously frightened.

'Well then, refuse,' I said, showing my CINEWS Inc. badge. 'I don't want to order anything else anyway, your prices are exorbitant. And under consumer law I have a perfect right to sit here and finish eating the ice cream I have paid for. I am a representative of the free media. And this isn't an Orkish satrapy, but Big Byz.'

'There's no filming or photography allowed here.'

'Were not filming anything,' I said. 'We're eating ice cream.'

Global Orks never know what's really going on around them. And they're constantly afraid that someone who does know will suddenly downgrade their assets into liabilities (to express myself in their language). And so no scandal ensued. The head waiter sat down at the table vacated by the affronted Global Ork, took out a notepad and started listening intently to our conversation.

Oh, he really frightened me.

It is sometimes said that many of the Global Orks are

members of the Orkish special services. Let them be my guests. In comparison with these children, Big Byz is one big secret service, which is simultaneously a tabloid newspaper, a washing machine, an ATM, a vibrator and a confessional. Let them spy away. Even if we expressly start explaining the set-up here to them, they still won't understand anything.

Anyway, we stayed there, sitting at the table – and then Kaya showed a rather unexpected side of herself. Realising that the Orkish head waiter was listening to her, she started telling Grim and Chloe, in a loud voice, about a squabble between the VERTU HIGH and BI GBEN restaurants – she must have spotted the information via her air link.

I've already mentioned that Big Ben is visible from the windows of VERTU HIGH. But it's not simply visible: the angle from which it's visible is as if we were floating in the air, very close to the clock on the parliament side

Apparently, Gben Mabutu had taken the Orks to court for visual defamation. If the view from their window corresponded to the notional reality, then the building in which VERTU HIGH is located would have loomed up right in front of the windows of BI GBEN, blocking out the parliament. But according to the historical 3D panorama, there had never been anything there.

The Orks swore that their view had been approved in the municipality – which could very well have been true; they have a lot of money. Most likely they bought an exclusive – the municipality has the right to do that. But our courts are not fond of Orks, so Gben Mabutu had every chance of winning his case, and then the Orks would have to bring the view from their window into line with the historical one: either move into the parliament, so that Gben Mabutu's restaurant would hover triumphantly above them, or clear out altogether – to somewhere in Belgravia, and be left without any bollocks.

The head waiter was obliged to listen to this story too. His ears turned red, and his ugly mug turned green. After several more Global Orks left the hall, he got the idea of turning the volume up to full on the manitou just below the ceiling. But the news bulletin was already over. He switched channels and hit on Slava TV.

They were broadcasting 'Songs of Ancient Childhood' – a concert by the Orkish War Orphans Choir of the Yellow Zone.

Daddy's fighting at the front.
Mummy's shagging in the rear.
We could see and hear it all
Through this big big hole here …

It was hard to understand what these touching, semi-transparent creatures were singing about in their crystal voices – was it the holes in the wall that are so typical of Orkish daily life, or their own terrible prenatal experience? I knew that the Orkish conspiracy theorists in Slava always exchanged meaningful glances with each other when they heard this song – because Orkish TV always, without fail, plays this recording when someone important dies, either one of ours or one of theirs. The ordinary Orks aren't always informed exactly who has died.

In order to make Grim feel at home, I tried to give him a meaningful look. But he was looking at Kaya.

The head waiter changed the channel. It was another programme from Slava – 'Urkish Stars'.

'What is the secret of your unfading popularity?'

'Why, you stupid fool, the secret is that they show my fat fucking face on the manitou every day! Ho ho ho!'

The head waiter switched channels again, and hit on a third programme from Slava: a report from the show trial of 'political killer technologists' (the event with which Torn Trojan had inaugurated his rule). The material evidence drifted across the screen: shards of old ceramics, scrolled and sealed propaganda posters, colourful wads of holographic manitous. It seemed like Trojan was planning on getting even not only on his own account but for the entire dynasty, and he had already become impudent enough to arrest several Orks from the Yellow Zone, entirely without consultation... It looks like there'll be a new war sooner than usual, I thought.

The fact that the TV channels here were like this was no cause for surprise. It's an Orkish restaurant, even if it is global. For the first half of their lives Global Orks fight each other for the right to leave Urkaine and go to London, and for the second half they sit in London and watch Urkainian TV.

Actually, I enjoyed it. I'm quite fond of Orkish broadcasts in general. I especially like it when their unshaven propagandists start explaining to their fellow citizens that up here all we ever dream about at night is how we can occupy Urkaine and force them to live according to our laws. Bernard-Henri was right when he called them a romantic child-nation, ever ready to believe in a fairy tale and a dream.

Grim and Chloe felt very relieved when we finally got up and walked towards the door. I tried to explain to them that there was nothing to be afraid of. That the Global Orks were only frightening down below, but here they behaved very politely and quietly, and they would give their lives for the right to sit in their restaurant above the grey waters of the Thames.

But Grim and Chloe simply couldn't believe that so many infuriated big shots were no kind of threat. What can you do? Freedom is like the sun – you have to be accustomed to it from childhood. Any later than that is hard.

We didn't go to that restaurant any more.

Although I did discover that Chloe had been there several times without us, with some Global Ork or other. We saw her less and less often – she spent most of her time with Alena-Libertina and was rapidly expanding her circle of acquaintances.

Grim was left all alone.

And Kaya, of course, took advantage of the vacuum that had been created.

I couldn't have been more amazed by the cunning with which she wove her web around him. At first I didn't think her efforts would be crowned with success – after all, Grim was an Ork through and through, without even the slightest veneer of globality.

In order to become a pupo, it's important to have a light, agile imagination that is permanently ready to burst into flames and lead your conscious mind off into an artificial world of joy and ecstasy. We don't actually need to learn this – we already know how to do it, only negatively. Something similar happens every minute in any case, except that the worlds into which fantasy leads us out of our immediate reality have absolutely nothing to do with happiness: most of the time they're cheerless and depressing regions, dominated by a brute of a boss, a dragon of a wife, illness or humiliating poverty.

However, the general opinion is that this is 'serious' and 'real', and the door to it stands wide open in welcome. But the world in which Kaya lives is a space that the normal Ork is prevented from entering by his own psychological road barrier with a skull and crossbones on it, standing guard over so-called 'moral precepts'. Grim was no exception – and after her unmasking Kaya had become merely a thing to him, rather like a coffee grinder, a harness or a spade.

Kaya couldn't contend directly with a mindset like that. But she could make a start by elevating herself to the very pinnacle of his hierarchy of inanimate objects. And after that... After that some kind of accident might happen to Grim – a programme crash of some kind (Kaya often used to say that we humans were simply tangles of worm-eaten, badly written programmes).

Such, from the look of things, was her strategy.

And so she never tried to challenge Grim's prejudices – especially concerning what Orks regard as 'perversions'. On the contrary, she played along with him all the time. And at every step she made skilful use of her own informational weaponry.

I remember, for instance, how we wandered into a certain mall where loud music was playing. Grim started wrinkling up his face and Kaya, of course, noticed. When we reached a relatively quiet spot and sat down for a bite to eat, she suddenly quoted *The Book of Orkasms* – the chapter about how 'queerasts serve the world government'. I don't want to reproduce it in full, it's too disgusting. But I'll have to say a few words about it.

According to the invaluable information in this source, the following mechanism operates here. A man, it appears, can seclude himself 'in quiet and solitude' and, by peering into 'inner darkness' after a while 'comprehend the inexpressible'. As a result, the world loses all interest for him, and so does the world government. But then the queerasts come along to give the world government a hand and 'having entrenched themselves across the river, they switch on their music machine', after which 'instead of eternal light, you behold only a squelching orifice'.

I imagined ancient Orks, flying a white flag and fording a nameless river, with the woofers and tweeters of fallen humanity aimed at them. Paradise lost. However, Grim didn't even smile – as he was listening to this raving nonsense the skin across his cheekbones tightened. He sat there, staring into the distance, as if he really had spotted the glimmer of Orkish truth way out there.

But Kaya immediately started telling him the story of how *The Book of Orkasms* came into being.

Apparently the nucleus of this book really had been written

337

very long ago, and to all appearances the author lived by the sea, because in the early strata of the text mention is made of *kebabs of frozen fish, which they roast on the esplanade to queerastic chanting,* and *a herd of naked loiterers plodding to the concrete beach through a corridor of red-hot braziers.*

Kaya adduced several more quotations from the archaic level. The following in particular stuck in my memory.

The Custodian of the War Music said: he who has heard music of the queerasts twice is already a queerast himself. Such men are called 'defiled by way of air and sound'. Therefore did the men of ancient times perforate their ear drums with nails and speak with each other in the language of gestures...

Of course, inventing something like that is beyond the powers of a pampered new age. Hence the sombre power of this text, which is felt by anyone who turns to it to seek advice. But later on, the frivolous trivia created by subsequent centuries were introduced into the simple, severe edifice of this ancient temple – all those postscripts about the light of truth, the stings of the mind and other ineffable stuff. And naturally, our sommeliers had a hand in this too.

Grim listened with his jaw hanging open and Kaya was happy. At least, that was how it looked from the outside.

I finally realised that she had won when I saw Grim discussing Chloe with her. It was incredible, but they were talking about her as a common acquaintance, and no more. Mind you, they weren't discussing Chloe herself, but derivative pornography.

Grim had already got used to Kaya's readiness to answer any question. And apart from that, she was simply a thing to him, and it wasn't likely even to occur to him to feel embarrassed. But in this case he didn't even know that embarrassment was in order.

He said:

'I can't understand it... Chloe's been watching this derporn for more than a day and a night now. One of her friends gave her it. I saw pictures like that ages ago, but this is an entire movie. The screen shows a table with men and women sitting at it. Ordinary people. A couple of policemen, a priest. Looking into the camera without speaking. And every now and then they pull faces as if someone's killing a kitten in front of them and they can't do anything about it. And Chloe stares at all this. And I can see she's bored, but she's pretending not to be... And that's not all she does... Is that really what your pornography's like?'

At this point I broke down and laughed. I was curious to see how my little darling would wriggle out of this situation.

I must say she handled herself pretty well.

'It's lucky for you, Grim, that you didn't bring this up with some other girl,' she said. 'You would have got a slap across the face. And then an hour of hysterics. But I'm a very broad-minded girl. On most things...'

She laughed quietly, and I noticed that without even realising it, Grim had already fallen under her spell – just like when they first met.

'You see,' Kaya went on, 'there's a specific cultural difference between the inhabitants of Big Byz and Orks. Orks perceive the erotic component of snuffs as pornography. To them it seems obscene and titillating.'

'Well, not always,' Grim muttered.

'But often. While for a topside person it's a dreary, routine religious agenda. If we take the word "pornography" to mean a video sequence that induces erotic spasms in the viewer, then the cultural clichés are quite different in a post-informational society. And that's why Chloe's trying to work up some interest in derp. You see, she wants to turn herself from a little Orkish fool into a fully adequate human being. The ability to be aroused by derp is one of the qualities that distinguishes upper people from Orks.'

'But why is it called that – derporn or derp?' asked Grim.

'Derivative pornography. To avoid saying "legal underage porn".'

'Underage porn? But all the people at that table are pensioners!'

'Derp isn't the banned product itself, but its legal derivative. It's not about the pensioners sitting at the table. It's about what the pensioners are watching.'

'A-a-ah!' said Grim, catching on. 'You mean they're not looking into the camera?'

Kaya shook her head.

'Big Byz actually once used to have a porn industry in which underage models were involved. A struggle was waged against it. Every time they found more material with minors in it, a special commission had to watch it before it was destroyed. According to legend, the manitou used by the commission had a small camera on it, as they often did in those days. And it filmed the faces of the members of the commission while they watched the confiscated material. The recordings started to be passed from hand to hand, because this aroused visually surfeited people even more powerfully than real underage pornography...'

'You mean those sullen mugs on the screen are watching underage pornography?'

'Not for a long time already,' said Kaya. 'Nowadays the derps use special actors who have spent many years studying Stanislavsky's system. During shooting they merely imagine that they are seeing underage pornography. That's stipulated in the disclaimer. But on the black market it's possible to buy derp in which the actors are watching absolutely genuine underage porn – the kind in which the models are less than forty-six years old. You won't be able to tell the difference. The same table with

340

a tablecloth, carafes of water, name cards. Exactly the same kind of men and women, wincing and spitting in exactly the same way. But a connoisseur realises immediately, after four or five minutes. Of course, it's shameful to keep films like that at home. But it doesn't break the law. While the underage porn carries a sentence of half a lifetime in prison.'

'And you mean some people really like it?'

'What do *you* think?' I put in, unable to resist. 'There are some who wank off to derp all their lives. If they don't have the money for a sura. Who wants to do time for underage porn? You should go to the court some time and have a listen. "The male model is only forty-two years old, and filming him beside a naked woman could cause him irreparable psychological trauma…" And crawling through bloody genitals, age zero, was OK for him? So let's put Manitou to jail for twenty years or so…'

'Oh, how vulgar you are,' said Kaya, wincing. 'I feel ashamed for you in front of Grim.'

I like it when she reacts to me emotionally. Even when she simulates this emotion for the sake of my symbolic rival. I chuckled and went on:

'Bernard-Henri had a collection of genuine derp, old stuff. And not on his manitou, but on photographic paper – the biggest hit of all for a connoisseur. He used to sort it by category – facial, anal and so forth…'

'Phoo! Phoo! Shut up immediately!' Kaya said and stamped her foot.

'What do you mean, shut up? Even children draw that sort of thing now. A table with uncles and aunties sitting at it, with their faces all skewed. And it's all coloured in with crayons – the table, the carafe. When the parents find it, it means instant tears and thrashings.'

'But why can't people watch snuffs?' asked Grim. 'I mean as erotica?'

I shrugged.

'Well, if you can't understand that and feel it for yourself, I don't know how to explain it. There's even an Orkish saying: "Often – puff, seldom – huff, never – wank to a snuff".'

'Phoo, you coarse brute,' Kaya snorted.

And she blushed.

Honestly, she blushed. And Grim was hooked immediately. And again he didn't notice how.

'I shouldn't have started this conversation,' he said, looking at Kaya. 'But what kind of Orkish saying is that?'

'In my young days I studied Orkish folklore,' I replied. 'In order to understand the soul of the enemy. I learned lots of new things. By the way, they're still making historical discoveries from your sayings.'

'How's that?' Grim asked in surprise.

'Well... for instance there was a Siberian proverb: "His son and his daughter put the kibosh on Darth Vader".'

'What's a kibosh?' Grim asked.

'Kibosh? I'm not completely sure,' I said. 'Perhaps this big black lacquered helmet. Like the one they put on you in the entertainment block. You remember?'

Grim nodded.

'And who is Darth Vader?'

'He ... Well, it's a long story and doesn't really matter. What matters is that we can conclude from this proverb that in the times when Urkaine was called the Siberian Republic, the fore-bears of present-day Orks had access to the Ancient Films.'

'And what other discoveries have they made from sayings?'

I suddenly felt curious about whether Kaya would continue making passes at him and took a few seconds to come up with something that would delight her. Fortunately it wasn't difficult – every Orkish saying is a good pretext for a duel.

'For instance, "Pissing without farting is like tea without tsampa". The historians conclude that the Orks once had a higher standard of living than today. And contacts with the Tibetan Plateau, through which they obtained barley flour.'

Kaya winced but kept quiet. But now she didn't need to open her mouth – her manipulations had already galvanised Grim. He spoke up himself.

'I'm sorry, Kaya. Another bad idea.'

'No,' said Kaya. 'Not at all. Everything's fine.'

But she looked as if she had been forced to undress in front of a battalion of Ganjaberserks. Grim looked upset too – that happened to him every time he came face to face with the abysmal hideousness of his own nation.

'I haven't heard a single one of these sayings,' he said.

That wasn't very surprising, because they had most likely been invented in the time of Loss Liquid by our sommeliers, who were assembling an anthology of Orkish folklore – in that period the Orks decided to buy in a bit more cultural history for themselves and paid pretty well for it. These sayings never infiltrated the broad masses, and down below it was mostly only philologists who knew them. But of course, that didn't mean that I couldn't study the soul of the enemy from them. On the contrary, it was very convenient – you got a clear picture in the minimum of time. If the Orkish masters of culture were capable of inventing anything themselves, they would have been certain to come out with much the same. But I didn't talk about that – Kaya would have found something to carp about even there.

'I'll find out all about Orkish sayings,' she promised Grim.

'No, don't,' he growled. 'But thanks, of course. It's very kind of you, Kaya.'

With tiny little steps like that my wily playmate advanced towards her goal – and soon reached it.

Oh yes. And how.

This one time we went to watch Ancient Films at the retro-hall, where they show them on the same apparatus as in the times when they were shot, which makes for total immersion in the historical atmosphere. It's an interesting experience. I usually take a seat in the first or second row, because I like the big picture. But Grim and Kaya sat right at the back.

I didn't look round, but I had a nanocamera with me, which I put on my collar specially to keep an eye on them. And somewhere in the middle of the film they started kissing. Long and hard.

So this was it.

I can't say that I felt jealousy. But when the kissing couple appeared in my mini-manitou, I started thinking about how I'd ended up with a life like this. And why, I wondered, had I adjusted my sura's settings to such a mode that she was ecstatically kissing this Orkish *untermensch*, while I could only get a kiss out of her by cunning and blackmail?

The answer, of course, was simple. When she kissed someone else, I believed in her sincerity, because it's always easy to believe in something bad. But if she started kissing me as ecstatically as that... I could achieve that with just three twists of a knob. But I could never have forgotten for a moment that it was the 'Cloud of Tenderness' mode kissing me.

These were our final outings in Big Byz. The introduction phase was over – Grim had got his bearings in the environment well enough now to carry on getting to know Byzantion independently.

From now on he could only see Kaya in my home. I didn't intend to deny him this small joy – if only because I didn't want

344

to deny myself the great joy that was waiting for me every time after he left.

I hadn't known before that the list of services provided by suras included this one: 'Non-symbolic triumph over the symbolic rival'. As amplified by dopamine resonance, too.

It seems to me now that those were the happiest days of my life. Kaya immersed herself in simulating her romance with Grim and was very glad that I didn't obstruct their occasional meetings (I even used to fly out on a mission sometimes, pretending that I didn't notice their whispering and kissing in the corners, but they didn't go any further than that). In response she gave me happiness readily and obediently. And also, I think, without any particular revulsion – insofar as that's possible under the sullen skies of maximum bitchiness.

One day I got a call from the manufacturer.

Apparently Kaya had acquired paid access to materials that weren't in the general info-library... The company wanted to know if I was aware that she was paying for it herself. The materials were entirely inoffensive in character – ancient religious treatises on human nature, information on the functioning of the brain and so on.

I decided that Kaya wanted to find out more about what makes us tick, so that it would be easier to manipulate us. And suddenly I realised that I was thinking about her as if she was alive.

I couldn't understand how she contrived to behave in such a way that all the time I saw before me a real personality, exactly like myself. After all, I knew that the light of Manitou wasn't in her, that this was simply an electronic mirror hanging in front of me.

But it was a mirror that could play chess. And when you're playing chess, can you tell who's sitting opposite you from the way the pieces move?

It suddenly seemed incomprehensible to me how I could have taken on trust, and for so long, the company's assurance that she was in no way qualitatively different from a complex domestic electrical appliance.

Of course, the reason why the company said that was clear enough.

Only was it really true?

Grim journeyed through the new world all alone – Chloe could have accompanied him, but she didn't want to, and Kaya was eager to, but she couldn't.

Getting around was easy. All he had to do was walk into a metrolift cabin and enter the address in the manitou with his finger. The list of options was refreshed after every new letter, exactly like in an on-screen dictionary.

If the destination was displayed in large font, it meant that there would be a large public space outside the door (these were mostly stations devoted to the great cities of antiquity – but despite the numerous tube exits, crowds of people rarely gathered there).

Smaller text led into malls, restaurants or cultural centres such as the memorial to Trig. They were usually empty. Byzantines hardly ever came here – only for a gala dinner, some kind of media event that required the presence of lots of people, or when a consumer wanted to touch a product with his own hands before buying it.

Really small text related to private addresses. Several times when Grim made a mistake the tube disgorged him into corridors exactly the same as the one where the door of his own residence was located.

It looked like the inhabitants of Big Byz preferred to spend their time in their own individual space.

Grim knew that there were also restricted zones, which weren't in the transporter's menu – to get to them you had to know the code. But for the time being the freely accessible world was enough for him.

He mostly travelled to the very biggest words – 'Florence', 'Carthage', 'Los Angeles', 'Jerusalem', 'St Petersburg' and so on. Every time he found himself in fantastically beautiful places that he had only seen before in the *Free Encyclopaedia* or on the manitou. Of course, if he really thought about it, he was seeing them on a manitou now as well – but he tried not to think about that.

The boundaries of physical reality could almost always be identified directly through the three-dimensional apparition. Points at which there was a danger of banging a head or an elbow were marked with little green perimeter lights; if they were anything to go by, reality was rather cramped. The cities consisted of several city squares, the squares were actually round halls with low ceilings, and what looked like streets turned out to be narrow tunnels. Apparently the underlying space looked like the scruffy corridor that Grim had seen on his first day on Big Byz, which hadn't been connected to a generator of illusions.

But the three-dimensional projectors transformed these crooked technical burrows into extremely convincing avenues with tall old trees and fairy-tale palaces. The illusion went beyond a simple three-dimensional mirage. If Grim was walking past dusty railings screening off a shady garden, he could even blow on the dust – and see it go flying up off a cast-iron flourish. The important point was not to touch anything with his fingers.

347

But the world was arranged in such a way that it left very few opportunities for unmasking it.

The space was always a joy to look at – but it was physically beyond reach, because he was separated off from it by either a fence, or a deceptively light screen, or a concrete parapet that coincided with a real wall. Distant parks, rivers and hills were quite literally no more than a fleeting glimpse – they existed only as they went fleeting by.

But the universe was cordoned off with such cunning that the unstated prohibition on crossing its boundaries never seemed as crude and offensive as in Orkland, where everything was real. And Grim was amazed to realise that all his life down below he had been taking what he saw on trust – but essentially the pathways along which destiny had herded him were every bit as crooked as in Big Byz.

The physical world coincided with the projected version at principal key points, the so-called 'sphincters'. For instance, the entrances to palaces and houses, marked with little green perimeter lights, were absolutely genuine – in the sense that they allowed Grim to enter a multi-storey space in which the electronic windows offered views from the height appropriate to each individual storey, and he could see the street that he had just left in order to come inside. The view was as illusory as the street itself – and just as convincing. Sometimes he could go out onto the roof and survey the city from above – but an unobtrusive barrier prevented him from getting too close to the edge.

The people he occasionally met during his walks were un-sociable – they often seemed to be simply part of the overall 3D-panorama. And soon Grim noticed that he was spending more and more time in front of his personal manitou at home – because the choice of illusions here was much wider than in the public spaces.

Firstly, the manitou allowed him to watch movies shot by people in the distant past without any restrictions – those self-same Ancient Films that were practically never shown down below.

In Big Byz they were regarded with religious reverence. Before every film Grim saw this caption:

THE HOUSE OF MANITOU
AND
THE ARCHIVE OF ANCIENT FILMS
ARDENTLY PRESENT

The Ancient Films were mostly two-dimensional, two-hour stories. They could be about anything at all – about wizards and the forces of evil that people had worshipped and prayed to before the coming of Antichrist; about a solitary hero in search of money; about love and the death that accompanies it; about the inhabitants of a concrete hell, trying to sell their jaded sex to the big city; about cosmic democraships and dictocracies and so on.

Chloe watched the movies with her eyes popping out of her head, but Grim himself rapidly lost interest in them. Possibly what he had heard from Bernard-Henri was hindering him. He really did find it hard to perform the inner act of will that the discoursemonger had called 'the suspension of disbelief'. Even if Grim made a conscious effort to suspend his disbelief, the sheer idiocy of what was happening on the manitou unfailingly brought the feeling back again. And the moments when the moviemakers' intentions showed through the picture were particularly unpleasant.

Ancient man was a happy child – he could believe in the reality of the rock paintings that he danced around with his spear, or in stories invented and acted out by other people, shot on a two-dimensional film camera and clumsily touched-up with electronic cosmetics on a low-speed manitou.

But Grim couldn't do that anymore. He knew that an illusion could take any form at all, and it wasn't worth a damn. Watching the Ancient Films wasn't interesting – as if the lie-infected light that the film had once captured had turned rank over the centuries in the round tin boxes where its coils were kept. A night dream was a hundred times more interesting and real, because it wasn't the work of people with their carefully calculated untruth, but of the gloriously inconsistent Manitou.

There was another reason why he found watching the old stories disagreeable.

The people on the screen were always getting into difficult and awkward situations. They experienced (or rather, portrayed) humiliation, embarrassment and fear. It was clear that things were arranged like this to provide some kind of logical basis for the action, some developmental impulse to keep the plot moving. But Grim couldn't give a damn for the logic of the lies on the screen – only critics in the pay of the cinemafia could take those seriously. In his view, it would have been better if the ancient shades had acted without any reason at all, instead of torturing him to death with their contrived dramatic effects.

The negative emotions portrayed by the actors were transmitted to his soul, not because he believed in them, but simply by virtue of the law of resonance. Every time the characters ended up in yet another ghastly situation, Grim pressed the pause button in reflex response: by doing that he could halt his own anguish – which was real, unlike the false anguish on the screen. And so he didn't even suffer with the characters, but instead of them.

Apparently, archaic man not merely believed in the reality of what he saw, but also fed off the false suffering of others – or used it in some way to spruce himself up before the new working day. But Grim, who didn't even believe in what was happening, pressed pause so often that it took a whole night to watch a two-hour melodrama. Chloe usually left him and went to another manitou.

Basically, Grim wearied very quickly of the antiquity that had been consumed by the nuclear fire – and he couldn't figure out why the Archive of Ancient Films was regarded as just about the most important religious shrine on Big Byz.

Another opportunity that the manitou offered was far more important. Now he could watch any snuffs at all in full – without any military censorship or Orkish spiritual oversight.

He finally discovered the meaning of that word – a subject on which even the *Free Encyclopaedia* remained silent, to say nothing of school textbooks. The on-screen dictionaries helped him here. The acronym 'S.N.U.F.F.' stood for:

Special Newsreel / Universal Feature Film

The phrase seemed clear enough, but there were subtle shades of meaning to it. For instance, in antiquity the phrase 'Universal Feature Film' meant 'a film from Universal Studios', and it only later came to be used with the meaning 'universal work of art'. The word 'universal' also had religious connotations relating to the word 'Universe'. But for the time being Grim didn't delve into that.

The forward slash in the decoded phrase was called a 'zhizhek' in honour of some legendary European thinker or other. The dictionary explained that it demarcated the particular and the general, which complemented each other.

This zhizhek seemed to carry a semantic loading that was almost greater than that of the words themselves. The article devoted to it in the on-screen dictionary was set in fine print for smart people and had this title:

351

Grim didn't try to read it, but he was quite impressed.

There were dozens, if not hundreds of similar articles on snuffs in the dictionaries and encyclopaedias. A countless throng of the upper people's discoursemongers and sommeliers had hastened to offer this resonant acronym their respectful, high-quality services – the tips that came with this were clearly lavish.

Grim discovered that the word SNUFF was really very old, and was already used in the Internet shitstorms of the age of the Ancient Films, with the meaning of 'inordinately arousing actual art' (one of the notes explained this definition as: 'a porn movie with a real killing shot on film'). The fine print explained that a number of linguists believed that the modern-day interpretation had been appended to it in the new age, like the interpretation of the word GULAG – when, in waging their war against the Orks, people felt the need to declare themselves the exclusive heirs to the great past.

In dividing a snuff, as it were, into two parts, the zhizhek corresponded perfectly to its inner structure.

Exactly half the screen time of a snuff was filled with sex.

It was performed by global celebrities who, although no longer young, were still rather attractive, such as the late von Trier and his partner of many years – de Auschwitz. Proceedings were diligently captured on celluloid and not one minute anatomic detail went unrecorded. Grim had known the faces of almost all the actors since he was a child – but until now he had never seen them completely naked, since the Orkish spiritual censorship hid the erotic action on the screen behind its logos.

Once he saw what had been concealed so painstakingly, Grim thought it would have been far easier to turn viewers away from sin by showing it in full detail.

The other half of the screen time was filled with death.

This part of the snuffs consisted of military chronicles that Grim hadn't seen in full either – this time because of the Big Byz military censor.

And these chronicles simply astounded him.

He saw the faces of Kagans of ancient times. He saw flags, the faded tatters of which were kept in the Museum of the Ancestors. He saw the deaths of heroes, of whom all that was left in his world were identical posthumous portraits, documents covered with a reddish-brown crust and baby shirts preserved by mothers – now yellowed and shrivelled with age.

For every war the Orks donned a new uniform, often in several versions. There were wars of classical tunics, wars of shorts, wars of black leather harnesses and wars of formal suits. There were wars that looked like gay parades and wars that looked like these parades being dispersed. The people's clothes didn't change so greatly, but on the other hand, they entered into every war with new weapons and machines.

More than anything else, Grim was astounded by the tanks, which he had already seen in the Ancient Films. About two centuries earlier the people had built about fifty of them from surviving design drawings and used them against the Orks. The tanks had proved so lethal that they hadn't even left behind any traces in oral folk tradition – there was no one to spread the word. The demographic gap had had to be made up by using artificial insemination, with which the people had helped after the ceasefire (the so-called 'girlie draft' – it was studied in school now as an example of female wartime heroism).

It was in this very battle with the tanks that the great Marshal Stug had got almost a million Orks killed. Now Grim could see the fighting from beginning to end with his own eyes.

The marshal, sitting on a white horse, kept giving the order to attack ad infinitum. The Orks ran forward and every single

353

one of the people's tanks was transformed into a shapeless blob by the bodies sticking to it.

Then this blob slithered about on the spot for a long time, grinding the heroes into a bloody pulp. A shot from a tank's gun mowed down an entire Orkish detachment. After this, Marshal Stug gave the order to advance into a new attack and the gates of the Circus sucked in a new serving of Ork meat. Although the delivery was ideally organised, it took many days for the gates of the Circus to let through all the actors in the drama, and afterwards there wasn't another war for three whole years.

The people called the period of the girlie draft 'the monotank years' because for three years they had to repeat one and the same shot from different angles in all the snuffs.

That time round the filming really was monotonous, because the people didn't use the flying walls and shot the panorama of the tank battle from high altitude. For the first half hour this snuff (or at least its war component) was fascinating and terrifying to watch. But after that there was nothing left but nausea that got worse with every close-up angle provided by the nosediving cameras. They fell out of the sky by turns, to go hurtling between the huge machines wallowing in red slurry and then soar back up for another wide-angle shot.

Panoramas of the tank battle alternated with bedroom scenes that completely failed to engage Grim's empathy – since then, the people's culture had gone through several complete cycles, and so the actors embodied a type of sexual attractiveness that had been obsolete for ages. Grim was equally disgusted by the shaven-headed, potbellied man – an enigmatic smile on his lips, the garland of flowers over flowing orange robes, and the timid woman with fading beauty, an unshaven pubis, stars tattooed round her nipples and a mane of wavy hair. They were at least two hundred years old by now, and it showed – so even the clay teapot that the man picked up every time he changed poses or the tiger skin on which coition took place were of no help.

Although the people's weapons changed, the Orks' tactics remained the same: first raise the flag on the Hill of the Ancestors and then, after dividing into three formations, repel the attack on the central front and the flanks, until the people had shot the material they needed. This manner of conducting the battle was probably chosen because it could be rammed, century after century and without any great difficulty, into the heads of even Orkish military men.

From the point of view of editing or storyline, the snuffs were more primitive than the films of ancient times. But they were far more interesting to watch – and the most boring snuff was far more gripping than the most absorbing film.

It seemed to Grim that the light which had imprinted recent history on temple celluloid was still alive and fresh, it was still flying off into space somewhere – unlike the dead light of the Ancient Films, which had faded forever. The great battles that drifted across the screen were genuine. And so was the Circus – Grim himself had only just passed through it, and it was simply astounding how little it had changed.

Everything in the Ancient Films was lies and play-acting. But everything in the snuffs was the truth. And not because the people had become any more honest over the centuries.

The very nature of love and death meant that you couldn't possibly engage in them as make-believe. It was irrelevant whether those participating in the procedure believed in what they were doing – the important thing was that it was really happening to them. Copulating and dying could only be done for real, either in domestic solitude or in front of hundreds of cameras in the arena. And so there was no longer any need to 'suspend disbelief', as the late Bernard-Henri used to say.

'The youth of great civilisations,' an unknown philosopher

explained in an on-screen dictionary, '*is characterised by the flowering of representative forms of government. Their maturity is characterised by the construction of a Circus which, at various stages of social development, can be informational and virtual, as well as physical and material. The mediacracies of the past were precarious because they oppressed man by constraining libido and mortido. Manitou the Antichrist forbade this on pain of love and death...*'

The embryonic plot present in each snuff was almost insignificant, and yet in some ways they resembled the melodramas of ancient times. They often told the story of two lovers. This could be a tragic love between one of the people and an Ork – Grim watched the snuffs like that first of all.

The 'Ork' was usually made up to look like a youthful man or woman of emphatically uncivilised appearance, and always had to have a straw sticking out of his or her hair (at first Grim thought this was a propagandist attack on his people, but then he guessed that it was more probably a symbolic indication of closeness to nature). The women's hairstyles and the way they applied their make-up changed greatly from century to century. For men the most significant change was in the design of their wallets.

There was something medical about the lovers' coupling – it was captured by a camera in every possible pose, including an obligatory close-up of genitals coupled together right in front of the lens (evidently for those who were bone idle, because the remote control included a little trackpad that allowed the viewer to adjust the magnification and viewing angle for himself).

The ancient news broadcasts that ended up in snuffs were like flies in amber – their authenticity and hideousness were amazing. Here too Grim quickly identified a repeated motif: an agitated anchorman in CINEWS uniform (which also changed over time) informed humanity of the latest obscenity committed in Slava – for instance, a mass killing of journalists, which drunken

356

Right Protectors had bragged about openly in the market, or something else of a similar kind.

That was followed by shots of the gruesome details – undoubtedly real (what Grim found interesting to look at were not the puddles of blood, but the way the market square and familiar streets used to look a hundred or two hundred years ago).

When the news section ended, the lovers started discussing what they had seen, and here the Ork usually gave vent to some vicious nonsense – for instance that Orkish journalists killed Right Protectors themselves, and to think that they were good while the others were bad was just plain stupid.

This was the point, of course, at which the unalloyed propaganda and brainwashing began. Grim couldn't imagine a compatriot of his who would come up with that kind of rubbish. Everyone down below realised that a journalist wouldn't dare say boo to a Right Protector. The Ork on the screen was telling massive whoppers, but for some reason he didn't tell the truth that Grim would definitely have told. For instance, that journalists were always stealing horses, and if they couldn't steal them they took turns to rape them, binding their feet and muzzles with wire, and afterwards the horses were ill for a long time, so the peasants often hired Right Protectors themselves. In Urkaine even the children knew that.

The only place he found an explanation for this intercultural misunderstanding was in an on-screen dictionary.

Journalist – Fr. Ch. Eng. – words implying daily activity (journal, diurnal). A thief who steals in the daytime – as opposed to a nocturnalist, or night-time thief. In olden times information sommeliers used to be called this, and in Church English the word 'journalist' still has connotations related to the information business. This is why for a long time the protection of journalists served as a reason for Circus wars.

There now – a reason for Circus wars.

Who needed the truth? Grim realised that the people didn't even set out to malign the Orks by showing them as malicious idiots, but were simply trying to encompass all the inconvenient complexity of their life in a single streamlined cliché that migrated from snuff to snuff, because that way it was easier to fill up the three minutes of time set aside for this – and any non-standard development of the subject would have transformed three minutes into five, or even fifteen.

Of course, there were welcome departures from the stereotypes, but the greater part of CINEWS Inc.'s output was cast in one and the same mould.

However, in a huge number of snuffs (shot, for instance on historical or mythological subjects), Orks weren't even mentioned. At first Grim couldn't figure out where the 'special newsreel' that had been promised was – and then he realised that it was the Circus section. Any war in the Circus was the main news of the year – and the most genuine event.

In visual terms the 'newsreel' was always segued perfectly with the 'feature film'. It was hard to say which was the chicken and which the egg: whether the costumes of the battling Orks had been chosen to suit the scenarios or the scenarios had been written to match the military uniform – but the transition from the chronicle of events on Orkish Slava to the love sections didn't require any additional bridges at all.

Every snuff began with a standard formula about the actors and models having reached the age of consent and the Government of the Urkainian Urkaganate bearing complete responsibility for all scenes of violence and cruelty. Basically, everything was clear. Apart from one thing.

What did the people shoot snuffs for?

Strangely enough, in all the numerous articles there was no direct answer to that question. All that was clear was that snuffs were somehow connected with the local religion, and for that reason they were shot on light-sensitive ritual film.

And they didn't simply have something to do with religion.

It seemed that snuffs were the central sacrament of movism.

Every Sunday the House of Manitou showed a fresh, or as they said here 'virgin' snuff. For the last hundred or hundred and fifty years not many people had gone to the temples, but on Sunday morning anyone could watch the new snuff at home. This tradition was so fundamental to the Byzantine identity that it was the usual thing to observe it – or at least pretend that you did.

That meant that CINEWS Inc. shot more than fifty snuffs a year. The footage in every one of them had to be original (although, as the story of the tank battle showed, the same event could be shot from various angles). That was why such a large number of cameras was required over the field of battle – the war had to be sawn up into a whole heap of different stories.

There was no information about the sacred mysteries of movism in the on-screen dictionaries. Nothing was even said about the symbol of the faith or the essence of the teaching – in response to all queries the on-screen dictionaries suggested seeking oral instruction at the House of Manitou.

Grim, however, had experience of using the *Free Encyclopaedia* and knew that grains of truth were sometimes to be found in articles devoted to debunking the wrong views of others. The on-screen dictionaries of Big Byz turned out to be organised in the same way. Although there was practically no information about movism as such, it was possible to get a glimpse of this religion from the articles about its heresies.

The most important of these was the sect of the 'Film Burners'.

The article about this movement, which had appeared about a hundred years earlier, was written in a tone of incensed loathing, and there was a lot in it that seemed obscure to Grim. But there were a few things he did understand.

The Film Burners taught that the external world is a projection of the inner world and the projector that creates the world is not located in the hands of Manitou, but inside man himself. The light of this projector is the light of Manitou, and the same in everyone. But the 'film' through which it passes is different for everyone and everyone lives in their own illusory world, where they suffer from loneliness. The primary spiritual task of a member of the sect was to find this 'film' and burn it.

The Film Burners believed that those who 'had burned the film' could be born in a different world after death. And some of them maintained that it was possible to go to that world even while still alive. In the end, the Film Burners, in perfect keeping with their own metaphysics, had tried to burn the Archive of Ancient Films. After this act of sacrilege their sect had been banned.

Grim found this so interesting that he even decided to visit Damilola at an unsociable hour.

Damilola received him seated at a table covered with tiny bottles of sake. This evidently wasn't the first day he had been drinking – the shadows under his eyes had turned into black circles. But on the other hand, Kaya astounded Grim once again with her beauty.

She was wearing a figure-hugging kimono of green silk and her hair was arranged in a black ponytail caught up with a rubber band that had funny little animal-bobbles on it. Her movements looked economical and precise – she occasionally came over to the table to wipe it down or to serve a bottle warmed to the required temperature, and immediately walked away again in order not to interrupt the men's conversation. But Grim received one long glance from under half-lowered

360

eyelashes, after which he started wondering what he had really come to Damilola's place for.

'Film burners?' Damilola asked with a frown. 'Yes, we used to have them. A very interesting sect. They said they'd found a way out of the world. And apparently they all took off through it, he he. There haven't been any here for ages. But they're still recruiting new members.'

'How?' asked Grim.

'Directly through the manitou. They send letters.'

'But how do they know who to send them to?'

'From queries. They have access to the net, they watch to see who's interested in the subject and start working on them.'

'But how can they send letters if they're not here anymore?'

'Elementary,' Damilola said with a wave of his hand. 'They left spambots behind.'

'Spambots?

'Yes,' said Damilola. 'It's from the word "spam". Advertising and all sorts of idiotic messages. It came from the expression "spiced ham". That was what they called dog food in the Age of the Ancient Films. A spambot is like a little kind of organism that lives in a manitou and adapts itself to changes.'

'So then,' Grim asked in fright, 'if I looked them up in a dictionary, does that mean those organisms will start on me now?'

'I don't know,' Damilola chuckled.

'And what do they write in their letters?'

'You should ask Kaya,' said Damilola. 'She's the one with an air link in her head, not me. Kaya, come here, baby.'

Kaya, who was following the conversation attentively, came over to the table and sat down, lowering her eyes. There was a kind of exalted sadness about her. And she also looked like a little girl who has broken an expensive vase and is waiting in terror for it all to come out, so that she will be punished. That

361

sort of thing never happened with Chloe – not meaning the vase, of course, but the shamefacedness.

'We were talking about the Film Burners,' said Damilola.

'I heard,' Kaya said with a nod.

'Can you tell us anything? I don't really know anything about them.'

Kaya thought for a moment and said:

'Their metaphysics had two main concepts. The "projector" and the "film". The projector is the light of consciousness. The film is the tenebrosities and obscurities of the soul that divide man from Manitou.'

'That's in the dictionary,' said Grim.

'Yes,' Damilola agreed. 'Hack a bit deeper, sweetheart.'

Grim didn't understand what that word meant, but Kaya evidently did. She closed her eyes and wrinkled up her face, as if she was trying to catch some barely audible sound.

'They taught that this film should be burned, right?' Grim asked impatiently.

Kaya shook her head.

'There's a slight confusion here. They didn't teach that the film should be burned. They didn't teach that anything should be burned at all. The word "projector" here is used in a different Old English sense, meaning "someone who makes plans, or projects". That was what they called a man absorbed in the unconscious activity of the mind. According to their teaching, one should stop being a projector and see reality as it is. To do this it was necessary to detect the "veil" of thoughts and move to the other side of it, to the pure, unadulterated light ... A specific mystical flight led to it ... I think that's it.'

She was silent for a while, flinching and wincing.

'Yes, that's it,' she said, 'remove the veil of thoughts from the eyes and behold the light of Manitou. They said that the human personality itself is simply the contamination and obscuration of

362

this light. Their teaching has nothing to do with movies. They called themselves "Film Removers". That's from John Milton's poem *Paradise Lost*. Shall I quote it?'

Damilola nodded, as Grim thought, with pride in his talking toy.

'"But to nobler sights,"' Kaya declaimed, '"Michael from Adam's eyes the film removed." The word "film" here can be translated as "movie" or "veil".'

'That's enough,' Damilola said with a wave of his hand. 'The conclusion?'

'They started burning films later,' said Kaya. 'At first several people committed self-immolation after winding temple celluloid round themselves. That really did happen, but it was a quite different sect, the "Witnesses of Manitou". And then there was the shady business with the Archive of Ancient Films, which members of the sect supposedly tried to burn in order to give everybody freedom. That was when they were given the name "Film Burners". One account suggests that the burning was invented exclusively so that they could be banned.'

'But what were they really banned for?'

'They used to leave here and live in Orkland. They lived separately from the Orks, on the very edge of the plain. Where the dumping grounds are... Now...'

Kaya wrinkled up her face as if she had a headache.

'An eye with a tear in it...'

'What eye?'

'It was their symbol – a round eye with a tear in it. That's what it says in the old versions of the dictionaries, but there's no image anywhere. No, here it is... I can't understand. There's no information, it's almost all erased. Aha, there it is... So that's it... That's clear...'

'What?' asked Damilola.

'It's nothing interesting,' Kaya said with a wave of her hand.

'All that's known is that none of the burners ever came back from Orkland. They all disappeared without trace.'

'That's easily done in our parts,' Grim remarked.

'That's all,' said Kaya. 'I don't see any more.'

'The Orks probably killed them all,' Damilola suggested. 'That's why the sect was banned.'

Kaya nodded, then turned to Grim and said:

'Grim, while we're here together, I want you to remember one thing. Whatever might happen, I'll never forget you. Never, do you hear?'

Grim was dumbfounded. Kaya was looking at him with her eyes wide open, and they were filled with such... such... Grim had absolutely no words for it. He hadn't even known that it existed at all.

Then, as if she had recovered her senses, Kaya lowered her eyes.

For a few seconds there was silence at the table. And then Damilola gave a deafening laugh.

'Oh, Grim, what a shame you can't see yourself. You're blushing! You're blushing!'

'She's blushing too,' Grim muttered.

'It's easier for her,' Damilola said and laughed again, so hard that he could hardly speak. 'You can't even imagine... you can't even imagine, Grim, what else she knows how to do!'

Kaya jumped up from the table and dashed out into the next room, provoking another paroxysm of laughter from Damilola.

'Don't take it to heart,' he said when he'd stopped laughing. 'All that cuddling and kissing in corners... She's provoking you in order to arouse stronger emotions in me. Jealousy, rivalry. She's good at it. But for the sole reason that I programmed her that way myself. Manual tuning.'

Grim nodded glumly.

'And as for your questions about religion,' Damilola went on,

'I've already had a word with Alena-Libertina. She remembers about you. She's expecting you the day after tomorrow in the park by her office.'

'In what park?'

'The House of Manitou Number 42,' said Damilola. 'A pleasant spot. In my young days I liked to go walking there. There's never anyone around. No one loves Manitou.'

On emerging from the tube at the spot 'House of Manitou No. 42', directly in front of him Grim saw a short dead end with a spiral staircase in it. The steps led up and out under an open 3D sky.

Climbing up, he found himself in the centre of a circular open area with white marble statues standing on pedestals round its perimeter – ten or more of them. The area was set out with rows of severe, straight-backed chairs; it was something like an open-air movie theatre, with a passage left between the rows. Evidently this was where they showed the fresh snuffs on Sunday.

There wasn't a single person anywhere to be seen.

The movie theatre was at the very centre of a star-shaped park – there were about a dozen alleys running off from the statues in all directions, with roundly trimmed bushes and trees growing between them. The alleys were blocked off by barriers, and Grim decided they must all be false – the park could hardly occupy so much space. But then he saw that in some places there weren't any barriers. After a moment's thought, he set off.

The bushes along the sides of the alley were genuine – Grim touched them with his hand and pricked himself on a thorn, drawing blood. He wasn't so sure about the trees, because it wasn't possible to reach them.

In this cool, shady space it was impossible to lose your way, but easy to lose yourself. All the paths led to a shoreline, where the sea splashed at the bottom of a steep cliff, fenced off by cast-iron railings.

It all looked as if he was on a small round island with high rocky shores. Grim realised that there wasn't any sea beyond the railings, but the sound of the waves was more than believable. And the hint of salty freshness, mingling with the familiar smell of heated plastic, was also convincing.

The sky was covered with uniform cumulus clouds and veiled in haze. Grim was already used to the fact that in large open spaces here the sun was scarcely even visible – although if you raised your head it was always possible to observe the cloud behind which it had just hidden. Apparently, imitating the lamp of heaven hanging in the sky overloaded the projection equipment.

Grim sat down on a bench beside the railings. He listened to the sound of the waves for a few minutes and breathed in the smell of the sea, trying not to think about its true nature. Then he dozed off for a short while and dreamed that an immense ancient machine with some obscure function was operating all around him and he himself was merely an incidental spot of living mould, an ant that had lost his way in a clock. When he woke up, he chuckled. Dreams come true, as they say. And then he saw a small figure in black walking towards him along the line of the shore.

It was Alena-Libertina.

When she got really close, a rapid tremor flickered across her, making it seem to Grim that she was also part of the mirage, but a moment later she sat down beside him, and he caught the aroma of a familiar perfume – Chloe smelled the same way now.

366

From close up Alena-Libertina looked cold and musty, as if she was filled with dead, stagnant blood. In Urkaine she would have been a regular old granny, but Grim already knew that people here measured age on a different scale.

'Hello, Grim,' Alena-Libertina said with a smile. 'You looked splendid in the entertainment block. A fine poem. Chloe must be very proud of you.'

Grim had already spent enough time topside to appreciate the depth of her irony – and at the same time realise that she hadn't intended to offend him at all. He lowered his eyes modestly.

'Damilola said you want to know more about the sacred mysteries. What for?'

Grim had his answer ready.

'I want to understand the world I'm living in better. Down below they never told us the truth.'

Alena-Libertina nodded.

'I'm a priest,' she said. 'And being a priest means revealing the truth to people. I'll be glad to tell you everything I can. Ask away."

Grim suddenly realised that all his questions had disappeared. He looked round helplessly.

'Why isn't there anyone in the park?' he managed to force out.

'This place is always deserted,' said Alena-Libertina. 'People don't like to come here. In this place you're on the open palm of Manitou's hand. No one believes in that now. But it's true.'

'A beautiful place,' Grim murmured. 'A very long shoreline.'

Alena-Libertina laughed.

'This shoreline and this park are actually only a moving walkway, Grim. To be precise, a number of separate moving walkways. You walk along them for an hour, or even two, but you're practically standing still.'

'But what if you walk fast?'

'When you walk fast, it whirls round faster. You set its settings yourself.'

Grim looked round at the park.

'And all the rest is an illusion?'

'You could put it like that,' Alena-Libertina said with a smile.

'But what about all these alleys?'

'Only three are genuine.'

'Three?' Grim exclaimed in amazement. 'But what will happen if someone walks along one that isn't real?'

'That can't happen. They're not alleys, but simply a corridor with bushes planted along its walls. A lot shorter than it looks, and also with a moving surface. But I myself don't know how it all spins and turns. Although I've been taking walks here for half a century.'

'Wait,' said Grim, 'But I saw you, you know, walking along the line of the shore. From a long, long way off.'

'You can see whatever you like,' Alena-Libertina replied. 'It might seem to you that I'm a long way off. But I could be within three metres of you. Everything here is very small and compact. Everything's close.'

And none of it is true, thought Grim, but he didn't say anything.

'Do you have any more questions?'

'Tell me, why are we the way we are? I mean the Orks. Who made us bad?'

Alena-Libertina nodded, as if she had been expecting a question like this.

'No one remembers for certain now, Grim. Only the general outline is clear. The holy books teach people to be good. But in order for someone to be good, someone else inevitably has to be bad. That's why some people had to be declared bad. After that, good had to be armed, to stand up for itself. And so that good could use its weapons to resolve any problems that

368

arose, evil had to be made not only weak, but stupid. The finest cultural sommeliers gradually created the Orkish pattern of life out of the heritage of mankind. Out of all the most deplorable things preserved in the human memory. I'm afraid that will seem cynical and cruel to you. But for our time it is simply a given.'

Grim had already heard something similar from the deceased discoursemonger.

'And why do they use that word – "sommelier"?' he said, asking another idiotic question. 'So many different professions and only one word...'

'That used to be what servants who brought the wine to the table were called. They had long lists of wine from which their masters could choose. And later they started using the name for people who do things that used to be considered creative work.'

'Why?'

'People had already invented everything they needed. At one time, long ago, mankind developed very rapidly – the things surrounding people changed constantly, and so did the words that they used. In those days there were many different names for a creative individual – engineer, poet, scientist, scholar. And they were all constantly inventing something new. But that was the childhood of mankind. After that, along came maturity. Creative work didn't disappear – but it started resolving itself into choosing from what has already been created. Metaphorically speaking, we don't grow grapes any more. We send someone to the cellar to get a bottle. The people who go for it are called "sommeliers".'

Grim got the impression that Alena-Libertina was speaking in a slightly irritated tone. He clearly shouldn't waste her time on things that the on-screen dictionaries could help him with. It was time to gather his thoughts and ask about the most important thing.

'Why do they shoot snuffs?'

Alena-Libertina laughed.

'It's our duty and purpose as people. It's what Manitou wants.'

'But people haven't always shot snuffs, have they?'

'That's true,' Alena-Libertina agreed. 'People haven't always shot them, because the will of Manitou wasn't yet clear to them on the conscious level. But they have always been shot *in* them. If you follow the metaphor.'

'But who are they shot for? After all, we ... That is, the Orks down below can't even watch snuffs properly. Everything's blocked out by the censor. But up here hardly anyone watches them.'

Alena-Libertina smirked again.

'You won't understand, dear boy.'

'Try it. Tell me.'

'You know, in the Age of Ancient Films there was a certain director. That was what they called the people who shot those films. And he was asked the same question – who do you make films for? For glory? For people? No, he replied. For Manitou.'

'For Manitou?'

'Yes, my boy. And we also shoot snuffs for Manitou.'

'And does Manitou know about it?'

'You won't understand that anyway until you enter the House of Manitou.'

'But where is the House of Manitou?' asked Grim. 'I thought I'd already got there.'

'Let's go,' said Alena-Libertina. 'I'll take you.'

She stood up and set off along the line of the shore. Grim got up off the bench and followed her, struggling with the fear that had suddenly flooded over him.

Probably it was what he had learned about the alleys that made the way back seem quite a bit longer. Grim found it hard to believe that there was a moving walkway under his feet. He looked down, trying to make out if that really was dense,

trampled soil down there, or if it was yet another apparition –
but he couldn't figure it out at all.

When they come out into the circular area with the statues,
where the chairs were standing, Alena-Libertina lowered herself
onto one of them and gestured for Grim to sit down beside her.

'Are you curious about who all these men are?' she asked,
pointing to the white statues.

Grim counted the pedestals – there were twelve of them,
matching the number of radiating pathways.

'I suppose they're ancient priests of Manitou?' Grim surmised.
'His servants?'

'More like His faces,' said Alena-Libertina. 'We call each one
of them by the name "Manitou". Because an entire era of human
history is behind each and every one of them, and every one of
them was the mouthpiece of eternal truth. In their time every
word they spoke shook the world, and volumes of notes with
commentaries were written about it. But now people don't even
remember their names.'

The only thing that interested Grim was what Manitou
needed so many faces for, if he never lied. Only he thought a
question like that might sound sacrilegious. But even so, he felt
he had to ask a few questions about these statues – if only out
of politeness.

'Who's that one?' asked Grim, pointing to a statue of a sly-
faced, slant-eyed warrior in boots with pointed toes, sitting
cross-legged on his pedestal.

'That's Manitou Buddha. A great warrior of ancient times. He
punished the enemies of Manitou by binding them to his wheel.
Do you see the wheel?'

'Aha,' said Grim. 'And these two?'

He pointed to two bearded men standing on pedestals beside
each other.

To look at them, they seemed like brothers – but one was

dressed in something like a sheet thrown over his body, and the other in a close-fitting bodystocking. The first was holding his arms out to the sides, and the second was stretching his up towards the sky, so that to Grim they looked like two fisherman – the first one showing what a big fish he had caught, while the second couldn't even raise his arms high enough for that.

'They are Christ and Antichrist,' said Alena-Libertina. 'A notable example of "yin-hegelyan", the mirror faces of Manitou. You Orks revere only Antichrist and consider us heretics and apostates because we accord other avatars equal respect. But we believe you are too narrow-minded. And they don't tell you the full truth even about Manitou Antichrist. He wasn't anything like a black hole with an accretion disk – the way he is depicted on your supraphysical icons "Manitou in Glory". Many illiterate Orks think that he once came to the city of Slava in that form. But in actual fact, he was just a human being, same as you and I. It's simply that he was the mouthpiece for Manitou, who has bound the Universe together with a string of black holes.'

'And what exactly did he say?' asked Grim.

'Antichrist taught people that Manitou lives in everything without exception, in both the high and the low. And it is the division into good and evil, into low and high that is the original sin. In order to nip all prejudices in the bud, he chose for himself the most reviled name that existed in human mythology, and he also chose the most discredited symbols.'

'I've heard that before,' said Grim. 'But what was he shot for?'

Alena-Libertina gave a thin smile.

'According to the rumours, it was because he spoke Spanish badly. In his native English he was always chattering nineteen to the number of the beast, and could cajole anyone into anything, but the cocaine naguals didn't understand him too well and decided he was a freak and perhaps a spy... In his lifetime English wasn't a church language yet.'

'In our parts they'd say you're blaspheming.'

'And in our parts, they'd say that your priests blaspheme. And another thing you should know is that he never made your spastika his emblem. The spastika was invented by the Orks, who wanted to show that only they had preserved the true faith. Possibly they were helped by our sommeliers, but certainly not by Manitou the Antichrist. If he hadn't been killed so young, he would have forbidden the worship of any symbols and icons at all... Please understand, we have nothing against your spastika, Grim. But we don't always like the doings that it blesses.'

Alena-Libertina paused, as if she was expecting an outburst of outraged feelings. Grim didn't react in any way to what he had heard. He pointed to the empty pedestal.

'And has that statue been removed?' he asked.

'No, that's the spiritual leader of Northern Europe, the prophet Muhammad. His only image was the absence of an image. Therefore the theologians asserted that his image was everywhere.'

'And who's this beside him?'

'That's the first Mashiah – Menachem Mendel Schneerson.'

'And this?'

'The second Mashiah – Semyon Levitan. The former lived in New York, the latter in Moscow and Palestine. The first was revealed to people, the second was hidden from them.'

The names of the fabled ancient countries sounded to Grim like magical spells that conjured up for just one second the image of something very familiar. He seemed to understand what Northern Europe, Moscow, New York and Palestine were – but a moment later the mirage dissolved like a cloud of smoke. And it was probably good that it did dissolve – far too much of all sorts of things had happened over the centuries for anyone to remember it and live...

'That's enough about the past,' said Alena-Libertina. 'Now it's time to enter the House of Manitou.'

'Do we have to go somewhere else?'

'You don't go to the House of Manitou. The House of Manitou comes to you. Are you ready?'

'Yes,' said Grim.

'Watch.'

For some reason Grim was expecting that a retro-screen would appear in front of them – of the kind on which they showed Ancient Films. But what did happen was that everything changed instantly.

The only things left in place were the stone incarnations of Manitou. But now they were in the niches of a circular wall that enclosed him and Alena-Libertina from all sides. There were no doors in the wall. And instead of a sky, veiled in haze, Grim saw a high dome ending in a round opening.

He was inside an immense building like the ancient temples in the *Free Encyclopaedia*. The walls and the dome were covered with frescoes. Grim guessed that they represented the history of mankind. There were battle scenes from snuffs, multi-headed beasts emerging from the sea, pyramids being built, iron birds flying in the sky and lots of other things that he simply couldn't put a name to. But it wasn't the pictures that made the greatest impression on him. And not even the implacable symmetry of the bas-reliefs and cornices, which set his head spinning.

Light suddenly flared up in the round opening of the dome. It was a globe of blue fire so bright that Grim spontaneously squeezed his eyes shut as soon as the rays tore into them.

Grim had never seen light from this strange spectrum before. In comparison with this, the yellow Orkish sun was mild and gentle. But here... This blue fire searing his eyes was probably the sword of Manitou, which the black cotton wadding of the universe mercifully concealed within itself. And now Grim had seen it with his own eyes – and realised that he couldn't look at it. The light was too pitiless. Even when Grim closed his eyes, the light continued to burn in them, as if the bright ray had cut a round hole in his eyelids forever.

When the light went out Grim was relieved to brush away the sweat that had sprung up on his forehead. Now he was surrounded by semi-darkness. He could see everything around him like before, although a vague black spot with a brightly glowing rim was floating in front of his eyes.

'Are you all right, Grim?' Alena-Libertina asked.

'What was that?'

'The Light of Manitou. That is how Manitou shines when He is young.'

'It would be terrible to live under a light like that,' Grim said.

'Many believe it is the most beautiful thing that exists in the entire world. The universe is born and disappears in this fire. And though we are condemned to be merely its shadow, this light still remains the anchor of our world. Such is reality.'

A shining yellow sphere lit up in the space in front of Grim, with other, smaller spheres circling round it. The third one from the centre was glowing brightly, and Grim guessed that it was the earth.

'Reality, Grim, has two aspects, which the people of the past called "yin-hegelyan". The first is matter. The second is con-sciousness. Our consciousness is always grounded in matter, and matter only exists in our consciousness. Reality is not reducible to either one or the other, much as electricity cannot be reduced to positive or negative. The ancient sages perceived that these two poles are linked together through blood.'

'Why?' asked Grim.

'It's very simple, Grim. Now you are alive and you see the physical universe around you. And you are a part of it yourself.

Matter and conscience are the two poles of the one Grim. But by spilling your blood, these poles can be separated forever.'

The planets and the sun went out, and Grim was left in the half-light again.

'The cosmic link between matter and spirit can only be maintained through the constant offering of sacrifice.'

Grim saw that one of the white statues had started glowing in the semi-darkness. It represented a strange being – a man with a snake's head, frozen in a complex ceremonial pose.

'This is Manitou Quetzalcoatl,' said Alena-Libertina. 'He had already served people before as Prometheus, and he was chained to a rock. Later he served them as Antichrist and he was shot in a Mexican ravine. Each time he sacrifices himself and becomes the sun of the world. The same one that shines over Orkland. It is the same fire that burns in all the other worlds. Any of the stars is Manitou's dwelling.'

'But surely a star is just a big atomic reactor,' Grim said in a tone that suggested he knew what an atomic reactor was. 'Isn't that right?'

'Grim, there is a material and a spiritual side to everything. The atomic blaze suspended in emptiness is the physical aspect of Manitou. Our ability to see Him is the spiritual aspect. The sun will only be able to warm us and feed us if we maintain a spiritual link with it through blood. That is the purpose of the sacred wars in the Circus.'

'So for you, then, we are just a sacrificial offering?'

'Only a very short time ago you were an Ork, Grim, and I understand your feelings," Alena-Libertina said. 'But now you are one of us. Don't forget that.'

Grim nodded.

'But why do you hold a war so often?'

'Why do you eat every day? The sacrifice has to be repeated, so that the Light of Manitou will continue to burn. We don't hanker after blood out of cruelty. We are nourishing Heaven. It is not we who need blood, Grim. Manitou needs it.'

'But why do we have to take care of him?'

'Manitou and this world are one and the same. Manitou creates it out of Himself. You know how they explain that to little children? If we stop taking care of Manitou, Manitou will stop taking care of us. The Light of Manitou will fade away. And then not only the sun will go out, all the screens on which children watch their jolly cartoons will go out too. And then the manitou in all the daddies and mummies' wallets and purses will run out. No one will be able to live anymore.'

'That's why people shoot snuffs?'

'Yes. Such is the sacred ritual of the birth of the world.'

'But what has the birth of the world got to do with this?'

'That is one of the supreme mysteries of religion, Grim. You can only obtain an answer through initiation into the Mysteries. By no means is everyone capable of comprehending it. It is especially difficult for the Global Orks – they are inclined to think that there is no spiritual reality higher than the stock market indices.'

'Perhaps I can manage it,' said Grim.

'All right,' said Alena-Libertina. 'I'll explain it once, and if you don't understand, don't ask me to repeat it.'

Grim gulped hard and nodded resolutely.

'Watch...'

A bright blue dot lit up in the semi-darkness in front of Grim. Then it exploded and was transformed into a vortex of stars and nebulae scattering in all directions. Gradually fading, these blazing spots hurtled further and further away from each other, until space became black and empty.

'That is how the scientists of former times imagined the conception and birth of our universe out of the Light of Manitou, and its death,' said Alena-Libertina. 'However, before they were

377

consumed by the atomic fire, the physicists of the Age of Ancient Films proved that time actually runs in the opposite direction. It seems to us that the Universe moves from Big Bang to heat death – but this is simply an error of human perception. In reality all processes move in the reverse direction. The fourth law of thermodynamics, that blend of statistics and religious faith, is actually merely a perceptual illusion – of the same kind as the sun appearing to rotate round the earth...'

Grim raised one hand, as if trying to halt the flood of incomprehensible words.

'Man imagines that Manitou has disintegrated into fragments that are scattering endlessly through space, and therefore since time immemorial people have proclaimed that God is dead. But in reality Manitou is returning home. Manitou is becoming Himself. The red shift that astronomers observe is an illusion. For Manitou it is blue – man is simply condemned to see the blue light of Manitou as his own crimson. In addition, although nothing can move faster than the threshold velocity, the threshold velocity itself changes depending on the configuration of the Universe. However, reality is structured so that all this can only be comprehended with spiritual vision – and only then will certain physical validations become manifest...'

Grim was no longer trying to understand these words. He was looking at the manitou where the same nebulae and stars had started lighting up in front of him again. They converged, blazing brighter and brighter, and in the end they merged into a single blinding blue ray of light, which winked at him and went out.

'In actual fact the world is collapsing into a point, and what we see as the past is the future. The age of the crimson sun is behind us. You didn't flee from Orkland, Grim. You appeared here, among people. Later you will advance backwards into your future, become a tiny little bundle of wailing flesh, enter your mother's womb, dissolve into it and merge with the fundamental principle. Or, as the theologians put it, you will once again become an information wave in perpendicular time. The Age of Ancient Films is in the future. That is why your icons show the primordial cosmic body of Manitou as a singularity. That is what it is – and we are moving towards a point at which everything shall become one again.'

'How can that happen?' asked Grim. 'So it means we don't know our yesterday, but we know our tomorrow?'

'You've driven a motorenwagen, haven't you, kid? You can see where you're going – that is, you know what is going to happen. But you can't see what has been left behind you.'

'But if it's true... It probably changes everything!' Grim said, none too confidently.

'It changes everything, Grim. And it changes nothing. Whether you know the secret or not, your life will remain the same. You won't start growing younger from this second on. In your distorted perception you will still carry on, advancing into a future unknown to you – although in a higher sense it is your past. Such is the fate of all people. But in our spiritual ministry we are able to overcome this riddle and rise above it. What do you think – why out of all the past it is only the Ancient Films that have survived?'

'I don't know.'

'The Ancient Films are blueprints of the future that we preserve by the will of Manitou. The day will come when the future will arise out of the films that we are saving. The Light of Manitou will pass through them, be coloured by them and create the reality imprinted on them. In the true dimension all will occur precisely thus. We are helping Manitou to return home, Grim, even though we are incapable of feeling the true movement of time ourselves. Could there be any higher service?'

Grim could feel his head spinning – as if Alena-Libertina's voice really had elevated him to an unimaginable height.

'Now do you understand?' asked Alena-Libertina. 'We're not shooting snuffs. We're creating the world by projecting them outwards. Snuffs are the seeds of the world and are pleasing to Manitou. In the higher reality they existed before the events that are shot on them. And on the physical plane they dissolve into the Universe when the Light of Manitou, passing through the temple celluloid, transforms the blueprint into reality. At the point where the future aligns with the past, we people become Manitou's instrument. We conceive the Universe time after time in the ardent embraces of our temple actors, and simultaneously nourish Heaven with the blood of warriors obtained as we do it. Have you perceived the meaning of the sacrament?'

'We nourish with the blood of warriors,' Grim repeated quietly. 'Right . . . But if time runs in the opposite direction, then how can we nourish . . .'

'No need to continue,' Alena-Libertina said with a smile. 'Believe me, my boy, if Manitou wishes to accept your gift, he will find a way to do it outside the bounds of physics, logic and reason. His chambers lie outside of time, and for Him there are no limits. But just now you perceived the other most profound mystery of our faith. That which looks like our sacrifice to Him is, in the higher reality, His gift to us. The warriors do not die during the Circus war. They come to life. Do you understand?'

'Yes,' Grim said uncertainly.

'This is why they say that despite all the blood that is spilled in it, the world is run by love.'

'And does Manitou really need blood?'

'Yes, Grim. And do not try to understand this with your own weak reason. When they try to abolish sacred war, Manitou starts taking the blood that is due to him through mass murders that are committed by solitary crazed individuals. Nothing like

380

that happens during a war. Nourishing Manitou with blood is a cosmic necessity. But only a servant of Manitou can comprehend this. Have you become one, Grim?'

Perhaps it was a matter of the peculiar tone of insulation in which the question was put, perhaps it was the dramatic nature of the moment in general, but Grim realised that his entire future – which, as it now turned out, was in actual fact his past – could depend on his answer. And moreover, he ought to reply not with a simple 'yes' or 'no'. The answer had to be such that no doubts remained about his sincerity. Grim strained to think so hard that everything went black in front of his eyes. And the answer suddenly came.

'Having come here, can I be anyone else?'

Alena-Libertina laughed softly.

'You're a clever little Ork,' she said. 'Perhaps too clever. But I don't regret having let you into our world. Live here happily until the day you die...'

She paused for a moment and added:

'Now you know that it makes no sense to ask where we go to afterwards.'

The dome above Grim's head disappeared and he saw the circular open space around him again, with the statues, the 3D sky and the trees. And the rows of empty chairs.

Alena-Libertina, sitting beside him, chuckled.

'Welcome to the desert of the real. Now we have to think what you're going to do as a servant of Manitou. I have plans for you.'

Grim stretched out his neck in a gesture of unmitigated attention.

'You should work with words,' said Alena-Libertina.

'Why?'

'I heard your poem. That's rather unusual for an Orkish lad – to write poetry.'

'I know,' said Grim. 'I did it out of fear. And they finished off the rough draft for me...'

Alena-Libertina fluttered her hand as if that was absolutely unimportant.

'I hope you will be useful to us.'

'How?'

'Learn to use a creative articulator. It's the application on which our sommeliers completed your poem. You're going to create the Orkish sense line for new snuffs. If you can handle it, you'll be well paid. You can start right away.'

'Will I manage it?'

'Of course. In this job your shortcomings will be your virtues. As soon as you get ideas for fragments like the ones you wrote on your tattered pieces of paper, just enter them in the manitou. It's not difficult. The important thing is, don't try to hold yourself back. You'll gradually master the articulator and you'll be able to earn more... That's what I'd like to think.'

'Should I do it every day?'

'When it just happens on its own. But it's highly desirable for it to happen on its own every day.'

'But what should I write about?'

'What you feel like writing about. We'll find a use for everything. It's not likely that you could be a discoursemonger. But you'll make a content-sommelier.'

Alena-Libertina looked Grim up and down again.

'Whether you'll make a decent job of it will become clear very quickly.'

Is Kaya capable of suffering and feeling as I do? Is there anyone living in the Chinese room inside her head? Or is it just a gaping black void that she's got within?

This question turned out to be a lot more complicated than I thought.

The manufacturer clearly had no interest in too profound a discussion of the subject because of the possible legal problems. For instance, the question of the age of consent for suras could quite easily come up.

The House of Manitou, CINEWS Inc. and GULAG could also do without the extra headache.

It was forbidden to shoot suras in snuffs because they couldn't be participants in a religious ritual. And they couldn't be used in porn, since they 'imitated individuals who have not reached the age of consent'. But if suras suddenly came under the law on the age of consent, it would be enough to hold a few suras in the stockroom for forty-six years and the entire temple porn business would be *down the tubes or up the spout*, as the Orkish poet had put it. Or perhaps the fat old feminists would push through a law, making it compulsory for suras to look like them, only worse.

It was hardly surprising that investigations of this kind had not been encouraged. Therefore I had only myself to rely on – and I got stuck into the on-screen dictionaries.

It immediately became clear that I wasn't the first to have taken an interest in this question. This enigma had first been encountered many centuries earlier, when people were only just learning to make machines that imitate certain aspects of human behaviour. And they had formulated the problem of the 'philosopher's zombie'.

The philosopher's zombie is not some kind of corpse, raised from the grave by reading *The Critique of Pure Reason* or *Les Feuilles Mortes*. It is an entity that looks, talks and generally, in every possible instance, behaves exactly like a human being. The only difference is that it has no human soul. No consciousness, no Light of Manitou – it doesn't matter what you call it. You can look at a zombie like this and you can listen to it – but you can't *be it* on the inside.

Everything indicated that the ancient sages, without even knowing it, were talking about my Kaya. When I realised that, I set about sifting through the available information with redoubled tenacity.

It turned out that a full-scale battle had broken out between the ancient sommeliers over this philosopher's zombie. But it looked like they didn't always realise what they were talking about.

A sommelier by the name of Chalmers, for instance, said:

'The logical possibility of zombies ... seems obvious to me. A zombie is just something physically identical to me, but which has no conscious experience – all is dark inside.'

For whom, one wonders, is it dark? For Chalmers or for the zombie itself? If it's for Chalmers, then how on earth can it be light for him inside someone else? And if it's dark for the zombie, then where is it light for it? Inside Chalmers?

The ancient sommeliers were atheists and they didn't understand that the Light of Manitou is the same everywhere. And they constantly tried to explain light through darkness, because this was happening before the coming of Antichrist and in those times it was impossible to get a grant any other way.

A sommelier by the name of Dennett actually introduced the concept of a 'zimbo'. This was a zombie that 'monitors its own

384

activities, in an indefinite upward spiral of reflexivity' and 'as a result of self-monitoring, has internal (but unconscious) higher-order informational states that are about its other, lower-order informational states.' So there we go.

This zimbo, Dennett asserted, could have believed (also unconsciously) that it was characterised by various mental states of which it could render an account. It would have thought that it was conscious, even if it did not possess consciousness...

At this point I became completely mystified as to how this zimbo could have believed in anything if by its very nature it was only capable of 'possessing informational states'. Like Kaya, it didn't have anyone inside it who could believe; there were only kaleidoscopic informational sequences and patterns at the output interface, and they could become a 'belief' or a 'thought' only if they were witnessed by some observer pickled since birth in human vocabulary and culture – someone like me.

Anyway, this sort of chitchat wasn't getting anywhere. And it probably wasn't any great disaster that quite soon afterwards, for reasons of a religious nature, these arguments were prohibited and all such philosophers were executed.

Manitou the Antichrist said, 'Everything is Manitou – Manitou, and a manitou, and manitou.' The holy rollers, naturally, set about adjusting reality to fit this great quote, gradually proscribing all live polemics and constricting the bounds of what was permissible to discuss to the narrow range of their own understanding. In the end the only content of the residual sediment was that from the legal point of view all these zombies and zimbos should be considered merely electrical devices.

The only school of thought that remained safe from the religious viewpoint was called 'behaviourism' – the intensive analysis exclusively of behaviour without any speculative attempts to understand what or who stands behind it. And this, incidentally, genuinely resembled an objective science that observed man, fly and sura with equal detachment.

And from this point of view it turned out that there was simply no difference between me and Kaya. Or if there was, it wasn't to my advantage.

All suras of Kaya's class carry a label that says: '333.33% Turing test passed' (not on the actual sura, of course, but in the documentation). A miniscule note below it adds: 'guaranteed only on factory presets'.

I realise that there is no affront to human intelligence to which a sales sommelier would not resort in order to earn another ring in his nose – but this set me wondering how there could be 'three hundred and thirty-three per cent' if there is only a hundred per cent in total.

I delved into the on-screen dictionaries again and discovered the following. In the Age of Ancient Films there was a sommelier by the name of Alan Turing. A lot of information about him has been preserved in the GULAG card index, by the way – he was a gay, driven to suicide by a hypocritical and inhuman society. Turing was a mathematician of genius. He was the first to try to answer the question of whether machines can think.

Since for Turing himself 'to think' meant something like 'to break military codes' (that was his principal occupation, thanks to which he saved many soldiers' lives) he approached the question with military efficiency.

He suggested trying to solve the problem experimentally. In his experiment several controllers posed random questions to invisible test subjects, some of whom were computer programmes and some, human beings. An attempt was made to determine who was who from the answers. Turing forecast that by the end of the second millennium (it is hard to believe that such machines already existed then), the programmes would be able to deceive thirty per cent of the judges after five minutes of this exchange. And then, in his opinion, it would be possible to say that a machine thinks. To pass this threshold was to pass the Turing test completely.

Aha, I realised, that's where the 333.33% came from. The sales sommeliers had used a simple arithmetic proportion – if deceiving thirty per cent of the judges means a hundred per cent pass of the text, then deceiving a hundred per cent of the judges gives three hundred and thirty three point three recurring.

The meaning of this elegant figure is that no Turing panel today could distinguish a sura ('on factory presets', as the label specifies) from a live human being.

How do they achieve this? I'm not a specialist, but I remember what the consultant surologist said: the same as in a human head. A large number of precedents are recorded in the memory and used as the basis for making a judgement on how to reply to a question, react to a new situation or elicit an unanticipated meaning from within oneself. This reaction can also be tuned – but I can't even imagine the mechanism involved here.

Basically, after ploughing through mountains of literature, I realised that there was no clarity waiting for me on the other side of them – only new mountains of literature, which would rapidly start looping round, referring me back to what I had already read. And I finally came up with the most obvious idea: I couldn't possibly find anyone better to consult on these matters than Kaya herself.

And this was where my sweetheart laid her ambush for me.

'Right, you talk about the Light of Manitou,' she said as soon as I started the conversation. 'You say you have it inside you and I don't. Do you really believe that Manitou is inside you?'

'Yes,' I replied.

'But doesn't he find it cramped in there? Squalid?'

'It's only manner of speaking. In actual fact...' I squeezed my eyes shut, trying to recall the Prescriptions '...Manitou has no inside or outside. You can say that we exist in the Light of Manitou. And we ourselves are that Light. But all you have inside you, my darling, are informational processes.'

'Correct. But why do you believe that the Light of Manitou is only capable of illuminating these informational processes through the agency of your six senses?'

'But how else?' I asked in amazement.

'There is no other way, if you regard Manitou as an invention of man. But if you regard man as an invention of Manitou, there's no problem. You simply don't know what it means – to be me.'

'Then you do exist?'

Kaya smiled and said nothing.

'Why don't you say something?' I asked. 'What's so bad about me trying to understand you better? To figure out what really controls you and where your next phrase comes from...'

'Your stupidity consists precisely in the fact that you try to understand that about me – but you don't try to understand what controls *you* and determines *your* next action.'

'Controls me?' I echoed, trying to grasp what she was getting at.

Basically, she was absolutely right. In order to understand how the imitation works one should first understand the original.

But Kaya was already moving in to attack this poor pilot.

'What motivates you? What makes you act from one second to the next?'

'Do you mean my passions?' I asked. 'Desires, tastes, attachments?'

'No,' she said, 'that's not what I mean. You're talking about lifelong metaphors. About good and bad character traits, about long-term personal inclinations. But what I'm talking about occurs in your mind so quickly that you don't even notice it.

388

Not because it's impossible. Simply because you don't have any training.'

When she starts saying things I don't understand, the best strategy is to play the idiot. I assumed a serious, intense expression (I know that she analyses the set of my facial muscles twice every second).

'Training? You think I need to go to the gym?'

She shook her head distrustfully. I twisted my face even further out of shape.

'Well then, in your opinion I don't aspire to the things that I ought to? I'm too caught up in the material side of things?' I asked, trying to give my voice an edge of intense uncertainty.

She smiled forbearingly.

'You really don't understand. You poor thing.'

She can sense when I'm trying to mock her – and in cases like that knocks my weapon out of my hands by switching to an intimate, compassionate simplicity. Which suits me just fine – when that happens, it means I've outwitted her maximum bitchiness for a little while.

Damilola one. Kaya nil.

'So are you interested in finding out what controls you? Or is that subject too complicated for you?'

Well, well. I felt a prick of irritation – outwitting my little darling wasn't so simple.

'Nothing controls me,' I said. 'I control everything myself.'

'What do you control?'

'You, for instance,' I laughed.

'And what controls you when you control me?'

I thought about that.

The best thing was to talk seriously.

'I choose what I like and reject what I don't like. That's how any human being acts. Although of course, in a certain sense my inclinations control me. Naturally, once again under my control. My attachments – yes, that's it. I said that right at the beginning.'

'That's almost right,' said Kaya. 'But only almost. People are inclined to interpret the word "attachment" as some kind of bad personality trait that can be got rid of. But we're talking about instantaneous reactions that take place constantly, controlling the electrochemistry of your brain.'

'I like Kaya,' I sang, slapping her on her little stomach. 'Kaya's my sweet little girl. Is that an attachment?'

'No,' she said. 'That's the mumbling of an imbecilic bloated voluptuary.'

She said it almost compassionately, and that particular nuance proved to be the tiny high-density core that pierced through all the layers of my armour. But I didn't show it and said:

'Well then, explain.'

'Your perception has a definite structure,' she replied. 'First your sense organs relay a signal about some event to your brain. Then the brain starts classifying that event, using its templates and schemata, trying to correlate it with existing experience. The result is that the event is recognised as being either pleasant, or unpleasant, or neutral. And subsequently the brain no longer deals with the event, but only with the tokens "pleasant", "un-pleasant" and "indefinite". In simple terms, everything neutral is filtered out, so there are only two types of tokens left.'

'The outline is clear,' I said. 'I just don't understand how it looks in practice.'

'Do you remember how you almost shot up an Orkish wed-ding?'

I really had told her about that one time after the dopamine resonance, when the words and the tears were pouring out of me like spring rain.

It happened during that war when Bernard-Henri and I lost the tender – I was in a really vicious mood, and getting caught in my sights was not a good idea. I had to eke out an income with paltry little jobs, and I flew out to film an Orkish wedding for an ethnographic programme. To shoot the footage I had to wait until the Orks got drunk. I cruised round in circles over the village, getting bored, and suddenly I fancied that they were singing 'No Fucking Way to Break Out from this Shithole'.

I hate Orkish folk songs with all my heart for their obtrusive homosexual subtext, and at that particular moment I also got the feeling that they were singing about my credit problems – I was just thinking about them. My insides instantly turned a double somersault and clenched up tight. I almost sprayed the wedding feast table with a burst from my cannon – and then I realised that in fact no one was singing. It was the creaking of a door, picked up by the long-range snoop system. And it was me who had transformed it into a reason for rage. I calmed down and no one was killed.

'I remember,' I said.

'That's what I'm talking about. You're not dealing with reality, but with the tokens that your brain issues to itself regarding reality – and often, in fact, mistakenly. These tokens are like the chips in a casino: some are exchanged for euphoria and others for suffering. Every time you glance at the world, the game on the green baize is continued. The result is pleasure or pain. These are electro-chemical in nature and are localised in the brain, although they are often experienced as bodily sensations. And for this game you don't even need the world around you. Most of the time you're busy losing to yourself, locked up inside yourself.'

She was right – so far I was on a straight losing streak in my casino.

'What next?' I asked glumly.

'Attachment is not induced by the objects themselves or the events of your inner world, but precisely by these internal electrochemical injections of euphoria and suffering that you give yourself on their account. Why are all the protests against the stranglehold of so-called "consumption" so bogus? Because what you consume is not the goods and products, but the positive and negative attachments of the brain to its own chemicals and circuits, and your poor blind souls are always jammed up against the same old internal gasket mechanism, which can be tacked on to any external projection you like – from Manitou to *kvasola*...'

It required a certain effort for me to recall that *kvasola* is the Orkish national drink.

'You're a hopeless junkie, Damilola,' she went on, 'and for you the whole world is nothing more than a set of excuses for your brain to shoot up or give itself an enema. The enema makes you miserable every time. But the spikes don't make you happy, they just send you off looking for a new dose. It's always like that with narcotics. All your life, second after second, is a constant search for an excuse for a fix. But there isn't anyone in you who could resist this, since your so-called "personality" only appears afterwards – as the blurred and bleary echo of these electrochemical bolts of lightning, an averaged magnetic halo above an unconscious and uncontrolled process...'

I didn't even know how to object. In cases like this I convert everything into a light-hearted joke.

'If all human beings are hopeless drug addicts, little darling, then why don't they put us in jail?'

She only thought for a split second.

'Because this is Manitou's own narco-business. Junkies are persecuted precisely because they muscle in uninvited. And then again, in reality you're doing jail time anyway. Only you're afraid to admit it, because then you'd immediately have to give yourselves an enema and call yourselves losers.'

The semantic hiatus was helpful – I finally realised what to say.

'You'll find it hard to believe, babe, but there's more to a man than just a drug addict serving his stretch inside himself. A man has ... I don't know – an ideal, a dream. A light towards which he advances all his life. And you haven't got anything like that.'

Kaya laughed affably. That's what I hate more than anything else, her affability.

'My route is inscribed inside me programmatically,' she said, 'and your route is inscribed inside you chemically. And when it seems to you that you're advancing towards light and happiness, you're simply advancing towards your inner handler to get another sugar lump. In fact we can't even say that it's you advancing. It's just the chemical computer implementing the operator "take sugar" in order to move on to the operator "rejoice five seconds". And after that, there'll be the operator "suffer" again – no one has ever deleted it and no one ever will. And in all this there isn't any "you".'

'Why do you keep repeating all the time that there isn't any me? Who do you think it is that screws you every day?'

'A blubbery, feeble-minded arsehole,' she replied with obvious satisfaction. 'Who else? But the fact that a blubbery, feeble-minded arsehole screws a talking doll every day doesn't mean that there is some real essence in any of this. What do you have in mind when you say "I"?'

It had been clear right from the start that once she'd run the whole nine yards on maximum spirituality she'd skip back over to maximum bitchiness. But I was sure that I knew how to make her switch back again, and that made me feel calm and self-possessed. And actually, why shouldn't a battle pilot have a heart-to-heart talk with his girl on his rare day off?

'I don't have anything in mind, Kaya. I say "I" because that's what I was taught to do,' I said. 'If when I was a kid I had been taught, for instance, to say "ribbit" or "woof", that's what I'd do.'

'All right,' said Kaya. 'A witty and correct remark. "I" is merely an element of language. But after all, do you genuinely believe that there is something inside you that was you ten or even fifteen years ago?'

Right, we've already been through this.

'Well yes,' I said. 'Everything flows, everything changes. A man is like a river. More of a process than an object, agreed. But this process is my "I". Although "I" is only a nominal label.'

'The point isn't whether it is a process or a label. The point is something quite different.'

'What?'

'Did anyone ask you if you wanted them to launch this process?'

'No,' I replied. 'No one asked.'

'In other words, you have no power over the start of the process, or the form in which it proceeds ...' she slapped me on my corpulent buttock with her little palm '... or over its length and its end?'

'No,' I said.

'Then in the name of Damilola, why do you call it yourself? Why do you use the word "I" for it?'

'I ...' I began, and started thinking about it. 'That's no longer a scientific question, but a religious one. You and I have different natures. To take the spiritual aspect, I'm a human being, and you're a domestic electrical appliance. The Light of Manitou is in me, but there's no one in you who hears these words of mine – all that's pure simulation. And it's because that light is in me that I can say "I". But you, in essence, are just a programme.'

'That's right,' she said. 'My reaction to your words is a pro-grammed event. And there isn't anyone in me who listens. But there isn't in you either. There is simply a manifestation of the nature of sound that for some reason you ascribe to yourself. And there is a manifestation of the nature of meaning in the nature of sound, which sometimes occurs to your adipose brains, triggering reactions conditioned by attachments. You're just another programme, only a chemical one. And there isn't any "I" in any of this.'

'Hang on,' I said. 'You say that I'm controlled by my chemical attachments. But there has to be someone who's attached, doesn't there? The one who is subject to their influence and decides how to act? Well, that is "I".'

'You still don't get it. The reactions that result in the appearance of what you call your "self" occur before they are consciously perceived. They are controlled by the same physical laws governing the way the entire Universe is being transformed. Where in all this is the self who is capable of deciding and doing something? How can an echo control the sound that gave rise to it? There isn't anyone in you who is in charge.'

'Then what is there?'

'There is only the constantly repeated act of a fly getting stuck in honey. But that honey only exists as excitation in the fly, and the fly only exists as a reaction to the honey. And that is the only content of your infinitely rich inner life... I know you're reading about all these "zombies" and "zimbos", you know. I've seen the tags. You think that you have consciousness and I don't. But in actual fact, there isn't any consciousness at all. There is only the single, universal means by which all the forms of information that constitute the world come into existence. That is why in ancient China they spoke of the universal Way of Things. And in India they said "*tat tvam asi*" – "thou art that". It's so simple that no one can understand it. There is only constantly changing experience. *It* is you. *It* is also the world...'

'And the attachments?' I asked for the sake of at least asking something.

'To what can an experience be attached? With what rope?

It will simply end, and another will begin. Do you understand that, stupid? Aagh ... I can see that you don't ...'

So there now.

That was the way it went with us almost every day. Can you imagine? You've come back from a war, you've had a bellyful of watching all sorts of stuff, and at home – this is what you get. Perhaps, I thought, it's not entirely normal to derive pleasure from this? Perhaps I am simply concealing my own innermost intentions and dispositions from myself, and I ought to buy her black boots and a whip? Raise aloft, so to speak, the fallen banner of Bernard-Henri?

'If you can ever get your feeble mind up to speed and see yourself as you are,' she went on, 'you'll understand the most important thing. Your thoughts, wishes and impulses, which make you act, are in reality not yours at all. They come to you out of a space that is totally obscure, as if out of nowhere. You never know what you will want in the next second. You are merely a witness in this process. But your inner witness is so stupid that he immediately becomes a party to the crime – and he rakes in the loot big time ...'

That made me tense up, because it was not only incomprehensible and offensive, it also sounded threatening. Perhaps she was trying to programme me subconsciously? I don't like to lose the thread in these conversations. Especially when I don't lose it, but she tugs it out of my hand.

'And if I can't get my feeble mind up to speed?'

'Then try examining your inner life on slow rewind. You'll see the endless repetition of the same old scenario. You're walking along the street and suddenly vague shadows start robbing the bank on the corner. You immediately get involved, because you need money for drugs – or at least for an enema, in order to forget about them for a while. The result is that you end up with a prison sentence, although you didn't really rob any bank

396

on the corner at all, because there aren't any corners anywhere. And every day you rob illusory banks, and for that you serve an eternal, non-illusory life sentence . . .'

I suddenly felt sad, because I sensed a glimmer of truth in what she said. After all, she hadn't thought up all of this herself. She couldn't have done. It had to be the wisdom of ancient mankind, packaged in accordance with the settings I had chosen.

'Then what do I do?' I asked in a quiet voice.

'You can't do anything. Everything simply happens – both inside you and outside you. Your military propaganda calls you and other unfortunates "free men". But in actual fact your life is merely a corridor of torments. There are no good people or wicked villains among you, only poor souls who want to keep themselves busy with something in order to forget about their pain. Life is a narrow strip between the flames of suffering and the phantom of joy, through which the so-called free man runs, howling in terror. And this entire corridor only exists in his head.'

'It seems as if you don't believe that free men exist.'

Kaya laughed.

'You even breathe in and out because the imminent onset of suffering makes you do it,' she said. 'Try holding your breath if you don't believe me. And who would breathe otherwise? And in exactly the same way you eat, drink, relieve yourself and change the position of your body – because after several minutes every pose it assumes becomes a pain. In the same way you sleep, make love, and so forth. Second after second you flee from the stick, and Manitou only occasionally teases you with a false carrot in order to clout you even more painfully when you come running for it. Where is the freedom in this? Any man has only one path – the one that he walks through life.'

'So I can't control absolutely anything at all then?' I asked.

'Of course not. Even the attention that you consider your own is controlled by Manitou.'

'In person?'

'Through his laws. But that's the same thing.'

'But can I at least pray for grace?'

She nodded.

'How?'

'For a start you can keep track of your own reaction without being drawn into it. That *is* prayer.'

If only they could hear her in the House of Manitou.

'But my attention is controlled by Manitou, isn't it?' I said. 'And in order to pray, I have to keep track of my reaction. So it turns out that in order to pray for grace, I already need that grace?'

'Of course. Prayer and grace are the same thing. Don't try to understand this. There's nothing to understand here and no one to understand it. Just stop robbing the bank. Remain a witness. That is the only spiritual act that you are capable of.'

'Then the robbers will try to kill me,' I joked morosely.

'Yes, they will try,' said Kaya. 'That is precisely why they shoot snuffs, broadcast news and are always cranking up their music machine on the other side of the river. But in actual fact the robbers can't do anything, because they're only shadows. And you could learn to see through them. And after that you would stop noticing them at all, and that would be the start of a whole new story. Only the trouble is, Damilola, that you yourself are a robber and a shadow. So you don't want to learn. But Grim could. He hasn't killed anyone yet.'

That was the bitchiness kicking in again, clearly in anticipation of an outburst of jealousy. Then seduction would immediately cut in – sure thing, we know, we've been there before. But the reason I set seduction to maximum was in order to give in to it at some point, right?

I tumbled her to the floor.

Her face mirrored the submissive weariness that maximum bitchiness always brings on its black wings. That usually got me even more aroused. But now, with her face right there in front of mine, I suddenly understood what she had been talking about.

I saw what had made me tumble her to the floor – the sweet tremor of anticipation running through my body, the flash in my brain that was a promise of eternal happiness. But because of what she had said I could no longer fuse unthinkingly with that flash in the way I used to. And that tiny delay proved fatal.

There was no pleasure up ahead any longer.

Its brilliance faded and it went out, like a flame doused with water. And I realised that the bright promise towards which I had rushed every time with my heart and loins in turmoil had no substance behind it – and it never did have. I remembered that I had realised this many times before... why damn, I realise it every time at the supreme point of gratification for a tiny little moment – but I immediately forget again.

What is all this for? I thought. There I go, heading towards the beacon of the closest joy – it glitters in front of me for a while and then disintegrates in a shower of counterfeit sparks, and I realise that I've been tricked, but I can already see a new beacon and I head towards that, hoping that this time everything will be different. And then it disappears too, and so on endlessly, ad infinitum...

It was as if I had been hit on an extremely sensitive point – a nerve centre that I didn't even know existed.

I had served this world as best I could, and I really had run along the corridor of torments that she talked about. I had despised many of the things that I had to do in my job – but there was supposed to be a reward for my labours, and Kaya was the most important part of it. And suddenly I had seen that there was no reward. She had taken my happiness away from me, but left the flames of suffering in place – and now they were blazing all around me.

Worse than that, she herself had become the blaze of suffering. She had turned from my inscrutable Kaya into a rubber doll WHO DIDN'T LOVE ME AT ALL. And when I realised that just a moment ago she had stolen my only joy, I hit her for the first time.

Suras can be beaten; they're designed to take it. They look up at the ceiling and don't resist. Sometimes a little synthetic blood bleeds out of them and a lip swells up. It all passes by morning.

The next day I had to go to the base and stay until evening to check the new gyroscopes for Hannelore – a real pilot always monitors that for himself. And when I got back, Kaya wasn't at home.

She had taken a large bag, her dresses and all her operational accessories, leaving me only the transgender phallo-simulator module. She had placed it in the most obvious spot. There was a message written in lipstick on the mirror in the hallway: 'Gone to Nirvana. Take care.'

I didn't even know we had any lipstick at home.

Every day when Grim switched on the creative articulator, a word woven out of transparent letters appeared in front of him for an instant.

This, as the dictionary explained, was one of the ancient names of Manitou. It proved to be entirely apt – there really was something supernatural about the articulator.

All he had to do was clumsily tap in some nebulous verbal embryo with two fingers, or even just start to do it – and in response the application immediately threw out several versions of the newborn thought, ready-formulated and rosy-cheeked, swaddled in the nappies of clever words that Grim had to keep delving into on-screen thesauruses to find.

The growing embryo looked like a small rotating cube – different versions of the text appeared on the sides that moved close to the screen Every time it was a well-formulated, complete sentence – it didn't require any further processing. But it was possible to change the nuances included in it, ad infinitum, and the most important thing here was to stop in time.

Grim didn't know exactly how the articulator worked, and no one else really knew. Damilola only said that it incorporated the same algorithm as Kaya had – the programme took into account everything that had ever been said by people, all of the countless semantic choices that had been made over the centuries and preserved in the information annals. Grim's fingers seemed to have at their command an army of dead souls, who moved the cubes of words for him.

It was like a game – as if he was tossing instantly sprouting seeds into a furrow. Their pattern of growth could be controlled in a most bizarre fashion. A newborn paragraph-cube could be moved along numerous axes with captions such as 'more complicated', 'simpler', 'angrier', 'kinder', 'cleverer', 'more naïve', 'more heartfelt', 'wittier', 'more ruthless' – and as you did it the text instantly changed in accordance with the route selected, and what's more, at new points of the endless trajectory new semantic axes appeared and the thought could be pushed further along.

Grim understood now how the unknown masters had finished off the 'Ork's Song Before Battle' for him – after experimenting with his own drafts, in just a few minutes he produced several other possible versions of his masterpiece, each one better than the last.

But what Grim liked most of all was that the articulator made him incredibly, dazzlingly clever. He deliberately entered a stupid, clunky phrase into the manitou, typed it almost at random – and with a few simple manipulations transformed it in a most radical manner.

For instance, in response to the embryo 'in Big Byz they're all cunts and fuckheaded wankers', after a couple of prods with a well-gnawed finger at the axes 'cleverer' and 'more refined', the articulator came up with the following paragraph:

'The inhabitants of Byzantion must be conceited and in-secure sexual neurasthenics, inclined to conceal their pleasure in other people's pain behind false sympathy and hypocritical moral preaching – simply because no other mental modality is compatible with life here. At all other points of psychological equilibrium the reality of existence here will immediately reveal its essential nature and start inflicting searing pain.'

And the obscure phrase 'without a manitou they're nobody, but with a manitou they think they're big time' was transformed by a number of more complex movements of the finger into this:

'And if all the manitous were stripped out of their world, we would see hallucinating termites, working in cells of steel, and if all the manitous' feelers were torn out of their minds, we would see decomposing protein bodies, feverishly generating one cerebral whirlwind after another in order to forget about their impending disintegration.'

Both paragraphs were sucked in by the grateful manitou,

402

which immediately transferred to Grim several thousand, which popped up at the top of the screen – when one of Grim's passages turned out well several columns of figures appeared there. Grim didn't understand exactly what they meant; all he knew was that the larger the figures were, the better he had pleased the system.

After only two weeks he heard his own words from the screen in one of the fresh naval snuffs, which Chloe was watching at full volume after coming home (she spent the night at Alena-Libertina's place a lot less often now). Both pieces were pronounced by an 'Orkish countess' (only people could have fallen for an idiotic title like that) in a break between oral caresses and making love lying on one side. After that the snuff showed the last war, which Chloe didn't want to watch.

Grim was very proud of himself. And Chloe, to whom he didn't bother to explain how such an impressive text had been produced, also gave him a respectful look.

But when Grim got to know the application a little bit better, it turned out that far more semantic axes opened up not in the area of 'refined subtlety' but in the zone of 'trusting simple-mindedness' – where touching naïvety merged into adolescent forthrightness, so to speak.

It was precisely these modalities of self-expression that were in greatest demand by the upper people, although Grim hadn't noticed that they were naïve or particularly frank. But for them complexly phrased intellectualising inevitably aroused associations with an underfed Ork – as his own creative success testified.

It could only occur to an Ork to pull the wool over the eyes of the person he was talking to by speaking in a sophisticated and abstruse way – people simulated simplicity for that. When anyone spoke to them in a complicated manner, they simply stopped listening, just as no one listened to the Orkish countess in the snuff as she shuddered from the jolting blows against her pelvic bone.

It was a mystery why CINEWS Inc. required the services of a screenwriter like himself if people had no trouble at all transforming any verbal stub into an expanded thought with any desired degree of resonance and depth.

Grim racked his brains over this for a long time and came to the conclusion that it was precisely a matter of the Orkish intention, the contorted verbal embryo and the distinctive spurts of venom that he could spew out, since this was something people weren't good at any longer. They were capable of lots of things, but not this. And in addition, even having created an embryo like that in their laboratories, they would never have moved the little cube of text along the axes of the creative articulator like he did. He was not simply unique, he was doubly unique.

Once he realised that, Grim calmed down – he felt that he had his own special niche in the world. And that, as he knew, was the most important thing for any man.

He finally realised that he had fitted into Big Byz when he noticed how time had speeded up.

He couldn't have said that it was moving too fast. It simply disappeared in entire chunks of the calendar. And then one day, after a whole week had vanished into nowhere, Grim guessed that all the rest of his life would disappear exactly like that.

He recalled Alena-Libertina's words – 'Live here until the day you die.' A rather strange thing to wish someone, if you thought about it. He wondered what she had meant.

Grim loaded the embryo of his perplexity and sadness into the creative articulator, prodded it in the directions labelled 'more heartfelt' and 'more sincere', and then along the sub-axis 'salinger', which popped up in the final sectors of the augmented 'soulful' mode. He didn't have even the vaguest idea of what this 'salinger' was, but just recently he had lost all qualms about simply copying all the cunning ruses of the upper people's design.

This was what came out:

'But if you understand that what remains between your physical death and the point at which you are now is only a slick of time as smooth as an ice rink, what difference does it make how long you will be skimming across it? The second just before death will be the same as now. Nothing else will happen, only once again the politely smiling waiter will come over and serve you a slightly different cocktail of familiar drinks that have made you vomit so many times already. Perhaps death was that point at which you realised this, accepted the sentence and travelled on?'

To Grim's eyes the little cubes were turning out better and better, almost like upper people's.

Only for some reason the manitou was scoring him fewer and fewer points. Because of this, Grim almost always had a dreary, bleak feeling and he gradually began to understand the nature of the force that had prompted the late Bernard-Henri to descend into the accursed lands of the Orks.

Grim hardly ever talked about his problems with Chloe – they were incomprehensible to her. And at the same time she kept insisting that he should 'get into the local social scene', and he made an honest attempt to do this, accompanying the sociable Chloe to all the parties that she was invited to.

People usually got together in some large space that was dark, with loud music playing and coloured zigzags of light running over the faces and the walls. Chloe really liked this dizzying, fresh darkness transfixed by bright flashes of light and filled with thunderous bass rumbling, but Grim just couldn't relax completely in it – he thought the problem here was his combat experience, in which a loud 'boom-boom' meant something different.

405

Some people hid in the corners, secretly sniffing various forbidden powders, and Chloe rapidly acquired a taste for this.

The powders weren't really forbidden seriously, but rather, as someone put it 'for the extra adrenalin buzz', which was more or less understandable, even though the words were unfamiliar. But after he tried the mixture once, Grim almost went out of his mind. He imagined that he was still in Orkish Slava, and everything that was happening was just another cunning attack by the people, who had paralysed his brain with an unknown weapon, and it was all going to end as usual, with an air strike, which he wouldn't be able to hide from now. While Chloe hopped about in the vivid, multicoloured splashes of light, he spent the whole night shuddering silently in a corner – and covered himself, as she informed him later, in everlasting shame.

On the other hand, at one of the parties Grim met another Ork who had established himself among people, an *orktivist* in exile by the name of Drip – ITN 1 5406 20 677 43 2. He was better known to people under his pseudonym of Andrei-André Gide Tarkovsky. He was a bald, bearded little old man with elusive eyes.

After the death of the legendary Ivan-Yves Montand Karamazov, whose pupophobia and brutal nationalism the upper people had learned to forgive for the sake of his exceptionally photogenic exterior, Andrei-André had become the foremost representative of the Orkish underground conscience on Big Byz. Grim even remembered his poem 'A Gecko on a Church Spastika', for which Andrei-André had been stripped of his Orkish citizenship.

Tell me, gecko gaily painted,
Answer, groves of cannabis,
Why one twentieth of the planet
Has to breathe a stench like this?

406

Andrei-André didn't like the word 'sommelier' and called himself a writer – just like the late Ivan-Yves, whom he still envied bitterly to this very day ('daily photosessions from the conspirative revolutionary underground – that's life and fate for you, brü …')

At first Grim took the word 'writer' to mean a sommelier whose little cubes weren't taken for even a single snuff. Andrei-André corrected him, saying that a writer didn't write for his contemporaries, but for eternity. Grim enquired if eternity had returned the gesture by agreeing to support Andrei-André, but the writer good-naturedly explained that he was sometimes quoted in the news – entirely without recompense, of course. But then, in parallel, and entirely independently of his social position, he received a small university welfare grant. He didn't keep any secrets from Grim – he was too old for that.

'Listen, kid,' he said, 'you're an Ork. They keep you here so that people can hear an honest Orkish voice when they need it. That's what they feed you for. So you have to pinpoint the precise moment when the honest Orkish voice should speak up and what it should say. And for that you have to watch the news and the snuffs all the time, and ideally read all the frontmen-gunlayers of the assault fleet, in translation from the Old French, right there on their special sites, to know which way the wind's blowing. Then you'll be able to get a small lead on things and astound everyone with the freshness of your views.'

'In other words I have to lie all the time?'

Andrei-André shook his head.

'On no account. Always give them the truth straight from the shoulder. But along the right trajectory, and up here there's only one of those, and you have to sense it with your butt. And be in the news all the time, in the news … In that department the late Ivan-Yves was a real ace, even though he didn't know Church English. And if you don't want to take any risks, there's an easier way. Repeat their morning headlines. Only in the first person and straight from the heart. You can give it a positive twist or a negative one. That makes no odds to them, we're Orks anyway.'

'But can't they tell us themselves what to say? At least roughly?'

Andrei-André laughed.

'No one's going to explain to you what to say, you've got to sense that for yourself. This is a high-class musicians' gig here, Grim. Has been for many long years. And there's only one thing they want from you – your honest voice mustn't disrupt the harmony of the orchestra. Fit in with the symphony. One note a month, and you can dine for free at buffet lunches for the rest of your life. But if you don't mind, please don't foul up that one single note – you've got to understand things for yourself . . .'

He worked his lips for a little while, contemplated the liver spots on the back of his hands and added sadly:

'Honestly, this smart free speech of theirs isn't for the feeble-minded. All that different bullshit you have to remember for three hundred manitous and a free burger . . . Do you know how the discoursemongers here keep themselves fed? Say some kind of event happens. And they all have to take turns to speak out about it. And what's more, they have to speak out about it incisively and boldly, so they'll get remembered and their grant will be renewed. And they all take turns to talk, and the others listen and filter it, to see if there's anything inappropriate or incorrect in there.

'And if anyone makes a slip because he's hungry, they all immediately swoop down on him and start pecking away at his liver. It's a frightening sight. If I was younger I'd fly the coop, go down below to pull in some money . . . But no, I'm wrong there. When I read those downside magazines, like that *Siberian Nights* or *Orkana*, I can't sleep afterwards. Revolution's a fine thing, of course, I gave half my life to it, but Manitou forbid

408

that we should ever lose our grip on the reins. We'll see some really first-class bastards creeping out of the woodwork then...'

'But do you believe in revolution?'

Andrei-André gave him a bleary look.

'Just don't you ever say this on camera, son, but remember it for yourself – every revolution in our Urkaine, without exception, ends in blood, shit and slavery. From century to century it's only the proportions that change. And freedom lasts exactly long enough to pack a suitcase. If you have anywhere to go.'

Andrei-André was a good-natured and sincere Ork – and he treated Grim as if he was his own son. He willingly shared his own professional secrets.

'You have to realise straight off that all you can sell here is snuff and derporn. You'll deal in derporn when you get old. But while you're still young and handsome, you should sell snuff.'

'How's that done?' asked Grim, puzzled.

'You have to portray the young green shoots of life that have broken through the concrete of social oppression and are intertwining above it in an exuberant dance of love, and while you're at it you have to show what's special about this particular generation's dance of love. And later you have to describe the steamroller of oppressive despotism snapping off the young shoots of life and rolling new asphalt over them. But you can't just prattle away at random here, you have to check everything against the news and the discoursemongers – so the asphalt will be the same kind as they showed in the news... Then they'll give you a bite to eat. Would you like us to do it together?'

He said a lot of interesting things. He also kept promising to give Grim a copy of his unpublished memoirs, titled after some Ancient Film *Don't Call Me Bwana*. Unfortunately, he got drunk very quickly, and it was only possible to make conversation with him for a few minutes. Grim spent the rest of the time feeling bored in some corner, waiting for Chloe to dance herself out so that they could go home.

He didn't enjoy parties.

And yet he couldn't even formulate exactly why – until the creative articulator helped him out when one day Grim spent a long time chasing around a little text cube that began with the words 'a bunch of party snakes'. The result produced was this:

'A party is a camouflaged social arena, a micro-coliseum that people come to supposedly to take a break and relax, but actually they all have gladiator equipment hidden under their clothes. They bring their own murky intentions along with them and dance to their tune all evening, and not at all to "a different drum" as they laboriously explain in conversation. And then, following a thousand supposedly casual moves in a freakishly lit aquarium, these bright-coloured reptiles end up twined together in a manner strictly appropriate for ingesting and inseminating each other. What appears to the naïve observer to be convivial merriment is a constant and unceasing struggle for existence laced with social ritual.'

Chloe felt right at home at these parties. She usually put on outfits for them that Grim thought were absolutely bizarre – some kind of blouse made of feathers, or a dress with large fabric flowers that looked like malignant tumours. But people liked that, although they didn't dress that elegantly themselves. Chloe acquired a lot of friends and she spent entire days bab- bling away to them over the sound link while choosing a new outfit on the manitou.

She went out to these parties on her own more and more often.

And then she left altogether.

It happened simply and prosaically, and it didn't come as a blow to Grim – a rather hostile alienation had already sprung up

410

between them long before. Grim was actually amazed to realise how well prepared he was for it.

Chloe moved in with a certain young snuff director who didn't have the slightest objection to her friendship with Alena-Libertina and promised her a part. Chloe had been dreaming about that for a long time.

She even acted generously: from the legal viewpoint Bernard-Henri's former residence belonged to her – but for the time being she let Grim have it. The view she now had from her new windows was Paris in springtime. Of course, Grim couldn't offer her anything like that.

Chloe sent him two or three letters – they were cold and insincere, or they just seemed that way because she wrote them without a creative articulator. Grim didn't reply. Not because he was hurt – he simply didn't have anything to say.

At this time an event occurred in his life that appeared insignificant from the outside but shifted all the social settings inside his head in a strange way.

He made himself business cards.

On Big Byz, of course, there was absolutely no need for them. Theoretically they could come in useful if he took off to Orkland on business. But he actually needed them for something quite different.

He thought up the design and the text himself. Or rather, he didn't think it up, he reproduced it – from the very same business card that used to hang above his desk in Slava for so many years.

After printing out a pack, he glued a sweet-smelling card to the upper frame of the manitou, so that it was in approximately the same place as his great-uncle Mord's used to be. Then he lowered his eyes, waited for a few seconds – and flung his head up sharply.

411

There in front of him was a cardboard rectangle with a text in simple, austere lettering:

Grim ITN 1 3505 00 148 41 0
Content Sommelier at Discourse
Big Byz 093458731 - 4091

It was a victory certificate.

Grim had earned it at a very young age, not even twenty – when the life and fate of most Orks who had survived in the Circus were only just coming together. But he didn't feel a thing. Just as late great-uncle Mord probably didn't feel anything about his own cards any longer.

Yes, down below there were many Orks who would have been wracked by envy at the sight of that white business card. But Grim couldn't care less about their feelings, because he no longer understood how the Orks' envy could be transformed into his own happiness.

Things were no better with the upper people. Every day it became more and more clear that for someone who didn't really like parties, the cheers of a crowd differed little from the crowing of a cock outside the window or the distant grunting of a pig – especially in those cases when these sounds were artificial.

He had no interest in a reward like that. But the world had no other rewards to offer – apart, of course, from money. But if you thought things through, nobody had any manitous anyway, apart from those who printed them. The others were only allowed to hold them occasionally – in order to convince themselves that manitous truly did exist, and keep on working. But Damilola advised him not to pursue this question in any greater depth – this was the point at which the quicksands of hate crime began.

Grim was in any case skirting closely round its very edge, and sometimes he overstepped it. Once he even reviled democraship, which Damilola said you should never do in a liberative society.

In a new snuff the anti-democraship passage was given to an enemy of progressive reforms – a spiteful Orkish farmer, who waved a trident and net about as he hissed at his sexual partner:

'Democraship made sense as an expression of the will of people who, to put it in agricultural terms, were "free-range organic fed" – and therefore in those days it was still possible to use the word "freedom". Everyone accumulated wisdom and experience drop by drop – and the sum of those wills gave the best form of government in the world, which was *organic*. But now it's become *orkanic*. Today democraship is the product of an expression of the will of worms that live in an iron honeycomb. Their only connection with the universe is via an information terminal that pumps through their brains a torrent of the mental chemicals, fertilisers and modifiers produced by the political technologists. Where's the choice? What difference does it make which of the cockroaches allowed to run in the race comes first, if they're all taken out of the same jar? Does it matter what colour the prophylactic is, as long as the dildo remains the same?'

Damilola advised Grim to stop making this kind of joke – from reading his attacks on democraship the senior sommeliers might draw the conclusion that he was in favour of the Urkaganate.

'The best porn actors of Big Byz have given their lives for the establishment of democraship in Orkland,' he said drily. 'If you live in our society, you should respect their memory. And don't use the word "political technologist", no one understands it here. You can't put a footnote into the snuff every time – "an electoral sommelier in a society without elections".'

Grim himself understood how stupid his candid comments made him look. And it was clear how he ought to behave – on

413

that point old Andrei-André had explained everything very precisely.

Only was it really worth pretending?

He thought about that for the first time when he noticed what had become of Tuscany in his window after his gaze had been grinding at it for so long. One by one, details had emerged that undermined all confidence in the landscape.

Firstly, a cloud that was always the same shape, resembling his late uncle Khor's profile, drifted over the distant mountains every few hours. Secondly, the wings of the windmill always turned at the same speed. Thirdly – and he was particularly irritated by that – the column of smoke from the chimney of the white house on the hill kept changing in such a way that after a very short while all its fluctuations were repeated in exactly the same sequence.

Grim finally understood the meaning of the expression 'a dead-end life' when he noticed that he was drinking for the third evening in a row with an unshaven Damilola in his empty apartment, which seemed to have gone mouldy all of a sudden. At first he complained to Damilola about feeling depressed, then for some reason he told him about his great-uncle Mord and showed him his new business card. Damilola examined it with interest for a few seconds and then tossed it onto the table.

'Don't let it get to you,' he said. 'You're still young, that's all. And youth is a period of life crisis and total hopelessness for everyone. It's all over, there's nothing left to strive for ... Ha ha ha ... At eighteen a man feels eighty, but then at eighty he feels twelve. If not four. You're just stressed out because of Chloe, Grim. It's stress and hormonal morning sickness.'

'But what should I do?' asked Grim, tying his tongue in knots.

'I'll tell you. Go to GULAG, to the rental centre. Find a sura that looks like Chloe. You can even order a temporary face for her from a photograph, if you don't mind coughing up the manitou. Rent her out for the weekend. Put her in "Desdemona" mode, chat with her a bit about snuffs and culture, you know, and about music. And then strangle her. Slowly, with real feeling. So that she pisses herself. Then reset her, and do it again. And do that five times, until it's imprinted in the subcortex. Only put a rubber sheet on the bed. You'll wake up a different man. Try it, seriously... Give it five, the pupo jive.'

Of course Grim had no intention of following Damilola's advice. But his company was better than being alone. Although it was pretty dismal too.

'Two abandoned failures...'

No one spoke those words out loud, but they seemed to hover in the air.

Not even what the manitou told him about the latest disturbances in Orkland was any help. As was only to be expected, the new Kagan was no better than previous ones and the fresh shoots of democraship soon became a farce. In the news Andrei-André appealed for support for the revolution, and they were already starting to bomb the outskirts of Slava a bit – more in homage to tradition than with any specific intent.

But Damilola was glad. After the period of leave that he had taken out of grief, there promised to be lots of work, and after that the next war. The purchase of a new Kaya was gradually shifting from the realm of harebrained scheming over into the zone of sober budgetary planning.

'I'll make do with derporn for a couple of years,' he said. 'And then I'll take a loan and buy. They say they're going to print a lot of money for the Orks soon, and I'll be able to get refinancing against the old equity. But with the new sura everything will be kept under warranty... Although... there's not much chance I'll be able to hold out, not really...'

Grim listened to this as he looked out of the window.

It looked as if Damilola was serious about it – since Kaya

disappeared he'd been economising on everything. He'd even moved from Naples to cheap New York, and now outside his window it was always night, seen from the window of an ancient 'skyscraper'.

That was what they called the buildings people used to live in – in the Age of Ancient Films. They looked like incredibly high cliffs, studded with the bright dots of windows. The view was enchanting and terrifying. Grim liked it on the whole, but Damilola explained that it was one of the ancient horrors preserved by human memory. These expanses of concrete cliffs aged far more quickly than traditional flat cities. Literally in two or three hundred years the conglomerations of skyscrapers had been transformed from a symbol of the future into a reminder of the dismal past.

'I want external reality to correspond to what I have inside me,' said Damilola. 'When I take a turn for the better, I'll change the view. But meanwhile...'

It occurred to Grim that the people in skyscrapers lived almost the same way as in the massive bulk of Big Byz – in boxes on top of each other, stretching up and down for level after level. Only now, instead of streets, there were tunnels. And the living units had no 'outside' any more– there was only 'inside' left.

This thought could have been twirled about on an articulator, and the sommeliers would probably have put it into the mouth of some Orkish character or other in a new snuff. But Grim couldn't be bothered even to write it down.

Sitting at home in front of the manitou, more and more often he left the screen idle long enough for it to go blank. And then his face and part of the room behind him appeared in its black mirror. The window was also reflected – and in the mirror-image behind him, Tuscany was significantly less plausible. The reflections of real windows – down below – looked different.

416

Well then, he thought, it looks like I've lived as far as death already. Let's see if there's anything else to come...

This embryo could also have been transformed into something beautiful and complex, but Grim didn't enter it in the creative articulator. His last phrase accepted for a snuff was this:

'All your cultural sommeliers and discoursemongers are just evil little skunks in the service of the world government. And as for your women... I used to think they were bitches. But now I've realised that they're just rubbery. In the bad sense of the word.'

Two strange things happened with this passage.

Firstly, in processing it on the articulator, Grim didn't add a single one of the flourishes suggested by the programme.

Secondly, for some reason in the snuff this text wasn't recited by an Ork, but by a man giving examples of criminal hate speech.

БB

My final insights into the tenebrous soul of the young Ork were already half the product of my own imagination. And I won't have a chance to entertain the reader with them now. But I don't have much more left to tell.

The words 'I've lived as far as death' are the last I remember from his babbling during our drinking sessions – simply because they sounded so exceptionally absurd, coming from such a young and vigorous creature. But nonetheless, they were entirely accurate – as far as I could judge from his confessions. I wasn't listening to the muscular little beast very attentively, since I got drunk a lot faster than he did. And apart from that, my thoughts were occupied with other things.

They couldn't find Kaya anywhere. And nobody could help me. But then, no one tried particularly hard. The supremely benign consultant surologist referred me to the breach of warranty – and suggested that Kaya had self-terminated in the central garbage disintegrator. There really had been cases of that happening, and it was the most convenient cop-out for the manufacturers. I was offered a serious discount on a new sura of the same class. All the details of physical appearance could be reproduced precisely – but it wouldn't have been Kaya. I promised to think about it.

It soon became clear that Grim had no prospects at all in our culture. He suffered two image disasters in quick succession, and they both involved inept quotations from Bernard-Henri, who seemed to be avenging himself on his enemy from the grave. First Grim was invited onto the programme 'Social Opinion', where he declared that in the modern world social opinion doesn't even exist, there is only a financial resource, absolutely teeming with a swarm of ravenous sommeliers, which shows itself on the manitou. Bernard-Henri hadn't written that in Old French by accident, but our little mongrel cur thought he could repeat it out loud.

When he was given a chance to put things right and explain himself a couple of days later, he told the people from the reception committee that he didn't want to go to any more broadcasts at all. They started trying to impress on him that it wasn't in his own interest to turn into a lone wolf but he replied with yet another quotation from the deceased discoursemonger – that 'sullen hermit', 'inner exile', 'lone wolf' and 'prima donna' was what a man was called in our time if he wouldn't shag a pig in front of the cameras for nothing. And if he wouldn't do it even for money, then they'd say, 'He's trying to surround himself with an aura of mystery...'

I tried to explain to him that Bernard-Henri himself had

never been a lone wolf or hermit, and he hadn't surrounded himself with any aura – quite the opposite, he simply wallowed in the manitou, and in manitou as well. So it was all the more important for a clueless young Ork like Grim to make a mighty effort. But it looked like Grim had fallen into a depression.

I was amazed by the strange parallelism of our destinies. We had both had loneliness forced on us and immediately run into financial difficulties. Of course, the reverse sequence of events would have appeared more logical, but evanescent and romantic girls who look like angels can sense approaching poverty every bit as keenly as rats abandoning their cosy familiar nooks before disaster strikes.

There were funny moments too. Grim already regarded himself as a fully fledged content sommelier, gliding smoothly round all the bends in the new world. He only realised that possibly this wasn't entirely the case when they cut off his hot water.

I remember him coming to share his strange discovery with me. The little sweetheart had spotted an interesting connection between the fact that the figures in the upper right-hand corner of his manitou had turned red and acquired a minus sign, and the fact that the water in his tap had turned cold. Only he still didn't seem to understand which was the cause and which the effect. I paid him a visit (it's interesting that after Chloe's departure the apartment of the late Bernard-Henri immediately ceased to resemble an Orkish pigsty) and delved into his accounts.

It turned out that the advance generously issued to him by the House of Manitou following his arrival had already run out. The CINEWS Inc. grant, paid after his memorable appearance in the entertainment block, had also been spent. Chloe had blown almost all of it on jewellery of some kind that Grim vehemently assured me he had never even laid eyes on.

The most interesting conclusion from the financial records was that Grim had already learned how to earn money for himself, and had been doing pretty well, especially at the beginning of his creative career.

But the poor soul had misunderstood his place in our culture. Instead of the bombastic Orkish phrases brimming with elaborate, barbarous complexity, which the snuffs needed so much, he gradually started feeding the senior sommeliers his juvenile fantasies about life, licked into shape on the creative articulator entirely in the style of our own people (not to say our own losers). Naturally they credited him with less and less manitou for this – although old Andrei-André had explained, with exceptional generosity for a competitor, how an Ork ought to earn his daily bread if he seriously intended to survive.

It ended the same way it always does – they cut off his hot water.

For several days the cleanly child of the lower plains came knocking at my door clutching a pathetic towel in his hand, until I finally had to explain to him that the home of a CINEWS Inc. battle pilot isn't an Orkish bathhouse. After that he apparently started washing with cold water and our joint drinking sessions fizzled out... But we carried on seeing each other, and soon he told me that he had found work down below.

I agreed that this was the best solution for him, since Chloe intended to sell Bernard-Henri's apartment eventually, and in any case with his unstable income he couldn't live in my neighbourhood any longer. He had two ways out – move to a three-square-metre cupboard room that looked like an enlarged copy of my privy (a toilet bowl with a shower, a coffee machine, a manitou right across the small wall and a twenty-four-hour view of night-time Manhattan), or find a risky job among the Orks, which would allow him to scrape together at least a little money. He chose the second option – and he was right, because his competition up here was an army of content-sommeliers who were up for anything and whose skills with an articulator and a dictionary of cultural codes were a lot better than his. But down below he was like a fish in deep... Creative articulator is not quite sure whether I should say 'shit' or 'water'.

And his business cards would come in handy too.

During our final meeting Grim was incredibly focused and calm – and I noticed for the first time that there was nothing of the Ork left in his external appearance. He looked exactly like a loser should look when he's sublimating an unsatisfactory sexual fling into low-budget romantic drama – all in black, with a fringe down to his eyes, a zigzag trimmed into the back of his head and tiny little metal skulls on his left sleeve – everything in the latest youth protest fashion (the poor soul really still hadn't understood that's the way those who are well past forty dress when they want to look thirty and roger those who are just over twenty). But it suited him.

He'll go down below, I thought, and find himself a new Orkish girl. Only they won't let her up here with him. Never mind, if need be, he can polish up her skull as a memento. Bernard-Henri's residence probably had that kind of karma. I think that was what my fugitive love called it...

When I learned what kind of work he had found for himself, I was surprised at first. Well, in another five years or so it could look pretty natural, but straight away... But at least it became clear what he was protesting against so elegantly.

It turned out that he had decided to become a child-dealer.

We need these people. And it's best if they're former Orks. Having your own children isn't encouraged up here for eugenic reasons – with the best will in the world it's hard to apply the rule 'don't look – don't see' to pregnancy and birth, which the law says are only legal after the age of forty-six. The high age of consent that has been imposed on society results in the production of sickly offspring. Therefore, in order to have children who are legal and healthy, people prefer to adopt them in

Orkland. This is better for us, for it ensures a constant influx of fresh blood into our melting-globe – although, of course, no one would dare to talk about 'fresh blood' in public.

The work is simple – you have to select little children according to a genome test that is carried out with a tiny little drop of blood by a special portable manitou. Every year different genetic combinations are required – depending on social planning needs and the preferences of the adopting parents. It's hard for the dealers to find the right material immediately – sometimes they have to spend a long time traipsing round remote Orkish villages. Basically the job's like being a travelling salesman, which suited my little friend's rebellious image just perfectly. Make a purchase, call a platform, load it in, give your hem a quick wash and move on, swinging the skulls on your sleeve.

Grim asked me to water the plants while he was away, and I agreed. But I forgot about this request as soon as he left to go down below. And I forgot simply because they almost cut off my hot water too and I was only saved by one tiny little loan secured against Hannelore (as my colleagues like to joke, you buy a sura secured against a camera, and a camera secured against a sura, and it's all paid for by the Orks, for whom they print five tonnes of fresh green manitous every spring).

I had good reason for saying that our destinies were strangely linked. I certainly had no grounds for mocking Grim – my sweetheart had managed to spend all my money just as cunningly as his Chloe, which was the final proof that a sura will never be outdone by a live woman in anything. And I had to abase myself by taking on low-paid hackwork.

Now I flew out on my Hannelore almost every night to launch a firework display over the upper hemisphere – where there is always restrained celebration in the air and battle cameras are forbidden to fly. Only thoroughly seasoned pilots are allowed

422

up there to work, and there aren't too many of those – so there were commissions to fill.

They came especially often through GULAG – from David-Goliath Arafat Zuckerberger. Notwithstanding all our gloomy solidarity, one could hardly call this work highly paid, especially taking my problems into account, and for the first time in my life I felt the full weight of the Orkish idiom 'sucking dick for food'. I don't wish to be witty on the subject of GULAG, as the creative articulator is suggesting, especially since everything's clear anyway.

On the other hand I had a rare opportunity to examine David-Goliath's residence. It was a copy of the Emperor Tiberius's home on Capri, where he lived at one time with Manitou Christ.

The villa was located slightly above the equator of Big Byz. It was a marble mansion lavishly embellished with statues and eagles, drowning in the greenery of absolutely genuine gardens. Immediately below its walls there was a steep cliff – everything just like on the distant isle of Capri. A long path for walks ran along the cliff top, and David-Goliath used to stroll along it in the company of his surs and hangers-on. But it wasn't this multi-billion open-air path, lined with live rose bushes, which really impressed me – it was his famous 'nooks of Venus'.

These were marble summer houses, set back among the greenery, in each of which two or three surs to his taste simulated an orgy of love twenty-four hours a day, waiting for David-Goliath, wreathed in roses, to wander in, during one of his strolls. I was unfortunate enough to witness all of this with my own eyes, but I must admit that it wasn't the erotic aspect of what was going on that set me thinking. Any one of those surs – any single one! – cost as much as my Kaya.

But someone even richer lived beside him. This man had twice as much land. And his own river. I'm not joking – his own river, flowing through a meticulously unkempt garden. It ended in a waterfall that fell into a steel inlet pipe, concealed in the bushes. And all this was real and alive, protected against the high altitude cold by an invisible screen. By the way, to this day I still can't understand how those screens manage to keep the air in, but let through cigar butts and champagne corks (of which I was regularly informed by the radar on my battle Manitou).

Of course, I pondered the economic basis for such great prosperity more than just once or twice.

The entire upper surface of the offglobe, which looks like an immense green hill, dotted with occasional external villas, belongs to either old porn actors (no mystery there) or to the lads from the Manitou Reserve. The guys who print the money for us and Orkland. Of course, the expression 'print the money' is only meaningful as applied to the Orks down below, where holographic pieces of paper really are in circulation. But on Big Byz manitou doesn't have any palpable material existence – it's just numbers on a manitou.

And to me, a person far removed from economics, it remains a mystery to this day how these persons unknown contrive to produce something completely immaterial and intangible – and use it to keep a tight grip on the balls of an entire material world, the existence of which they strictly forbid us to doubt through their sommeliers. There's clearly a good reason why the words 'Manitou' and 'manitou' only differ by the upper case of a single letter.

But I was rescued from the path leading into the dark abyss of hate crime by a timely sighting. One day I saw David-Goliath out on his strolling path – he was wearing a light toga and walking with his arms round two terrifying boys like the one that I had seen at the opening of Trig's memorial.

While working on commissions like this, it's forbidden to engage the filming apparatus. But in launching fireworks one uses the same system as for launching rockets. You have to set

424

the sight on the spot where the client is located and press the trigger – after that you don't have to worry about anything else. There's a chip in every firework that calculates the flight trajectory and the moment of detonation so as to optimise the view.

Well anyway, taking my aim on the strolling path, I saw David-Goliath's greatly magnified head in the cross-wires. And I noticed earplugs in his ears – and a very glum scowl on his face. I activated the external microphones for a second – and understood everything. The air was throbbing with thunderous music from a party being thrown by his porn-actor neighbour who lived in the green paradise beyond the artificial waterfall. And a trustee of the Manitou Reserve – the great Arafat Zuckerberger himself – couldn't do a thing about the queerasts who had dug in on the other side of the river and were cranking up their music equipment. That's how the world government bites itself on the tail with its venomous teeth – that is, if Orkish divinatory books can be trusted.

I didn't particularly trust them. But it was hard not to recall Kaya's words about the corridor of torment. It turned out that a nonentity like me wasn't alone in wandering along it: the most august David-Goliath was too. *Sic transit gloria mundi* from point 'A' to point 'B'. It probably is not earthly glory any longer, it's airborne – but as we can see, there isn't any difference. There's no point in getting jittery over petty preferences here.

In my free time I tried to understand how Kaya had contrived to spend my money and what on. It wasn't all that easy – but in the end I succeeded.

It had been enough for Kaya to obtain access to the control manitou just once. Judging from the dates, it had happened on the same day that the war began – when I had wanted to change her settings for the last time. Evidently the stress had been too great, and I forgot to log out of the system before I flew off.

While I was fighting in the sky, she slipped into the happiness room and copied all my passwords and digital signatures.

Since then she had been able to spend my manitou. She only needed the hundred and seventy-five thousand that she scrounged from me as a blind – so that I wouldn't start wondering what mazooma she was using to order things. And she had used my final resources to splash out on something completely incomprehensible. She had bought...

There was a whole list of it.

Several large rolls of synthetic fabric. Like the kind that nomadic Orkish herdsmen use for their yurts, and in the same colours – grey and black. Was she planning to raise cows?

And also a pair of large-meshed fishing nets – and the most expensive kind too, made of practically weightless, super-strong thread. Was she planning to catch crocodiles?

And also a whole heap of odds and ends of building materials and tools: plastic panels and fasteners, several kinds of assembly paste and so on. It would take two screens to list it all – and along with all the rest there was an aqualung breathing apparatus, gas burners and a mountaineer's watch.

All in all, a pretty bizarre selection.

Perhaps she needed one of these things and she had bought all the rest as a blind, trying to set me thinking about cows and crocodiles?

She had paid for all this on some kind of complicated instalment scheme, so that the bills only arrived after a long delay. My little darling had clearly decided not to distress me too soon, and with good reason. But now I had the receipts, and that made things significantly easier for me.

I entered codes into the manitou and started rummaging through databases. And pretty soon I found everything. The purchases had been delivered to the address of a transport terminal in the Yellow Zone. Two years of storage had been paid for – at absolutely crazy rates. I contacted the terminal and received a short reply: 'Received by the addressee'. The addressee was an Orkish woman by the name of Hama ITN 1 5052 09 043 12 7. She had also claimed the unused payment for storage and received it in cash.

Kaya was down below.

And she had money too – far more than her daddy did. Not because she had so very much. It was just that her daddy didn't have any at all now. The whole operation had been very easy for her – a Slava Certificate (the Orkish identity card) could be bought on every corner in Urkaine. For any name and number (you could even have the ITN re-perforated, if you had the manitou).

But after that her tracks vanished.

First I had to understand how she had got down below.

I checked to see if any excursions to Orkland had coincided with her disappearance, and found two departures for the Circus, both with stops in the Yellow Zone. The tourists on these routes are counted with a biometric implant scanner, it happens automatically while they board the trailer. The checking apparatus only reacts to people – you can carry a vacuum cleaner or a juice extractor through under your arm. So my little darling had given the scanner a wink, like sister to brother, walked through and sat down in a free place. Nobody had noticed anything. Now it was impossible even to find out which of the excursions she had left with to reach the Yellow Zone.

She had stayed down below, but it was impossible to find her.

After this doleful discovery I binged for two days. A substantial portion of what I drank left my body in the form of tears. I pictured my little darling sitting somewhere in an Orkish bazaar, wearing a widow's headscarf for disguise, with a heart-rending little suitcase containing all of her simple girly belongings – three

427

replacement pussies, *Fury of Aphrodite* gel and a greasy wad of manitous lifted from my account.

But why did she need the materials for building a yurt? Was she really going to join the Orkish cattle-herders? Or did she want to make Orkish one-piece baby suits, lighting her basement workshop with gas? Lunacy. Sheer lunacy.

And it was only on the third day that my drunken brain put two facts together: Kaya was down below and Grim was down below. Until then I'd clearly been thinking that they'd gone down to two different Orklands – or I'd been thinking about them with different hemispheres. It had never even occurred to me that they could have arranged to meet.

But as soon as I realised that it was possible, the conjecture metamorphosed into dismal certainty. And I remembered that Grim had asked me to water the plants – and I hadn't done it even once.

Once inside Bernard-Henri's apartment (I still hadn't got used to thinking of it as a den of Orks), I dashed for the manitou. The trusting Grim hadn't protected it with a password. I slipped into the inbox. It was full of spam from jewellery and cosmetic firms, which Chloe was still attracting after she'd left – like some extinct star, still enticing dreamers with its light.

There was a lot of correspondence, and I didn't even know what to look for. Fortunately I thought of looking in Grim's sent mail – and I saw that he had answered one of the advertising messages.

That was strange, even for an Ork. I opened the letter and read it carefully.

And I realised how events had developed.

About a month after Chloe left, Grim had received a letter from the Film Burners. Or at least a message that was very much like such a letter. Perhaps some had arrived earlier too, but this was the first one he had read. It said:

'Grim will like his new manitou!'

The picture attached to the letter probably seemed strange to Grim – it didn't have any manitou in it. It was a girl in a yellow dress standing in a meadow. In one hand she was holding a burning clump of transparent plastic, and in the other a placard with the words:

OPEN WITH AN EDITOR!

I didn't understand this caption myself – I had to delve into an on-screen dictionary. It turned out that the word 'editor' didn't mean only a person who corrected someone else's work. It had another meaning as well, a manitou programme that processed text. The creative articulator also fell into this class of applications, but I wasn't able to open the picture with it.

There were other text editors in Grim's manitou. He himself used an old Orkish programme 'Kompøzer!' and I made another attempt using that. The manitou asked if I was certain I wanted to do it. I confirmed that I was.

A moment later the picture opened up as text and a chaotic conglomeration of symbols appeared in front of me. There were ordinary letters. There were Church English and Upper Mid-Siberian letters. There were some that I had never even seen before. But what there was most of, was the strange kind of symbols that mad scientists in the Ancient Films used to write in chalk on blackboards as they prepared to train their death ray on mankind.

There were very many symbols and letters. I patiently looked through several pages – and suddenly saw the word 'grim' in a gap.

After scrambling through the forest of incomprehensible squiggles, I finally ended up with the following text:

grim – the manitou reads all letters – this way the manitou
doesn't see – if you've read this, reply – manitou not needed

I think that by force of Orkish habit Grim took fright and tried to be cunning. Instead of writing the terrible words 'manitou not needed', he sent a slightly different reply:

Thank you for your letter.
Manitou sees – at the present moment the Manitou that I have suits me perfectly well. I don't need a new one.

The Orkish warrior had probably written 'Manitou' with a capital letter deliberately, so that he couldn't be accused of sacrilege. At the same time he had hinted to his unknown correspondent that he was concerned about the secrecy of their correspondence. And if he was called to account, he could have said that he had replied to a commercial mailshot out of naïve inexperience. The poor soul still didn't know that the world around him lived according to different laws that were cruel and simple, and if anything went wrong this stupid Orkish cunning wouldn't help him one tiny little bit.

The next letter addressed to him had arrived two days later.

This time it didn't have any external signs at all of a message from the Film Burners – apart from the same return address. It was a typical roaming advert with the words: 'crazy reductions on an extravagant window view'. The attached photograph of a black volcanic plain covered with streams of crimson lava was clearly that self-same view – so it was immediately obvious why there were crazy reductions on it. It was a genuine worthwhile offer. If things get really tight, I thought, I'll move there from New York.

I opened the picture with the editing program, like the last time, and after painstakingly sifting through many pages of incomprehensible code I filtered out the following:

grim – there is a way out – you can do it – it's all in the next letter – kaya

After the word 'kaya' there was a little black heart in the line. In fact they occurred quite often in the jumble of symbols.

A little black heart. A little black heart. Nothing could have been more appropriate.

The letter with the final instructions had arrived three days after the second one. There had obviously been a direction to delete it and then empty the recycle bin, which Grim had done. Only his reply had been saved – it consisted of just two words: 'Got you'. The address was the typical kind of one-day barakadabra used by distributors of spam – I didn't even bother to check it in the database.

I didn't need any addresses. If my hunch was correct – and I had no doubt about that – I needed to find Grim in order to see my little darling again. And finding Grim couldn't have been easier.

The thing is that buying children is a rather risky business and it's not so easy to find volunteers for it. Sometimes the buyers are covered from the sky, in which case a deduction is made from their account. Of course, pilots of my class don't lower themselves to that kind of trade – you won't even make back the cost of the cannon shells. But in the military register you can find the contact signatures of all the buyers working in Orkland. They spray special markers onto them so that if anything happens they can be located rapidly from altitude.

What a pity that no one had thought of marking Kaya in the same way. But it was forbidden to export suras to Orkland anyway – because of problems with batteries. Clearly the fact that that they could go there by themselves had never entered the manufacturers' heads...

The atomic battery could still help me though. For some

431

technical reasons or other, it had an electronic passport – a signal detectable within a radius of a hundred metres. At that distance my instruments ought to pick it up. But trying to find Kaya in the Orkish swamp from that super-quiet squeak was like searching for happiness in a haystack. On your own, I mean.

I needed to find Grim.

I gave myself a day to sober up, loaded his data into Hannelore and on a murky Orkish morning I flew out on my search. I say 'a murky Orkish morning' because our people had intensified the camouflage cloud and so that day in the Orkish capital had turned out rather dismal indeed. But while Hannelore was diving towards the clouds, the weather was perfectly sunny.

Several circles above the Orkish capital and around it didn't turn up anything. I started panicking – it occurred to me that Grim could have got rid of his marking. Putting Hannelore on autopilot, I took off my battle goggles and clambered over to the control manitou – in order to find out if that was possible.

No, the system replied, as long as the patient (or, as the Orks literally translate it, the 'sufferer') is alive, the markers will be identifiable at long range. Grim had either departed for Alkalla (or whatever it is the Orks call it) or he was too far away from the capital. I couldn't check the first possibility, so I decided to work on the second one.

It took me five whole days.

I'll spare the reader an account of my wanderings above the dreary Orkish expanses, with their villages that look like swamps and swamps that look like villages, with their identical rice fields, with here and there a grey old nag plunking a hoof in the liquid mud (and the way they breathed, the creative articulator adds – ' the pale horse! the seventh seal!'), with their miserable banana plantations, with their terrified scarecrows, vainly imploring a pilot to take them out of their hempen hell, with their chapels camouflaged as haystacks, not daring

432

to exhibit their semi-proscribed spastikas to the jaunty barrels of our cannons, with their destitute lakes, bankrupt rivers and insolvent coconut groves... Especially since the creative articulator has already described it all for me.

Grim's signal showed up on the southern border of Orkland. Not far from the area where the boundless ancient dumping ground begins. It was located in a little Orkish border village with the ancient name of 'Shliudyanko'. The very sound of it made me feel depressed.

Grim clearly wasn't here to work – the instructions forbade the buying of children in this region because of the radiation.

Of course, this prohibition was an unnecessary precaution because the radioactive dumping had happened two or three hundred years ago and now there was practically none of the radiation left. Besides, a north wind was always blowing here, so the background radiation level would be normal in any case. But even so, Grim had violated his instructions.

I was shaking all over – I was certain that any moment now I would see Kaya. But Hannelore's batteries were running very low and I decided to return to Big Byz in order to prepare for the final act of the drama. The autopilot could do that.

Five hours later I was back at the controls. There had been enough time to take a rest, have something to eat, recharge and reload all the battle systems and have a bitter wank. The reader can see how difficult it is for me to separate myself from Hannelore. But only Manitou is capable of comprehending what it was like for me to lose Kaya – and what I felt for the Ork who had brought this disaster down on my head. My finger was simply dancing on the trigger. Grim was very lucky that his signal disappeared from the manitou screen as soon as I dropped lower.

I released the stress by shooting up a scarecrow on the edge of a meadow where two cows were grazing (they ran off at such a clip that one stumbled and, I think, broke its leg). May Manitou Shiva forgive me – I've heard that he feels a special affection for these animals. After calming my nerves, I set out to look for my little friend – I wasn't worried that I would lose him, because there was naked steppe on all sides and he couldn't have got away. He could only get lost in the folds of the relief. Although how could there be any hollows in the steppe?

The village itself consisted of little houses stretched out along a country track. Some of them served as dwellings for Orks and others as quarters for cattle, and in fact it was practically impossible to distinguish their functions even in zero-altitude flight. On the main street I came across a couple of chickens, a pig relaxing in a puddle and a drunken agricultural Ork in a coarse, dirty kaftan, with a pitchfork in one hand and a bottle of *volya* in the other. Honestly, if I'd seen him in the news, I'd have frowned and thought that military propaganda ought to be less crude.

I decided to gain a bit of height and Grim's signal appeared on my screen again. Now I realised why he kept appearing and disappearing. Not far from the village there was an ancient quarry where they used to extract something or other in the Age of Ancient Films. It had subsided and was overgrown with dense green vegetation now, but it was still possible to climb down into it. There was a half-ruined shed standing in its bottom. I pinpointed Grim when he had already climbed up and was heading towards the village.

Cautiously moving in closer, I skirted round him and then followed, trying to keep my distance – despite his youth, Grim was already an experienced Ork in the military sense. My camouflage was engaged, naturally, and I performed all the usual precautionary manoeuvres, taking the sun and the wind into account.

But once he reached the centre of the village, Grim suddenly turned towards me and raised one hand with the middle finger extended. His eyes were looking straight into mine, as if he really could see Hannelore – although I was approaching downsun and he shouldn't have been able to see me, even without optical camouflage.

To anyone watching it was a strange sight – a young Ork suddenly swung round in the village street, gave the sun the finger, spat and walked on. But from the approving grunt emitted by an Ork sitting on a roadside bench (I think it was the same agricultural Ork with the bottle, only without the pitchfork now), this gesture was entirely in keeping with the national spirit.

Grim could hardly have spotted me. Perhaps he had been prompted by some kind of instinct, but most likely he had simply assumed that I could be following him and realised where my camera would be in that case. After all, I myself had explained the basics of flying tactics to him during our binges. He had nothing to lose, this young Ork, except perhaps the finger dispatched in the direction of the sun. But could anyone possibly count how many of them had already dissolved in its ancient yellowish-white fire? Shut up, creative articulator, shut up.

Grim disappeared into a hut on the edge of the village. I waited for several minutes, flew in closer and tried glancing in through the window. Grim was sitting at a table and cutting a circular patch out of material that looked like leather with big rusty scissors. Lying on the table in front of him were a tube of glue, pieces of rope and offcuts of shiny fabric. The boy was making something. Sometimes he raised his head and answered the person sitting opposite him. I couldn't see the other person and a chilly tremor of anticipation ran down my spine.

I activated the long-distance microphones.

'What does that mean, "they believe, they don't believe"?'

435

Grim was saying. 'That's the Orkish approach. Their news isn't for people to believe or disbelieve anything, it's for knowing which way the wind's blowing and what smells it's carrying.'

'Then why do they make news for us?' his invisible companion asked. 'We won't understand anything anyway.'

Kaya wasn't there, it was some Orkish peasant.

'Well, it's like as if they replaced the signals from our sense organs with different ones,' Grim replied. 'Just imagine that you're crawling towards the slaughtering table in a butcher's yard. Creeping through blood on your belly. But your eyes show you a garden, your ears hear a little river splashing, and your nose smells flowers. And you've got this thought hammering away in your head that you need to buy some canned meat. But if, Manitou forbid, you really do crawl into a garden like that by chance, your eyes will immediately show you a bloody butcher's yard. It's all been fixed.'

'You mean they show us nothing but untruth?'

'Aha,' said Grim. 'But they don't show us just one untruth – it's at least two different ones. Ours and theirs...'

He carried on talking after that, but I wasn't interested any more. I flew back a bit from the window and activated the hyperoptics. The hut started shimmering with all the colours of the rainbow and two coarse-grained silhouettes appeared on the manitou – Grim and a paunchy man sitting opposite him. But he didn't arouse my usual feeling of empathy with fat men.

Kaya wasn't anywhere there.

Now I knew that for certain, because if I hadn't located her from her outline (it's the same as people have), I would have seen her battery's signal on the manitou.

I flew over the village, dropping down to each of the different-coloured houses. The hyperoptics presented to my gaze quite a lot of drunken Orks, several children crawling around on the floor and even a copulating pair. Kaya's signal wasn't anywhere.

436

Then I flew to the old quarry out of which Grim had appeared. He could have hidden my little darling there – and that was my last hope. But soon it was dashed too. There was no one at all in the shed on the bottom of the quarry. Inside it there was some kind of cluttered workshop – through the window I could see a large work table with pieces of fabric, lengths of rope and plastic shavings. The villagers obviously worked here sometimes. But Kaya wasn't there either.

Beside the workshop I could make out the remains of ancient cabins – at first I thought the Orkish miners must have lived there at one time. But then I noticed a large, crude bas-relief on a stone wall – an image of an eye with a tear. I remembered that was the symbol of the Film Burners. Perhaps it wasn't a tear, but blood, Kaya had said something about that. It wasn't important. If they had hidden here at one time, that time was long past.

Moving up a little higher, I scanned the quarry again – and saw only the silhouettes of small rodents in one of the cabins. I went back to the village and combed it again. A waste of time. Then I started cruising round it in ever-increasing circles, watching the manitou closely. Kaya's signal wasn't anywhere.

When it got dark, I went back to the house where Grim was holed up, put Hannelore on autopilot, glued my eye to the sights and started waiting.

I was woken by a cock crowing in my earphones.

Turned out I had fallen asleep at my post – and slept for a long time. My camera was still hovering beside the house, but it was already light. Day had come.

Grim had had enough time to send me a greeting.

There was a dirty grey bed sheet stretched out on the wall of the house, with mocking, angular letters gazing out at me from it.

DAMILOLA!
KAYA HASN'T BEEN HERE FOR AGES.
SHE FLEW OFF TO THE SOUTH.
HONESTLY. GRIM.

My eyes were still racing over the sheet, my brain was still analysing the meaning of the black squiggles – but I already knew that it was true.

She had flown away...

Never, do you hear me, never put your sura on maximum bitchiness. Because maximum bitchiness is when you realise that you can never get her back.

I noticed that I was yelling at the top of my lungs and firing from both cannons. I couldn't remember how it had started – I only became aware of what was happening when I saw the smoking sheet slip to the ground.

Then the Orkish hut started falling apart, as if wasn't made out of logs but dried-out sand. First the wall was blown away, then the shells started chewing up what was behind it. The table and benches, pots, bottle, trunks and chest of drawers all shattered into splinters and only the large white stove (Orks build them for religious reasons of some kind) withstood the blows of my shells for the time being, losing its shape as it shrank rapidly.

Grim wasn't in the house any longer. I only realised that when I ran out of shells and an Ork who was hiding from my fire behind the stove darted out into the field in nothing but his shirt. It was the man Grim had been talking to the day before – the priest from the local chapel, I think.

There was absolutely nothing left of the hut apart from the stub of the stove, still rising up out of the wood dust and fine chips. I never even suspected that Orks could make such strong bricks.

Then I remembered about the workshop on the bottom of the quarry. Grim could be there. I swung round...

And in the distance I saw a balloon rising up into the air.

It looked like a cloud of smoke. I engaged the light filters and magnification – and I made out a plastic cube, with a gas burner working away at full power above it. The flame ran up into a grey-and-black sphere, inflated inside a fishing net, to which the gondola was attached. The sphere was black on top, apparently so that the sun would perform part of the work of warming it. And it also looked a little bit like an eye – on its grey flank there was a black spot that was reminiscent of a pupil constricted by some kind of hallucinogen. Perhaps a valve or a patch.

Everything suddenly fell into place – the fabric, and the gas burners, and even the Film Burners' symbol.

It wasn't any kind of eye with a tear in it.

It was a hot air balloon.

In a single second I understood everything about her deception, about the 'mystical flight' and even the 'burning of the film' (possibly some members of the sect really did burn ancient celluloid to fill the envelope with hot air). If she really had flown south on a balloon like that – and since the wind here always blows from the north, it's hard to fly anywhere else – it meant that she was no longer in Orkland.

Grim's balloon was rising higher rapidly. I flew towards it, gaining altitude. I could shoot it down at any second – although I had no shells left, I still had the rockets. But then I would have lost the final thread that linked me to Kaya – and that thought prevented me from acting emotionally. Really, if Kaya had flown

439

off on the same kind of balloon, where could Grim fly except after her?

I glanced at the instruments. The battery had lost only a quarter of its charge overnight. A forced landing in Orkland was no problem – it had happened to me before. I could call an evacuator from Big Byz, although that had become an expensive option for me now. But if the battery went flat faraway over the dumping ground... No one would fly out there, for sure. And I was already right on the border. But Hannelore should hold out for twenty-four hours – and that meant I could fly away from the border for almost a day and still be able to return.

I decided to go for it.

I had to conserve energy, so I disengaged the camouflage. But I took every precaution to prevent Grim from seeing me. I kept behind and below him, trying to make myself just an indistinct dot against the ground.

The balloon was gaining height. When Grim had risen above three kilometres, he started switching off the burner temporarily – he clearly had precise instructions on when to do what. His balloon continued rising by inertia. I realised that he was entering the zone of strong wind and I had no choice but to follow him.

Soon the ground speed indicator started showing some very serious figures. But at altitude I could barely feel the wind at all, because we were flying along with it: Grim's balloon hung in front of me as tranquilly as a Christmas tree decoration. I switched Hannelore into automatic tracking mode. I was clearly going to be flying for more than just an hour or two, and I decided to pay a visit to the kitchen for a bite to eat. After that I got washed – I can't stand it when I start feeling itchy during a flight.

This was all frayed nerves, of course.

When I got back, I saw that Grim had risen higher and now

he was flying even faster. That was risky, because of the wind
– at high altitude there were vertical gradients that could tear
the balloon off the gondola. But Grim was acting cautiously.

Watching the box he was sitting in wasn't interesting – the
hyperoptics showed that he was squeezed in between the gas
cylinders, wrapped in blankets, and every now and then tugging
on the ropes leading to the burner – they served as his control
levers. He was obviously keeping track of his altitude and the
time on a mountaineering watch, checking with his instructions
– and breathing through a respirator.

The poor wretch was feeling very cold, of course, and every
now and then I got the urge to warm him up with a precisely
targeted rocket. I wasn't planning on denying myself that satisfaction, but it was still too early yet.

An hour later the dumping ground below me came to an end
and the Great Desert began. I never expected that I would ever
see it with my own eyes – I'd always thought it was much further away from Orkland. Not even reconnaissance probes had
been sent out here for quite some time – what was the point?
The desert looked like a sea, covered with a film of brown scum.
Here and there the stumps of ancient wind turbines stuck up
out of it – as if giants who had been buried here were giving the
bygone finger to the sky and me. And to the creative articulator
too, probably.

After an hour, contact with Hannelore deteriorated badly.
That frightened me, because I hadn't thought about it at all
– over Orkland, there are relay stations hovering everywhere,
but in the region where I was pursuing Grim there hadn't been
any technological civilisation for many centuries. The final relay
station was too far behind me and any moment now we would
move out of its range. I was all ready to fire a rocket salvo and
turn back, but just then the system switched over to an ancient
sputnik – after warning me how much it would cost.

I just gritted my teeth even harder.

But now the communications link was working perfectly. I even picked up a satellite radio channel – they were broadcasting a memorial programme about Nicholas-Olivier Laurence von Trier. They played excerpts from the last long interview with the deceased.

'It can't be easy – being number one in sales in the "first teen fucks" category for a whole forty years. How do you manage it?'

'Well, honey, if there was any simple answer to that question ... Let me put it this way – the very second I wake up, I'm already working on myself ...'

Soon I noticed that patches of green had started appearing below me. They were getting denser all the time. Little rivers flickered by. And then a forest started. Did that mean the Great Desert was already over? Or we had just cut across the very edge of it? It seemed strange to me that we had covered such an immense distance, but at that moment I didn't attach any significance to it.

I really, really ought to have thought about it! But I didn't.

The problem was probably that for most of the flight my brain had been balancing between three states. I was reckoning up my losses, thinking about how I would kill Grim and imagining my meeting with Kaya. In the end I'd started dealing with these tasks simultaneously, as if I was making things up with Kaya, killing Grim while I was at it, and signing yet another loan deed with his blood. I kept an eye on the time – and when the moment came I noted that I would have to turn back soon – so it was possible that I wouldn't see Kaya again and would only manage to kill Grim. But then his balloon started to descend, and I decided I still might get everything done.

The strangest thing of all was that I had no clear idea of what I would do when I saw her. Lurking somewhere at the bottom of my mind, of course, was a vague hope that was absolutely insane from a technical point of view – that at the moment of meeting she would repent, come up close and embrace my Hannelore, and the only thing I love would bring back home the only entity that is dear to me. Or vice versa; it's not important – I'm not a discoursemonger, after all, but a battle pilot... Of course, the load would have been too heavy for my Hannelore to lift, but I felt as if everything would change at the moment of meeting, even the laws of physics.

Grim had already descended to one kilometre, and now his balloon was flying fairly slowly – the wind had almost completely died away here. I thought to myself that the Film Burners, whoever they were, really had found a very convenient way of travelling – a balloon's speed could be regulated simply by changing altitude, because lower down the wind blew gently, but above four kilometres it got up so much speed that not even my Hannelore could have kept up with it.

And then I suddenly felt as if my brain had teeth that had been chewing on semi-liquid porridge for a long time – and all of a sudden they'd hit a steel ball bearing. Which shattered them instantly.

I realised that I couldn't go back.

I'd forgotten about the wind.

With fingers that suddenly felt feeble I instructed the manitou to calculate the reverse course. It turned out that I wouldn't even get as far as the dumping ground – I'd bellyflop somewhere in the desert.

Every battle pilot faces the risk of losing his camera every day, but you have to act as if the danger doesn't exist. This is no profession for cowards, and I had never lost my composure in battle, in the very thick of blood and death. Only then losing my camera had been no more than a statistical probability – but now...

443

Now it was inevitable. There were only a few hours left before Hannelore would be a wreck.

This seemed all the more absurd because there was absolutely no palpable danger emanating from the world around me. Hannelore was alive and well, all her systems were functioning normally, and even the prehistoric sputnik communications link was working amazingly well – like some ancient genie, whose long wait for a client had finally been rewarded.

I shouted out loud and my head started bobbing about furiously in all directions, as if it was trying to snap the stalk of my neck. Tears flooded my battle goggles, turning the world around me dim and blurred. I was even afraid that I might not be able to control Hannelore.

I just couldn't get my head round the fact I had gone and lost this second, or rather, first body of mine so easily. The pain was as bad as the day when Kaya left. I was convulsed like an Ork caught in a burst of cannon-fire from the sky.

It was especially unbearable to realise what Kaya would have said about my torment (I had spent enough magical nights with her to know this almost verbatim): 'If you think about it, you flying lard-arse, your drama comes down to the fact that one machine can't find another with its groping electromagnetic fields, and a bloated seal who's receiving reports from a rusty sputnik is sobbing in his faraway sealer...'

Then I calmed down – and the Pilot in me awoke. As if the spirit of one of the ancient Asiatic airmen, who flew off coolly into the attack knowing that there was no way back, had descended unto me.

I understood what they felt at that moment. Every second was transformed into a little lifetime, the figures on the manitou were filled with incredibly precise meaning, little Kaya came to life in the photograph above the altitude sensor – and sent me a smile from the dazzling peak of bitchiness and seduction.

444

And then I understood what had been hidden away at the bottom of my consciousness right from the start. I understood why I wanted to find her.

Not so that she would come back to me. That was impossible. And naturally, not in order to kill her – that was also unachievable, for her ontological status, as the late Bernard-Henri would have said, had been non-existence from the very beginning. But if I couldn't bring Kaya back into my existence, my Hannelore could take her along.

And Grim was perfect in the role of an escort.

As soon as this decision crystallised in my mind, everything that followed became simple. I calculated the time I had left with camouflage engaged or disengaged: with interim usage, the result ought to be somewhere in the middle. I was really hoping that I would have enough time, since Grim had descended a long way and was now flying really slowly – his destination was obviously already close.

It was getting harder and harder for me to stay below him – and flying at the same height as him was risky: I would have stood out against the bright stripe of the sunset (*last day in the sky*, someone said in my ear). When Grim went down even lower, I moved sideways and gained some height – and I had to engage the camouflage. The sky was still too bright.

I had absolutely no idea what region this was – I could only see mountains in the distance, lit up by the blaze of the setting sun. There was blue mist eddying between the mountains, and it occurred to me that it looked like the clouds going to bed (that's not the creative articulator; I really did think that at that moment). Open space, a beautiful, boundless expanse – and every glance at it reminded me that my magical eye was about to close forever.

And then I spotted lights ahead.

In fact, it would have been hard not to spot them in the

445

gathering twilight down below. The bright electric lamps glowed in a long dotted line, one lamp every hundred metres or thereabouts. Evidently Grim was expected – or perhaps these lights burned here all the time. As a pilot I noticed that despite being so primitive, this was a convenient navigation system – it was impossible to miss a long chain like that from altitude. All Grim had needed to do was rise into the air from the old quarry – and the wind, like a river, had delivered him to his destination. Probably the time of departure had also been calculated so that he would reach his goal in the twilight, when the signal lights were easy to make out.

Grim had clearly noticed the lights – his balloon started descending sharply.

The gondola touched the ground at the edge of the forest, and he immediately jumped out.

They were already running towards him.

At first I didn't understand where these people had come from. Then I spotted a canopy covered with bark – on the boundary line between the field and the forest, with several horses tethered under it. I assume that Grim's heart must have rejoiced, since the men meeting him looked more or less as 'ancient Urks' could have looked – if we accept that this nation ever really existed somewhere outside the bounds of Orkish historiography.

They were wearing dark robes with belts round them. Some were armed with crossbows and had knives hanging on their belts. Enlarging the image, I noticed that they had strange hairstyles – a knot of hair on the back of the head, tied round with a bright-coloured ribbon.

They surrounded Grim and the young Ork explained something for about a minute, waving his arms in the direction of the still-bright western sky. They seemed to understand him. It seemed to me that his appearance wasn't really a great surprise. Soon there were only two of them left beside Grim, while the others surrounded the balloon, which had already metamorphosed into half of an immense onion, and started dismantling it into its constituent elements. The deftness with which they removed the burner suggested that it wasn't the first time they had done this.

The two men led Grim to the canopy. I was afraid that they would keep him there for the night and my plans would collapse, but fortunately they only let him drink his fill and take a rest, and then they mounted their horses. They gave Grim a horse too – the Orks know how to ride them (it's part of their military training, in case cavalry scenes might be required in the snuffs). Then all three of them galloped into the forest.

It was already completely dark in there. Grim's guides put on headbands, and two bluish-white beams shone from them onto the road. The light wasn't too bright, but it lit up their way perfectly well. My Hannelore has a headlamp... That is, she used to have one. Doesn't matter. I only mean to say that the forest men not only had electricity, which many primitive tribes have, but also things like this, obviously not manufactured in our Yellow Zone. Because of the crossbows behind their backs, it hadn't even occurred to me that they could produce something like that themselves.

When we finally arrived, the red 'battery low' sign was already glowing on the manitou. The system usually worked for an hour or two after that, but it could hold out for a little bit longer. I was starting to get nervous already. They seemed to take too long dismounting from their horses.

They had stone houses. At least, partly stone: the walls and the roofs were made of wood and bark, but the foundations and supporting columns were made of stone and cement.

It was something like a village hidden away in the forest – the houses stood in the gaps between the trees and the paths connecting the houses ducked under their crowns. Our apartments for the ecologically minded middle class have similar views in the window ('among the giant sequoias', 'a thousand years before Antichrist'), but for obvious reasons, it would be hard to get close to the trees there...

They led Grim to a house with a large terrace, lit up with yellow paper lanterns that looked like huge mandarins. Men were sitting cross-legged on the cushions below them – unarmed and dressed rather colourfully. There were about twenty of them. However, I didn't examine them for long, because...

Yes. She was sitting on the same kind of cushion, facing them – my stolen joy. She was wearing a long garment in gold and green – a kind of dress made of a single piece of fabric, wound round her body (the Orks call it a sarifan). And of course, she was doing what she liked best, brainwashing these guys the same way she had been brainwashing me only recently. They were listening to her attentively. I pointed the microphone at her – and managed to record a few phrases.

I think that during our last days she had been pouring an extremely similar detergent into my cerebral convolutions:

'When you feel anger or pain, you appear. It seems to you that there is someone who is smitten by them – and afterwards it is he who acts and suffers. You simply do not know that you are not obliged to react to these sensations and thoughts. But the reaction begins with you agreeing to consider them your own. However, the chemical whiplash cracking in your brain is by no means your supreme master. You have simply never subjected to doubt its right to command. If you learn to perceive its blows, they will lose their power over you. And they can only be seen from one angle – when the one who accepts them as his own disappears. There is an ancient Orkish saying: "Where is best? Where we are not..." What does it mean? As long as you view the world from the little hillock that you have learned to regard as "yourself", you will pay a very high rent for it. But what will you receive in exchange? You do not even know which cracks of the whip will drive your "I" into its nightmare journey in a moment's time...

'The ancient gays told their enemies the same thing as today's Ork brutes – "Know thyself". For good reason, they regarded this as a terrible insult. For there is nothing in the "self" that can be known, just as there is nothing that can be known in the shifting patterns of a kaleidoscope. There is not even anyone within you who can remember this impossibility for five minutes. But to shout out on every corner that no "I" exists is even more stupid. Not because it does exist, but because it is this very non-existing apparition that will pretend that it does not exist. Do not take on a burden that is beyond your strength, and do not accuse Manitou of dumping it on your shoulders. Let Manitou bear this burden Himself – that is what Manitou is there for...

'Why do you want the monstrous responsibility for the play of the light and shade that have never asked you for anything? Why grow your hair and nails with a terrible effort of will, if they grow of their own accord? You have no more power over yourself than over the weather – and if you can occasionally predict it correctly, that does not mean that the rain falls because of your incantations. Do not take on yourself any of those things that become visible when the thread of life unravels. And do not fear to offend Manitou by your lack of understanding – when He wants something from you, you will be the first to know...'

And then she saw Grim.

She immediately got up and walked towards him. They met on the path, smiled at each other as if they had parted only a minute ago, joined hands and walked into the forest without speaking. Someone managed to give them two headbands with lamps, and they put them on. Kaya could see in the dark, but I remembered that her programmes were wary of frightening

449

off the client by demonstrating this ability: when we were still together, my little darling often asked me to turn on the light.

They walked a long way into the forest – two bluish-white spots on the uneven ground, two vague black silhouettes. Then one ray of light tilted up into the black sky and other turned down into the nearby ground, sometimes snatching Kaya's laughing face out of the darkness. And then they switched off their lamps.

In the infrared spectrum they didn't look so romantic. Especially to me – every one of the bleached-out details inflicted unbearable pain on my heart. So I only looked at them out of the corner of my eye. I evaluated the position (I mean Hannelore's, not theirs), trying to view reality with the eyes of a battle pilot and not a cuckolded husband, because cuckolded husbands often miss when they shoot.

They had snuggled down on a spot at the edge of a large clearing. I flew into the centre of it, rose another four metres into the air and carefully fixed my sights on them, setting up a salvo of all six rockets. I even checked the distance to the target to see if the camera might be damaged by debris, although that wasn't really important now.

At this point my camouflage disengaged itself – that meant Hannelore had only ten minutes left to live at the most. And although Kaya and Grim were swaying smoothly to and fro in the red 'target locked' square, for an instant I forgot all about them – and tears sprang to my eyes. I don't know which of them I loved more – Hannelore or Kaya. And now I had to lose them both in a single instant. And all because of this Ork.

They didn't notice anything, because I was hovering in darkness – but now I wanted them to see me, right at the end. See me and hear me. And not even fearing any more that it would drain Hannelore's final strength, I switched on the headlamps and navigation lights and then cut in the music too, the good old

'Flight of the Valkyries' that has served so many generations of battle pilots. Let the Orkish hero depart to Alkalla to the sounds of the music machine that he hated so much.

Then I zoomed in on their faces that were turned towards me and switched the image to standard light mode. This was probably the only time I ever regretted that my camera was a Hannelore and not a Sky Pravda. If I'd had a Sky Pravda, I would have seen them exactly as I would in daylight. But now the colour distortions made it seem as if I was looking at a rubber boy lying on a rubber girl. Never mind, I thought, that will do for a last glimpse.

Kaya had never seen my Hannelore so close up. Now look, I thought vengefully, take a last look at the flying lard-arse, my little sweetheart. Now you can see what I'm really like. Look at who it was that you embraced treacherously for so many nights in order to swap him for this Orkish freak. Depart into non-existence together with him. Or rather, meet him there, do...

But Kaya knew that I was looking into her eyes, and she gazed up into the black sky in order not to give me this final joy. And her face set in a calm, even scornful half-smile.

Bitchiness on maximum, what else can you expect?

But Grim looked straight at me. I enlarged his face so that it filled the entire sight. He remembered my Hannelore without camouflage – that was how their acquaintance had begun. He had already heard that fragment of Wagner before, when he froze in my sights without his trousers for the first time. But standing. How miserly life is with her inventions.

When I saw his eyes, I realised that he had recognised his own death. As if this instant in the night-time forest and that instant by the stream in Orkland had merged into a single long second, during which the poor little kid dreamed that he had almost slipped out of death's bony grasp. But death always keeps his promise. And now here he was – and at that moment Grim probably clearly realised that all this time death had been waiting patiently beside him.

And then I pressed the launch button.

The starting flash was reflected in Grim's eyes and his face contorted in a grimace of revulsion in the face of death. I had caught this final transformation of Orkish features on celluloid many times, after which everything disappeared in a swirling vortex of fire.

Only I didn't see any vortex.

Grim gaped in wild confusion, and I realised that he wasn't looking at Hannelore any longer, but somewhere higher and off to the side. Kaya was looking in the same direction, and for the first time I saw her jaw drop in surprise – until then I had never managed to trigger this subroutine...

And then six dull booms exploded in my earphones, one after another. I raised my battle goggles to look at the distant sky.

Six huge flowers were blossoming in it – a red one, a green one, a blue one and three in bright rainbow colours. They were all different shapes – and they looked like new universes that had just been born in the blackness of non-existence, each one now living according to its own laws. Then the second round of charges started detonating, and the sky around the six large flowers was lit up by small coloured zigzags, arrows and spirals of multicoloured fire. *Ba-boom! Ba-boom. Ba-boom*!

I had forgotten to change the programme on the control manitou. And at the last reloading the base had given me fireworks instead of battle rockets – just as they had done every night recently, when I flew out to earn some easy night-time money above David-Goliath's villa.

I was in the habit of thinking of myself as a sky warrior – but for the system I was already... I don't know what it's called. You know, the one who stands by the bed holding a candlestick.

452

And then the six universes in the black sky burned out, Wagner fell silent of his own accord, and my battle goggles went dark forever. But before Hannelore tumbled into her infinitely distant green grave, I just had time to notice the most insulting and intolerable thing of all.

They weren't looking in my direction any longer.

They...

They were carrying on.

I took off my blinded flying goggles, climbed down off the battle cushions and fell onto the floor. I cried all night long, only stopping to take a dose of alcohol. And then the alcohol started pouring back out of me again.

EPILOGUE

I only have a few words left to say about myself – and about what happened to our world. Conjointly I shall explain why at the commencement of these artless sketches, as the creative articulator puts it, I called this a tale of revenge.

But all in good time.

My Hannelore didn't die completely. She has a reserve battery that powers a recovery radio beacon. It will last for many months, and it can occasionally be used to maintain contact via the sputnik. And the sweet couple didn't forget about me. Kaya linked in to Hannelore via her air port and sent me a message that unexpectedly popped out of my orphaned battle manitou.

'Happy birthday, Damilola, and thanks for the firework display! We love you! Kaya and Grim.'

It's probably no problem for Kaya to connect to Hannelore's memory. It still has a lot of interesting and amusing things stored in it. Take Grim's graduation essay, for instance, filmed from his manitou through the window. Or the photograph of the document in Upper Mid-Siberian, which the wind tumbled past his nose at Orkish Slava.

Strangely enough, I don't regret in the least that Grim wasn't killed. On the contrary, I'm extremely glad about that turn of events. It's the very thing that makes my revenge possible. The

455

only thing I can't understand is how my premonition could have misled me so badly. After all, I've seen death clearly reflected in his eyes, not just once but twice.

But what's to be done? It means I was wrong. It happens to everyone. All sorts of things can be discovered in the depths of Orkish eyes. Perhaps it's simply the imprint left by a difficult childhood.

Grim was a greatly hyped media figure, so his flight could have got into the news. But the story was skilfully hushed up. Chloe helped.

By that time things were going wonderfully well for her – she had been given a supporting role in a snuff that they started shooting as material for the next war. A supporting role isn't porn, so age doesn't matter here. There are usually semi-naked creative young people with candlesticks standing around the conjoining aged celebrities. The viewer loves close-ups of chaste, youthful eyes, with the copulating stars reflected in their pupils – it's pretty much like derporn, only in reverse, and without any moral ambiguity. While the creative young people hold the candlesticks, the senior sommeliers select their future giants from among them – it's a long process, and it's important to get the right start in it.

Excerpts with Chloe in them were shown in the entertainment block (she even allowed herself the liberty of several hip move-ments approved by a lawyer), and then the presenter asked her about Grim. And Chloe, the clever girl, shed a little tear and complained in a thin little voice:

'He used to raise his fist to me and once, when he was drunk, he said, "Go away, you stupid fool, you've got the face of war."'

The presenter's answer to that was:

'Perhaps we were too hasty in inviting him up here.'

And that was it, Grim didn't exist in this world any longer.

But military men, of course have their own particular reality, and facts don't fall out of it so easily.

I sent my boss a report of what had happened – and I was summoned for a talk. It immediately became clear that no evacuator would be flying out to get my Hannelore. And my future prospects came under consideration.

From now on I would be working only with rented equipment – that is, as I've already said, sucking dick for food. If I happened to take another brilliant long shot like the black Orkish octopus, the company would simply pay itself three million. And as for a new sura, I could forget about it – with zero collateral there was no real chance of getting a new loan. At the very best it was renting for the weekends. Taking some disinfectant-smelling blue-eyed blonde, with a sealed tuning block, from a rental outlet and hearing her say things like: 'Right then, fatty, how about we play the birds and the bees? I really love our intrepid warriors of the air!'

After the talk with my boss I got the feeling that up here they had always known about our neighbours. And feared them. There could be wizards living among them, capable of bringing down our offglobe by tootling on a reed pipe, the way it had already happened in Brazil. I was ordered to keep my mouth shut. The idiots, the blind, greedy idiots. It wasn't wizards with reed pipes that they ought to be afraid of, but their own immediate business partners.

And this brings me right up to the point in space, time and destiny at which I find myself now.

A month after Grim bolted, we were bombed.

That is, Big Byz itself wasn't bombed, of course. They blew up the wall of the Circus.

It was done by that self-same Torn Trojan from whom all our news channels were expecting changes. So he went ahead and arranged that. Now there will be very big changes.

457

Why did he do it?

Well, because Torn Durex was killed. Our people thought it was a lesson that would intimidate all future Orkish Kagans, and no one would ever dare to use gas as a weapon again.

But Torn Trojan drew the exact opposite conclusion – he decided that in the end he would be dumped head-first into Orkish Slava in exactly the same way. And he decided to raise the stakes. He watched *Star Wars* again – to get his courage up (Orks who have access to Ancient Films have been comparing the offglobe to the Death Star for centuries), soused his noggin in durian (probably not the simple stuff, but free base – for half the Orkish budget) and resolutely blew up the wall of the Circus with a gas bomb.

The most bizarre and galling thing about this whole story is that it was the report on the opening of Trig's memorial that gave him the idea.

It showed a cross-section of the mine that the Orkish secret police had supposedly dug under the home of the martyred pupo. A very fine drawing, thorough, and they showed it for a long time – they were obviously reluctant to let such a fine piece of work be wasted. And it definitely wasn't. The Orks themselves would never in their lives have come up with that. But now they started thinking – why shouldn't their repressive regime really throw out a challenge to the global community? Since they were chattering about it in the news anyway, and the regime itself was already in the process of being flushed down the drain...

The Orks know how to dig, and they have gas too.

Never drive dogs into a corner, not even your own working dogs. They start to bite. But it's too late to recall this ancient wisdom now.

They moved the bomb in through a tunnel dug from Slava. Not a single one of our cameras spotted this work going on – no one approached the wall on the surface, and they simply weren't expecting a tunnel. Why not? Well, because everyone who could give the nod for it to be done kept his manitou with us.

Not one can understand how our special services could slip up over something like that. After all, we record all of the Kagans' communications. I recall a conversation in which the Orkish secret police tried in all seriousness to persuade the Kagan not to carry his emerald Vertu around with him, because the people could always tell where he was. Our sommeliers were just rolling around the floor with laughter.

'Anyone would think we couldn't do it without the phone. If necessary, the Kagan will call in himself to report...'

Well, now what have they got to laugh at? Torn Trojan didn't talk to anyone about the bomb on his mobile. And he didn't call us.

Actually, some discoursemongers said that the rationale behind it was all to do with economics. In former years Global Orks could steal down below and hide what they stole up above, because it could be magically transmuted into a special non-material condition. This is a complex alchemical mechanism, comprehensible only to people such as David-Goliath Arafat Zuckerberger. The wealth that a Global Ork possesses is like points awarded to him by the Manitou Reserve. So naturally, this can only be kept with us.

Global Orks had been doing that all their lives. And then suddenly they noticed that the high-flyers in the Reserve had inconspicuously awarded themselves a lot more of these points, with the result that the Orks now seemed to have very few of them, although for a long time before this they had had more and more points every year. Of course, they felt insulted by this injustice. So their top brass started wondering why they had to steal and go for each other's throats day after day, while the topside guys, based on annual results, simply pronounce themselves ten times richer – a feat that they achieve by prodding

459

elegantly at the keyboard with their well-manicured nails. So it all went bang.

But our vibrant Orkish community didn't celebrate for long. It turned out that our security people had a detailed plan of action in case of sabotage. And the doors of all London apartments that belonged to Orkish top screws suddenly locked solid. At the same time the water, electricity and air were cut off. And then the London outside the window went out. And for the remainder of their lives (from some units, with a large volume of air inside, tapping was still heard for another five days or so) what they saw through their windows was no longer the gloomy and magnificent city on the Thames, but the sulphurous campfires of Lower Shitfall, their religious hell – programmed in perfect keeping with Orkish iconography, only realistically and in high definition, together with infrasound croaking of the Toads of Retribution and a pungent faecal smell. All this had been prepared by the House of Manitou a long, long time ago, for use if required.

The rich Global Orks were lucky – they died quickly, after jumping from their open balconies onto Orkish Slava. A couple of them even took the balcony 'bollocks' with them on their final journey – and the news channels found time to laugh at that ('You've already heard about the *Kagan's prayer*, dear viewers, but now we'll show you the *Kagan's jump* as performed by a group of Orkish investors.'). Orks have never been really liked in London. The people who say that our media have played a certain role in this might possibly have a point here.

I'm joking, in case you haven't realised. Everyone everywhere is joking now.

The explosion damaged the support solenoid of the gravity drive, or whatever it is that the sommeliers call it. Nothing can be repaired, because to do that everything has to be switched off. And if everything's switched off, we'll fall straightaway.

Basically, we're going to fall anyway now – the technical sommeliers gave us one month after the explosion at the most, and that month has already passed. It's hard to believe in the inevitability of a catastrophe, because there aren't even any cracks in the wall of the Circus – it looks the same as before. There's just black smoke rising up from under the ground in two places. Only a very little bit. But because of that smoke the manitou is now showing scenes from *Titanic* – that was one of the Ancient Films.

Evacuation is ongoing. But we won't be able to transfer our critical technologies down below in the time that's left. And that means that very soon we shall be fighting the Orks on equal terms. There'll be probably enough shells for my generation. But after that they'll simply devour us.

The most interesting thing is that it took them a whole two days to kill Torn Trojan, because he buried his emerald mobile phone in the forest, in a false dugout with several gas cans. When three battle cameras homed in on his signal, they were blown up too. The guys were experienced enough pilots, but they immediately dropped straight down to ground level – since they were competing with each other. Each of them wanted to shoot the villain in person and sell the close-up for a good fee. They were thinking of what a big bang they could make in the news. And they made one – probably even bigger than they wanted. I wouldn't have got caught out like that. But for the basic wage other people can do the flying.

Pilots, never forget: under any circumstances the most important thing is to have altitude in reserve. It can always be converted into speed. But speed can't always be converted into height. And the worst thing of all is when you have neither height nor speed.

Which is the situation we'll all find ourselves in soon. Big Byz will no longer exist. But Orkland... Eschatological conspiracy

461

theory has been in fashion with the Orks for hundreds, if not thousands of years. But their Urkaganate is so vile that there's not much chance of it ever being in any real danger. The problems will start if they ever want to improve.

Of course, some people will survive in the new world. Take Chloe, for instance. Before being evacuated she came running home and looked for things to take down below. I remember her well. Three layers of make-up, five platinum chains with diamonds and a gold brooch. Grim was exactly right when he said she had the face of war, that's exactly what it is. She'll find herself something to do.

But how the aged porn stars with their lapdogs and trailers will settle in down below is a great puzzle. On the other hand, our crack discoursemongers will have an excellent opportunity to learn for themselves in the Orkish marketplace how much their free word weighs without close air support.

The unidentified patriots who have being printing manitous for us – and, naturally, themselves – all this time (and are possibly still continuing with their labours even at this moment) will probably get by all right. Bernard-Henri, I recall, compared them with spiders that digest flies by pumping spittle into them. As long as there are flies, the spiders will still be around. But even so, it's not clear from where they'll be injecting manitous into the world now, and to where they'll be sucking out the vital strength of mankind, dissolved in their venomous emissions. However, it's best not to go too deeply into this subject, since no one has rescinded the law on hate speech – and it would be doubly stupid to fall victim to it in these terrible days.

Basically, no one will have an easy time of it down below.

And there are even some who have decided to stay.

I'm glad that I am one of them.

Everything that I loved in this world is already in the past – so what good is a future to me? What would happen to my clumsy, fat body in Orkland? Thanks for the offer, but no. I've observed this life through a gunsight for far too long.

Throughout this final month that the technicians gave us I haven't been scurrying about or packing things, but calmly setting my jottings in order. Of course, I've been greatly assisted by the creative articulator, and now my work is practically completed. I'll be polishing it right up to the last minute – but there might be something I don't have time for, so please don't be too hard on me. As soon as the farewell sirens order me to put in the final full stop, I'll send this book via the sputnik to the address of my paralysed Hannelore, and then my little darling can download it via her air link, and the local scribes will write it on bulls' skins, or whatever the fashion is there nowadays.

Let Kaya and Grim not pity me, for they have nothing to love me for (naturally, as applied to Kaya the words 'love' and 'pity' signify only imitative patterns – but there's no other way to say it).

It's entirely possible that in a hundred years their new tribal kinsmen – those sullen guys with crossbows and coloured ribbons in their hair – will be grabbing my composition out of each other's hands. And by that day it will be the final monument to our great culture.

But then, my little darling would ask, what is any culture if not a pre-programmed sequence of electrical impulses passing through human synapses, which allows some people to laugh and crack jokes as they kill others? The word 'great' is only appropriate because any human greatness has the same electro-chemical nature...

And now for the most important thing.

I have asked myself many times: why, oh why did my only love choose Grim, without even waiting for me to pay off the loan I took out for her? The answer is so simple and obvious that I would never have thought of it myself if the compassionate consultant (he is also staying here) had not enlightened me.

463

Simply because that's the way she's programmed. Her control codes include a series of operators that make her simulate sexual preferences in a specific way. This sub-programme orders her to select well-proportioned young males and to do it demonstratively – in the timid hope that all the other males will fight with each other over this, and there'll be lots of flesh and blood all over the place.

That's all there is to it. But we spend so many years writing insightful verse and poems, we just can't calm down, and worst of all, we hide the truth from ourselves, because it threatens investments that have already been made... Although when you get right down to it, the truth is well known to everyone – at least in its practical, everyday aspect.

A woman is not a human being. And a prostitute is the only thing that can save a man from a woman.

The articulator advised me twice to remove the word 'rubber' in the previous paragraph. What if an elderly, socially active feminist, one of those who raise our age of consent year after year, should come across this page – perhaps she might croak right on the spot.

Okay, so I'll do it – simply out of my love for art.

The articulator still doesn't know what's in store for elderly feminists even without any effort on my part. But the floor is already healing over noticeably, and there is very little time left.

The consultant said there was another reason why Kaya might have left. After all, bitchiness wasn't the only parameter that she had set on maximum. It turns out that the maximum spirituality setting includes an algorithm that orders the sura to share this spirituality of hers with those 'whom she can still help', as the consultant put it. Possibly my little darling looked straight through me with an indifferent gaze and then, like an ancient torpedo, performed a spiral search in the dark depths of our world, and that mongrel cur appeared in her sights.

Or perhaps she really was stricken by love.

That seems a particularly bitter possibility to me – and a highly probable one. After all, human love is also a programmable event, a particular kind of tunnel effect – impelled by the sexual instinct, it punches straight through all the matrices of consciousness. Something similar could quite well have happened inside Kaya. Ultimately, electrical circuits behave according to the same laws whether it's a simulation or not.

But I don't see anything exalted in this. Love is a repulsive, egotistical, inhumane feeling, because obsession with its object is accompanied by ruthless indifference to others. And in any case, it makes no difference now.

As I said, I don't regret at all that Grim is alive. I'm even glad of it.

Do you know why?

Because I myself could not have devised a more terrible revenge.

Grim was my symbolic rival, who got all the affection and loving caresses stolen from me by maximum bitchiness. But what will happen when I depart? The full weight of maximum bitchiness will come crashing down on him, it's inevitable. So may his skeleton crack under this hammer of the witches! I think the day is not far off when Chloe will seem to him like an angel who flew through his life, and at the mention of Sacred War No. 221 nostalgic tears will course abundantly down his flaxen eyelashes. The fun will start when Kaya realises that I'm not around anymore – and now Grim is not the symbolic rival, but the new target.

That's why I have spent so many days working on the articulator, honing this stiletto, this posthumous firework display, which will allow me to surprise my little Orkish friend even from the next world. And what a joy it is that I shall be helped in this for the last time by my old Hannelore, every bit as dead as me.

465

Kaya, can you hear me? Yoo-hoo!

Grim will like his new manitou.

Admittedly, after Kaya managed to get into my control terminal and copy the passwords, she acquired the ability to change her own settings herself. But I doubt very much that maximum bitchiness will ever allow her to take herself off maximum bitchiness – no matter what pseudo-spiritual mumbo-jungo her speech synthesisers might process day after day. If anybody has studied that rubber soul closely, I have.

But that's enough about Orks and their battlefront girlfriends. I want to say something else that's important.

The whole of Big Byz thought that it was carrying out the will of Manitou – but then why is our world crashing down, why is the universe slipping out from under our feet? What should a sincerely religious man make of this?

Probably Manitou no longer wishes us to believe that we are acquainted with him in person, and especially that we know his plans and secrets.

Manitou does not wish to have professional servants and proclaimers of His will, and our sacraments are repugnant to Him. He does not want us to nourish Him with the blood of others, offering Him our immaculate gerontophilic snuffs as a gift. How can He love us if even our own devices for concupiscence, created in our own image and likeness, flee from us? Why would He want a world where only a rubber doll is capable of unconditional love?

We are vile in the eyes of Manitou, and I am glad that I have lived to see the moment when I am not afraid to say this out loud. Everything will be different now. But in what way – only Manitou knows.

What will remain of me in the universe when I go to a place where no rubber woman will ever break my heart again? Perhaps a certain likeness of a multidimensional information wave.

Possibly this wave will splash up onto the sand of other worlds, and what I have heard from Kaya will help the new me to start my ascent into the heights, where I shall acquire peace and my spirit will become free and light. Or perhaps I am destined to become an Orkish pig and end my days in a sty (with or without a 3D manitou). In any case, it will no longer be me, because that 'I' never existed at all – right, Kaya? So is it even worth guessing?

Will I be remembered on earth?

I'm sure that my emblem for Sacred War No. 221 will be included in many creative textbooks and historical annals. But for how long will mankind annalise them, or whatever it is they do with them annals? I couldn't give a damn anyway. What difference does it make whether the world will remember me or not, if I shall be only too glad to forget it, and myself, too?

And how impetuously the finale approaches. I still have half an hour – just enough to write in a full stop and transmit this book to Hannelore. The creative articulator is suggesting to me several entirely worthy options for a final phrase, including quotations.

Here, for instance, from the ancient composer of texts Ivan Bunin, who, when it was his turn to kick the bucket (I don't entirely understand the articulator's joke, but there's no time to go into it), decided to say something regal and magnificent in conclusion, and quoted an even more ancient sommelier by the name of Maupassant.

The passage is already on my manitou:

A freshening breeze drove us over a tremulous wave, I heard a distant bell – somewhere they were pealing, the Angelus was ringing out… How I love this light and fresh morning hour, when people are still asleep, but the earth is already awakening! You breathe in, you drink, you see the corporeal

life of the world being born – life, the mystery of which is our
eternal and great torment...

'Bernard is thin, agile, exceptionally devoted to cleanliness
and order, attentive and vigilant. He is a pure-hearted, faithful
man and a superb sailor...'

That was what Maupassant said about Bernard. But Ber-
nard said the following about himself:

'I think I was a good sailor. Je crois bien que j'etais un bon
marin.'

He said that as he was dying.

But what did he wish to express with these words? Joy in
the knowledge that, living on this earth, he was of use to his
neighbour by being a good sailor? No: it was that, together
with life, God gives each of us one talent or another and
imposes on us the sacred duty of not burying it in the ground.
To what end, why? We do not know this. But we must know
that everything in this world that is incomprehensible to us
definitely must have some meaning, some exalted divine inten-
tion, directed towards making this world 'a good place', and
that the zealous fulfilment of this divine intention is always
our merit in His eyes, and therefore both joy and pride to
us... I think that I, as an artist, have earned the right to say
about myself, in these final days of mine, something similar
to what Bernard said as he was dying.

Thanks for the hint, dear manitou, but here my path and that
of the articulator must part.

The articulator suggests that I crack a witty joke about Bernard and Bernard-Henri (say, for instance: What difference does
it make what all these Saint Bernards whinged about before they
died?) and then conclude with the phrase: *I think I was a good*
pilot. Je crois bien que j'etais un bon pilote.

But I don't want to be like the people of the past who earned their bread with their brows so soaked in sweat that even on the edge of the grave they were tormented by their professional complexes (my remorseless little darling would probably add that they were simply looking for an excuse to get off on an inner high one last time). As the free and enlightened horseman number four (farewell, Dürer above my work station!) I wish to pose the question more broadly. So that my words could be repeated in his final moment by any Damilola of this world – both ancient, and contemporary, and the one still to come hereafter.

Kaya was sent to be my comfort and joy – although she was, of course, just a rubber doll. But if she told the truth about how my mind is arranged, why would Manitou want a rubber doll by the name of 'man'? And why would Manitou wish us to feel pain when smouldering butts are stubbed out against our skin?

Alas, there are no answers. Or rather, there are – but of such a kind that even more riddles spring up.

Then again, Kaya used to say that we ourselves are the answer.

We ourselves – and what we do with life, our own and that of other people.

Or perhaps I'm confusing things. Perhaps it was the late Bernard-Henri who said that – during the war before last, when he was fraternising with the Orks who had passed the auditions and I was filming him on temple celluloid. Words are the same for everyone, after all, and who on earth hasn't tried putting them together this way or other?

That's all, there's no time left. I take my leave.

Manitou, I hope I have done my work well.